"There is nothing nice about you, Mister Corey."

He smiled and in that smooth, half-mocking voice that only added to his magnetism, said, "You can be so cruel. Anybody ever tell you that? Real cruel."

"I have had excellent tutors," Ellen coldly informed him.

"Well, if that were the case, why didn't you…?"

"Don't start with me! You know nothing of my life or the circumstances that govern it and I will not be appraised by a common carnival barker!"

For a long moment Mister Corey said nothing as he watched the expression on her face. When he spoke, it was in low, soft tones. "We live not as we wish to, but as we can. Or so the philosopher says."

"Really?" she answered hatefully. "And if I want to hear any more of your trite little platitudes, I'll be sure to let you know." She gave him a smug look, pleased with herself.

But as usual, he surprised her. Leaning close, he said, "What about when you want me to kiss you again? Will you let me know?"

"Oh! That will never happen, I assure you. I did not want you to kiss me that morning at the station. And the day will never come when I do want you to kiss me!"

"What about the night?"

"Neither morning, noon or night. Not ever."

He grinned wickedly. "Say that to me again in twenty-four hours."

**"The pages burn as Nan Ryan works her magic creating a hot, hot, hot love story…sensual, steamy, titillating."**
**—*Romantic Times***

# The Seduction of Ellen

## Nan Ryan

**MIRA® BOOKS**

*MIRA is a registered trademark of Harlequin Enterprises Limited,
used under licence.*

*First published in Great Britain 2002
MIRA Books, Eton House, 18-24 Paradise Road,
Richmond, Surrey, TW9 1SR*

© Nan Ryan 2001

ISBN 1 55166 814 9

58-0502

*Printed and bound in Spain
by Litografia Rosés S.A., Barcelona*

For
my dear sister
Glenda Henderson Howard

With love, affection and most of all,
gratitude for being there with me
during the bad times as well as the good.

# PART ONE

# One

It was growing dark when Ellen Cornelius stepped down from the hired coach before a gloomy tenement house in London's West End. Ellen gazed at the dilapidated building and inwardly shuddered. She did not want to go inside. She dreaded knocking on the door, dreaded meeting the person behind it. Nervous, doubtful, Ellen longed to climb back inside the carriage and return to the safety and comfort of the Connaught Hotel.

She didn't dare.

She hadn't chosen to come here. She had been sent by her indomitable aunt, aging American heiress and industrialist Alexandra Landseer.

Alexandra, with Ellen in tow, had come to London from her Park Avenue home seeking a medical miracle. Desperate to slow the aging process, Alexandra seemed convinced that money would buy her longevity.

"*Why* can't I live forever?" Alexandra had often

asked with an arrogant sincerity. "I don't intend to die like everybody else. I intend to stay young and vital!"

Now, after spending a week in a famed London clinic, Alexandra was both angered and disappointed by the results. She had been outraged when the team of noted Harley Street physicians bluntly told her that there was absolutely nothing they could do for her. She was, they pointed out in forthright terms, only mortal.

Nor did they sugarcoat their prediction that although she seemed to be in fairly good health, she could not expect to live many more years past her present age of eighty-one.

So now Ellen, Alexandra's only niece, had come alone across the city of London to this strange place to do her aunt's bidding. Just as always.

Ellen would, she knew, continue to endure and acquiesce to her self-centered aunt for as long as the old woman lived. She would cater to her every whim.

She would do it for Christopher—for her son who was now a cadet in South Carolina.

Resigned, long ago, to her lot in life, Ellen Cornelius looked older than her thirty-six years. And felt older. Especially tonight as she stood alone and frightened in this squalid section of London. She did not even know why she'd been sent to the West End. Only that she was to instruct the tenant in #203 to contact Alexandra Landseer at the Connaught Hotel in Mayfair as soon as possible.

Ellen summoned up her courage, stepped smartly

up the weed-choked front walk and entered the building. It was dim and foreboding inside. The light was inadequate and as she looked up the shadowy stairway, Ellen felt the fine hair rise on the back of her neck. She clamped her teeth together, forced herself to climb the rickety stairs and, squinting, soon located the correct room.

Her heart in her throat, she lifted a hand and knocked. She waited, listening for sounds of movement inside. She heard nothing. Seconds passed. Ellen knocked again, more forcefully this time. Still no answer. Apparently no one was in. Beginning to relax, Ellen tried one last time.

Secretly delighted that no one was home, she hurriedly skipped back down the stairs and out into the deepening dusk. Once in the carriage she instructed the driver to return her directly to the Connaught and then she settled comfortably against the plush leather seat, relieved that one more unpleasant task was behind her.

Halfway to the hotel, the coach slowed as it passed a noisy street fair. Ellen's green eyes began to glow slightly as she watched the gaily colored lights and the crowds of people and the shouting pitchmen hawking their games and wares. On a lark, she behaved impulsively, uncharacteristically. She decided to seize the opportunity to stay away from the Connaught—and her demanding aunt—for at least another hour.

"Driver," she called out excitedly. "Please stop the carriage. I...I am going to visit the fair!"

The coach stopped quickly and the smiling, ruddy-faced driver helped Ellen down.

"You will wait for me?" she asked.

"Why, I certainly will. Stay as long as you want, madam," he said, then eagerly confided. "I took my wife to this very fair last night and she had such a good time she's still in high spirits." He winked at Ellen and grinned.

Ellen smiled back at him and replied, "Perhaps it will sweeten my mood."

"Guaranteed," he assured her.

Nodding, feeling uncommonly buoyant, Ellen turned away and hurried toward the bustling fair to join the milling crowds.

The night was mild and the slight breeze that touched Ellen's face and lifted wisps of her chestnut hair was pleasantly warm. She was glad she hadn't brought a wrap as Alexandra had instructed.

Ellen found herself smiling as she made her way in and out of groups of starry-eyed children clinging tenaciously to strings supporting high-flying balloons. Her smile broadened when she noticed a trio of pretty girls, giggling and sticking their tongues out to taste the huge pink balls of cotton candy they carried. Ellen noted that the girls were well aware of a group of admiring young men following them at a distance, the bashful boys elbowing each other and laughing and blushing.

Young and old were obviously enjoying themselves and their happiness was contagious—soon Ellen realized that she, too, was having a good time. As she strolled leisurely past the many booths, a palm reader's tent caught her eye and her interest.

Ellen had never in her life visited a fortune-teller. A little shiver of excitement skipped up her spine as she took a couple of decisive steps forward, pulled back the heavy scarlet curtain and stepped inside. Immediately feeling anxious and wishing she had not been so adventurous, she nonetheless took a seat in the shadows directly across from a turbaned old crone.

For a long tense moment the bony, wrinkle-faced woman stared at Ellen, making her extremely uncomfortable. Then the soothsayer took Ellen's right hand in her own and studied it carefully. When she finally looked up, there was an odd expression on her face.

She made a strange prediction.

Her voice gravelly and coming from deep inside her narrow chest, the fortune-teller said, "I see a pretty young woman with glossy chestnut hair, flawless fair skin and large eyes that shine with excitement and anticipation. Green eyes they are. Vivid emerald eyes that sparkle with fire and mischief." The old woman paused and gazed unblinkingly at Ellen, then told her, "This emerald-eyed woman is soon to meet a man of great mystery and charm. A dark stranger who sees into her secret heart. A tall, spare man with lustrous coal-black hair and dark liquid eyes who will put the bloom of the rose back into her pale cheeks and—"

"No, wait. That's enough. Stop," Ellen interrupted, swiftly withdrawing her hand and waving it dismissively. "I know all too well about the past. Tell me of the future."

The garishly painted Gypsy looked Ellen straight in the eye and said, "It is not of the past I speak. It is of the future."

Rejecting her comment as utter foolishness, Ellen shook her head in annoyance, dropped a coin in the fortune-teller's hand, rose to her feet and left the tent.

Back outside, Ellen continued to saunter between the bunting-draped booths, stopping abruptly before a stall where a tall, spare man with lustrous coal-black hair stood on a raised platform. Torchlight falling on his chiseled face revealed squint lines that radiated outward from his eyes, forming grooves on either side of his nose down to his mouth.

A long, curving scar on his tanned right cheek gave him a villainous appearance. So did his eyes. Eyes as black as midnight. Eyes from which not one bit of light shone. Eyes that had seen too much of life.

Dressed entirely in black—suit, vest, silk shirt and leather shoes—the man held a bottle of patent medicine up to the crowd. In a tone as lifeless as his eyes, he extolled the many benefits to be derived from the secret elixir.

He glanced down, catching sight of Ellen standing directly below. Without a smile or change of expression, he crouched and held the bottle out to her. "What about you, miss? Shall I put the bloom of the rose back into your pale cheeks?" he asked in a low, flat voice.

"No, I...I..." Confused and momentarily tongue-tied, Ellen quickly turned away and left.

But she couldn't get the stranger out of her mind. All the way back to the Connaught, Ellen saw his tanned face and heard his low voice saying, "Shall I put the bloom of the rose back into your pale cheeks?" Ellen blushed as she guiltily acknowledged that he could probably do that and more.

She was surprised at herself. And perplexed. That she could have such a profoundly unsettling reaction to a stranger—a common carnival barker no less—was totally out of character. Besides, she had been so certain that her ability to feel any kind of attraction to the opposite sex had died years ago.

Perhaps not.

Ellen shivered involuntarily in the closeness of the carriage. Then she shook her head and smiled at her schoolgirl silliness. Still, she was glad she had gone to the fair. Glad she had seen the dark, dangerous-looking man and that he had made her pulse quicken. No harm had been done and it *had* been rather exciting. Lord knows there was precious little excitement in her life.

Ellen's foolish smile began to fade and she sighed wistfully as a rush of memories washed over her. Painful memories of an unhappy girl so anxious to get away from her domineering aunt that she had married the first young man to come calling. Vivid memories of the hurt and disappointment she'd felt when she'd realized that life with her neglectful husband,

Booth Cornelius, was no better than it had been with her cold, uncaring aunt.

Terrible memories of Booth Cornelius walking out on her some twenty years ago. Abandoning her with an infant son to raise alone. Hurtful memories of having to return, shamefaced and repentant, to Aunt Alexandra.

There were bitter memories of that one time—years ago—when she had made a brave attempt to break away from her aunt. But, she'd had Christopher to care for and no skills with which to earn a decent living. Within a few short months she'd been forced to return to Alexandra's where she had been ever since.

Where she would stay forever if that's what it took to ensure her adored son's inheritance. Ellen had been cheated out of her own fortune. She wouldn't let it happen to Christopher.

The last traces of Ellen's smile had disappeared. Now melancholy from recalling her empty past, the young woman silently cursed the cruel fates that had allowed her widowed father, Timothy Landseer, to be killed in the War Between the States. And as if her beloved father's death had not been devastating on its own, his wealthy widowed mother had died less than six months later.

Her grandmother's will had never been changed. A dead man could not inherit. The entire Landseer fortune had gone to Alexandra, Timothy Landseer's older sister and only sibling. Young Ellen was left beholden to Alexandra for the very roof over her head.

Ellen felt fatigued by the time she reached the Connaught. Climbing out of the carriage, she hoped against hope that Aunt Alexandra would have retired for the night.

She hadn't.

"Well?" Alexandra rose from her chair and placed her hands on her broad hips, when Ellen entered their suite. "Did you do as you were told?"

"I did," said Ellen flatly. "But it was a wild-goose chase. No one was home at the given address."

"No one home? Then you will return there tomorrow!" declared her disappointed aunt.

"Not unless you tell me the purpose of the visit," said an exasperated Ellen.

The frowning Alexandra suddenly began to smile like the cat who got the cream. She picked up the late edition of the *London Daily Express* from a table beside her armchair. The paper contained an advertisement that had captured Alexandra's attention and prompted her to send Ellen across the city.

Excited, Alexandra attempted to read. Squinting, she held the paper farther away, then finally said, "I don't have my eyeglasses. Here, you read it."

Ellen took the newspaper and read aloud, "'Do you long to turn back the clock? To rejuvenate your aging flesh? To replenish brain cells? If so, come drink of the Magic Waters and recapture your youth! Contact Mister Corey.'"

Ellen looked up from the newspaper.

"The address is listed, the one I sent you to," Alexandra pointed out. "You will go there again in the morning."

Calmly, Ellen said, "Aunt Alexandra, you know very well that these so-called Magic Waters will not make you young again and—"

"Did I ask for your opinion? I did not. You will go there tomorrow, do I make myself clear?"

Too weary to argue, Ellen simply nodded, dropped the newspaper back on the table and retired to the blessed privacy of her room.

But sleep eluded her. As she lay in bed in the still darkness, she thought only of the man with the unforgettable cold black eyes.

And for some odd, unexplained reason, the vivid vision caused her eyes to smart with unshed tears and her lonely heart to ache with a reawakened regret for what never was.

And would never be.

# Two

As soon as the sun rose the next morning, an impatient, robe-clad Alexandra Landseer knocked on Ellen's bedroom door.

"Wake up, Ellen," Alexandra called loudly. "Get out of bed *now!* I want you at that West End address in time to catch Mister Corey before he leaves. Get up, Ellen. Get up."

Ellen grimaced, gritted her teeth, but dutifully rose and began to dress. When, moments later, she entered the suite's spacious drawing room, Alexandra looked up from the sumptuous breakfast she was hungrily devouring.

Chewing and swallowing quickly, Alexandra explained, "I didn't order anything for you. There's not enough time. You can have breakfast when you return." She patted her mouth with a large linen napkin and added, "The carriage is waiting downstairs. Go now and find out all you can from this Mister Corey."

"Good morning, Aunt Alexandra," Ellen said flatly.

"Yes, yes, good morning," Alexandra muttered distractedly. "You tell Mister Corey he is to come to the hotel and meet privately with me at eight sharp this evening. Don't take no for an answer. I must speak with him.''

Ellen gave no reply. Alexandra was still firing off commands when Ellen left the suite.

The journey across London wasn't as nerve-racking in the daytime, but when she reached her destination, Ellen found the building and its unkempt surroundings even more depressing than she'd remembered. It was glaringly obvious that anyone who lived in this run-down tenement was impoverished.

One would assume that the person who held the secret to eternal youth would be incredibly wealthy. Ellen rolled her eyes heavenward, silently damning Alexandra and her latest exercise in idiocy.

When Ellen stood before the door to #203, she took a deep breath and knocked. This time her knock was promptly answered. Answered by a tall, spare man with lustrous coal-black hair and eyes to match.

The carnival barker from last night's street fair!

Ellen's eyes widened in surprise and alarm. Again she felt the racing of her heart, a weakness in her knees. Struck speechless, she started to turn away without stating the purpose of her call.

But the man who'd opened the door took her arm and drew her inside.

''I'm Mister Corey,'' he said in a low, flat voice with a hint of a drawling Southern accent. ''And you are?''

''I...ah...Ellen Cornelius,'' she managed, her voice slightly shrill.

''To what do I owe this unexpected pleasure?''

asked the unsmiling Mister Corey, releasing Ellen's arm.

Nervous, rushing her words, she explained, "My aunt, Miss Alexandra Landseer, saw your advertisement in the newspaper and she...ah...she asked that I come here to learn more about this...this...water you claim is magic."

Mister Corey nodded. "Come with me," he said and directed her into a sparsely furnished sitting room where a small, bald, coppery-skinned man awaited.

Mister Corey made the introductions and offered Ellen a chair. He remained standing. Ellen sat down and listened politely as Padjan told her that he was an Anasazi Indian whose home was far away in America's great Southwest. He spoke eloquently and excitedly of Magic Waters in the Lost City of the Anasazi, a city hidden high in the rugged canyonlands of Utah.

"The location of the Lost City," he said with great authority, tapping his chest with a forefinger, "is known to me alone." Ellen could hardly hide her skepticism, but she said nothing. Padjan continued, his dark eyes aglow, "In that secret place are Magic Waters from which a person can drink and stay forever young." He paused, as if waiting for her to speak.

Not knowing how to respond, she said, the cynicism evident in her tone, "That I would like to see."

"And you can," said Padjan. "I will take you there if you so desire." He smiled at Ellen then, his teeth very white in an incredibly smooth, youthful-looking face. "Drink of the waters," he told her, "and the passing of time stops."

At that, Ellen said resolutely, "I've no desire to make time stand still." She glanced nervously at Mister Corey who was quietly watching her, arms folded, lifeless dark eyes fixed on her. "Nor is there any part of my youth I would wish to reclaim," she continued, returning her attention to Padjan. "As I told you, my aunt sent me here. She's the one who wants to live forever, not me." Ellen abruptly rose to her feet. She looked from Padjan to Mister Corey and said, "My aunt has instructed me to bid you to visit her this evening. Can you do that? Both of you?"

"We can and we will," said the smiling Padjan, rising to face her.

"Very good," she said, turning away, then pausing and turning back. "Be at the Connaught Hotel at eight this evening." She looked at Mister Corey. "The Connaught is in Mayfair by the—"

"I know where the Connaught is," he said, his eyes narrowed ever so slightly.

"Oh. Well, good. I just supposed that…"

"…someone like me had never been in the *better* part of London?" he finished for her.

"No, I… That isn't what I meant."

"That's exactly what you meant," he coolly accused and she flushed hotly because it was true.

Eager to get away from him, Ellen tensed when Mister Corey followed her to the door. He reached around her to open it. For a split second she stood directly before him, trapped between his tall, lean frame and the closed door. Instantly plagued with a bad case of the jitters, Ellen was terrified she would start trembling and that he would notice her nervousness.

Her anxious eyes fixed on the hand gripping the brass doorknob, she felt as if all the oxygen had been sucked out of her lungs.

Mister Corey languidly opened the door.

Ellen bolted into the dimly lit hallway and, without looking back, rushed down the stairs as if fleeing the devil himself.

Mister Corey stood in the open doorway looking after her, mildly amused by her obvious aversion to him. A slight smile briefly touched his lips.

But it never reached his eyes.

Alexandra Landseer, wearing her finest, was ready and eager to receive her invited guests. Her steel-gray hair had been dressed elaborately atop her head and she wore an expensive creation of silver-gray silk that would have been stunning on a younger, slimmer woman. Her wrinkled face had been liberally dusted with powder and her cheeks sported twin spots of rouge. Sparkling jewels graced the crepey folds of her neck and dangled from her fleshy earlobes.

On joining her aunt in the suite's drawing room, Ellen had commented that it might not be wise to wear so many valuables for this particular occasion.

"After all, Aunt Alexandra," Ellen reminded her, "I told you when I returned this morning that this Mister Corey is nothing more than a common carnival barker. I saw the man last night hawking his magic potion at a street fair.''

The gussied-up old woman made a sour face. ''You had no intention of telling me about stopping at the fair, did you?''

''But I did tell you,'' Ellen defended herself.

Alexandra replied, ''Not last night you didn't.''

''Last night. This morning. What difference does it make?''

Alexandra toyed with a priceless rope of pearls-and-diamonds dangling from her throat and pursed her lips. ''Tell the truth, if you hadn't recognized Mister Corey this morning, you would *never* have told me about going to the fair last night.''

Ellen crossed her arms over her chest. ''And shame on me. I hadn't realized that doing something as daring as going to a street fair on my own should be immediately reported.''

''Don't you get smart with me, Ellen,'' Alexandra warned, pointing a finger at her niece as the younger woman turned and left the room.

Alexandra ignored her niece's surprising show of audacity. The heiress was in too good a humor to be bothered by Ellen's reaction. Alexandra was as excited as a child waiting for Santa on Christmas morning. She was zealously looking forward to this evening's meeting. It was to be, perhaps, the most important meeting of her entire life.

''Ellen,'' Alexandra shouted loudly, ''our visitors should be here soon. Where are you?''

Ellen, attired modestly in a simple white piqué

dress she'd worn for several summers, returned to the drawing room.

"Right here," she said, managing a smile.

While Ellen dreaded seeing the intimidating Mister Corey again, she wanted to be present for this little conference so she would know exactly what ensued. Alexandra, who successfully dealt daily with titans of rail, steel and telegraphy, seemed to lack all common sense when it came to the issue of staying young.

Ellen was afraid that the two scheming strangers would easily convince Alexandra that they held the secret to eternal youth. And, therefore persuade her aunt to pay an astronomical sum of money to take her to their so-called Magic Waters.

"They're here!" Alexandra announced excitedly at the knock on the door. She waved a bejeweled hand at Ellen, "Go let them in, please. No, wait just a minute."

Alexandra always insisted on staying seated when greeting guests. She preferred to play the role of a monarch on a throne, expecting her lowly subjects to come forward to bow and beam and fawn over her.

"Ready?" Ellen asked, barely concealing her annoyance as Alexandra fussed with the shimmering silk skirts that swirled around her feet.

"Yes, you may admit them," said the queenly Alexandra and Ellen went into the foyer to open the door.

The smiling Padjan entered the marble-floored vestibule. In his arms was a large green paper bag that he held as gingerly as if he were carrying a piece of fragile crystal. He was followed by Mister Corey who was clean shaven and surprisingly immaculate in a white linen shirt and neatly pressed dark trousers. Ellen felt her stomach contract.

"Good evening, Padjan, Mister Corey," Ellen calmly acknowledged. "Won't you come inside and meet my aunt?"

Padjan, the crown of his bald head gleaming in the light of the wall sconce, nodded eagerly. But first, he turned and carefully placed the bag on the table beside the door. Then he and Mister Corey followed Ellen into the suite's large drawing room.

"Aunt Alexandra, this is Padjan," Ellen indicated the smaller man. "Padjan, may I present my aunt, Miss Alexandra Landseer."

Grinning from ear to ear, Padjan stepped forward, bowed from the waist and, taking the hand Alexandra offered, said with sincere enthusiasm, "It is a true pleasure to meet such a great lady, Miss Landseer."

Charmed, she said, "Forget the formalities, call me Alexandra."

Nodding, Padjan released her hand and moved aside.

"And this," said Ellen, glancing up at him, "is Mister Corey. Mister Corey, my aunt, Alexandra Landseer."

Mister Corey was not impolite, but he did not grin or bow to the seated heiress or take her outstretched hand as Padjan had done. "Miss Landseer," he said and almost imperceptibly nodded.

Within minutes Alexandra and Padjan had their

heads together, talking like two old friends. Padjan knew exactly what Alexandra wanted to hear and he wasted no time telling her about his Lost City and its Magic Waters.

Mister Corey said little.

Ellen said even less.

The two of them sat at opposite ends of a long brocade sofa. Ellen, paying close attention to the conversation taking place between Padjan and her aunt, was nevertheless vitally aware of Mister Corey's strong masculine presence.

Occasionally casting covert glances at him, she wondered what he was thinking. He looked bored. Disinterested. And he looked as if he was bored and disinterested much of the time. He was, she surmised, a man who was experienced and world-weary. She got the impression that he had been everywhere and done everything and that he expected life to hold no further surprises or joys for him.

How, she wondered, had he ended up living in an old tenement building far from his native America? Hawking magic elixirs at street carnivals?

"Just you wait right here!" Padjan was saying as he nimbly rose to his feet and hurried out into the foyer.

In seconds he was back with the green paper bag. Gingerly placing the bag on the footstool before Alexandra, he looked up at her and said, "Here is proof that I am who I say, a member of the Anasazi, the Ancient Ones who the world believes have disappeared." Dark eyes flashing, he opened the bag,

swept it aside and withdrew a beautiful pottery artifact. He placed the artifact on the stool before Alexandra. "This came from the mystical Lost City," he
proudly declared. "You will see nothing like it anywhere else in the world."

Alexandra sat up straighter in her chair and reached
out to touch the exquisite urn. An avid collector of
pre-Columbian art, she immediately recognized that
the piece predated many within her own collection,
that it was authentic and not some modern reproduc-
tion.

Her bejeweled hands running admiringly over the
precious artifact, she said, "Ellen, perhaps you'd like
to retire to your room now. The gentlemen and I have
some business to conduct."

"If you don't mind, Aunt Alexandra," Ellen tried
to sound casual, "I'm finding this so fascinating that
I'd prefer to stay and—"

Alexandra looked up from the relic she was admiring. "I do mind," she cut Ellen off.

Ellen, mortified, felt Mister Corey's dark, disap-
proving gaze touch her. Without meeting his eyes, she
was certain they held an expression of mild disdain.
He was, she felt sure, silently rebuking her for meekly
allowing her aunt to dismiss her as if she were a child.

Well, she didn't care what he thought. He knew
nothing about her relationship with Alexandra or why
she allowed the older woman to order her about. She
was not surprised that her aunt had insisted she leave.
She had expected it.

She was always banished from the room anytime finances were to be discussed.

Alexandra patiently waited until the door was shut and her niece was out of earshot, then said, "Gentlemen, let's get down to business. I want to hire the two of you to take me to the Magic Waters and—"

Interrupting, Padjan shook his head. "Miss Landseer, there are four in our party. If one goes, we all go."

Alexandra frowned. "Four? We've no need of four people. Can't you just leave the other two here?"

A deep shade of red appeared beneath Padjan's smooth copper skin. "Never," he said and he was no longer smiling. "If you are ever to see the Magic Waters, you will take all four of us."

"Oh, all right," said Alexandra. "You *will* take me to your Magic Waters."

"I will," said Padjan, nodding solemnly.

"Then give it to me straight, please. Tell me, how much?" Alexandra asked. "How much is this entire operation going to set me back?"

The terms were promptly laid out. The deal was quickly made. Alexandra told the pair she would, come morning, have her niece book passage to America for them all within the week.

"Tie up any loose ends you have here in London and be ready to sail to America when I send word," she instructed Padjan and Mister Corey.

"We'll be ready," said Padjan. "The sooner, the better."

"I agree. I can hardly wait," enthused Alexandra as she showed them out.

She closed the door behind them and clapped her hands with glee.

# Three

In top cabin staterooms, very near to their own, was the strange carnival contingent that was to guide Ellen and her aunt to the Lost City of the Anasazi.

After having met all four, Ellen wondered how such a diverse group of people had ever come together.

Mister Corey was obviously a loner who needed no one. If he had any feelings, he never revealed them. He said little, rarely smiled, kept his own counsel, went his own way. His rugged sensuality, heavy-lidded gaze and devil-may-care attitude was repellent and appealing at the same time.

A man best left alone.

Enrique O'Mara was the exact opposite of the somber Mister Corey. He was a sunny-dispositioned, carefree half-Latin, half-Irishman, who everyone called Ricky. Of average height, Ricky was a sturdy, muscular man in his early thirties. He had dark wavy hair, snapping green eyes and an ever-present smile that could melt the coldest of hearts.

There was Padjan, of course. A man who loved to talk to anyone who would listen, he could speak for hours on any subject under the sun. Seemingly better educated than most university graduates, he impressed both Ellen and Alexandra with his vast wealth of knowledge. Alexandra was clearly fascinated by Padjan and the two spent long hours together talking.

Rounding out the quartet was the birdlike Summer Dawn, a tiny Indian woman who was so old and so weak she could not walk unaided and no longer spoke. Shriveled and extremely frail, she had tried to smile when Padjan had introduced her, saying simply, "This is our sweetheart, the precious Summer Dawn." Nodding, smiling, both Ellen and Alexandra had assumed that Summer Dawn was a close relative of Padjan's. His grandmother, or perhaps even great-grandmother.

Having met the entire foursome, Ellen's concerns had only increased. Did Alexandra actually expect these down-on-their-luck characters to lead her to the fountain of youth? There was no doubt in Ellen's mind that they were a bunch of charlatans whose sole aim was to fleece Alexandra of her fortune. And she dreaded the prospect of spending the next several weeks—perhaps even months—in the company of such disreputable people.

Especially in the company of the disturbing Mister Corey. Ellen wouldn't allow herself to even think about the treacherous trek across the rugged country of western America when there would be nowhere she could escape his presence.

It would be all she could do to avoid him on the long voyage home.

As feared, Ellen encountered Mister Corey on shipboard.

Often.

She simply couldn't bear to stay in the stateroom forever listening to the constantly complaining Alexandra. She had to get away from her aunt for a few minutes now and then if she were to maintain her sanity. But every time she ventured out to stand at the railing to feel the mist on her face or take a leisurely stroll around the deck, the unprincipled man she held personally responsible for this entire costly charade mysteriously appeared.

And immediately gravitated toward her.

"Enjoying the voyage?" he asked that sunny afternoon as he stepped up beside her.

"I *was*," she said pointedly, "until now."

"Does that mean you'd rather I hadn't joined you?"

"How quick you are," she replied.

He cocked his head to one side. "You don't like me, do you, Ellen?"

"If I ever gave you a thought," she responded, "I'm sure I wouldn't."

"Oh, you've given me a thought or two."

Her head snapped around. "I most certainly have not! I have much better things to do than—"

"Like what?"

"Like…oh, for heaven's sake, Mister Corey, what is it you want from me?"

"I don't know, Ellen," he drawled. "What are you offering?"

Ellen felt her face flush hotly. Anger rising with her growing discomfort, she said, "Nothing for you. Get this straight, Mister Corey. You may be able to hoodwink my aunt, but I am not quite so gullible."

An infuriating half smile touched his full lips and he said, "You don't want me to put the bloom of the rose back into your pale cheeks?" He lifted a hand and lightly brushed her face.

She stiffened and pulled away from his touch. "I want nothing from you," she said firmly, "except to have you out of my sight!" Lifting her chin, she added, "If you think for one minute that I intend to stand idly by and let you and your band of thieves steal all my aunt's money, you are sadly mistaken."

"How do you know we are thieves?" He was unfazed by the accusation. "What if we're telling the truth and there really are waters of magic?"

"You stopped recognizing the truth years ago, Mister Corey. Your entire life is a lie."

"And yours isn't?"

The offhand remark cut too close to the bone. Flustered, Ellen said anxiously, "If you'll kindly excuse me." She turned and hurried away.

Ellen blamed Mister Corey for this whole outlandish fiasco. The others were merely pawns in his elaborate con game. It was, she felt certain, Mister Corey who had hatched the far-fetched scheme. He who had rounded up the players and he who would claim the lion's share of the money they managed to swindle out of Alexandra.

Ellen strongly suspected that the cold Mister Corey would not be content with the sum—however great it was—that her aunt had agreed to pay.

- He had undoubtedly read about Alexandra Landseer's visit to London in the *London Daily Express*. He knew that her aunt was an extremely wealthy woman and extremely vain. It was as if he had purposely placed the advertisement in the paper knowing that Alexandra would see it and respond.

Would a man like that be satisfied with what he'd been promised or would he try to relieve Alexandra of the bulk of the Landseer fortune?

These doubts were nagging at Ellen on the fourth evening at sea when she accompanied Alexandra to a shipboard dance. She found herself hoping that the cool, confident thief wouldn't be there.

But despite the fact that she knew exactly what he was, she couldn't deny the attraction he held. A fact that shamed and frightened her.

She shuddered to think that such a flawed man could nonetheless so perfectly symbolize the fortune-teller's prediction and the mysterious, dreamlike vagueness of her own romantic fantasies. Fantasies that had long been forgotten until she'd had the misfortune of meeting Mister Corey.

Thank God he couldn't read her thoughts.

Midway through the evening's dance, Ellen finally

began to relax. How foolish she had been to worry about Mister Corey appearing at this gala affair. Surely his kind had not been invited. And even if he had, he couldn't possibly own the proper attire for such an occasion.

Bored and growing warm in the stuffy, crowded ballroom, Ellen told Alexandra that she was going up on deck for a breath of fresh air.

"Don't stay out too long and catch a cold," her aunt berated.

"I won't," Ellen dutifully replied.

# Four

Lifting the skirts of her well-worn ball gown, Ellen made her way toward the wide center staircase, paused at the base and looked up.

And lost her breath.

His lean, tanned hand resting carelessly on the smooth marble balustrade, Mister Corey stood at the top of the stairs. He was elegantly dressed in dark evening clothes and a pristine white ruffled shirt. His hair had been carefully brushed and was shimmering in the light from the crystal chandeliers. The curving scar on his right cheek shone pale white against the darkness of his olive skin. The left corner of his mouth was lifted in the hint of a teasing smile, but his black, brooding eyes were as lifeless as ever.

Mister Corey was looking directly at Ellen and she at him. She wished she could return to her chair. But it was too late. Holding her gaze, Mister Corey leisurely descended the carpeted stairs, took her elbow and guided her onto the polished dance floor.

In his arms, Ellen was more than a little uncomfortable. His nearness—the closest she had been to a man, other than her son, in ages—was so intimidating she was momentarily tongue-tied and unduly flus-

tered. Heart pounding, face flushed, she made a misstep. Mister Corey caught her, held her tightly and
suggested she relax.

Which made her all the more nervous.

Fully aware that she was behaving like a foolish,
frightened old maid, Ellen realized—miserably—that
the perceptive Mister Corey had already picked up on
her involuntary response to him.

But Ellen was also an astute woman.

While Mister Corey had that insolent, nothing-
bothers-me manner of a totally secure man, she
sensed that his caustic wit and sardonic grin likely
masked some deep, underlying pain.

She knew enough about concealing pain behind a
brittle facade to easily recognize the practice in others. Somewhere in Mister Corey's past, he had been
hurt. Badly. She would bet her life on it.

But that was his problem, not hers. Her once-fragile
heart had long since hardened. This dark, mysterious
man warranted no compassion from her. He was, after
all, a thief and a fraud and she had no use for him.

Mister Corey didn't know what was going through
Ellen's mind at that moment, but he was well aware
of his unsettling effect on the lonely woman. Her dislike of him was elemental and impersonal. She firmly
believed that he was after her aunt's money. Ellen
Cornelius clearly didn't approve of him, didn't like
him.

But she was attracted to him on a purely physical
level. It was not a mutual attraction. While he had no

doubt that she had once been quite beautiful, there was now little about her that was appealing. She was too thin to suit his taste. With his arm around her, he could feel her ribs and there was no generous swell of bosom rising above the square-cut neckline of her sadly out-of-fashion pink ball gown.

Her brown hair didn't gleam with golden highlights and she wore it pulled severely back from her face and twisted into an ugly pinned-up knot at the back of her head. Her green eyes were large and almond-shaped, but they held no spark, no glow. And her lips seemed to be permanently drawn into a stern line of disapproval that strongly discouraged any temptation to kiss them.

The years had been unkind to Ellen Cornelius and she obviously was not a happy woman. But he had no real interest in learning the cause of her disillusion. Her problems were the last thing he needed.

Feeling awkward and anxious and wishing the dance would end, Ellen was conscious of the fact that dozens of ladies in the ballroom were far prettier than she. She wondered why Mister Corey had chosen to dance with her. Was it simply that he was mean-spirited and cruel and enjoyed upsetting her, liked having her make a fool of herself in his arms?

Her forehead pressed against his cheek, Ellen nervously glanced around, convinced that everyone was watching them. She wasn't that far off the mark. Within minutes of his late arrival, a number of interested females were twittering and smiling, intrigued by the dark, enigmatic Mister Corey.

As soon as the dance ended, Ellen found herself back in her gilt chair beside the elegantly gowned Alexandra, who wasted no time critiquing her niece's performance. "You never did learn to dance properly. You haven't any natural grace, Ellen. You are clumsy and uncoordinated and you'd do well to just stay off the floor and stop embarrassing yourself and me."

Ellen was so accustomed to her aunt's belittling, she paid her no mind. Her undivided attention was on Mister Corey and his new dance partner, a tall, stunning, expensively gowned beauty with dark hair, fair skin and a voluptuous body that she was eagerly pressing against his.

Even Alexandra noticed the striking couple. "Ellen, look who Mister Corey is dancing with now!"

Endeavoring to sound nonchalant, Ellen said, "Mmm. Who is she? Do you know her, Aunt Alexandra?"

"I know of her," sniffed Alexandra. "She is Mademoiselle de Puisaye, a rich, spoiled French beauty who does exactly as she pleases. They say all the eligible bachelors on the Continent are after her." Alexandra clucked her tongue against the roof of her mouth. "Looks like she is enjoying the dance with Mister Corey a bit too much." She shook her head and exhaled loudly, "What could any sensible woman see in that rude, scowling man?"

"I can't imagine," said Ellen.

And then she felt her heart squeeze painfully in her

chest as the music ended and the French beauty whispered something to Mister Corey.

He nodded.

She laughed.

And the couple hurriedly left together.

Waiting just long enough to make certain she wouldn't bump into the pair, Ellen claimed a raging headache and escaped to the stateroom she shared with her aunt. Inside, she paced about, restless and edgy.

And wondering, miserably, if Mister Corey had only seen Mademoiselle de Puisaye to her stateroom where he had said a gentlemanly good-night. Or had he gone inside?

Instinctively, Ellen knew the answer. She sighed and sank down onto the edge of the bed.

Just a few doors down, in the well-appointed stateroom of Mademoiselle de Puisaye, Mister Corey and the French beauty sank down onto the edge of the bed.

"I saw you the minute you walked into the dance," said the confident Gabrielle de Puisaye, "and I said to myself, 'That man is going to make love to me tonight.' You are, aren't you?"

Mister Corey leaned down and placed a kiss on the bare swell of her breasts above her low-cut bodice.

"Tonight. In the morning. Tomorrow afternoon. Whenever. Whatever you want."

"I want you to undress me and I want you to tell me your name."

"Mister Corey," he said, urging her to her feet before him.

"I know that," she said. "I mean your given name."

"Doesn't matter," he said as he turned her about and began to deftly undo the tiny hooks going down the back of her lush satin evening gown. He urged her opened dress down to her waist and was amused to see that she wore absolutely nothing beneath the gown's bodice. Curious, he pushed the dress to her hips and revealed her naked backside. "My, but you're a brazen lady, Gaby. No underclothes of any kind?"

Giggling, Gabrielle shoved her shimmering egg-shell gown to the carpet, stepped out of it, kicked it aside and turned to face Mister Corey. Naked, save for her shoes and stockings, Gabrielle quickly discarded her dancing slippers, peeled the stockings down her legs, and tossed them aside. She sank to her knees before him and quickly removed his shoes, but not his black stockings. She then rose to her feet, bent to him, kissed his lips, then eagerly climbed astride his lap.

"I'm not brazen, I just plan ahead," she told him, running her hands through his hair and tracing the long white scar down his cheek with a red-nailed finger. "This way you don't have to fuss with all that cumbersome silk and lace to get to the real goodies."

"I do admire a woman who is well organized," he said, his hands spanning her bare waist. "Now, if you'll just give me a minute, I'll get undressed." He started to lift her up off his lap. She resisted, clinging to his neck.

"No, not yet," she begged. "Do it to me while you're still fully dressed. I like it that way. It's so…naughty and exciting."

Her hands went to the waistband of his dark trousers. Looking into his cold black eyes, she promptly freed his throbbing erection and said, "Oh, God, I knew it. You're so big and hard and hot. Put it in me, Mister Corey. Hurry, hurry, I can't wait to feel you moving inside me."

Mister Corey willingly obliged.

"Ahhhh," Gabrielle moaned with delight as he slowly impaled her on his hard, pulsing flesh.

With his hands on her firm thighs, he guided her, lowering her soft, yielding body down onto him until he was buried in her.

She loved it.

Gabrielle immediately began rocking and thrusting her hips and Mister Corey quickly caught her rhythm. Her bare, full-nippled breasts pressed against his dark face, the Frenchwoman murmured teasingly, "You've done this before, Mister Corey."

"As have you, Gaby," he replied.

Unashamedly experienced, needing no extra time and mindless of her partner's stage of arousal, Gabrielle quickly climaxed, letting herself go, crying out in her ecstasy. Damp with perspiration, heart pounding beneath her naked breasts, she collapsed against him, wrapping her arms around his neck and clutching his sides with her knees. She was aware that he'd not yet attained release and she was glad.

She wanted more.

Sighing, smiling foolishly, Gabrielle finally sat up, looked him in the eye and said, "You're still hard, Mister Corey. Soooo deliciously hard."

"Guilty as charged."

"Do you like games?"

"Try me."

"Let's see if we can manage to get all of your clothes off while you're still inside me. Wouldn't that be an enjoyable challenge?"

It turned out to be just that.

The couple tumbled about on the bed, rolling to one side so that Mister Corey could get his arm out of a jacket sleeve. Gabrielle busied herself with the buttons on his white ruffled shirt. Working furiously, Gabrielle laughing all the while, they contorted their bodies, reaching around each other, tugging at clothing, taking care to not come apart.

Finally Mister Corey was as naked as she, except for his dark stockings.

"Here's how we'll do this," he said, lying on his back with Gabrielle seated astride him.

He slowly rolled up into a sitting position facing her as she drew her legs around his back. Checking to see if she was comfortable, assured that she was, he bent his right knee and brought it up close to his side. Immediately taking her cue, she twisted about, reached out, and peeled off his black stocking. She tossed it to the floor and said, "Now give me your other foot."

"We did it!" Gabrielle cried jubilantly, when the last black stocking came off. "Now, let's do it."

# *Five*

"Good morning, Miss Cornelius. May I join you?"

Ellen turned from the ship's railing to see Enrique O'Mara approaching.

Nodding, Ellen said, "That's *Mrs.* Cornelius, Mr. O'Mara."

He laughed and said, "That's Ricky, Mrs. Cornelius."

His warm, friendly manner and infectious grin disarmed her. She laughed too and said, "That's Ellen, Ricky."

"Ah, *sí,* Ellen," the good-natured Ricky replied as he stepped up and rested his muscular forearms on the railing beside her.

Spanish on his mother's side and Irish on his father's, Ricky O'Mara possessed the good looks and fiery spirit of both parents. He was one of those rare individuals who enjoyed every minute of his life, no matter where he was, who he was with, or what he was doing. He took genuine delight in things others hardly noticed. To him, a spectacular sunrise was cause for celebration. As was the dazzling sight of the vast Atlantic Ocean stretching before them. He found joy all around, which made him a joy to be around. People liked Ricky O'Mara because he liked them.

Ellen Cornelius was no exception. Circumstances being what they were, she had honestly expected to dislike him. But it was impossible. The happy-go-lucky Ricky was a naturally sweet, kind, fun-loving man who cared about others. He was so amicable, Ellen wondered why on earth he chose to be friends with the sullen Mister Corey.

Ellen lifted a hand to shade her eyes and said, "Tell me, Ricky, how have you been entertaining yourself these past five days at sea?"

Ricky's broad grin grew broader still. "Oh, it has been easy. There is so much to do and see. So many delicious meals." He winked at her and added, "So many pretty women on this ship, Ellen."

"Yes, I've noticed," she said dryly. "Anyone in particular that you—"

"No, oh, no," he said emphatically, shaking his dark head for emphasis. "I love *all* women." He flung his long arms out in an encompassing gesture. "I could *never* love only one."

"How can you be so sure?"

"I *am* very sure. I will never marry. It wouldn't be fair, since I could never be a faithful husband."

"No, no, it wouldn't," Ellen said. "At least you know yourself and admit it."

"Yes, I do. I have never been in love," he stated, then reasoned, "I am thirty-four. If it hasn't happened to me by now, it never will." Laughing then, he touched Ellen's hand where it gripped the railing and said, "What about you, Ellen? You are Mrs. Cornelius, so you must have been in love once. Will you fall in love again?"

She answered quickly. "Never in a million years."

She laughed then and Ricky laughed with her. They fell silent for a moment, then Ricky needlessly cleared his throat and said, "Ellen, I know that you do not approve of me, of us, but—"

"I really don't want to discuss it, Ricky," she stopped him. "Whether I approve or not is unimportant. You were contracted by my aunt, not by me. My opinion, as usual, is of no value. So, you'd be wasting your time trying to convince me that this upcoming excursion is on the up-and-up."

"But it is," he said, his expression earnest. "Padjan knows where—"

"Ricky," she interrupted, "please. Let's change the subject."

Ricky wisely heeded her advice. The disarming smile back on his lips, he said, "You know something? I like you, Ellen Cornelius."

Ellen raised an eyebrow at him. His flashy grin suggested both his amusement with the world and his fondness for it. And for himself. But on him the expression was somehow boyishly charming.

"I like you too, Ricky."

In the following days—and nights—Ellen saw Mister Corey and Mademoiselle de Puisaye together regularly. Bristling each time she spotted the laughing French beauty seated beside Mister Corey at dinner, or at a gaming table, or on a railside bench in the moonlight, Ellen reminded herself she was far too sensible to care.

While there was no denying that Mister Corey had a certain menacing charm, Ellen knew instinctively that he had found the kind of woman he preferred in the bold French beauty. The kind of woman he deserved. A woman who was much like himself. A woman who shared his values—or lack thereof. The counterpart to his toughness and vulgarity and sensuality.

They were, Ellen decided, a perfect pair and they had her blessing!

After ten full days at sea, the SS *White Star* slowly entered the New York harbor. Ellen hadn't realized how homesick she'd been until she saw the imposing Statue of Liberty rising to meet the clear New York sky.

Once again, Ricky O'Mara stood beside her at the railing. "Glad to be home?" he asked, his dark-eyed gaze on the Manhattan skyline.

"You have no idea," Ellen said.

"Ah, but I do," said the smiling man who had been away from his beloved America for more than a year.

Still in her stateroom, Alexandra was giving Mister Corey instructions as the ship inched its cautious way toward the dock, several tugs urging it into its proper berth.

"I will be ready to leave for the West in ten days," Alexandra told him. "You are to make all the traveling arrangements for the journey. I own a private rail car, but there's only enough room for Ellen and me, so you will engage additional cars to transport your group.''

"I'll see to that this very afternoon," said Mister Corey.

"How far can we travel by train?"

"To Grand Junction, Colorado."

"And after that?"

"By wagon, on horseback," said Mister Corey. "And at the very end—on foot."

"On foot?" Alexandra was nonplussed. "You can't expect *me* to walk! Perhaps you are not fully aware of just who I am. I am Alexandra—"

"Doesn't matter who you are, Miss Landseer. If you want to reach Padjan's Magic Waters, you may have to walk the last few miles."

Her face red, an angry Alexandra said, "Don't ever interrupt me again, young man! And don't be telling me what I will and will not do. You, sir, are insolent and disrespectful and I've half a mind to banish you from my sight right now and let Padjan take care of everything and…" Mister Corey casually got to his feet and walked away. "…what are…wait a minute! You come back here! Where do you think you're going?"

At the door, Mister Corey paused, turned, looked her squarely in the eye and said, "If you want to dismiss me, that's your prerogative."

"Well, now, not so fast," said Alexandra, suddenly anxious, afraid the highly anticipated expedition might fall apart without the man who was coldly looking at her. "I...I didn't mean it, really. We need you. *I* need you. I want you to stay and help guide us to Padjan's Lost City."

"Fine. But get this straight, Miss Landseer. I do things my way, not yours. I make decisions based on what will be best for everyone, not just on what will be best for you." A muscle danced in his lean jaw when he added, "If anyone is to be carried when we reach the rugged, almost impassable gateway into the Lost City, it will be Summer Dawn, not you."

Alexandra Landseer stared at him, nearly swallowing her tongue. No one had ever talked to her the way this impudent man was talking to her. Her position of power, her great wealth had successfully insulated her from tactless upstarts like him. She was so accustomed to having people grovel to get in her good graces that she couldn't believe that someone like him, a man who was obviously poor and without resources, would dare challenge her.

"If I escort you to your destination," continued Mister Corey, "I run the operation. What I say goes. My authority is absolute and will not be questioned and my orders will be obeyed by everyone. Including you. You are no different than any of the others who will be in my charge. Obviously, you are used to bossing people about, but you won't boss me. Not ever. So, it's up to you. You have exactly one minute to make up your mind."

"I want you to stay," she said meekly, barely audible.

"What was that? I couldn't hear you."

Her voice strengthened and her eyes flashed with anger when she repeated, "I want you to go with us!"

Mister Corey nodded, but he did not come back across the room. "Where are we to stay while we're in New York?" he asked, and caught the perplexed expression that immediately came into her light-colored eyes. She was, he knew, terrified he might expect that they'd be staying in her home. He knew better, but he said innocently, "Will we be staying with you and Mrs. Cornelius?"

"Certainly not. This is a business arrangement, you are not a friend. Book yourselves some rooms at a nearby hotel."

"Will do," he said and was gone.

Alexandra Landseer was in high spirits.

After a couple of days of rest, she invited Mister Corey and Padjan to her Park Avenue mansion for lunch and the opportunity to discuss, in depth, their exact route to the Lost City.

When the pair appeared empty-handed, carrying no maps or charts, Alexandra's hands went to her broad hips. "Where are the maps?" she demanded. "I had hoped to lay them out on the dining table to study them."

Padjan said calmly, smiling as he spoke, "The Lost City can be found on no map other than the one in my head." Seeing her disappointment, he said, "Do not trouble yourself, Alexandra. I know the way and I will take you."

"Oh, I just can't wait to get there," said Alexandra as they went in to lunch, Alexandra and Padjan leading the way, Ellen and Mister Corey following. "Tell me again what it will be like and how long I will need to drink of the Magic Waters before I become young again."

Padjan chuckled, pointed a finger at her and said, "That, Alexandra, will depend on you."

As she was anytime she was in Mister Corey's presence, Ellen was extremely uncomfortable. She sat directly across from him and, while she made it a point not to look in his direction, she could feel his eyes examining her. When finally she could stand it no longer, she glanced at him.

He was staring unblinkingly at her, those obsidian eyes fixed on her. He wore a jet-black shirt and it suited him perfectly. Everything about him was dark. Dark strength. Dark sexuality. Dark heart.

Ellen felt a chill skip up her spine and she quickly looked away. She reached for her stemmed wineglass and drank thirstily. She had the awful feeling that, without making a sound, Mister Corey was laughing at her.

Damn the dark demon.

By the time the luncheon ended, Alexandra was in such a good mood, Ellen decided this was the right time to broach the subject of visiting Christopher.

As Padjan and her aunt continued to discuss travel plans, deciding on the day they would depart, Ellen waited for an opening. Finally she said, "Aunt Alexandra, since once we leave for the West we may be gone for months, I would like to go down and visit Christopher for a couple of days.''

Ellen held her breath. She badly wanted to see her son. But Alexandra could easily prevent her from making the trip.

To Ellen's delight, Alexandra was perfectly agreeable. She said, "Why, yes, of course. Go see Chris. Have Mister Corey go with you."

"Certainly not!" Ellen was quick to protest, casting an anxious look at him.

Ignoring Ellen, Alexandra turned to Mister Corey and said, "Ellen's son, my great-nephew, is a cadet at the Citadel. You will accompany Ellen to South Carolina to visit him."

Ellen was looking directly at Mister Corey. She caught a brief, puzzling flickering in his dark eyes and the minute tightening of his jaw before that familiar half smile touched his lips and he said, "Ellen's a big girl. She can go alone."

# *Six*

Ellen was not pleased to learn that Mister Corey would be driving her to Grand Central Station.

It was, of course, Alexandra's idea.

Ellen had not been consulted.

Ellen hadn't found out until late Thursday afternoon when she hurried down the stone steps of the Park Avenue mansion. Before even glancing toward the carriage, she'd been distracted by a black Persian cat that was sitting on the bottom step. The beautiful cat belonged to the Winstons who lived across the street. Ellen would have given anything to own a cat, but Alexandra wouldn't allow it. So Ellen contented herself with petting the Winstons' Persian anytime she got the chance.

Smiling, she sank down onto her heels and rubbed the cat's head. "How are you today, Prince," she addressed the purring feline. "You come to say goodbye?" She remained as she was, stroking the cat and talking to him for several minutes before reluctantly rising to her feet.

It was then that she looked up and saw Mister Corey lounging against the parked carriage. Watching her, as if amused.

"What are you doing here?" she asked sharply as he took her valise.

"Driving you to Grand Central Station. What else?"

"What have you done with Jerome?" She looked around for the faithful old Landseer driver.

"We gave Jerome the day off," said Mister Corey as he reached out, encircled her small waist and lifted her up onto the carriage seat.

Ellen exhaled with annoyance when Mister Corey slid onto the seat beside her and gave her a sly, side-long glance. She knew then how he was going to behave. Or misbehave. She was tempted to jump down out of the carriage and hail a hired conveyance to drive her to the train depot.

Her apprehension escalated rapidly. The carriage wheels had hardly begun to turn on the pavement before Mister Corey was teasing and deviling her. She realized he arrogantly assumed that he could easily upset her, just as he had at the shipboard dance.

But he was wrong.

Now that she was back home and in familiar, comfortable surroundings, Ellen had regained her rigid composure. She could and did hold her own with her needling tormentor and, in fact, took secret pleasure in triumphantly putting him in his place.

Subtly, but directly, so that there was no misunderstanding, Ellen let Mister Corey know that she thought he was far beneath her in social status and class. She made it clear that she was of the upper echelon and did *not* associate with his kind.

Mister Corey seemed to take her disdain in stride. He smiled when he said, "You really think you're better than me, Ellen?"

"Yes and don't you ever doubt it!" she replied sarcastically.

And then took a great degree of satisfaction from seeing the distinct hardening of his tanned jaw. She wanted to laugh out loud. She had managed to penetrate that ever-present armor of indifference. Taking pleasure from her small victory, Ellen suddenly realized that she needn't fear Mister Corey. He was human after all. Despite his impervious demeanor, he obviously had feelings that could be hurt, just as she did. That valuable bit of knowledge would work to her advantage. It was simple, really. All she had to do was to never let him forget that she felt nothing but contempt for him.

"Ah, but I do doubt that you're any better than me," he said, "and so do you."

"Not for a minute, Mister 'Carnival Barker' Corey!" she replied cuttingly.

"There are worse ways of earning your daily bread."

"I can't think of any."

"I can."

Ellen gave him a smug look. "Pray tell, what could they possibly be?"

"Constantly kowtowing to a disagreeable old woman, for one."

"You have no right to judge me."

"Nor you me."

The two continued to spar all the way to the train depot.

When the carriage finally reached busy Grand Central Station, Ellen felt a great sense of relief. While she was now confident that she could successfully put Mister Corey in his place, it was taxing and she was eager to get away from him.

As soon as he had helped her out of the carriage and retrieved her valise, Ellen said, "I can manage from here."

"I'll go inside with you," he stated flatly.

Ellen made a face. "What about the carriage? You can't just leave it unattended."

Mister Corey looked about, motioned to a young boy who was selling fresh-cut flowers. Flipping the boy a shiny silver dollar, Mister Corey said, "Watch this carriage until I get back and I'll give you another dollar."

"Yes, sir!" said the boy, then beamed when Mister Corey withdrew a bill from his pocket as he reached for a bouquet of fragrant ivory roses.

"For you," Mister Corey said and held out the roses to Ellen.

The frown still on her face, she reluctantly took the flowers, not wishing to cause a scene in public.

Inside the huge terminal were crushing crowds of people, all seeming to be going in different directions and all in a hurry to get there. Ellen was bumped by a big, stout man before she had taken two steps.

"You okay?" Mister Corey asked. She nodded. He took her hand and said, "Follow me."

Running interference, he managed to get her safely through the terminal and out onto the platform where the trains arrived and departed. Pointing out the locomotive that would take her to Charleston, he looked up and down the tracks and asked, "Where's the private rail car? I thought those private cars were usually added to the rear."

"I'm not taking the private rail car," Ellen said, dreading what she knew was coming next.

"Not taking it? Why? What's the use of having…?"

"For your information, Mister Corey," Ellen said, "it costs a great deal of money to transport a private rail car. The price is equivalent to eighteen first-class rail tickets, plus an additional fee."

Mister Corey's dark left eyebrow lifted. "Jesus, that rich old woman makes you travel in a day coach like the poorest of travelers?"

"It isn't that far to—"

"It's seven or eight hundred miles," he corrected. "It will take nearly twenty-four hours."

"I enjoy visiting with the other travelers," she said, wishing he would mind his own business.

"Sure you do," Mister Corey said, "and trying to sleep in one of those hard chairs is really delightful."

"All aboard for Philadelphia, Salisbury, Norfolk, Wilmington, Charleston, Savannah and Jacksonville!" shouted a portly uniformed conductor.

"That's me," said Ellen. "It's time for departure. You may go now."

She made an attempt to take her valise from him.

He withheld it. Travelers were pushing forward, eager to board the train. They were surrounded by people.

"I have to go," she said, again reaching for her suitcase.

She had no idea that Mister Corey had decided to have his last bit of fun at her expense.

Purposely speaking loudly enough for most of the crowd to hear, he said, "Goodbye, dear. Don't worry about a thing. I'll keep close watch on the children while you're away."

As she stared at him round-eyed and openmouthed, he wrapped an arm around her waist, drew her into his embrace so swiftly the bouquet of ivory roses was caught and crushed between them and kissed her soundly.

"All aboard," called the chuckling conductor, spotting the kissing couple as he stood in place beside a set of portable steps. "All aboard!"

Vaguely, as if from far away, Ellen heard the conductor's shouted appeal for all passengers to get on board. But she was far too captivated by the warm, smooth lips moving on hers to respond to anything or anyone but the dark, devilish man who was kissing her as she'd never been kissed in her life.

Mister Corey held nothing back. He kissed her as if they were all alone, two lovers who were hot for each other and about to make love. His sleek tongue slid deep inside her mouth, exploring, touching, conquering in an intimate invasion that shocked, thrilled and scared her half to death.

Then all at once, the hot, intrusive kiss ended as unexpectedly as it had started.

"All aboard that's going aboard!" shouted the perspiring, shiny-faced conductor.

"Better get on board," said Mister Corey coolly as if he had done nothing more than shake her hand.

Ellen gave no reply. Her face was bloodred and her heart was racing. She was furious. She was shaking. She was half-dazed and confused. Mister Corey took her arm, guided her to the train steps, handed the conductor her valise and said to the man, "Look after the missus for me, won't you?" He peeled off a bill and handed it to the rail employee.

"I'll sure do that, mister," said the beaming conductor. "Don't you worry about your little wife, we'll take real good care of her."

Her face a study in silent fury, Ellen made her way down the aisle as the locomotive's wheels began to slowly turn on the tracks. She found her seat and dropped down into it, the crushed bouquet of ivory roses still gripped tightly in her hand. She gritted her teeth and closed her eyes.

Then jumped, startled, at the faint rapping on the train window. Mister Corey stood there mouthing the words, "See you soon, Ellen."

Her head snapped around and she faced straight ahead. She silently begged the train to start moving. To leave the station. To hurry and take her far, far away from this cocky carnival hawker who had dared to kiss her against her will!

Or had it been against her will?

As the train finally began to pick up speed, Ellen miserably searched her soul. Had she participated in the disgraceful caress? Could she have freed her lips from his? Had he physically forced her to stand there locked in his close embrace? As he kissed her with such devastating intimacy, had she shamelessly kissed him back?

The southbound train left Grand Central Station—and Mister Corey—behind and was moving toward the outskirts of the city.

But Ellen couldn't leave behind what had happened there.

She kept reliving that blazing kiss as the miles clicked away. Over and over again she felt those hot, smooth lips moving aggressively on hers, felt the incredible hardness of his broad chest pressed against her breasts, felt the powerful strength of his arm around her waist.

Ellen gave herself exactly a half hour to behave like a silly young girl. During that time she carefully plucked one of the ivory roses from the bouquet, withdrew a book from her reticule and placed the rose inside the pages. She closed the book.

Then closed her eyes and sighed and squirmed and daydreamed and pretended that she was someone else and he was someone else and that the two of them were madly in love and could hardly bear being parted from one another, even for a few short days.

At the end of her allotted half hour, Ellen's blood had cooled and her equilibrium had returned. She was herself again, a wise, sedate, rational woman who placed the book in her reticule where it belonged.

She also placed Mister Corey where he belonged.

Out of her thoughts.

Ellen was weary.

Tired to the bone.

She had been sitting up all night and all day in an uncomfortable wooden day chair and her back was aching mercilessly.

But her exhaustion magically departed when, less than twenty-four hours after leaving New York City, the train began traveling across the beautiful South Carolina lowlands toward the coastal city of Charleston. Hardly able to contain her excitement, Ellen lowered the window to look out. She inhaled the heavy, humid air and could have sworn it carried the faint scent of magnolias. Soon she could see the tall spire of St. Michael's Church. Her heart raced. She was almost there.

Ellen considered Charleston, South Carolina, to be a beautiful, unique, seductive city, unlike any other. The city proper was built on a peninsula between two rivers, the Ashley and the Cooper, which flowed together to form the busy Charleston harbor. The earliest settlement in South Carolina, it was an enchanting, semitropical city where gracious living prevailed, good manners were requisite and some of America's oldest, wealthiest families lived.

The pace was much slower here than in New York City. The content Charlestonians took the time to enjoy life's pleasures and the pleasures were many. Chris had told her that Charleston was often referred to as an American Venice by the proud citizens. And she knew why.

The train was fast approaching the downtown depot. It was nearing three in the afternoon. In less than one hour she would see her son. When she'd wired Chris that she was coming, he had wired her back, saying, apologetically, that he would be unable to meet her at the station. It was a long-standing tradition that Fridays at 3:45 was parade at the academy and all the corps marched. His general leave wouldn't start until 5:00 p.m. Then he would be free until midnight.

Ellen was glad he wouldn't be at the station. She knew she looked a sight and she wanted to freshen up and change clothes before she saw her son or his friends.

She didn't want Christopher to be ashamed of his mother.

# Seven

Ellen hired a carriage to take her to the Mills House on Meeting Street. Chris had made reservations for her at the imposing five-story hotel in downtown Charleston a few short blocks from the harbor.

As the uniformed doorman stepped forward to help her down from the carriage, Ellen asked the cabdriver if he would kindly wait and drive her to the Citadel. She wouldn't, she promised, be more than fifteen minutes. The driver agreed.

Once inside her fifth-floor room, Ellen went hastily about throwing open the windows. She paused before one for a moment and looked out, viewing the Battery and the sailing vessels on the calm waters of the Ashley River. And out in the harbor, the big parrot guns of Fort Sumter, that historic place where the War Between the States had begun.

It had been, legend claimed, cadets from the military academy her son now attended who had opened fire on a Northern supply ship attempting to deliver supplies to the garrison at Fort Sumter. The first shots fired in the war.

Ellen turned away.

She didn't want to think about war and destruction.

She wanted to dwell entirely on the next two carefree days she would be spending with her son.

Humming happily, Ellen took a hurried bath, redressed her long chestnut hair neatly atop her head and put on her best summer frock, a sky-blue poplin with elbow-length mutton-chop sleeves, tight waist and narrow skirt that flared at the knee. Taking one last appraising look in the mirror, Ellen frowned and sighed. She certainly wouldn't win any beauty prizes. Her cheeks were too hollow, her complexion too sallow, her hair too dull.

She turned away, grabbed her gloves and reticule, rushed downstairs, out onto the street and up into the waiting carriage.

"The military academy," she said. Then, unable to keep her maternal pride to herself, she added, "My son is a cadet at the Citadel."

"Is he now?" the cabbie responded, then drove several long blocks down Meeting Street until he reached the section of the old rampart called Marion Green. Once a state arsenal and guardhouse, it was now the remodeled, three-story Citadel.

Quickly paying the fare, Ellen was out of the carriage with the agility of a young girl. She was ushered through the gate and onto the academy grounds by the Cadet Officer of the Guard.

Her heart aflutter, Ellen hurried toward the parade ground to join other visitors and natives who were watching the South Carolina Corps of Cadets marching in full-dress parade. Ellen stood at the perimeter of the quadrangle with the other onlookers, shading her eyes against the strong Carolina sun, searching a sea of bright young faces for the one dear to her heart.

The marching cadets wore their crisp summer whites. The tight-fitting waist-length jackets with their stiff stand-up collars had a triple row of brass buttons adorning the chest. The neatly pressed trousers had gold stripes going down the outside of each leg. Those stripes were now moving as one, as feet were lifted and lowered in flawless cadence by the well-trained cadets.

On their heads were tall, plumed hats with chin straps worn just below their noses. The cadets' white-gloved hands swung back and forth in perfect precision. They were, Ellen thought, America's finest sons and her heart swelled with happiness at the knowledge that her own precious son was one of their elite number.

Awed, she watched the proud corps pass in review while the regimental band played and the crowd of visitors applauded and waved American flags. Ellen continued to anxiously hunt for Chris. Finally she spotted him. Her hand went to her breast and she exhaled with pleasure.

Christopher marched with the skill and expertise of one who'd spent many long hard hours on the parade ground. His back was rigid, his shoulders straight, chest out, stomach in. He was staring straight ahead. Lean. Proud. Erect.

A true cadet.

When the dress parade ended, Ellen stayed where she was. She spotted Chris looking about and knew that he was hunting for her. She raised a hand and waved. He caught sight of her and a wide boyish smile instantly spread across his face. He yanked off his plumed hat and started running toward her, dodging other cadets as he came.

Ellen didn't move. Just stood there admiring him as he sprinted toward her. Tall and blond and incredibly handsome in his crisp summer whites, he was the precious child of her heart, the light of her life, the one thing in this often dark, dismal world that had made it all worthwhile. The mere sight of him coming toward her erased all the pain and loneliness she'd ever known. The brilliant sun in her universe, he was, and always had been, the sweetest, kindest, most loving child in the world.

But he was no longer a child, she realized almost sadly as she watched him approach. He was no longer her little boy. He was no longer a boy. That nervous, slender eighteen-year-old who had entered the academy last autumn was gone. In his place was a sleek, efficient, confident young man.

Chris reached his mother, threw his arms around her, lifted her off the ground and swung her round and round while she laughed, somewhat embarrassed.

Chris Cornelius was the opposite of Ellen. Where she was by nature prim, sedate, timid, submissive and distrustful, her only son was gregarious, friendly, trusting, outgoing and fun-loving.

When at last Chris put Ellen down, he gave her an affectionate kiss on the cheek, not caring who saw, and said honestly, "I'm glad to see you, Mother."

"I've missed you so," she softly replied. She drew back to look up at him. "You've grown," she said as if surprised. "You're taller than you were at Christmas break."

"I have," he said proudly, "Guess how tall I am."

"Six foot?"

"Six-one," he said, laughing. "Come on, I want to introduce you to my friends."

"Are you sure?" Ellen asked hesitantly. "I don't look my best after all those hours on the train."

Chris's blond eyebrows shot up. "Aunt Alex didn't let you come down in the rail car? You had to sit up in a day coach the entire way?" Ellen nodded sheepishly. His brilliant blue eyes momentarily flashed with anger, then he quickly smiled again and said, "I sure hope God threw away the pattern after he made her, don't you?" Ellen laughed. Chris laughed with her, squeezed her waist and said, "Mother, you look beautiful. Let's go meet my friends."

Chris introduced Ellen to his roommates, three young men who had been through the grueling plebe year with him. They were mannerly, attentive, and made easy, amiable small talk.

After several minutes of pleasantries, Ellen said, "I've heard the first year at the academy can be quite difficult." She smiled at Pete Desmond, a big, muscular cadet from Richmond, Virginia, and said, "Tell me, were the upperclassmen mean to you knobs?"

Pete glanced at Chris, who stood behind his mother. Chris shook his head. Pete grinned and said,

"No, ma'am, Mrs. Cornelius. They were most helpful and kind."

Ellen didn't believe Pete. She had heard the stories of how the upperclassmen at military academies were sometimes quite brutal to the plebes. She had worried about Chris since the day he had come here, had wondered what he was going through.

"You hear that, Mother? What did I tell you?" Chris said.

Chris, not wanting to worry her, had never told his mother of the demeaning torment and physical misery he had suffered at the hands of some sadistic upperclassmen. He had never once, in his weekly letters, mentioned his agonizing loneliness, his intense fear, his constant exhaustion. His biggest fear had been that he would be branded a coward and drummed out of the corps like so many others who had come here with high hopes, only to be sent home in shame.

He never would tell her.

He had made it.

The first year was almost over and he had survived the rigors of the institute and had never complained, except to the three cadets who were his roommates. They had been through the torture with him. They had shared his terror and had understood his fear. They had comforted him when he was in danger of breaking and he had done the same for them. The experiences they had shared had drawn them closer than brothers. The four of them were good friends. The best of friends. Chris loved these three brave, loyal men with whom he had been through the fires of hell. He knew that they would be his friends for life.

Chris invited the roommates to join his mother and him for dinner that evening, but they respectfully declined.

Jarrod Willingham, a slender, red-haired, freckle-faced cadet from Memphis, Tennessee, said, "We do appreciate the invitation, Chris, but I know if my mother came to visit, she'd want to have me to herself for a while." Jarrod grinned and winked at Ellen.

Ellen smiled and nodded.

The visit to Charleston was everything Ellen had hoped for and more. After an excellent dinner that evening, she and Chris strolled toward the Battery in the bright Carolina moonlight. Their pace leisurely, their conversation inconsequential, they soon reached South Battery and continued beneath the tall oaks to the seawall.

Chris took Ellen's hand as they ascended the steps of the seawall. At the top, they stood in silence for a time before the railing, watching the glittering lights of houses along the shore of James Island and listening to the unique sounds of the sea.

The tide was going out. The powerful beams of the moon were now in command of the ocean's current. It was a warm, beautiful, starry night, perfect for promenading along the old seawall.

Deeply inhaling the heavy, moist air, Chris said, "It's nice here, isn't it, Mother?"

"Mmm," she murmured. "Breathtaking. I wish I could spend the rest of my life here."

Chris laughed. "You don't mean that."

"Oh, but I do. I would love to live in these warm lowlands near the ocean."

"Who knows? Maybe someday you will," Chris offered. Left unsaid was that it would have to be after Alexandra had passed away.

"Perhaps," she said dreamily, not really believing it.

On leaving the seawall, they walked down the Battery to East Bay and Chris pointed out the stately mansions on the tree-shaded streets South of Broad, where the aristocracy resided.

"The old Charleston families dwell in these houses," Chris told his mother. "I know a couple of cadets who came from here."

Although she had been raised around great wealth, and presently lived in an opulent town house, Ellen was awed by these splendid southern residences that were guarded by ancient towering oaks and surrounded by lush, verdant gardens. It was the gardens that most impressed her. Accustomed to the starkness of the plain concrete sidewalk outside the Park Avenue town house, she was enchanted by the profusion of flowers and leafy vines and velvet lawns before her.

"This incredible garden," she enthused, gazing at one particularly well-tended, flower-filled terrace sloping down to the street. "These grounds must be the most beautiful in the entire state of South Carolina."

"They are exquisite, but you should see Middleton Place," Chris said offhand. A pause, then, the idea abruptly striking him, he said, "How would you like to see Middleton Place, Mother? It's an old, uninhabited plantation that was once one of the glories of the Low Country. The gardens and ponds are still there. Would you like to see them?"

"I would love to see them."

"Tomorrow at noon, as soon as general leave starts, I'll hire a carriage and we'll drive out into the country. You have the hotel pack us a picnic lunch and we'll make a day of it."

"I can hardly wait."

The ride out into the lush, green countryside of South Carolina was highly enjoyable for Ellen. Along the narrow dirt road, tall pines grew and several bountiful orchards were filled with blackberries, grapes, persimmons and plums. Birds sang sweetly in the trees and the occupants of passing carriages waved as if greeting old friends.

It was early afternoon when the pair reached Middleton Place on the banks of the Ashley River. Ellen was eager to explore the estate and Chris was only too happy to point out where the plantation house had once stood. He told her the home had been built in the mid 1700s in the style of an Italian villa.

"What happened to it?" Ellen asked. There was nothing there but a pile of rubble.

"A detachment of Sherman's army occupied the plantation in the war. When it was time to move on, the soldiers ransacked the house, then set it on fire. Then the walls finally fell in the earthquake of '86.''

"Such a shame," said Ellen.

"Yes," Chris agreed, "but the gardens are still here and someone—I don't know who—tends them regularly. Come."

Chris showed Ellen the most magnificent grounds that she'd ever imagined. Classical in concept, geometric in pattern, the gardens featured parterres, vistas, allées, arbors and bowling greens. And everywhere, among the live oaks and Spanish moss, was water, reflecting in its depths the clear Carolina sky.

There were broad-terraced lawns and butterfly lakes and a rice mill pond. Azaleas and magnolias and camellias in full bloom sweetened the air with their fragrance.

Chris told his mother the history of the house and its family while they ate cold chicken and ham and cheese and rolls as they sat on a blanket in the shade of a tall oak.

Feeling lazy after the meal, they stretched out on their backs to talk and doze and enjoy the serenity and beauty of the warm May afternoon. A time or two Ellen considered telling Chris about the upcoming adventure—or misadventure—that Alexandra had planned. But she didn't want to spoil this perfect spring day. She would tell him tomorrow.

On Sunday, Ellen and Chris attended church services at St. Michael's. Afterward they had lunch in the Mills House dining room. It was during the meal that Ellen told her son of Alexandra's latest folly.

"Chris, you know that Aunt Alexandra hates the idea of getting old," she began.

Chris laughed and said, "Somebody should tell her that she's already old."

His mother smiled, then was serious. "I know. But she doesn't want to get any older, so…"

Ellen drew a deep breath and related the entire story. She told him that Alexandra had been furious with the physicians in London when they'd told her there was nothing they, or anyone else, could do to slow down the aging process. That she was an old woman and couldn't expect to live many more years.

Ellen went on to explain that Alexandra had seen an ad in the newspaper promising magic waters that would keep a person forever young. Ellen talked and Chris listened intently, seeing the worry in her eyes.

When her story was finished, Chris did his best to console Ellen, to jolly her, to make light of the situation, although it worried him that his mother and aunt would be traveling with strangers, people who were obviously of less than sterling character.

"I just wish Aunt Alex would wait a month," said Chris. "Then I could go with you, watch out for you."

"It isn't our physical safety that most concerns me, Chris. These people are nothing but liars and thieves. And Alexandra wants to be young again so badly, there is no telling how much money they've taken from her. Don't you see, they know how foolish she is and they may be planning to rob her of the entire fortune.''

"Now, Mother," Chris soothed, "I'm sure you're worrying needlessly. Aunt Alex may be behaving foolishly, but she hasn't lost her mind. Surely she'd never let anyone get their hands on all that money."

"I'm not so certain," Ellen said. "I believe she'd give away the bulk of her estate if she thought it would get rid of a few wrinkles and buy her ten more years." Her eyebrows knitted, she said, "For heaven's sake, it is *your* inheritance we're talking about here, Chris. The Landseer fortune should go to you and—"

"Mother, I wish you would stop worrying about my inheritance and—"

"Never!" Ellen said, interrupting. Her chin raised pugnaciously, she said in a cold, level voice, "I have tolerated that ill-tempered old woman all these years and I mean to see to it that you are not cheated out of what is rightfully yours." Before he could reply, she softened and said, "It will be a long, difficult journey we'll be making. We're going all the way to the canyonlands of Utah. The lead guide, Mister Corey, has said that near the end we may have to walk and—"

"Corey?" Chris interrupted. "Did you say Corey? What is this Mister Corey's full name?"

"Ah…I really don't know. I've never heard anyone call him anything but Mister Corey. Why? Is the name familiar to you. Have you heard of Mister Corey?''

Chris paused with indecision, then said, ''No. No, Mother, I haven't.''

He quickly changed the subject, turning the conversation to the activities at the academy. No more was said about the journey or the man leading it.

But after Chris had seen his mother off at the train station, he hurried back to the Citadel. Its quadrangle was nearly empty on this warm spring afternoon, very few cadets on the grounds. Chris went into the silent building that housed the Hall of Honor.

In a glass display case he examined the sun-faded outline of a Silver Star, the nation's second highest award for bravery. The medal was no longer there. Nearby, a framed photograph of the graduating class of 1882 hung on the wall. In the third row, standing fourth from the right, a cadet's face had been crossed out.

Chris read the name below, scratched through, but still discernible.

Cadet Captain Steven J. Corey.

# *Eight*

The contentment, the happiness, the warm glow that had enveloped Ellen during the long, lovely weekend in Charleston was rapidly slipping away. No matter how hard she tried, she was finding it difficult to retain that wonderful sense of well-being she'd felt from the minute she'd stepped off the train in Charleston on Friday afternoon.

But now it was Monday.

Blue Monday.

And the northbound train on which she rode was moving steadily closer to New York City and the terminal at Grand Central Station. The joy of the past three days was behind her, already a sweet, fading memory.

Ahead of her was a long arduous journey to the inhospitable West with her cranky aunt and a motley group of unprincipled characters led by a disrespectful man who had kissed her at the depot as if the two of them were lovers.

Ellen's eyes opened.

A little tremor surged through her slender body. She told herself it was a shudder of revulsion at the memory of that audacious kiss.

But was it?

The train was now slowly rolling into the station. Dread was rising, creeping through her bones, tightening her throat, giving her a slight headache. Anxiously she peered out the window, praying she would *not* see a tall, lean man with coal-black hair and a long white scar on his right cheek waiting on the platform.

Her prayer was in vain.

Leaning lazily against a wide, square column that supported the depot roof's overhang was Mister Corey. He was wearing a white shirt, buff-colored snug-fitting trousers and freshly polished leather shoes. Clothes that were no different from the ones worn by many of the other gentlemen on the platform. At least a half-dozen men were dressed similarly. They all looked neat, clean, harmless. Except for Mister Corey.

He looked neat.

He looked clean.

But he didn't look harmless.

Ellen realized she was holding her breath. She didn't want to get off the train. She didn't want to encounter Mister Corey. She didn't want to talk to him. She didn't want him to drive her home. And she sure didn't want him to kiss her.

As she made her way down the narrow aisle toward the car's door, Ellen stiffened her spine and silently lectured herself. *Never let him see that you are nervous. Insult him before he has a chance to upset you. It's the only thing his kind understands.*

Ellen stepped down from the train, tensed, expecting the dark devil to hurry forward, grab her off the steps and attempt to kiss her again. To her surprise, nothing of the kind happened. She looked about and saw that Mister Corey was still leaning against the pillar, unmoving, his arms crossed over his chest. What kind of game was he playing now?

Frowning, Ellen stepped down onto the platform, lifted her valise with effort and headed into the busy terminal. She glanced at Mister Corey out of the corner of her eye and felt her temper rise. He was making no move to come to her, to relieve her of her heavy suitcase, to assist her in any way.

Ellen went completely through the huge, crowded terminal and out onto the sidewalk in front of the station. She was raising her hand for a carriage when Mister Corey stepped up beside her, took the valise and said, "Welcome home, Ellen."

She did not return the greeting. "Where is the carriage?"

Inclining his head, Mister Corey took her arm. "Just down the sidewalk about twenty yards. Think you can walk that far?"

"I can walk all the way home if I have to," she warned, pointedly freeing her arm from his loose grasp.

"Then why don't you?" he coolly challenged.

Her head snapped around and she glared at him. "Oh! I have," she said in clipped tones, "had just about enough of you and—"

"I don't believe you," he cut in smoothly. His gaze

briefly lowering to her lips, he said, "I don't think, Ellen, that you've had nearly enough of me."

"Are you blind and deaf?" she said, flustered and annoyed. "Don't you know that you disgust me?"

They had reached the parked carriage. Mister Corey stepped close, put his hands to Ellen's waist and lifted her up onto the leather seat. He placed her valise in the back and climbed up beside her.

"Your kiss," he said softly, looking directly into her eyes, "was not the kiss of a woman who finds me disgusting."

Ellen's eyes narrowed. "I did *not* kiss you, you kissed me and I most certainly—"

"You kissed me back."

"For heaven's sake! Try and get this through your thick skull, Mister Corey, I did *not* want you to kiss me. I did *not* kiss you back. And I forbid you to *ever* kiss me again! Now, please, kindly just drive me home!"

Mister Corey smiled, nodded, unwrapped the long leather reins from around the brake handle and guided the horse and carriage out onto the busy thoroughfare. He made several attempts at small talk, but Ellen refused to respond.

He knew how to get a rise out of her.

"Was your homesick baby boy happy to see you?" he asked. No reply. Ellen stared straight ahead, acting as if she had not heard him. He knew she had. He pressed on. "Is he a mama's boy?"

The insult of his question unleashed an angry diatribe from Ellen. Turning, she snapped, "My son is not a baby and he most definitely is not a mama's boy. Christopher is a man and he has proven it.'' She gave him a sneering look and added, ''But then, that's something you would know nothing about. You've probably never even heard of the Citadel, much less know what a great honor it is to attend the prestigious South Carolina military academy. Only the brightest and the best enter those gates and many of them are gone within days or weeks, unable to stand up to the rigid rules of the institute.''

''Is that a fact?''

''It most certainly is! And that is exactly as it should be. Those who are weeded out, and there are many, do not belong there. The academy's goal is to make brilliant, steely-nerved officers of fine, intelligent young men like my son. I assure you that no fools or cowards or weaklings graduate from the Citadel.'' She gave his lean frame an assessing glance, and asked, ''Do you think you could have made it, Mister Corey?'' Her tone, as usual, was condescending. ''Could you have withstood the harsh discipline and intense punishment a plebe endures? Or would you have been too much of a coward?''

Ellen was looking directly at him when she asked, so she noticed the tension in his jaw. She immediately recalled the same thing happening the day Alexandra had suggested he accompany her to Charleston.

She was curious, but in an instant his expression changed and he said in a flat, drawling tone, ''Looks like you've found me out, Ellen Cornelius. Yesiree, the truth is I'm a sniveling, quivering, trembling coward." He laughed then.

She did not. "It isn't funny, Mister Corey. I would think you would at least have enough pride to be ashamed to admit that you are a coward."

"There was a time, long ago, when I was. But now I'm used to the label and it doesn't sound that distasteful anymore. There are worse things to be called."

"Yes, I suppose there are. Like swindler or cheat or thief," she said hatefully, a smirk on her face.

"Perhaps, but I know some that are worse." He pinned her with his night-black eyes. "Like toady or bootlick or kowtower."

Ellen's face instantly flushed with hurt and anger. Her green eyes flashing with fury, she said, "Insult me if you will. What you think of me is of no importance whatsoever. I do not need—nor want—your approval."

"I don't believe you," he calmly replied.

In the 1890s America's privileged took great pride and pleasure in showing off the expensive toys their vast wealth could provide. And so it was a period of the most splendid and ornate private railroad cars man could imagine. The wealthy all owned them, even if they seldom or never traveled. For the snobbish upper crust, the private rail car was an absolute necessity. The quintessential exhibition of ostentatious elegance.

Of all the private rail cars, none were finer than the sleek, gleaming ebony car with the gold script lettering on the door. The elegant car belonging to one of America's richest women, Miss Alexandra Landseer.

Commissioned by the Pullman Company at the beginning of the decade, it had taken the company more than a year to finish the luxurious conveyance.

The delay was not the fault of Pullman, but of the persnickety lady who was to own the car. The interior had been changed no less than half a dozen times because Alexandra couldn't make up her mind as to what she wanted. The harried workmen would think that they had finally completed the Landseer job, only to be told by a frowning Alexandra, bejeweled hands on her hips, that "No, this just won't do! The bedroom is too large, the sitting room too small! All these walls must be torn out. You'll simply have to start over. I will not pay you a penny until I get *exactly* what I want!"

And so it had gone for the entire year.

But, giving the devil her due, when finally the rail car had passed Alexandra's discriminating inspection, it was a rolling wonder.

Inside, intricately carved boiseries exhibited the craftsmen's infinite capacity for detail. A composite observation-sleeping car, the *Lucky Landseer* boasted a marble bathtub with gleaming gold fixtures. In the spacious sitting room, beneath a vaulted ceiling heavily embellished with Gothic fretwork, sat a handsome, oversize sofa and two matching easy chairs. The pale blue velvet furniture rested upon a thick, plush Aubusson carpet of blue and beige.

At the rear of the handsome room, a door opened

onto an observation deck. A waist-high railing of beautifully carved iron lace bordered the small open-air deck. A narrow steel ladder went from the floor of the deck to the car's top.

There was no furniture of any kind on the observation deck, although there was plenty of space. Alexandra saw no need for chairs or a settee. She had absolutely no interest in sitting out in the open, and it was always her own comfort that concerned her, no one else's.

If Ellen or any invited guests wished to spend time on the observation deck, they simply would have to stand.

On the other side of the living room, in the car's opulent bedroom, all the windows were draped with ice-blue velvet curtains. Alexandra never allowed those heavy drapes to be opened. She stated unequivocally that when she was inside her boudoir, she did not want some unwashed peasant along the tracks looking in at her.

The bedroom was capacious and comfortable and decorated with heavy carved furniture, gold-framed mirrors, marble statuary and handsome globed lamps and sconces. Beautiful artwork graced the wood-paneled walls.

Alexandra thought the room ideal.

Ellen did not.

It would have been, had it been hers alone. But the room was Alexandra's and Ellen was forced to share with her aunt. Two specially built beds, covered in pale blue velvet spreads, were separated by only a small night table. The lack of privacy made Ellen dislike traveling in the splendid car.

But, tomorrow she would be trapped inside the velvet prison for several long days and nights as the train rolled westward.

Ellen exhaled loudly. Tonight, the eleventh of May, 1899, was the last night she'd spend in the quiet serenity of her own bedroom for many weeks.

Slipping her nightgown over her head, Ellen sank down onto the edge of the bed. It was well past midnight, but she wasn't sleepy. Her anxiety was rising steadily as departure time neared. The last thing on earth she wanted to do was to go out West on this outlandish, expensive lark.

It was more than just the senseless waste of money that bothered her.

She had a nagging premonition that once the journey westward was under way, nothing in her life would ever be quite the same again. She felt as though she would be caught up in some clandestine web of danger from which she could never escape. She had the frightening feeling that she might never return to the safety of this Park Avenue town house.

And, that even if she did, she would not be the same person she was when she left.

Ellen shook her head and silently scolded herself. She was being unforgivably silly. *Nothing* was going to happen to her. Nothing more than a long, boring trip across the country and a senseless trek to some ordinary water hole where Alexandra would learn, too late, that there was no such thing as a fountain of youth.

Then, at last, back home to her sheltered, well-ordered existence.

Ellen sighed, took the pins from her hair and let it spill down around her shoulders. Without aid of a mirror, she swiftly plaited it into a thick braid. She yawned, blew out the lamp and got into bed.

There was nothing to worry about, she assured herself. She had cleverly managed to avoid Mister Corey since the morning he had met her at Grand Central Station. Four pleasant days without seeing him.

And in that time the memory of his burning kiss had faded until she could hardly remember what it had felt like.

Out of sight, out of mind was actually true. And she would keep him out of sight on the long train trip to Grand Junction, Colorado. All she had to do was to constantly stay inside the close confines of the *Lucky Landseer.*

It wouldn't be easy, but she could do it.

She would do it.

She *had* to do it.

Ellen's resolve strengthened as Mister Corey's arrogant words came back to her, "I don't think, Ellen, that you've had nearly enough of me."

# Nine

At the last minute, Alexandra had decided to not take any servants along on the train trip. It was customary, when she traveled in the *Lucky Landseer* to have at least the chef and her personal maid, Esther, accompany her. She decided against it for this journey and, as usual, her decision was a selfish one.

She worried that if her servants were on board, the group with which she was traveling might assume that they, too, could avail themselves of their services. The outsiders might mistakenly take it for granted that her chef would cook for them and that her maid would tend their needs.

That would be the day!

Now as she excitedly rushed around on the morning of departure, Alexandra congratulated herself on electing to leave the servants at home. She was aware that their absence would not make the trip any easier. But she could do it. She would take her meals in the dining car, just like any common passenger. And, after all, she had Ellen.

"It's them!" Alexandra cried out as a knock came at the mansion's massive front door. Her uniformed butler, the solemn, long-suffering Dunwoody, immediately appeared. Alexandra put up a hand and stopped him. "No, Ellen will answer the door. You should be seeing to the luggage." Turning to Ellen, she said, "Don't just stand there, let them in! What in God's name are you waiting for?"

Ellen couldn't tell her aunt that she was waiting for the pounding of her heart to slow its beat. Ellen was sure that when she opened the door, Mister Corey would be standing there, tall, dark and intimidating.

Ellen squared her slender shoulders, lifted the skirts of her cotton summer dress and proceeded across the black-and-white marble tiles of the spacious foyer.

She opened the door and immediately smiled.

She was greeted by Ricky O'Mara who said cheerfully, "Good morning to you, Ellen. Are you and your aunt ready to leave?"

"We most certainly are," came Alexandra's distinctive voice from behind Ellen. "Now get in here and get this luggage loaded! Where's Mister Corey? You'll need his help to—"

"No, Miss Landseer," said Ricky, coming inside. "I can take care of the luggage." Alexandra made a face, went to the door and looked out. Ricky quickly explained, "Mister Corey and the others will meet us at Grand Central Station."

"Oh," said Alexandra, mollified. "Good. Yes, that's fine."

Ellen wanted to echo her aunt. She felt she had been temporally reprieved and was grateful. With any luck, she would not have to see Mister Corey this morning. She and Alexandra would board the *Lucky*

*Landseer* with Ricky and a porter's help. And if she played her cards right on the journey, if she ate her meals at either an early or late hour, she likely wouldn't encounter Mister Corey more than a time or two on the entire train trip.

It was, she figured, more than two thousand miles to Grand Junction. With all the stops the train would make along the route, it would take several long days before they reached their destination. Several peaceful days in which she would *not* have to contend with the troublesome Mister Corey.

Feeling herself relax, Ellen finally began to smile. When Ricky and Dunwoody had loaded the many valises and cases and heavy trunks into the waiting carriage, Ellen went back up the steps of the town house to say goodbye to the servants.

She hugged Ida, the housekeeper, a big, rawboned woman with a ruddy face, salt-and-pepper hair and a kind heart. She shook hands with Dillon, the portly chef. Next came Alexandra's personal maid, Esther, a small, agile, middle-aged woman with gray-streaked red hair and a saucy manner.

Esther wrapped her short arms around Ellen and whispered in her ear, "Don't be waiting on bossy old Alex hand and foot while you're gone. She's the one wanting to go off on this asinine adventure, so just tell her to make her own bed and comb her own hair."

"I will," Ellen promised, smiling. "You take care of things here while we're gone."

"That's what I'm here for, honey," said Esther.

She and the others followed aunt and niece to the front door. Alexandra turned, gave Esther a half-hearted pat on the shoulder and commanded, "You'll see to it that Ida and the cleaning girls keep this place immaculate, just as if I were here."

"No," teased Esther. "Once you're safely out the door we're throwing a big party. All the servants up and down Park Avenue are invited. You get back here, you'll find empty champagne bottles and cigar butts all over the place."

Alexandra didn't bother responding. Just frowned, waved a dismissive hand and went down the front steps. Ricky lifted Ellen up into the carriage and turned to Alexandra.

"May I assist you, Miss Landseer?" he asked politely.

"You'd jolly well better, young man!" she snapped.

The wide smile never left Ricky's handsome face. Stepping forward, he placed his powerful hands at Alexandra's thick waist and effortlessly lifted her onto the seat. Solicitously arranging her skirts around her feet, he grinned at her and said, "Why, you're as light as a feather."

"Don't waste your time trying to butter me up, O'Mara. It won't work. You know your place. See that you stay in it."

"Sorry, Miss Landseer," Ricky apologized and Ellen wanted to choke her inconsiderate aunt.

But Ricky was neither hurt nor insulted. He had realized early on that Alexandra Landseer was a shallow, rich, self-centered woman and that dealing with her would often be unpleasant. He didn't mind. Her rudeness didn't bother him. In fact, he almost felt sorry for her. She was undoubtedly a miserable person.

His sunny smile still firmly in place, Ricky swung up onto the seat beside the aging heiress, and asked, "Now, are we ready to leave?"

"I've been ready from the moment I read Mister Corey's advertisement in the *London Times*. Let's be on our way!"

"At your service, madam," said Ricky, reaching for the reins.

"No! Wait!" Alexandra abruptly grabbed his arm. "Stop. Wait a minute. I'm not ready after all! Good heavens, I was about to get off without my chalice."

"Your chalice?" said Ricky, dark eyebrows lifting in question.

"Yes!" Alexandra said irritably, almost shouting. "My goblet. My golden goblet!" She looked sharply at him and said, "I *must* take it with me! I have it all planned. It is from the golden goblet that I will take my first drink of the Magic Waters!"

Alexandra turned to order Ellen back inside, but Ellen had already scrambled down out of the carriage and was rushing up the steps of the town house. In seconds she returned and in her right hand was a deep-blue velvet bag with a drawstring pulled tight at the top. Inside was Alexandra Landseer's golden goblet. Ellen held it up for her aunt to see.

"Now we can leave," said Alexandra.

"You're welcome, Auntie," Ellen said quietly. Ricky lifted her back up into the carriage and the two of them exchanged knowing looks. Ellen was suddenly very glad that a man as nice as Ricky O'Mara was going on this long journey. She felt as if she had a friend in the likable Spanish-Irishman.

At Grand Central Station, Ricky quickly engaged a porter to transport the luggage through the crowded terminal and out to the tracks. When Ellen exited the building and stepped onto the platform, she automatically looked for Mister Corey.

She immediately caught sight of the bald, beaming Padjan. The wiry little man was standing on the steps of a rail car near the end of the train, slowly backing up the steps and gesturing to someone below.

Mister Corey moved out of the crowd and up to the car. In his arms was Summer Dawn. He cautiously carried the old Indian woman up the train steps, deftly turning to one side to ensure that she wouldn't hit either side of the door as he eased her into the waiting car.

In seconds Mister Corey reappeared in the car's doorway, and Ricky, having instructed the porter to load everything into the *Lucky Landseer* looked up, saw Mister Corey and motioned him over.

Mister Corey swung down from the train and headed toward them. Ellen stiffened as she watched him approach. He moved with quiet assurance, as if incapable of taking a clumsy step. A fact that irked her no end. His natural grace made her feel all the more awkward.

Hoping to save herself from an encounter with the disturbing man, Ellen said, "My goodness, Auntie, we'd better get on board. Let's hurry and get in out of this heat."

"Yes," Alexandra agreed, but added, "O'Mara, have Mister Corey come to the *Lucky Landseer*. I've some last-minute things to discuss with him." Ellen's heart sank.

"I'll tell him," said Ricky.

Alexandra and Ellen headed for the *Lucky Landseer*. Just ahead of it was the leased rail car in which Ricky O'Mara and Mister Corey would be traveling. Directly in front of that car was the car in which Padjan and Summer Dawn would be lodged. In each of the two rented conveyances was a long, narrow hallway to one side that stretched the length of the entire car. Doors along the hallway opened onto private sleeping quarters.

The cars were designed so that other passengers could walk through without intruding upon the privacy of those inside. A necessity, since the cars in question were not always located at the end of the train. Passengers had to have access to the club car, the dining car and the sleeping cars.

There was, on this long train, only one completely private car. The *Lucky Landseer*. For that reason, it was the very last car on the train.

Once Ellen and Alexandra were inside their elegant conveyance, Ellen, eager to avoid Mister Corey, said sweetly, "I'll go into the bedroom and start unpacking."

"There's no hurry. We'll take care of that later," said Alexandra.

Ellen tried again. "Very well. I'll just check to see if there are plenty of towels and—"

"There are and you know it. Why are you so fidgety?" said Alexandra. "Sit down, you're making me nervous. I want you to be here when Mister Corey shows up."

"Why?" Ellen asked.

"Because, quite frankly, the man scares the daylights out of me and I don't wish to be alone with him." She shrugged and added, "There's something sinister and threatening about Mister Corey. I wish he were not going with us. I wish it was just that smiling Spaniard and Padjan. Padjan is the one who knows the way, so I don't see why we need Mister Corey, but Padjan says—"

The sound of a booted foot on the train steps stopped her. Her head jerked around. Mister Corey stood in the open doorway.

"You sent for me?" he said with the slightly bored, agitated air of someone who had heard it all before.

"I did," said Alexandra. "Come inside, please."

He advanced, and Ellen, standing beside one of the blue velvet chairs, nodded but did not smile. Nor did he.

"Morning, Ellen," he said, his eyes resting on her for a split second, then dismissing her.

"Have a seat, Mister Corey," Alexandra instructed.

"Sure," he said. He sank down onto the velvet sofa and sat there with one long leg thrown over the other in an attitude of indifference. "What's on your mind, Miss Landseer?"

"This journey, of course," she said and sat down on one of the matching chairs. "It's still not clear to me exactly how we're to proceed once we leave the train."

"Then let's go over it one more time," he said as he withdrew a cigarette from the breast pocket of his pale-blue cotton shirt, struck a match with his thumbnail and lighted the smoke. He shook out the match, then looked around for an ashtray.

"There are none, Mister Corey," Alexandra haughtily informed him. "We do *not* smoke in this conveyance."

"You don't?" He shrugged wide shoulders. "Well, I do." He took a long drag from the cigarette, then blew out several perfect smoke rings.

Annoyed, Alexandra said, snapping her fingers, "Ellen, quick, get him a dish so he won't be dropping ashes all over the Aubusson carpet."

Ellen complied, then took the chair beside her aunt, directly across from Mister Corey. In a low, flat voice he explained, again, that once they reached Grand Junction they would take at least a couple days to rest and purchase the supplies they would need.

He had, he assured Alexandra, been in touch with a rancher there who had agreed to sell them several saddle ponies, along with a sturdy team to pull a specially equipped wagon. The wagon was being customized and they would pick it up at a local carriage maker's shop.

"Most everything has been taken care of," said Mister Corey. He glanced from Alexandra to Ellen. "Now, you really do ride, don't you, Ellen?"

"I've told you that I'm a very capable horsewoman."

"Tell me again. I don't want to get there and find out your idea of horsemanship is a ride on one of the tame nags they rent out at Central Park."

Ellen bristled. "For your information, Mister Corey, I have, since I was a child, been riding blooded animals on the Landseer country estate in Connecticut. I can ride as well as any man, so don't be worrying about me."

"That's the idea," was his reply. His attention returning to Alexandra, he said, "Padjan will drive the wagon. You will sit on the seat beside him. Summer Dawn will rest on a bed inside the wagon out of the sun."

"What if I get tired and want to lie down?" said Alexandra.

"What if *I* do?" was his calm comeback. "Miss Landseer, I've tried to warn you that this is going to be a very difficult journey for you. We are going to be traveling through some of the roughest, most inhospitable country in the entire United States. It will take great sacrifices on all our parts. If it's too much to ask, then you should reconsider."

"I am going!" stated Alexandra emphatically. "You are taking me to those Magic Waters just as promised."

Nodding, Mister Corey continued, "There's a big outfitter in Grand Junction where we can pick up everything we need. Cooking utensils, blankets, tents, and…"

As Ellen listened to the low, deep timbre of Mister Corey's voice, she covertly studied him. He must have once been very handsome. Now that long white scar slashed down his right jaw, giving his unsmiling face a fierceness that sent chills up her spine.

She noticed his strong brown hand holding the lighted cigarette, idly rolling it between long, tapered forefinger and thumb. His hands were beautiful, perfectly shaped, deeply tanned. She involuntarily shifted in her chair when, suddenly, in her mind's eye, she could see those dark, artistic hands on her own pale shoulders, could almost feel the warmth of his touch.

"Something wrong, Ellen?" Mister Corey caught her sudden movement.

"Not a thing," she said and folded her arms over her chest.

"I thought I saw you jump and—"

"Perhaps you need your eyes checked by a professional, Mister Corey. I haven't moved."

"My mistake," he said, snuffed out his cigarette and rose to his feet. "If that's all, ladies."

"Yes, you may go," Alexandra dismissed him.

Ellen continued to guiltily examine him as Mister Corey headed, unhurriedly, toward the door. He moved with the measured kind of grace that only predatory jungle animals possess.

He looked like a predatory animal. Like a dangerous panther, dark and sleek and graceful.

Ellen bit the inside of her lip.

Watching him made her clothes feel uncomfortably tight. She had begun to perspire at the hairline. Her stomach contracted and her nipples tightened. She felt the muscles in her thighs jump involuntarily and her breath grew short.

Ellen Cornelius was not an experienced woman, but she recognized what was happening to her for what it was. A strong, undeniable sexual attraction to the unprincipled Mister Corey. She was horrified that his mere presence could evoke such powerful physical yearnings.

"You look pale and overwarm." Her aunt's accusing tone broke into Ellen's painful reveries. "Are you feeling well?"

"I'm fine," said Ellen. "Just fine."

# PART TWO

# Ten

*Aboard the* Lucky Landseer
*May 1899*

At long last, the contingent departed for the West, traveling in grand style across America in three private rail cars.

But as luxurious and comfortable as her quarters were, it was not an hour after leaving Grand Central Station that Alexandra turned to her niece, who was occupied with the unpacking, and said, "I'm bored. Bored to tears. Go up ahead to Padjan's car and tell him to come back here and visit with me."

"Now, Aunt Alexandra," Ellen said, taking one of her aunt's fine dresses from a large trunk, "you know very well that Padjan is not going to leave Summer Dawn alone."

"I hadn't thought of that," said Alexandra, rubbing her chin and making a face. Then she smiled and said, "You can stay with Summer Dawn. Tell Padjan you'll be happy to sit with the old woman for a couple of hours."

Ellen exhaled heavily but didn't argue. She carefully hung up the expensive dress, closed the trunk and left without saying a word.

Ellen stepped out onto the open platform between the *Lucky Landseer* and the car just ahead. She held her breath when she went inside the forward conveyance. She looked cautiously down the long narrow passageway before venturing any farther. Praying Mister Corey wouldn't pick that particular moment to come out of his quarters, she hurried through the car as if demons from hell were after her.

She gave a great sigh of relief when she exited and was again standing in the warm sunshine between two rail cars.

Padjan was surprised to see Ellen.

"Ellen! Come in, come in," he said warmly. Then quickly asked, "Is something wrong?"

"No," Ellen assured him, then said, "Well, actually, yes, something is. You see, Aunt Alexandra is at loose ends, so she insists that you come entertain her."

The bald little man immediately began shaking his head from side to side. "She knows better than that," he said, smiling, his ebony eyes twinkling. "Summer Dawn can't be left alone for a few minutes, much less two hours."

"I know. My aunt suggested that I watch Summer Dawn while you visit with her." Ellen's slender shoulders lifted, then lowered in a shrug. "I'll be more than glad to—"

"My dear child," Padjan interrupted and Ellen found it amusing that this man, who could not be that many years older than she, would call her "child."

Padjan hurriedly continued, "I wouldn't dream of asking you to waste your afternoon in such a manner." He gently took her arm and said, "You should be enjoying yourself, Ellen. Why don't you go along to the dining car? Mister Corey and Ricky are there. You can have a nice long lunch with them."

"Oh, no, I…I'm not hungry. I'll wait until the last seating."

Padjan nodded. "Then, please go back and tell Miss Alexandra that if she wants to visit with me, she knows where to find me. I will not leave Summer Dawn."

"I'll tell her," Ellen said, smiling now, "but she won't like it."

Padjan chuckled and confided, "I know. She is not used to having her will thwarted, is she?"

"Not at all."

Together they laughed and when Padjan saw Ellen to the door, he prophesied, "It will not always be so. Once Alexandra has drunk of the Magic Waters, you will see a remarkable change."

Highly skeptical, Ellen raised a well-arched eyebrow and replied, "I'll believe it when I see it."

Padjan was confident. "You *will* see it. You will believe it. She will change. And, she will not be the only one. Whoever drinks of the Magic Waters is forever changed."


Alexandra and Padjan, having hit it off from the beginning, spent a great deal of time together on the long train trip. In Padjan's rail car. Not Alexandra's. Padjan stubbornly refused to leave Summer Dawn,

except for hurried visits to the dining car. On those
occasions, either Mister Corey or Ricky, or both, willingly stayed with the weak old woman.

Ellen was glad that Padjan stuck to his guns and
made Alexandra come to him instead of the other way
around. It was novel indeed. In thirty-six years, she
had never seen her aunt bend to another's will.

Ellen was glad for another reason. She welcomed
the long hours alone in the *Lucky Landseer*. With her
domineering aunt out of the way, she could relax,
read, rest, do just as she pleased. Which certainly
wasn't the case when Alexandra was present.

When the two of them were there together, Alexandra was constantly ordering her about, saying, "Get
me this, get me that. Make my bed. Comb my hair.
Press my dress. Rub my neck. Open the drapes. Close
the drapes." On and on.

And Alexandra constantly complained.

It was too warm in the *Lucky Landseer*, she was
sticky and uncomfortable and totally miserable. The
food in the dining car was terrible, not fit for human
consumption. The interminable blowing of the train's
whistle as they passed through stations was driving
her mad. Would it never stop?

Her aunt's continual whining was not the only
thorn in Ellen's side. She had foolishly assumed that
she could, for the most part, avoid Mister Corey on
this journey. It had not worked out that way. It
seemed that no matter what hour she chose to go to
the dining car, he was there.

Her intense dislike and unwanted attraction for him

grew steadily with each encounter. Ellen was afraid of him and of the way he affected her. She never felt entirely safe in his presence. There was a compelling sexuality about him that both repelled and beguiled her. She involuntarily responded to his raw masculinity and each time she was around him she felt as if she were being helplessly lured into some exotic web of sexual danger.

Or exquisite pleasure.

Or both at once.

She vainly attempted to safeguard herself from him with a patronizing manner and an acid tongue. Every chance she got, she spelled it out in no uncertain terms that she believed him to be an unscrupulous swindler, a man without morals whose aim it was to embezzle her aunt out of her fortune. Ellen never passed up an opportunity to heap insults on his dark head.

Which was a mistake on her part.

Mister Corey was not especially attracted to the too-thin, buttoned-up, socially inept Ellen Cornelius. He had, at the beginning, looked on her as a rather pathetic figure, a lonely young woman, apparently disappointed by life, forced to live under the thumb of a tyrannical aunt. He had once felt no small degree of compassion for the forlorn Ellen.

Not anymore.

She had called him a thief and a liar one time too many. Although he very carefully hid his feelings, her words rankled him. That, and the fact that she constantly looked down her aristocratic nose at him as if he were riffraff. Southern white trash. The scum of the earth. So far beneath her she abhorred being in the same room with him.

The inexperienced Ellen had badly miscalculated her opponent. Mister Corey was a world-wise man. He had seen and done just about everything and he could read most people with ease. He could certainly read her. He knew there was a great deal of fear related to her contempt for him. Not actual fear of physical harm. But fear of herself and her perplexing attraction to him. He was certain she repeatedly told herself that she disliked him, despised him, loathed him.

He knew better.

While she did not approve of him, she was definitely intrigued. She was drawn to him against her better judgment and she blamed him for it. Thus, she went out of her way to offend and humiliate him. Had she been more sophisticated, had she known more about the nature of men, she would have ignored him. And he, in turn, would have left her alone.

But she didn't and, therefore, he couldn't.

Truth to tell, Mister Corey grudgingly appreciated Ellen's sarcastic wit, which was similar to his own. She was good at mocking and ridiculing him. She was quite adept at delivering stinging verbal jabs.

Still, he sensed her true feelings and so he relished testing her fragile poise. She'd become somewhat of a challenge for him, something to help alleviate his trainbound boredom.

If she delighted in insulting him, he took pleasure in saying things to her that no gentleman would say to a lady. Things he knew no other had ever dared say to her. And it worked. He infuriated her. He shocked her. He repelled her. He excited her. And he'd decided it was about time he showed her more about herself than she'd ever known before. More than she ever wanted to know. She'd lose some of that rigid smugness, that patronizing patrician manner once he had.

She had no respect for him? Well, the feeling was mutual. She considered him to be a charlatan and thief. Was she, a spineless sycophant who catered to a mean old woman for filthy lucre, any better? She considered herself to be far, far above him? He knew how to bring her down to his level.

She deserved it. And, although she didn't realize it, she was asking for it. Before the train reached Grand Junction, he was going to give it to her.

Those less-than-gentlemanly thoughts were running through Mister Corey's mind when, on the fourth day of the journey, Ellen entered the dining car as the summer sun was setting. She spotted him immediately and frowned, clearly displeased with his presence.

Which pleased him very much.

He rose to his feet and motioned her over. The other diners had turned to stare, so Ellen gritted her teeth and started toward Mister Corey. When she reached him, he stepped around the table, took hold of her arm, whispering something so suggestive her face flushed bloodred.

She jerked her arm free and said, "I will not stand for this!"

"Then sit down," he said and pulled out a chair.

Feeling prying eyes on them, an angry Ellen quickly complied as she wondered how she could get herself out of this troubling situation.

"Where's Ricky?" she asked, hoping the answer would be that he would be along any minute.

"He couldn't wait, had dinner at the first seating."

"That's too bad. He seems like such a nice man."

"And I'm not?"

"You said it, I didn't."

"But you don't think I'm nice, do you, Ellen Cornelius?"

"How many times must I say it," she was quick to reply. "No. No, I do not. There is nothing nice about you, Mister Corey."

He smiled and in that smooth, half-mocking voice that only added to his magnetism, said, "You can be cruel. Anybody ever tell you that? Real cruel."

"I have had excellent tutors," she coldly informed him.

"Well, if that were the case, why didn't you...?"

"Don't start with me! You know nothing of my life or the circumstances that govern it and I will not be appraised by a common carnival barker!"

For a long moment Mister Corey said nothing, just regarded her with cold black eyes that held no trace of light. When he spoke, it was in low, soft tones. "We live not as we wish to, but as we can." He smiled. "Or so the philosopher says."

"Really?" she answered hatefully. "And if I want to hear any more of your trite little platitudes, I'll be sure to let you know." She gave him a smug look, pleased with herself.

But as usual he surprised her. Leaning close, he said, "What about when you want me to kiss you again? Will you let me know?"

"Oh! That will never happen, I assure you. I did not want you to kiss me that morning at the station. And the day will never come when I do want you to kiss me!"

"What about the night?"

"Neither morning, noon nor night. Not ever."

He grinned wickedly. "Say that to me again in twenty-four hours."

"Gladly!"

# *Eleven*

Later the same night.

The westbound train chugged across the state of Kansas. Topeka had been left behind hours ago and there was now nothing until Salina. Nothing but the flat, windswept Kansas plain stretching endlessly in every direction.

Midnight came and went.

Ellen was still wide-awake and agitated, lying in bed in the dark, wishing she could fall asleep. Wishing it were not so warm and stuffy in the car's bedchamber. Wishing morning would come. Wishing her sleeping aunt would stop the infernal snoring that was driving her half-crazy.

Wishing she could stop thinking about the man asleep in the car next to theirs.

Ellen frowned worriedly.

The enigmatic Mister Corey was too often in her thoughts, the recollection of his stirring kiss impossible to forget. She was, she realized, helplessly drawn to him and that knowledge frightened her as nothing ever had.

Finally Ellen exhaled with exasperation, turned onto her side and glared at her peacefully slumbering aunt. Alexandra lay on her back, hands folded over her chest, fast asleep, snoring so loudly that the irritating sound reverberated throughout the shadowy suite.

Ellen could stand it no longer.

She threw back the covering sheet and got out of bed. She reached for her robe, then tossed it back on the chair. She wouldn't need it. It was the middle of the night and the train was traveling across the vast barren plains of Kansas. No cities, no houses, no people along the route.

Ellen often sought refuge on the observation deck. On those occasions when she couldn't stand one more minute of her aunt's griping and grumbling or gossiping, she slipped out onto the open-air deck to get away if only for a few minutes. She often wished that there was a seat on the deck so she could stay longer. As it was, she had to content herself with standing at the railing.

Ellen tiptoed from the bedroom, quietly closing the door behind her. She was barefoot and her long hair was braided into one thick plait that hung over her shoulder. She wore a white batiste nightgown that reached her ankles and nothing else, but she wasn't worried.

No one would see her.

She hurriedly crossed the car's darkened drawing room, anxious to take several deep breaths of the fresh night air. She unlocked the door, opened it partially to slip through, and carefully closed the door behind her.

She sighed with relief as she slowly turned around. And then she saw him.

Mister Corey, shirtless and shoeless, his broad bare shoulders gleaming in the moonlight, his raven hair shimmering with silver highlights, stood leaning against the observation deck's railing, calmly smoking a cigarette. Stunned, caught completely off guard, Ellen was, for a second, totally speechless. She couldn't believe her eyes. He *couldn't* be on her aunt's private observation deck. He had no access. Surely she was imagining him. Perhaps her yearning heart had conjured him up.

As she stared in dazed incredulity, Mister Corey took a long drag off his cigarette. The glowing tip momentarily illuminated the scar on his cheek and his full lips. Ellen felt a familiar tingle surge through her body and knew this was no illusion. He was there and he was dangerous and it was imperative she hurry back inside to safety.

She never made it.

Mister Corey took the cigarette from his mouth and carelessly flicked it onto the tracks. Orange sparks flew in the warm wind and Ellen felt as if the showering embers were igniting a virulent blaze deep inside her. Unsettling heat quickly spread through her immobile body and the blood singed through her veins.

Mister Corey moved and Ellen had little will to fight what she knew was about to happen. Still, she made a vain, halfhearted effort.

"What are you doing here?" she said, attempting

to sound authoritative. "You have no right to be on this private observation deck!"

"Why, Ellen, I came for you," he drawled, moving catlike, slowly, toward her. "I came because you wanted me to come."

Ellen's face flushed hotly, but she was quick to deny it. "You know better than that," she said. "How did you get here? There's no access to…"

"By magic. You envision me and I appear," he said. He then looked pointedly at the iron ladder she stood beside. She glanced at it, understood and said, "You crawled atop the rail car?"

"No, I didn't crawl." He could almost reach out and touch her. "I walked atop the rail car. I risked my life just for you."

Flustered and foolishly flattered by his teasing statement, Ellen knew she was in peril. At great risk. She had to get away from this darkly appealing man immediately, or…

"Don't," she warned, her voice shrill, "Please, don't come any closer, Mister Corey."

He came closer.

Didn't stop until he stood only inches from her. Ellen involuntarily trembled when he raised a hand, wrapped lean fingers around the braid of hair lying on her shoulder and said, his voice deep and low, "Ellen, my full name is Steven J. Corey. Call me Steve."

"W-why?" she asked nervously.

He gave the braid a gentle tug and said, "Because

it would be a bit formal to call me Mister Corey when I'm making love to you.''

Ellen swallowed hard. ''You're not...I won't allow...you're not going to make love to me, Mister Corey...Steve.''

He released her braid, swept it back over her shoulder. He raised a hand above her head, laced his fingers around the side-rail of the iron ladder.

''You're wrong,'' he said as his dark head slowly descended and his lips lowered to hers. ''I am going to make love to you.'' He paused and gazed at her trembling lips for a long moment before adding, ''And you, Ellen, are going to make love to me as you've never made love to anyone.''

Before she could reply, he kissed her, and just as it had been that day at Grand Central Station, Ellen felt her knees go weak, her heart race in her chest. It was an invasive, demanding kiss of such fierce animal passion she felt as if they were already intimate. Surely no lovemaking could be any more carnal than this blazing, penetrating kiss.

With one strong arm around her waist, Mister Corey held her close against his naked chest and kissed her ardently, hungrily. His smooth, full lips were blazing hot on hers and his sleek wet tongue was deep inside her mouth, teasing, tasting, conquering.

That's all it took.

Just one devastating kiss.

By the time that prolonged, overpowering kiss ended, Steve Corey knew she was his to do with as he pleased. Ellen knew it as well. Her will to stop him had melted in the heat of his kiss and already she was malleable clay in his hands. She knew very little about lovemaking, and what little she had once known had been mostly forgotten in the long, lonely years of celibacy. But she felt certain that the man who was kissing her had enough experience for them both.

Ellen sighed and her weak arms went around his neck when he tipped her head back and began kissing the sensitive hollow of her throat. Trembling, thrilling to his caresses, Ellen hardly realized he was moving her over to stand directly in front of the ladder. Vaguely she could feel the ladder's rungs against her back.

Then she felt nothing but his burning lips slipping lower into the half-open bodice of her nightgown and the hardness of his trousered thigh pressing between her legs. Soon his mouth was back on hers, thrilling her, pleasing her, showing her how to kiss with the total abandon of an uninhibited lover, which he intended to make of her.

With him as her teacher, Ellen learned quickly. She eagerly sucked at his tongue and shivered with delight when she heard him groan. And when he withdrew his tongue but kept his lips on hers, she knew instinctively what he wanted. She wasted no time in plunging her tongue into his mouth and felt a quick flash of feminine pride when he shuddered against her.

Ellen was so caught up in their deep, desperate kissing, she wasn't aware of the exact moment when he started easing her soft batiste nightgown up her slender legs. She was licking his lips when all at once she realized the night winds were stroking her bare thighs and that her nightgown was bunched up around her waist.

She should have been appalled.

She wasn't.

She tore her kiss-swollen lips from his, looked into his night-black eyes and let out a little gasp of shocked pleasure when she felt his hand rise to cup a warm breast. His dark gaze holding hers, he rubbed his thumb back and forth across the stiffening nipple while she squirmed and sighed and leaned back against the ladder for support.

"Noooo," she halfheartedly protested when he deftly eased the gown up over her head and took it off. "Mister Corey…" she murmured, shocked, when he opened his hand and released the gown. She watched as the wind caught it and for a few seconds the frothy garment was airborne.

"Mister Corey," she whispered breathlessly, "what will they think when someone finds my nightgown?"

"That you're such an impulsive lover, you couldn't wait one more second to be naked in my arms."

Ellen smiled nervously. She stood trembling and vulnerable in the pale moonlight, knowing she should be angry with him, but finding that anger was the furthest thing from her mind when he bent his head and captured a nipple with warm lips.

"Steeeeve," she sighed, putting both hands into his

raven hair to hold his dark face close. "Steve, Steve, Steve," she repeated as he ran his tongue around her throbbing nipple and at the same time slipped a warm hand between her legs.

She gasped when he touched her in that most sensitive spot, and when he began to caress her, she felt as if his fingers were literally setting her on fire. That she was surely erupting in flames that would consume them both.

He abruptly released her nipple to look into her eyes, but continued to gently touch and tease the tender feminine flesh between her legs, and said huskily, "You're hot, Ellen. You're hot and wet. For me."

She swallowed and nodded vigorously.

"Say it," he instructed in a low, seductive voice. "Tell me you want me. Tell me you're hot and wet and you want me inside you."

"Steve, don't...I...I...can't..." she began.

"Say it," he demanded, taking his hand from between her legs and lifting it up before her face. She saw that his fingers were glistening wetly from the liquid flowing from her. "Now say it to me, Ellen. Tell me that you're wet and hot and that you want me to make love to you."

On fire, so aroused and excited she was no longer capable of logical thought, Ellen anxiously clutched his bare arms and said, "Yes, oh yes, Steve, yes. I'm hot and wet and I want you to make love to me. I want you, I want you now."

''And you will have me,'' he said, bending to brush a kiss to her open lips.

Ellen's eyes widened in surprise and question when Steve took her arm and turned her about so that she was facing away from him. His tall lean body pressing close against hers, he took both her hands, raised them high above her head and wrapped her fingers around the twin side-rails of the iron ladder.

He stood directly behind her, leaned down, kissed her on the nape of the neck and instructed, ''Hold on tight, Ellen.''

Ellen cast a curious glance over her shoulder, wondering what he intended, then winced when he filled his hands with the twin cheeks of her buttocks and spread them apart. Her eyes slipped closed and her fingers tightened on the ladder as she felt his hand come between her legs to touch and toy and spread incredible pleasure.

She shivered when his other hand came around to rest for a second on her bare, trembling belly before sliding down to part the coils of chestnut curls between her thighs and caress that responsive button of flesh where her sexual hunger was centered.

Ellen's eyes slowly opened and she sighed with wonder. Fingers clinging tenaciously to the ladder, breath coming in quick little spurts, she couldn't believe what she, the highly respectable, less-than-sensual Ellen Cornelius, was doing. And enjoying. She was standing on the observation deck of a moving train, naked as Eve in the garden, with the balmy night wind caressing her bare tingling flesh, while a tall, dark man she hardly knew was turning her into a willing wanton.

The thought struck Ellen that it wouldn't matter if the train were to roll through a station at this moment in time. She was not at all certain she could make Steve stop caressing her, or if she would even try. His warm stroking fingers on her throbbing flesh felt too wonderful. His sensual lips pressing kisses to the curve of her neck and shoulder were too enjoyable. The sweet anticipation of having him buried deep inside her was too thrilling.

Let them look.

Let the whole world look.

She didn't care. Not when she was more aroused than she'd ever been in her life. Not when Steve's talented fingers were spreading amazing heat where he touched her. Not before she reached the awesome release she knew he could give to her.

Abruptly his loving hands left her burning flesh and Ellen moaned her protest at the desertion. But she sighed with approval when she felt his hand slip between their bodies. Quickly he flipped open the buttons of his tight trousers and immediately she felt his hard, throbbing flesh surge and seek the cleft of her bare buttocks. He stood stock-still for a long moment with his body pressed to hers, his ragged breath hot on her shoulder.

Then Ellen lost her own breath when his hands firmly spanned her waist and he urged her up onto tiptoe. Again, he ordered, "Hold on tight."

"Yes, yes, I will," she assured him, wondering

when he was finally going to turn her about to face him.

He never did.

To her shock, her intoxicatingly exciting lover took her from behind, bending his knees slightly and guiding his hard, hot flesh inside her. For the astounded Ellen, sharp pain and hinted-at pleasure mixed as she felt his rock-hard erection slide up inside to stretch and fill her until she felt she would surely be torn apart.

Then all at once he was fully inside her and he began the slow-seeking movements of erotic love-making. Ellen began to relax, to move with him, to take joy in the fact that he filled her so completely. Any discomfort departed. Pleasure increased. The two of them moved together in easy, languid rhythm.

What he was doing to her felt so sinfully good, Ellen wondered anxiously if perhaps they were doing something depraved. But soon she no longer cared as passion went unchecked and she gave herself completely to the wishes and desire of her experienced lover and her own eager self.

If this was wicked, then she wanted to be wicked. If this was perverted, then she was happy to be perverted. If what they were doing was deviant, then all lovers should be deviant now and then.

Ellen's rising elation was heightened when Steve's strong hands gripped her hips and he began to accelerate his thrusts. What had been undeniably enjoyable became exquisite rapture. Faster and faster they moved, his hard, heavy flesh thrusting and driving into her; her responsive body gripping and squeezing him until both were moaning with frenzied joy.

The tempo of their fierce lovemaking began to match the clickity-clack of the wheels turning on the tracks. Their bodies were like well-oiled machinery, his fitting perfectly inside hers, the two of them moving as one. The train, starting down a low grade, began to pick up speed. The naked lovers picked up speed as well. The clicking of the wheels on the tracks quickened to a lively, grinding rhythm. The cadence of the lovers' heartbeats soon matched.

With the train's abrupt acceleration, the private rail car shifted and swayed and danced dizzily on the tracks. The lovers' enjoined bodies ground and undulated and battled to keep their balance on the swaying observation deck.

It was a wild, exhilarating ride. The train roaring across the countryside. The lovers riding the train and each other in a celebration of unleashed passion. Ellen wished it would last forever. She wished that she could spend the rest of her life standing naked on the observation deck of this moving train while Steve Corey stood behind her and moved so sensually inside her.

Too soon Ellen could feel her climax beginning. Steve could feel it, too. He gave her all he had and Ellen squeezed her eyes shut, clung to the ladder and thrust backward, feeling the sexual bliss rise higher and higher until she began to explode in joyous delirium. She screamed as the powerful waves of sheer ecstasy buffeted her, frightening her in their intensity, thrilling her beyond belief, revealing the mysterious secrets of fulfilling lovemaking that she had never known.

And her undiluted joy intensified when she felt the hot, thick liquid of her lover's potent climax fill her to overflowing.

# Twelve

Hours had passed since a dazed, dewy-eyed Ellen Cornelius had slipped, naked and fragrant with the distinctive scent of sex, back inside the darkened *Lucky Landseer*. Grateful that Alexandra was a sound sleeper, Ellen had bathed, put on a fresh nightgown and gotten into bed.

But she hadn't slept.

For the first couple of hours she had lain on her back, sighing and smiling and happily reliving the wonder of being in Steve Corey's arms. Blushing in the darkness, she recalled with embarrassing clarity the delightfully taboo things that they had done together.

But by the time dawn's first gray light began to seep into the rolling rail car, Ellen was no longer a dreamily satiated woman whose contentment was absolute. Steve Corey had once again become Mister Corey and she was no longer eager to see him again. She was, instead, tense and worried and ashamed.

In the cold light of day, harsh reality intruded and Ellen couldn't believe what had happened last night.

But the unfamiliar tenderness between her legs was silent testimony to her scandalous indiscretion. It had actually happened. She had let it happen. Hadn't even tried to keep it from happening. She, a woman who had always prided herself on her morals, had behaved like a brazen trollop with an immoral man who cared nothing for her and whose sole aim was to steal the Landseer fortune.

By eight o'clock that morning, Ellen was beside herself with regret and despair. And cold dread. What would she say, what would *he* say, when she saw Mister Corey again? The blood chilled in her veins at the frightening prospect. Would the unprincipled carnival barker let everyone know what had happened between them? Had he already told Ricky O'Mara? Had the two of them laughed about it and made fun of her?

"Let's get dressed and go to breakfast," said Alexandra on awakening, startling the distraught Ellen.

Ellen's head snapped around, she looked at her aunt, who had risen onto her elbows in bed and was yawning.

"Why don't you go on, Aunt Alexandra. I'm not the least bit hungry and I'm still rather tired," said Ellen, hoping the reason for her exhaustion wasn't written on her face. "I believe I'll just skip breakfast this morning."

Alexandra levered herself into a sitting position, rubbed her eyes and said, "That's up to you, but get out of bed and help me dress."

Ellen's agony did not abate throughout the day. Claiming she had an upset stomach, she staunchly refused to visit the dining car or to leave the confines of the *Lucky Landseer*. She couldn't bear the thought of seeing Mister Corey. She shuddered on recalling the conversation they'd had in the dining car yesterday just hours before meeting on the observation deck. She'd pompously assured him that she would *never* want him to kiss her, not ever. And he had coolly replied, "Say that to me again in twenty-four hours."

What a simpleminded fool she was. And what a cruel bastard he was. Oh, how she hated him. Oh, how she hated herself. She had fallen right into his evil trap and allowed him to take advantage of her. He had, she presumed sadly, seduced her just to prove that he could. That was the kind of man he was. A heartless, profane man who had taken obvious delight in defiling her.

Ellen's heart squeezed painfully in her chest.

She took a small measure of consolation from the thought that he would likely leave her alone from now on. He had proved that he could have her, proved that he could make her his willing whore, proved that she would do anything and everything he wanted her to do.

Surely that knowledge would suffice and he would no longer bother to tease and torment her. He had, she imagined, wasted no time thinking about her after their clandestine encounter, while she had lain awake all night thinking of him.

Well, to hell with Mister Corey!

She would show him that he was not the only one

who could be cold and uncaring. If he expected her to gaze adoringly at him or to stammer and blush simply because they had been intimate he had another thing coming. The lovemaking meant nothing to him? Well, she'd make it very clear that it meant even less to her.

Her resolve surfacing, Ellen rose from the chair where she'd spent most of the long, miserable day. It was nearing six in the evening and she had not been out. She was so weary, so heartsick, she felt as if she might, any minute, start screaming. She had to get outside for a while. She had to get away from her chattering aunt who'd spent the afternoon in their car. She anxiously rose to her feet.

"Feeling better?" asked her aunt, looking up from a book she'd just started to read.

"Much better, thank you," said Ellen. "My stomach ailment has passed, I'm myself again."

"Good. Now tell me where this came from." Alexandra held up a pressed flower that had fallen from the pages of the book she was reading. A book she had borrowed from Ellen.

Ellen felt as if someone had brutally thrust a sharp-bladed knife directly into her solar plexus. It was all she could do not to clutch her stomach in agony. She immediately recognized the ivory rose from the bouquet that Mister Corey had bought for her the day she had departed for Charleston.

"I have no idea," she lied, in no mood to explain anything to anyone, least of all her aunt.

"Well, then I'll just throw it away," said her aunt, tossing the wilted rose into the trash basket.

Trying very hard to show no emotion, Ellen said, "If you'll excuse me, I believe I'll step out onto the observation deck for a few moments."

Alexandra nodded, then frowned and asked, "Ellen, I've been meaning to ask you, did you hear anything last night?"

"Hear anything? When? Where?"

Alexandra shrugged her shoulders. "I don't know what it was, but I'm almost certain I heard strange noises in the middle of the night. Coming from the direction of the observation deck."

Ellen smiled calmly. "It must have been a dream, Auntie."

"Maybe," Alexandra responded, not totally convinced. "You don't suppose someone on the train found a way to get back there, do you?"

"Heavens no," Ellen assured her. "They'd have to come directly through the *Lucky Landseer* to get to the observation deck, you know that."

Alexandra nodded. "That's true," she said, then scratched her chin thoughtfully and added, "Of course, there is that ladder that goes to the top of the car, but surely, with the train under way, nobody would…"

"Certainly not," Ellen said with calm control. "Such a harebrained stunt would surely end in disaster." She smiled, stepped outside and exhaled heavily.

For several long moments, the sad, shamed Ellen

stood at the railing, staring off into the distance, seeing nothing, wishing more than anything in the world that she could turn back the clock by twenty-four hours.

Ellen's heavy heart lifted somewhat when, blinking and shading her eyes with her hand, she got her first glimpse of the imposing Rocky Mountains rising majestically to meet the cloudless Colorado sky on the far western horizon. She had never been out West, but she had read many books about the awesome scenery of the western states and had always hoped to see it for herself.

Had the circumstances been different, she would have been excited and eager. As it was, she gazed in solemn awe at the towering monoliths rising from the flat plains in the distance. She wished—for the hundredth time—that Alexandra had placed chairs on the observation deck. She would have liked to stay right out here until the train reached the Queen City of the Rockies, mile-high Denver.

It was dark when the train rolled into Union Station in downtown Denver, Colorado, at shortly after nine o'clock. In and out for the past three hours, Ellen was again out on the observation deck as the locomotive slowly came to stop on the depot tracks.

Alexandra had said that there was to be a two-hour stop in the Denver terminal. The engineers and mechanics would be going over the locomotive and each of the cars, preparing the train for its laborious journey up and over the soaring Rockies.

With a couple of hours to kill, Ellen decided she'd like to explore the city. It would do her good to get off the train. It might help her forget her troubles for at least a little while. Ellen turned and went back inside the *Lucky Landseer*.

"Aunt Alex," she said, "since we're to be here for two hours, why don't we take a walk? See the shops and restaurants."

Alexandra laid her book aside. "After watching you mope about all day, I'd welcome any diversion." She struggled to her feet. "You think it's safe for us to…?"

"Perfectly. It's early. The streets will be full of people. Let's hurry."

"Oh, all right," said Alexandra. "Fetch my shawl."

As they stepped down off the train, Ellen looked anxiously about, terrified she'd see Mister Corey. He was nowhere in sight and she supposed that he intended to remain on the train. Thank heavens.

Union Station was right in the heart of the city, bordering its southern edge, so the two women only had to walk a couple of short blocks up Sixteenth to reach the many shops and eating establishments along both sides of Larimer Street. Gaslights lined the sidewalks and a uniformed policeman, nightstick in hand, patrolled the busy thoroughfare.

Hurrying past a noisy saloon, Ellen and Alexandra went in and out of stores, ending up in the huge two-story Wagonwheel Emporium that carried everything imaginable.

While Alexandra admired a lace tablecloth, Ellen gingerly lifted an exquisite porcelain tabby cat from a shelf filled with tiny treasures. It was a small, fragile, beautiful work of art, a coal-black cat with gleaming golden eyes. The craftsman who had shaped it was so talented, the cat looked real. As if it were alive. Ellen instantly fell in love with the miniature creation.

"I'm growing tired, let's get back to the train," her aunt said as she stepped up beside her.

"Look, Aunt Alex," said Ellen. "Have you ever seen anything so beautiful in your life?"

"Hmmph. It's okay, I guess, if you like cats. Which I don't."

"I know you don't and that is why I've always respected your wishes never to have a cat live in our home." Ellen gave the older, shorter woman a hopeful look, and said, "So I'd really like to have this one."

Alexandra frowned and snatching the porcelain cat from Ellen, she turned it over, hunting for the price. A helpful clerk appeared, smiled and said, "Ladies, this elegant piece is only twenty dollars."

"Only twenty dollars!" Alexandra's voice boomed through the store, causing people to turn and stare. "Why, that's highway robbery. I'm not about to spend that kind of money for a silly little trinket."

"No. No, of course not," said Ellen, resigned. She gazed wistfully at the shiny black cat and taking it from Alexandra carefully placed it back on the shelf.

"Let's start back to the train. I'm suddenly quite tired myself."

"Well, I didn't want to come here in the first place," said Alexandra.

Ellen sighed and gave the miniature tabby one last loving look. Then the two women started up the wide aisle toward the front door, Alexandra frowning and grumbling about having to walk all the way back to the station, Ellen silent and submissive, her deep melancholy clearly written on her face.

Neither noticed the man watching them from the far side of the store. A hip leaning against a table filled with fine china, arms crossed over his chest, the man's cold black gaze rested squarely on Ellen and remained riveted on her until the two women had exited the store.

Once they had gone, a half smile touched his lips. He uncrossed his long arms and pushed away from the table, going directly to the shelf of knickknacks where he'd first spotted Ellen.

He reached out and picked up the miniature black porcelain cat with the gleaming golden eyes.

"Elegant, isn't it, sir?" A smiling clerk stepped up beside him.

"It is," he said. "How much?"

"Only twenty dollars."

Mister Corey nodded. Then grimaced slightly. He had a sizable bankroll, money he'd won gambling on the crossing from England. But he'd left it on the train.

Mister Corey set the cat back on the shelf. "Afraid

I don't have that kind of money on me," he said truthfully.

"I'm sorry," said the clerk.

"Me, too," he said. He turned and shoving his hand in a trouser pocket idly fingered the twenty-dollar gold piece resting there.

He stopped walking.

He took the gold coin out of his pocket and stared at it wistfully. It wasn't just any gold coin. It was the twenty-dollar gold piece his father had given to him on the day he left for the Citadel when he was eighteen. He had carried it all these years, had never considered spending it. It was the last thing his father had ever given him. And the last time he'd ever seen his father alive.

Mister Corey frowned, turned and shook his dark head regretfully.

# *Thirteen*

The train left Union Station at precisely 11:00 p.m. and began the climb into the Front Range of the Rockies almost immediately. Alexandra had retired shortly after reboarding.

Weary to the bone but still too distraught to sleep, Ellen sat curled up in an easy chair in the darkness of the car's elegant drawing room. She would have liked to go out onto the observation deck, but she didn't dare. She couldn't risk meeting the dark seducer of her dreams.

She couldn't risk falling into his arms again.

The possibility so disturbed her, Ellen rose from her chair, hurriedly crossed the shadowy room and checked to make sure the door was securely locked. She then returned to her chair to gaze out the window at the twinkling lights of the city they were rapidly leaving behind.

An hour after leaving Denver, the train's whistle blew loudly as it reached the mountain hamlet of Golden. The train stopped to discharge passengers and Ellen got a brief look at the peaceful alpine village. Gazing at the lighted businesses and homes dotting the darkened valley, Ellen wished that this trip westward had been scheduled so that they would be crossing the magnificent Rockies in broad daylight. She would have loved to have seen every inch of their spectacular journey on a bright sunshiny day.

Shortly after the train climbed up out of Golden, exhaustion finally drove her to bed where she was asleep the minute her weary head touched the pillow. Even Alexandra's thunderous snoring didn't keep her awake. Nor the dark, provocative man who filled her last waking thoughts.

"Tell me again, Padjan," said Alexandra, sipping her third cup of strong black coffee. "Exactly what will it be like for me in the Lost City? Will I be content there? Will there be proper accommodations for me? Are the chefs capable of fixing decent meals?"

The two oddly matched friends were seated in twin easy chairs, Padjan's chair pulled up beside the bed of the sleeping Summer Dawn. Alexandra had come here as soon as she'd finished breakfast. She was getting more and more excited as they got nearer to their destination and she enjoyed hearing Padjan talk about his mysterious Lost City high above the clouds.

His hand idly patting Summer Dawn's bony shoulder, Padjan smiled and said, "My home is unlike any-place you have ever been before. There is no other village like it on earth. It is a secluded, remote, secret paradise where beautiful, youthful-looking people reside happily together. There is no crime there, no murders or robberies or meanness of any kind."

"That's all well and good," said Alexandra, impatient, "but I want to know more about where I will be staying and whether it will please me or not."

"Ah, Alexandra, Alexandra, you constantly concern yourself with unimportant things," Padjan scolded gently. "Do not worry. You and Ellen will share a private domicile where you will be quite comfortable." His dark eyes twinkled in his smooth bronzed face.

"Will there be servants to wait on me?"

His twinkling eyes narrowed slightly at the impertinent question. "You will not call my people servants. In the Lost City, there are no servants. All are equals."

Alexandra frowned. "If there are no servants, then who will…?"

"My people, the Anasazi, will do things for you because they are gracious hosts, not because they are servants," he said. "In the Lost City you will be my invited guest. I am respected and admired by my people, therefore you will be treated like…like visiting royalty."

Alexandra smiled. "Which is as it should be, my good man."

Padjan chuckled and said, "Alexandra Landseer, you may be old in years, but you still have much to learn."

"I? What could I possibly learn that I don't already know?" Her eyebrows shot up and she straightened in her chair.

"In time you will see," was his reply. His next

words were lost in the sound of the train's whistle blowing sharply.

"That infernal whistle," whined Alexandra when at last it stopped briefly. "Half the time I can't hear myself think."

The whistle gave another loud blast. Alexandra banged her palms on the chair arms in annoyance and gritted her teeth.

Padjan waited for silence, then said, "It appears we are arriving in Glenwood Springs. I understand your famous outlaw, Doc Holiday, spent his last days here, taking the waters, attempting to cure his malady."

"Well, it didn't work. He died here and good riddance."

Padjan shook his bald head. This petty, mean, bullying, sharp-tongued woman whom he liked nonetheless never failed to surprise and disappoint him. "Have you no compassion for anyone? Have you never felt sympathy for some poor unfortunate soul?"

"I'm as benevolent as the next one, but—"

Padjan's loud shout of laughter silenced her in midsentence. Alexandra stared at him, openmouthed, totally puzzled.

Tears of laughter rolling down his cheekbones, Padjan said, "You do not know the meaning of the word, Alexandra. But soon you will learn. Soon you will become a kind, caring person who gives of herself and ask nothing in return."

"Ha!" she snorted. "I'm perfectly content with myself just as I am. So don't be thinking you can change me."

"*I* can't," he said, then smiled. "But the Magic Waters can. And will."

The train reached Grand Junction, Colorado, on the western slope of the Rockies at ten minutes past noon on Tuesday, the thirteenth of June 1899.

As the slow-moving locomotive approached the depot, Ellen braced herself. There was no escape. She would have to get off the train and encounter Mister Corey. She could not avoid him. Dear Lord, how would he behave? How would she?

"Are you going to stay on board forever?" Her aunt's voice snapped her from her troubled reverie. "We're here, Ellen. We've finally reached Grand Junction. End of the line. Aren't you anxious?"

"You have no idea," said Ellen.

Paying little attention to what her niece said, Alexandra, jewels sparkling on every short, fat finger, jerked the door open and stepped out onto the observation deck. She shaded her eyes and looked about for Colonel Stanley Lord, the chief agent for the Landseer Western Mining Enterprises. The Colonel, an old family friend and trusted employee, had promised to meet the train.

Spotting the tall, silver-haired gentleman, Alexandra let out a loud whoop and began calling his name. Ellen followed her aunt out onto the observation deck. She was about to descend the steps when Ricky O'Mara and Mister Corey came walking down the platform.

Ellen automatically glanced at Mister Corey. When

his eyes met hers, she purposely fixed him with a haughty, disdainful look, eager to spurn him before he got the chance to rebuff her. Then felt her already aching heart swell with fresh pain when their gazes held for a moment. His midnight eyes were as lifeless and icy as ever and his face held no emotion.

He looked at her, but he might as well have looked through her. Any inkling of hope she'd held out that maybe she had been wrong about him, that maybe their lovemaking had meant something to him, was killed in that chilly glance.

"Let me help you, Ellen," said Ricky, hurrying forward to lift her down from the steps.

"Thank you, Ricky," she said, and then stared, dumbfounded, as the respected Civil War hero, Colonel Stanley Lord, turned and warmly greeted Mister Corey as if he were a long lost friend.

"Steve Corey!" said the smiling Colonel. "I had no idea you were with Alexandra's party. How in the world are you, son?"

"Never better," said Mister Corey. "And you, sir?"

"Few complaints," Colonel Lord replied, releasing Mister Corey's hand after pumping it firmly several times.

Wishing the ground would open and swallow her up, Ellen stiffened her spine and ventured forth. The distinguished Colonel caught sight of her, smiled and said, "Ellen, my dear, how good to see you," and swept her into his arms for a fatherly hug. With his long arm still around her waist, he shook hands with

Ricky O'Mara when Mister Corey introduced the two. Then the Colonel, smiling at Mister Corey, said proudly that he had once been Steven Corey's commanding officer.

"Oh, really?" said Alexandra with no real interest, and Colonel Lord knew the spoiled heiress well enough to quickly suggest they retire to the hotel.

Ricky and Mister Corey stayed behind to help with Summer Dawn and the luggage while Colonel Lord escorted Alexandra and Ellen to the Powderhorn Hotel on the north side of the town square.

In the two-story hotel lobby, the Colonel said, "I hope your accommodations will be satisfactory, Alexandra. The Powderhorn is the finest hotel in Grand Junction."

Alexandra gave no reply, just looked around with a telltale expression on her face as if she had detected some unpleasant odor.

"I'm sure the suite will be more than adequate, Colonel," Ellen said graciously. She smiled at the tall, elderly gentleman and added, "After all the time spent on the train, a room that stands still will be heaven to me."

He laughed, stepped up to the marble counter and checked the group in, instructing the desk clerk that the others would be along shortly to pick up their keys.

He turned, handed the key to Ellen and said, looking at Alexandra, "You ladies must be exhausted. I'll get out of your way now and let you get some much needed rest. Could I interest the two of you in dinner this evening?''

''Where will we dine?'' Alexandra wanted to know.

Looking a bit sheepish, Colonel Lord said, ''I thought we'd have dinner right here. The Powderhorn serves the best roast beef and Rocky Mountain trout in town.''

Before Alexandra could speak, Ellen said, ''Sounds lovely, Colonel. Say, eight o'clock?''

''Perfect.'' The silver-haired man nodded and smiled kindly at the tired, too-thin Ellen.

She no longer looked like a young woman, although he figured she couldn't be much past thirty-five. No doubt all those trying years spent tending to the irascible Alexandra had taken their toll. That, and the loneliness she had suffered. Ellen's disastrous marriage had ended shortly after it had begun and he had never heard of her having another suitor, which was sad. He felt very sorry for Ellen. He had been a widower now for more than five years and it was hard enough, at his age, to be alone, with no one to come home to. It was downright tragic to see a sweet, good-hearted woman like Ellen alone and unloved.

Colonel Lord pushed back his chair and rose when he saw Ellen and Alexandra appear in the dining room's arched entrance shortly after 8:00 p.m. He noticed Ellen looking anxiously about, as if searching for someone she did not wish to find. Then suddenly, she smiled, as if relieved.

"How elegant you both look this fine evening," said the Colonel when they joined him.

"I should look elegant," said Alexandra, sliding heavily down into the chair he held out for her. "This particular gown is supposedly one-of-a-kind and for the price I paid, it had better be."

Ellen and the Colonel exchanged looks and when he came around to seat her, he gave Ellen's slender shoulders an affectionate, understanding squeeze.

It was, for the most part, a pleasant enough evening. Or at least, it started out that way. Alexandra and Ellen had rested all afternoon and Ellen was feeling a little better.

The meal was superb, and the Colonel, a man who had traveled widely and had many interesting friends and acquaintances, entertained the two ladies with amusing stories of his adventures.

As Ellen listened and laughed, she kept waiting for an opening. She desperately wanted to hear more about the Colonel's association with Mister Corey. She wanted to know all that he knew about the man. But she was hesitant to act too interested. She hated to ask. And, as it happened, she didn't have to. Alexandra brought up his name.

"So, Stanley, you know Mister Corey?"

"I do," said the Colonel. "Although it's been a long time."

"I hope he's not as mean as he looks," Alexandra said and laughed. "What can you tell me about him?"

Ellen felt her body go rigid. She held her breath.

The Colonel chewed slowly, patted his mouth with his linen napkin and shook his silver head thoughtfully.

When he spoke, there was a hint of a frown on his weathered face. "I always liked and admired Steve Corey. When he served under me, he was a model soldier, never gave me a minute's trouble, was always respectful and cheerfully willing to undertake any task, no matter how tough or dangerous. In my opinion, Steven Corey was one of the finest cadet officers to ever graduate from the Citadel."

At the mention of the Citadel, Ellen immediately recalled the strange way Mister Corey had behaved when Alexandra had suggested he go with her down to Charleston to visit Chris. And she remembered Chris asking what Mister Corey's full name was. Had Chris known something about Mister Corey? Something he didn't want to tell her?

"How'd Mister Corey get that nasty-looking scar on his face?" Alexandra was asking when Ellen snapped back to the present.

"I have no idea," said the Colonel. "It wasn't there when last I saw him. But, bear in mind, it's been more than thirteen years since I last saw Steve Corey—Fort Richardson, Texas, it was—and at the time he was just a young, enthusiastic lieutenant." He frowned, shook his head slowly and said, "Steve's aged prematurely. I hardly recognized him. Looks older than his years. And it seems to me there's an underlying sadness about him that wasn't there before. Back when I knew him he was a handsome, strapping youth who was always laughing and happy." The Colonel sighed softly. "Guess life has a way of catching up with us all."

Ellen studied the Colonel's face and knew, by his somber expression, that there was something more about Mister Corey, something he wasn't telling.

"I know you too well, Stanley," she heard her aunt accuse. "You're withholding something from me. You know more about this man than you're telling. What is it?"

The Colonel exhaled, clearly reluctant to speak. Finally he said, "Steve Corey got into serious trouble several years back." He paused, as if hating to continue.

"Well, go on," Alexandra prodded. "Trouble? What kind of trouble? Did he murder somebody? Robbery?"

"No, no, nothing like that. But for the military, something worse. It happened up in the Dakotas. Steven Corey was court-martialed and cashiered out of the army for cowardice in the face of the enemy at the Battle of Wounded Knee."

"By the saints above! You mean to tell me that I have a yellow-bellied coward heading up my expedition?" thundered Alexandra.

Aghast, Ellen asked, her eyes wide with disbelief, "Exactly what happened at Wounded Knee? What did Mister Corey do? Or not do?"

"I honestly don't know the details," said Colonel Lord. "Such a shame, such a shame. As I said, when Steve served under me, he was as brave as any man

I've ever known. I just can't imagine..." His words trailed away. Then, quickly changing the subject, he asked, "Where is Corey's wife? Didn't she make the trip?"

Ellen felt all the blood drain from her face. "His wife?" she said, horrified. "Mister Corey has a wife?"

"Why, yes, didn't he tell you?" stated Colonel Lord. "Married a beautiful Southern aristocrat more than a decade ago. Absolutely mad about her, so they say."

# *Fourteen*

Steve Corey married?

Oh, dear God! She had made love to a man who was not only a liar and swindler but a coward and an adulterer as well!

Ellen suddenly felt as if she was suffocating. Her lungs refused to fill with air and she assumed that any second she would pass out. Which is exactly what she hoped would happen. How blissful it would be to feel the blessed darkness envelop her and rob her of all thought and feeling.

"My dear, are you all right?" She heard the Colonel's concerned voice as if it was coming from far away. "Are you ill, child?"

"What, I…I'm sorry, I…?" Ellen looked at him with glazed eyes, clearly dazed and disoriented.

"Has something I said upset you, Ellen?"

"It's not you, Stanley." Alexandra waved a bejeweled hand irritably and made a sour face. "She's been acting peculiar for the past thirty-six hours." She turned her head, fixed Ellen with a probing, narrow-eyed stare and asked, "Has it got something to do with Mister Corey? You're not making a fool of yourself over that man behind my back?"

A lifetime of quelling her emotions made it possible for Ellen to quickly rally and say with studied aplomb, ''I am not the kind of woman to make a fool of herself over any man.''

''You did it once,'' Alexandra reminded her. ''You married Booth Cornelius when I had warned you not to.''

Ellen laid her napkin on the table. ''That was nearly twenty years ago and I was a girl of seventeen.'' She looked from her aunt to the now-embarrassed Colonel and said, ''It was a lovely dinner, Colonel Lord. Thank you so much. Now, if you'll excuse me.''

''Of course, my dear,'' the Colonel said, rose to his feet and pulled out Ellen's chair. ''I'll see you tomorrow then and—''

''No,'' Alexandra broke in. ''You'll see only me tomorrow. You will come to the hotel to pick me up at 9:00 a.m. sharp. You will take me directly to your office where I intend to go over all the pertinent journals if it takes all day.''

The Colonel came around to help Alexandra up out of her chair. ''I know, but won't Ellen be coming with us?'' he asked, glancing at Ellen.

''No, Ellen will be going out to Sonny Johnson's ranch tomorrow with Mister Corey and Ricky O'Mara to choose some saddle ponies for the trip into southern Utah.'' The Colonel could tell by looking at Ellen that this was the first she'd heard of the plans. ''When they get back from the ranch,'' Alexandra went on, ''they'll go to the outfitters and pick up the needed supplies.'' She shot a sly glance at her niece and asked, ''Have you any objection to spending the day with Mister Corey and the Irishman?''

Ellen detected the mischievous twinkle in Alexandra's eyes and knew the older woman was hoping to hear her pleading protests. She wouldn't get the satisfaction.

''None whatsoever,'' Ellen said, smiling easily. ''It should be a most productive day.''


''You're late,'' Ellen accused as Mister Corey walked into the hotel lobby at twelve minutes past 9:00 a.m. ''What kept you?''

''My butler failed to wake me,'' he said.

Ricky O'Mara, watching the exchange, wondered at the seeming animosity between the two.

''Well, we're all here now.'' He stepped forward, smiling, looking from one to the other. ''Why don't we get on our way?''

Without a word, Ellen turned on her heel and headed for the hotel's entrance. At the curb, a rented buckboard waited, the two harnessed horses shuffling and swishing their tails. The June sun was already sticky hot, shining down with a vengeance from a cloudless Colorado sky.

Making no effort to assist Ellen, Mister Corey swung up into the buckboard, sliding down onto the back seat. Ricky turned to Ellen and said, ''I'm driving, so you can sit back there with—''

''No,'' she quickly corrected him. ''I will sit up front with you.''

"Whatever you say." He lifted her up and climbed onto the seat beside her.

The restless horses began moving the minute Ricky picked up the reins. Guiding the buckboard out into the dusty street, he turned the corner at the square's west side. Nodding and smiling to a couple of pretty young women who were on the sidewalk in front of the apothecary shop, Ricky O'Mara decided to ignore the puzzling tension between Ellen and Steve. He was determined to enjoy the day.

And every day.

As they left behind the city nestled at the confluence of the Colorado and Gunnison Rivers, Ricky pointed out the Grand Mesa, some thirty miles away.

"They say the Grand Mesa is the world's largest flat-topped mountain," he told Ellen.

Gazing at the huge tableland shimmering with the fierce heat of mid-June, Ellen nodded, awed by the mesa and by the great mountains beyond, snowcapped against the clear blue sky. It was indeed breathtaking country and the prospect of riding horseback through walled canyons and beside rushing streams and into deep, dark forests excited her senses.

The spell was broken when Mister Corey said, "We've all seen the mesa now, Ricky, how about moving on?"

Ricky immediately flicked the long leather reins across the horses' backs and they quickly picked up speed. The wheels turned faster on the dusty trail and Ellen held on to the seat with one hand, checking with the other to see if the neat bun at the back of her head was securely pinned.

"Have you ever seen a more perfect June morning or a more perfect place?" said Ricky, undeterred.

"It's truly enchanting," Ellen managed to say, feeling Mister Corey's cold gaze resting on her.

Ricky continued to make small talk on the four-mile ride out to the Johnson ranch, telling Ellen that this wild, magnificent country had once, not too long ago, been home to the Ute Indians. As soon as the Ute were expelled, white settlers had rushed in and founded the town of Grand Junction.

Ricky got little response from her. She seemed distracted, as if she had something on her mind. As he spoke, Ricky turned occasionally to glance over his shoulder in an attempt to draw Mister Corey into the conversation. With no success.

So Ricky was relieved when the outbuildings of the Johnson ranch came into sight. Maybe Johnson would be a bit more talkative than his two curiously sullen companions.

He was.

Richard "Sonny" Johnson, a big, strapping man with a long, hound-dog face, protruding ears and a mouth full of teeth came running toward the slowing buckboard waving his sweat-stained Stetson, grinning from ear to ear as if he had just heard a good joke. He wore a chambray work shirt with large sweat circles under each arm, a pair of ragged, faded Levi's that dipped low under his bulging belly and scuffed cowboy boots badly in need of a polish.

"Been 'a-waiting for you!" he said in a whiskey-roughened voice. "Got some mighty fine saddle ponies for you to take a look at."

Introductions were made and Sonny Johnson invited his guests into the house for a drink of whiskey or a cup of coffee.

"No thank you, Mister Johnson," Ellen spoke for them all. "We haven't the time."

Sonny Johnson's broad grin faded and he looked disappointed. "I was hoping y'all might spend the day with me. I don't get much company out here and my wife's visiting over in Denver with the kinfolks, so—"

"I wish we could," Ellen interrupted. "Now about those horses."

The smile was instantly back on Sonny's sun-wrinkled face. "Come with me," he said and, clamping his dirty Stetson back on his head, led the way out back to the stables.

Ellen stayed outside as Mister Corey and Ricky followed big Sonny Johnson into the plank-board corral. A dozen or so horses trotted around, neighing and whinnying, their sleek coats shining in the sun. Ellen looked with interest at the frisky ponies, quickly spotting the one she wanted for herself.

A beautiful saffron-colored dun gelding with white stocking feet and a white blaze face. He raced around the perimeter of the corral with his proud head held high, his long mane and tail trailing out behind him, clearly showing off for his audience.

"What about the saffron dun gelding?" she heard

Mister Corey ask Sonny Johnson. "He easy to handle?"

The big rancher had his back to her so Ellen strained to hear what he said. "Broke him myself," said Sonny Johnson. "He's smart, has amazing stamina and is so gentle a child could handle him."

Mister Corey nodded, reached out and took a coiled lasso from a nearby post. He walked into the center of the corral and began to whirl the lasso above his head. The horses, knowing his intent, raced anxiously around the corral, wild-eyed, trying to get out of harm's way. Mister Corey threw the looped rope and it fell over the dun's head.

"Come here, boy," Mister Corey gently coaxed, and the big saffron dun, whinnying loudly, ears forward, soon calmed and walked slowly to him.

Ellen, watching, felt her jaw harden. She might have known the selfish Mister Corey would take the very horse she wanted. She stiffened when, after patting the horse's jaw and whispering to him, Mister Corey turned and led the big gelding directly toward her.

Ellen stood on the bottom rung of the corral's fence, her arms draped along the top plank. Without a word, Mister Corey stepped up close and the beautiful dun gelding stuck his head out and pressed his velvet muzzle against Ellen's bare forearm.

For one magical moment all her troubles were forgotten. A wide smile spread over her face and she stroked the gelding's blaze face with genuine affection and joy.

"You like him?" Mister Corey asked. "Why don't you come in here and try him out?"

Ellen's attention immediately left the gelding and went to Mister Corey. "Are you blind? I'm wearing a dress, in case you hadn't noticed. I can't very well be expected to—"

"If you don't give him a short ride to see if you can handle him, you'll have to pick another horse."

Ellen's eyes narrowed. "I want *him!*"

"Then come inside and ride him."

"I'll just do that!" she snapped, backed down off the fence and stalked into the corral.

Big Sonny Johnson had already lifted a saddle onto the gelding's back and was tightening the cinch under its belly while Ricky slipped the bit into the creature's mouth. Finished, the two men backed away.

"Ready?" Mister Corey asked Ellen.

"I am. If you'll kindly step out of my way."

Instead of stepping back, he stepped forward, put his hands to her waist and lifted her into the saddle. Her face turned scarlet when she saw that one side of her dress had risen past her knee, revealing her stock-inged leg and worn, faded garter.

To her astonishment, Steve Corey lowered the dress before she could reach it and said in a voice barely above a whisper, "Don't worry, they didn't see a thing," referring to Johnson and Ricky. Then, his dark, lifeless gaze holding hers, he casually laid a hand atop her knee. Ellen felt the heat of his touch through the fabric of her dress and her pulse instantly quickened.

"Show him—" Mister Corey nodded to the gelding "—and me, what you can do."

Ellen yanked up on the reins and spun the big dun around, causing Mister Corey to have to jump quickly out of the way. She dug her slippered heels into the gelding's flanks and trotted him around the corral. She soon put him into an easy lope and finally into a fast, ground-covering gallop.

It had been ages since she'd been on a horse and she had forgotten how much she enjoyed riding. Momentarily forgetting the three men watching her, Ellen happily put the gelding through his paces and knew within minutes that the two of them were meant for each other.

On ending the exhilarating ride, she ignored Mister Corey when he stepped forward to help her dismount. Awkwardly, because she had to try and keep her dress from flying up, Ellen swung her leg over and dropped to the ground. But Mister Corey did not back away and she found herself facing him, standing very close. Too close. As much as she despised him, and she did, she was overcome with the strong, irresistible urge to throw her arms around his neck and press her yearning body to the hard, ungiving length of his.

Upset by her involuntary response to him, she anxiously stepped back and glanced nervously up at him, praying he couldn't read her guilty thoughts.

A hint of a sardonic smile touched his full lips and he said, "Me, too."

"I beg your pardon?"

"I know just how you feel."

Outraged, she leaned in and said, "If you know how I feel, then you know that I feel nothing for you."

"Nothing?"

"Nothing! You just stay away from me, Mister Corey!"

He shrugged wide shoulders and reasoned, "If you feel nothing for me, why must I stay away from you?"

She gritted her teeth. "Because I said so!"


The trio headed back to town with a half-dozen horses they had bought from Sonny Johnson. The saffron dun for Ellen, a paint stallion for Mister Corey, a big black gelding for Ricky and three extras. A red sorrel mare, a pinto stallion, and a golden bay.

Why, Ellen had asked, did they need that many horses? It was, it seemed to her, a waste of money. Mister Corey had remained silent. Ricky O'Mara had explained that on the kind of journey they were taking, it was prudent to have some remounts. And besides, what if something should happen to one of the ponies they regularly rode? Or if one or more of the tethered horses broke their restraints and got away? It wasn't safe to be left afoot in the rough, rugged country where they were headed.

Other than the six saddle ponies, there was the team to pull the wagon and a couple of burros to be used for pack animals. The horses and burros were tied to the back of the buckboard and as soon as they got back to town, Ricky drove to the livery stable to board them.

"Now, it's on to the outfitters," Ricky said when the last horse was led into Packard's Livery Stable. Ellen made a face and he said, "It's just around the corner. This will be fun, you'll see."

On the south side of the town square, between a dentist's office and the High Country Saloon, rose a huge two-story, false-fronted building with a large sign mounted on the roof that read simply The Mountaineer.

Ricky hurried to open the door for Ellen. She stepped into the vast, barnlike building, paused and looked curiously around. Soon she ventured forward into the cavernous room where table after table was stacked high with a myriad of merchandise.

Mister Corey stepped past her, saying, "Look around. Pick up anything you'll need. This'll be your last chance."

Ellen didn't reply. She sauntered over to a glass-enclosed display case filled with nostrums. She read the labels with amusement. Dr. Jacob's Female Tonic. Sure-Help Toothache Drops. Oriental Wart Destroyer. Electric Rheumatism Syrup.

She turned away, headed to a table filled with all kinds of hats. She tried on a flat-crowned straw with a wide brim and a drawstring. She took it with her as she looked for a pair of gloves.

She glanced up and saw that Ricky and Mister Corey were loading the back counter high. Blankets

and saddles and revolvers. Rifles and boxes of am-
munition and a couple of sharp-bladed hunting
knives. A pair of shovels and a sledgehammer. A canvas tent, neatly folded. Rolled bandages. Several can-
teens. Skillets and pans. A big tin coffeepot.

After almost an hour spent at The Mountaineer,
Ellen had chosen only the straw hat, a pair of soft
suede gloves and a colorful bandanna.

"That it?" Mister Corey inquired when she
brought her choices to the counter.

"Yes," she said.

He leaned back against the counter and crossed his
arms over his chest. "So you already have the proper
riding attire?"

"I do. I have a riding skirt that's good as new."

Mister Corey's arms came uncrossed and he
pushed away from the counter. He walked over to a
set of tall shelves that were filled with trousers of
every size and fabric. Men's trousers. He searched for
the smallest sizes, came up with a pair of soft chamois
trousers.

He came back to Ellen with the pants tossed over
his arm. "Try these on," he instructed.

"I certainly will not," she said. "I do not wear
men's trousers."

He stepped closer, held the pair of chamois trousers
up to her slender frame, cocked his head to one side.
"These should do," he said as much to himself as to
her, and tossed them up onto the counter.

"I do not appreciate you—"

Interrupting, he said, "Before this trek is over, you
will."

# Fifteen

The trio left The Mountaineer as the summer sun was westering. The two men flanking Ellen, they leisurely strolled down the wooden sidewalk toward the Powderhorn Hotel in the gathering twilight. Ellen was grateful that this long trying day was finally coming to a close.

Fearful that any minute her hard-fought-for self-control would crumble, she battled the strong desire to quicken her steps, to hurry to the hotel.

To hurry away from him.

The strain of spending more than ten long hours with Mister Corey had left her with a raging headache and a numbing lassitude that went all the way down to her toes. She was exhausted and he was responsible. She was also confused and upset. Deep, gut-wrenching guilt over their careless sexual interlude had become almost a physical pain upon learning that he was a married man.

Yet, at the same time, despite the terrible guilt and self-loathing, to her dismay, she was still helplessly attracted to this amoral man whose strong animal-like masculinity had proved to be her undoing.

As they reached the hotel Ellen gave an inward

sigh of relief, turned, smiled at Ricky O'Mara and said, "Good night, Ricky. And thanks for everything."

"You're not going to retire, are you?" Ricky asked with a grin. "It's early."

"I am and you should, too," she told him. "If we're to leave at dawn tomorrow…"

"I will be ready tomorrow. But tonight—" he winked at her "—there's a pretty little blond banker's daughter waiting patiently for me to keep an engagement." He lifted wide shoulders in a playful shrug.

Ellen recalled Ricky telling her, on the crossing from England, that he loved all women. Would never love just one. She believed him. On the crossing he had been with a different woman every night. Last night it had been a redhead. And back in Denver on the two-hour layover, no telling.

"What about you, Steve?" she heard Ricky ask. "Want to see if my young lady has a friend?"

"Thanks, but no thanks," said Mister Corey, and Ellen, knowing she shouldn't care one way or the other, was absurdly glad that he had declined.

"Well, good night again," Ellen said, glancing at Mister Corey before she crossed to the stairs.

She let herself into the spacious corner suite and wanted to cry when her aunt Alexandra, obviously dressed for the evening, came out of her bedroom in a cloud of expensive perfume. The woman looked anything but pleased.

"Well, it's about time! I was beginning to think you were all lost somewhere out in the country. Did you buy the horses? Get the supplies? How much was the bill?'' Not giving Ellen an opportunity to answer, Alexandra said, "Hurry on into your bath, a hot tub's waiting. But don't dally, you must get dressed for dinner. The Colonel's likely already waiting downstairs.''

"I'm not going to dinner," Ellen said flatly.

"You're not going...? Why, you most certainly are! Where are your manners? The Colonel is hosting us and we—"

"I am not going," Ellen repeated, turned and walked away, with her flabbergasted aunt staring, openmouthed, after her.

"I don't like the way you're behaving, Ellen, and I simply will not tolerate it!" Alexandra called after her. "Do you hear me? You're no help to me at all, I might as well have left you back in Manhattan."

At her bedroom door, Ellen paused, turned and said, "Oh, how I wish you had."

"Well, that makes two of us, missy!"

Ellen said no more. She went into her bedroom, closed the door behind her and leaned back against it for a long moment. Just beyond, an angry Alexandra, shouting now to be heard, continued to hurl threats and warnings to the ungrateful niece who'd have no home of any kind if not for her aunt's kindness.

When the diatribe finally ended, Ellen knew that her aunt had gone downstairs. She exhaled, pushed away from the door, kicked off her leather slippers and began undressing as she walked toward the bathroom.

She stood in the middle of the square, white room and finished disrobing. Naked, she turned toward the filled tub and caught sight of herself in a freestanding mirror. She straightened and carefully examined her bare, slender body. She was too thin. Her hipbones protruded and her stomach was almost concave. Her breasts were high and firm like those of a young girl, but small. Too small. Hers was not the kind of soft, ample bosom men admired. Her legs, she decided, weren't bad at all. A little too slim perhaps, but long and rather shapely.

Staring at her reflection, Ellen reached up and took the pins from the bun at the back of her head. Her chestnut hair fell down around her thin face in dull, stringy locks. She shook her head about, attempting a seductive pose.

It didn't work.

There was, she sadly admitted, nothing provocative about her. If she looked less than alluring fully clothed, she was even more unappealing unclothed.

Repelled, Ellen turned from the mirror and stepped into the tub. She sank eagerly into its depths and reached for a perfumed bar of soap and a washcloth. In seconds a froth of rich, thick suds fully concealed the pale, slender body beneath the water.

Ellen laid the soap and washcloth aside. She sighed and sank farther down into the hot, soapy water, leaned back against the tub's padded headrest and closed her eyes. She would, she decided, stay right here for the next hour, totally relaxing, thinking of absolutely nothing.

But with her eyes closed, her body bare and the hot soapy water gently lapping at her breasts and thighs, Ellen found herself thinking of Mister Corey. Of his sensual lips that could so carelessly kiss her into sweet submission. Of his artistic hands that were capable of easily igniting her tingling flesh. Of his lean, hard body that had given her a kind of ecstasy she'd never before experienced.

Ellen moaned softly at the vivid recollection. She raised a wet hand, touched a slippery breast and found the nipple rigid and aroused. She swallowed hard, ran the tip of her finger back and forth over the hardened nipple and felt her bare belly flutter. Her eyes remaining safely closed, Ellen allowed her hand to move down from her breast, trail across her ribs and come to rest on her slippery stomach. She paused with indecision.

Then did something she had never done before.

Hoping to mimic the magical way Mister Corey had touched her, Ellen carefully guided her fingers between her legs, parted the wet curls and touched herself, just as he had done. It took only a few short moments. Eyes tightly shut, nervous fingers teasing and touching, she pretended Mister Corey was stroking her, loving her. She climaxed, and it was pleasurable, though nothing to compare with the total release he had given her.

Ellen's eyes opened and she drew a deep, slow breath. She realized, finally, exactly what had happened to her. Why she was behaving in such a carnal, unconventional manner. And why she had never before felt this way. It was really quite simple once she used a degree of logic.

She was a thirty-six-year-old woman who had, for the very first time, been sexually awakened by a man.

Ellen sat up in the tub, pushed her dampened hair back off her face and felt as though she'd made a real breakthrough. She understood now. It wasn't that she actually cared about Mister Corey. Of course she didn't. How could anyone in their right mind care for a man who was a charlatan, a liar, a coward and some other woman's wayward husband?

She couldn't and she didn't. It had just so happened that he was the brash, hot-blooded male who had shown her the thrilling secrets of lovemaking. It could have been anyone. Any man who was brazen and experienced.

Ellen felt as if a great burden had been lifted from her shoulders. It was, she realized, quite natural for her to feel a degree of attachment to him because he was her first real lover. Her long-departed husband, Booth Cornelius, didn't count. He had known little more about the art of lovemaking than she, and he had certainly never given her any real sexual pleasure.

Ellen was smiling as she climbed from the tub and began to towel herself dry. She felt as if she had crossed a dangerous bridge and was now safely on the other side. Circumstance had caused her to slip and fall into Mister Corey's arms, but it wouldn't happen again. Not now that she realized it wasn't *him* who had so dazzled her, but simply that he had been the one to hold her and show her the mysteries of her own body. Any one of a thousand men would surely have been capable of the same, had they had the inclination and the opportunity. They never had because she had never been alone with a man other than her husband.

Never.

When Ellen crawled into bed and blew out the lamp, she knew she would sleep like an innocent baby because she was finally becoming a logical adult. With her newfound maturity, she knew she no longer needed to be afraid of Mister Corey.

He belonged to another woman? So be it. She was glad he did. That knowledge would most certainly keep her from *ever* desiring his touch again.

Sunrise.

The specially built covered wagon, ordered from Grand Junction's best carriage maker, was brought around to the front of the Powderhorn Hotel at dawn. The high, wide canopy covering the long wagon bed was fashioned of dark leather that successfully kept out the hot sun. Beneath that protective leather hood, a large, soft mattress took up most of the wagon bed. Directly before the mattress, under the canopy, were cushions and pillows and places to sit. In front of the little sitting area were heavy black drapes that could be pulled to shut out any and all light.

The driver's seat, high up off the ground with its own folding-leather hood, was wide enough to seat three people. It was plushly upholstered and had a high, padded back for comfort. At the wagon's rear, beyond the large mattress, was a storage space for many of the supplies the contingent was taking on their journey.

Despite the early hour, a curious crowd had gathered on the town square. All had heard about the Landseer expedition and many had regularly checked on the progress of the one-of-a-kind wagon as it was being built right there in Grand Junction.

Now as the dawn was breaking, the townsfolk were gathered around, talking, watching, speculating. Colonel Stanley Lord was there to see them off. He had, when he'd been alone with Alexandra, questioned her judgment about this undertaking. And had been soundly upbraided and told to mind his own business.

He had taken the advice, knowing it was hopeless to do otherwise. But he was profoundly puzzled by this senseless quest of Alexandra's. She had been so shrewd, brilliant and decisive in the business world that, under her stewardship, the Landseer estate had grown into a sizable fortune. How could such a woman be so foolish as to think a pond of water somewhere in the Utah canyonlands could make her forever young?

The Colonel stepped forward to greet them when Ellen and Alexandra came out of the hotel. They stood talking, and Alexandra was giving him last-minute instructions when Mister Corey stepped onto the sidewalk carrying Summer Dawn. The assembled crowd buzzed with curiosity and jockeyed for better position.

Ignoring the nosy gathering, Mister Corey went directly to the back of the wagon. The tailgate was lowered. With the agility of a cat, he stepped up inside and disappeared beneath the leather canopy. The nimble Padjan was right behind them.

Inside, Mister Corey went down on his knees and very carefully, lest he hurt the sick, fragile woman, laid Summer Dawn on the mattress that had been covered with a silky sheet.

"You all right, sweetheart?" Mister Corey asked, looking at her creased, shrunken face.

Summer Dawn said nothing, but her obsidian eyes sought his face and spoke for her.

"She'll be comfortable here," said Padjan, kneeling on the other side of her. "Yes, she will," he said, smoothed her hair and helped Mister Corey spread a warm blanket over her thin frame.

Touching her shoulder, Mister Corey said, "We're going to get you home. I promise."

But the sick old woman had fallen asleep.

Mister Corey and Padjan looked at each other, looked at the sleeping woman. Mister Corey said, "I promise you as well, my friend. We'll get her home. We'll make it."

"I know we will," said Padjan and the two men clasped hands across Summer Dawn.

Back outside, Mister Corey shook hands with Colonel Lord while Padjan climbed up on the high driver's seat of the wagon. "It's been a pleasure to see you again, sir," said Mister Corey.

"Same here, son." The Colonel continued to

firmly shake the younger man's hand, reluctant to let it go.

There were so many things he wanted to ask Steve Corey, but he didn't dare. Steve was not the kind of man to confide in anyone. Steve had been, even in the army, a bit of a loner. Minded his own business. Kept his own counsel. Never complained or revealed much about himself.

"You'll take good care of the ladies, Steve?" the Colonel finally said.

"I'll get them there and back," Mister Corey replied.

# *Sixteen*

The sun swiftly climbed into the brightening azure sky as the group departed, leaving a waving, cheering crowd calling after them. Mister Corey, mounted on his paint stallion, led the party out of town. Directly behind him, Ellen, atop her blaze-faced dun gelding, rode alongside Ricky and his big, shiny black.

Behind the riders came the custom-built wagon with Padjan driving the sturdy bay team and Alexandra sitting on the seat beside him, a wide-brimmed straw hat on her gray head, a wide smile on her wrinkled face. Inside the wagon, Summer Dawn slept peacefully. Tethered to the back of the wagon were the remounts and the pack burros.

Away from the town square, Mister Corey angled southwest. A half hour after leaving the outskirts of Grand Junction, he pulled up on the paint and turned him about in a tight semicircle. The others stopped, waited.

He said, "We're all well rested, so we'll go as far as we possibly can this first day out. If we ride due west, we'll pretty much be able to skirt the foothills of Uncompahgre Plateau. With any luck, we'll reach the Colorado River by sundown, where we can make camp for the night.'' He stopped speaking, stood in the saddle, shaded his eyes with a hand and gazed off into the distance for a long moment. He lowered himself back into the saddle and said, ''Once we reach the river, we'll be in Utah territory where we start heading south.''

''When will we get to the Lost City?'' Alexandra called out excitedly.

''That depends on you, Miss Landseer,'' Mister Corey replied in a low, level voice.

''On me?''

''On you and all of us,'' he said. ''On how far we are willing to travel each day.''

''Perhaps, young man, I haven't made myself clear enough in our many conversations,'' Alexandra quickly responded. ''I do *not* want to dillydally because someone in this party might get a little weary. Your job is to get me to Padjan's Lost City as soon as possible.''

''That is my intent,'' said Mister Corey and Ellen saw that familiar sneering half smile touch his lips.

She easily read his thoughts. He knew which one in the group would be guilty of slowing their progress. And it wouldn't be poor, sick Summer Dawn.

Sure enough, less than two hours into the journey, Alexandra was shifting on the seat, sighing loudly and complaining of the damnable heat, the irritable buzz of insects and the total lack of comfort this expensive wagon offered.

Padjan, eyes fixed straight ahead, paid her no mind. He hadn't time to humor her now. He was focused on one thing and one thing only. Getting Summer Dawn to the Lost City before it was too late.

He was not surprised that Alexandra was already whining. He had known it would be this way and was prepared to tolerate it as best he could. He had not forgotten, nor would he forget, that without Alexandra Landseer, and her money, he wouldn't have been able to bring Summer Dawn home.

Up ahead, Ellen, garbed in an old black wool riding skirt and long-sleeved white blouse, was hot and uncomfortable. Miserable really. She could feel the perspiration pooling behind her knees and between her breasts. The riding skirt's heavy black fabric attracted the heat of the sun and she felt as if she were on fire. But she was determined to keep her discomfort to herself.

She felt like kicking herself for not listening to Mister Corey and dressing more appropriately. He had warned her that it would be hot and dry and that she should dress accordingly. She should have taken his advice and worn those soft chamois trousers he had held up to her at The Mountaineer. She wondered where the trousers were. She was pretty sure that he had purchased them, but had no idea what he had done with them.

She wasn't about to give him the satisfaction of asking.

Ellen was determined to keep her eyes and her thoughts off Mister Corey. She turned her head this way, then that, gazing at the grandeur and beauty of the wide mountain meadow they were crossing. The trail led them alongside the rocky, crumbling foothills of the Uncompahgre Range of the Rockies. The great jagged walls of the mountains were covered with wildflowers at the lower elevations. Above, tall green pines scented the thin mountain air, and higher still, on the plateau country at the very top, pines gave way to quaking aspens.

It was some of the most dramatic scenery she'd ever seen, yet it couldn't quite make her forget the presence of the man riding directly in front of her. Ellen soon gave up on pretending to observe the panorama surrounding her and focused squarely on Mister Corey.

Brim of her straw hat pulled low, drawstring pulled tight beneath her chin, she quietly studied him through lowered lashes. He was totally relaxed, slouching comfortably, his Stetson pulled low over his eyes. He had the wide shoulders and narrow hips of a born horseman and was, obviously, totally at home in the saddle. As she watched, he slowly slid his left hand around and under his belt at the small of his back. The movement caused his pale blue shirt to pull across his shoulders and Ellen felt her throat grow dry. She quickly looked away and clamped her teeth together.

Mister Corey is a married man, she painfully reminded herself. He's married. He belongs to someone else. She had made love to another woman's husband and she was heartsick about it. Damn him. Damn him to eternal hell, the careless cad! Had she known he was married, she would *never* have made love to him!

Or would she?

She had proven, to her remorse, that she was weak and submissive where he was concerned. His for the taking. Would the fact that she had since learned he was a coward and a married man make any difference if he took her in his arms again? She wasn't totally certain and that nagging doubt frightened and shamed her.

Staring at him through narrowed eyes, Ellen once again firmed her resolve to snub and ignore him at every opportunity. To stay out of his way at all times.

Throughout the long, hot day, Ellen conversed easily with Ricky. Ricky regaled her with tales of his youth, stories of his many siblings and of the good times they had had together, despite being dirt poor.

Behind them they could hear the continual complaining of an irate Alexandra and smiled conspiratorially at each other. They even sang for a while to pass the time, laughing at themselves and their total lack of musical ability.

Ahead, Mister Corey rode in silence, taciturn and withdrawn. He was strangely annoyed by the sound of Ellen and Ricky's laughter and singing. And he was further annoyed by Ellen's stiff, chilly attitude toward him. He recalled with displeasure the way she had glanced at him when she stepped down off the train in Grand Junction.

She had visibly recoiled at the sight of him. Looked at him as if he were a dirty, disgusting animal who had brutally forced her to do unspeakable things.

Made it quite clear that she blamed him, not herself, for what had happened and wanted nothing more to do with him.

Or so she thought.

He knew better.

Mister Corey's eyes narrowed, a muscle danced in his lean jaw. He knew just how to take the starch out of that stiff backbone.

The summer sun was sliding low toward the horizon when the caravan finally reached the Colorado River. The wide ribbon of deep turquoise water lay a hundred feet below. Mister Corey, telling the others to stay put, cantered the paint up and down the rocky bluffs until he located a wide, gentle incline that would take them down to the banks of the river.

He returned and said to Padjan, "There's ample room on the trail down for the wagon, and the descent is not that steep. We should make it to the river in half an hour. We'll set up camp there."

He turned the paint about and led the way down a gentle sloping path from the rocky bluffs to the wide river. Soon all had reached the smooth, level banks and could hardly wait to stop for the night.

They were sure they'd found the perfect campsite when, just ahead, they heard and then spotted a beautiful waterfall cascading from out of the rocks high above. The falls splashed into a wide, shallow rocky shelf several feet above the river, then poured down into the main waterway. The sound and sight of the falls splashing over the sunbaked rocks was pleasing beyond belief.

Ellen and Ricky exchanged puzzled looks when Mister Corey, as if he hadn't noticed the falls, continued to ride on. The group dutifully followed. Soon they rounded a bend in the river, leaving the splashing waterfall behind.

Completely out of sight.

Shortly, Mister Corey pulled up on his paint, dismounted and said, "We will set up camp here."

Ellen, disappointed at not lodging beside the falls, drew rein and looked around. It was quite nice here, she had to admit. The grassy banks of the river were incredibly inviting, as was the river's calm, blue-green water gliding peacefully southwestward.

A stand of tall cottonwoods and emerald willows offered pleasing shade. Dismounting, Ellen turned round and round, admiring the quiet, verdant oasis. Hot and tired from the long hours in the saddle, she was tempted to just toss the dun's reins to the ground, collapse where she stood and lie down on the soft, grassy banks of the river. Or better still, strip off all these hot woolen clothes and jump into the water.

An exhausted Alexandra, scolding him and warning him to be careful, allowed Ricky to help her off the wagon. Straining under the load, the veins in his neck standing out, he carefully lowered her to the ground. Alexandra rudely pushed him away. Only to learn that she was none too steady on her feet. Ricky grabbed her before she could crumple, wrapped a sup-

portive arm around her thick waist and guided her
toward the cottonwoods.

Out of sorts, as usual, Alexandra groaned as Ricky
eased her onto the soft bed of grass. Seated, she called
out loudly, "Mister Corey, will you kindly come
here! I must speak with you at once."

Mister Corey, turning his saddled paint over to
Ricky, was starting toward the wagon to help with
Summer Dawn when Alexandra called out to him. He
stopped and walked over to her.

"Yes, what is it, Miss Landseer?" he asked, looking at her.

"Bend down here," she instructed. "I don't want
to break my neck looking up, for heaven's sake."

Mister Corey crouched on his heels, rested his forearms on his thighs. "What's on your mind?"

"The falls," she said emphatically. "Why the Sam
Hill didn't we stop back around the bend and camp
beside that lovely waterfall? If there's some explanation, I'd like to hear it." Her mouth puckered with
displeasure and she added, "Don't unpack. We'll go
back and—"

"No," said Mister Corey decisively. "We won't.
We will make camp right here."

"Well, that beats all I've ever heard of!" said Alexandra, exasperated. "Maybe you got too much sun
today and aren't thinking clearly. Just give me one
good reason why we—"

"There are those among us who might wish to
bathe beneath the falls once it gets dark," he said.
Listening as he spoke, Ellen inwardly shivered. It was

as if he was announcing—for her benefit—that he intended to be at the falls come nighttime. "In that event," he continued, "the bather would have total privacy, since the falls are around the bend and out of sight of our camp."

Alexandra frowned and said, "I'm not about to go over there and take a—"

"You are not the only one here, Miss Landseer," he pointed out. "Some of us may wish to bathe in the falls. Make sense?"

Alexandra grudgingly nodded. "Oh, I suppose so, but I—"

"Good." Mister Corey dismissed her, came to his feet and walked toward the wagon. But he stopped where Ellen was struggling to unsaddle her dun gelding several yards away. He said, "Here, let me help you with that."

"No, thanks," she was quick to protest, not bothering to look at him. "I can do it myself."

"Fine, but once you get him unsaddled, let me rub him down for you."

"I can do it myself."

"I'll lead him down to the river for a drink."

Her voice rose an octave. "I can do it myself!"

He nodded, was silent for a long moment. Then said, barely above a whisper, "Eleven."

Ellen finally straightened, looked at him, puzzled. "Eleven?"

"The falls. Meet me at the falls at eleven."

"Meet you at the...?" Her face flushed hot and her heart began to pound so that she could hardly speak. But she managed to fix him with an icy stare and asked, "Why on earth would I want to do that?"

"Because," he said, "there are some things you *can't* do for yourself."

She was taken aback for only a second. Then, guiltily recalling how she had touched herself in the warm, sudsy bath, said, "You're wrong!"

"Am I?" His dark eyebrows lifted quizzically.

"Yes, you are. You're dead wrong!" She gave him a smug look and added, "And you hate being wrong, don't you, Mister Corey?"

"Like the devil hates holy water."

# Seventeen

Once the horses were watered, fed, rubbed down and loosely tethered, Mister Corey, Ricky, Padjan and Ellen went about setting up camp. While Ellen unpacked the coffeepot and skillet and various eating utensils, Ricky took a fishing pole and went to the river to catch their supper.

Padjan, never straying too far from the secured wagon where Summer Dawn rested, gathered twigs and got a campfire going. Alexandra, making no offer to help, kept asking how long before they ate. She was hungry. Didn't anybody care?

Mister Corey, having discarded his pale blue cotton shirt, was rhythmically swinging a sledgehammer, driving stakes into the grassy ground to secure the canvas tent that he had skillfully erected.

Ellen, on her knees preparing food a few yards away, watched him covertly. His naked torso gleamed with a sheen of perspiration and each time he lifted the heavy hammer, corded muscles bunched and slid beneath the smooth satiny skin of his long arms and back.

On his bare chest, diamond drops of sweat beaded in the thick hair covering the flat, well-defined muscles. The crisp curly hair thinned to a heavy dark line that went down his smooth washboard stomach. His faded Levi's rode low on his slim hips and his belt buckle fell well below his navel.

Ellen turned back to her chores, knowing that it was unwise to watch him. The mere sight of the man—bare-chested, sweating, looking oh-so-potently male—ignited a newfound passion in her. An acute passion she'd never felt for anyone else. In Mister Corey's arms, she had, for the first time in her dull, quiet life, experienced hot raging desire and unbelievable sexual pleasure.

Therefore it was impossible to forget the memorable night on the train's observation deck when he had given her a delicious taste of sweet ecstasy. Already she was hungry for more. God, she was starving for more.

"Look what I caught." Ricky's voice, very near, snapped Ellen out of her guilty reverie. Proudly, he announced, "A half-dozen rainbow trout, skinned and ready for the frying pan!"

"Good for you, Ricky," she said, smiling.

She took the plate from him, rolled the fish fillets in cornmeal and dropped them into a skillet of hot bacon grease bubbling over the campfire.

Everyone but Alexandra agreed that the deep-fried trout was nothing short of superb. Alexandra's disapproval surprised no one.

"Is there anything else to eat?" she asked petulantly, turning up her nose at the golden-brown trout and setting her plate aside. "I never liked fish. You know that, Ellen."

Her mouth full, Ellen shrugged and made no reply.

Mister Corey, shirt back on but half unbuttoned down his dark chest, sat leaning against a tree trunk, long legs crossed and stretched out before him, enjoying the hot supper.

"There's bacon and beef jerky and bread and canned beans and cheese and crackers," he said.

Alexandra looked sharply at him. "You expect me to eat such ungodly foods as beef jerky?"

"It's up to you," said Mister Corey. "You're not in Manhattan, Miss Landseer. There are no restaurants here."

Alexandra exhaled heavily, lifted her plate and began picking at the trout. It was, she found, quite tasty, but she kept that discovery to herself.

Supper was finished. The dishes had been washed in the river and put away. Full darkness had fallen and a million stars had come out to twinkle overhead in the black night sky. The hot dry air had cooled and a gentle breeze blew off the river. The campfire burned low. A pleasing lassitude had settled over the tired group.

"If no one objects," Ricky said, rising agilely to his feet, "I think I'll be the first to take a cool bath under the waterfall."

"Well, don't stay too long," said Alexandra. "I'll need help getting to the tent."

"Be back in ten minutes," he promised.

And he was.

Whistling merrily, Ricky, his dark hair still damp, came sauntering toward the smoldering campfire.

"Ah, what a treat that was," he declared. "Ellen, you should try it. If you like, I'll go partway with you, stand guard."

Ellen automatically exchanged glances with Mister Corey. "I believe I'll pass," she said. "I'm just too tired."

Ricky nodded. "Maybe in the morning."

"Maybe."

They fell silent again. Soon Padjan rose and said his good-nights. He went directly to the wagon and swung up inside. He would stay in the wagon and watch over Summer Dawn until morning.

Alexandra was next to give up the ghost. With Ricky's help, she rose, stiff and groaning, from the blanket. Then, without so much as a by-your-leave, made her way to the roomy tent she was to share with Ellen.

Ricky returned and for a time the three who were left, Ricky, Mister Corey and Ellen, sat before the dying fire, gazing into its orange embers. They said little, each lost in their own thoughts.

Mister Corey, seated directly across from Ellen, smoked in contemplative silence, watching her from hooded eyes above the low flickering flames of the campfire.

Ricky sat close beside her, hugging his knees and beginning to yawn. Ellen took that as her cue. If

Ricky was getting sleepy, he would soon go to bed and she'd be left alone with Mister Corey.

The prospect so unnerved her, she jumped up and said, "It's been a long day and I'm exhausted. Good night."

"Night, Ellen, you sleep well," Ricky said.

"Thank you. I'm sure I will," she said, seriously doubting the possibility.

Mister Corey remained silent.

Ellen crossed the grassy bank to the tent that was located about thirty yards from the campfire and twenty from the wagon. Mister Corey and Ricky were to sleep beneath the stars without benefit of shelter. She supposed they would bed down by the dying campfire.

Inside the tent, Ellen found Alexandra already sleeping. And snoring. Ellen glared at her aunt, sat down and began tugging off her boots and stockings. She could hear the low murmur of voices as Mister Corey and Ricky talked.

She was unbuttoning her white, long-sleeved blouse when she heard Ricky say, "Steve, old buddy, I'm getting sleepy. Think I'll turn in. You going around to the falls to take a bath before bed?"

Ellen held her breath waiting for his answer. "In a while," said Mister Corey. "It's early yet."

Seated on the floor covering of the canvas tent, Ellen undressed in the darkness, her back to her sleeping aunt. Naked, she bemoaned the fact that she was badly in need of a refreshing bath. There was sand and grit in her hair and her body was fragrant with stale perspiration from a day spent riding under a broiling alpine sun.

Cursing herself for not thinking to bring a pan of water to the tent so that she could at least wash up a little, Ellen reached for her nightgown. Too late now. She didn't dare venture out and down to the river.

Ellen pulled her gown down over her head, shoved it past her hips and then stretched out on the ground, taking care to leave plenty of room between herself and Alexandra.

As usual, Alexandra was flat on her back, blowing and snorting and putting up such a racket Ellen wondered how she could possibly get any rest. As she lay there, sticky and miserable for what seemed like hours, she saw that the moon had risen. Its silver light was seeping in through the thick canvas fabric of the tent.

She wondered what time it was.

Had eleven come and gone? Had Mister Corey come and gone from the falls? Or was he there? Waiting. Waiting for her to come to him. At the thought of him waiting in the moonlight, Ellen's breath grew short and her heart pounded. She closed her eyes and balled her hands into tight fists at her sides.

But his image wouldn't go away. She could see him clearly. Could almost feel his arms come around her, his lips take hers in a long moist kiss. And then at last that release of all her pent-up loneliness.

Ellen wrestled with her conscience. She told herself she couldn't do it. She couldn't go to him. She simply could not. The promise of ecstasy did not alter the fact that the man had no morals. He was a disgraced coward and an unfaithful married man. She didn't like him, really, had no respect for him. Nor him for her. He had shown her a part of herself that she hated. A terrible weakness, a personal failing of which she was ashamed.

Mister Corey was everything bad in this world.

But, oh, being bad with him had felt soooo good.

Ellen's eyes opened.

Suddenly she felt as if her nightgown were choking her. She wished she was alone so that she could tear it off and put an end to the suffocating sensation that was overwhelming her. At the same time she knew nothing would stop the disturbing pulsing of her tense body. A gentle throbbing tempo was centered in her groin and was steadily building in intensity.

In mental and physical agony, Ellen stared up at the tent's sloping canvas ceiling. She told herself she didn't need what Mister Corey could give her. She had lived without it for thirty-six years, she could live without it another thirty-six. She had to be strong, to fight her dark desire. To shun the enticing evil that emanated from him. To forfeit the sure promise of stolen rapture for the sake of her own self-respect.

# Eighteen

Ellen was still telling herself that she *had* to stay away from Mister Corey when, glancing at the sleeping Alexandra, she sat up, unable to deny her deep yearning for one more minute. Her desire for him had become a constant driving force, coloring every thought she had, swaying every decision she made.

Ellen crawled over to the tent's entrance and pushed back the flap a few inches.

Squinting, she looked out.

Ricky O'Mara, using his saddle for a pillow, lay sleeping soundly beside the cold campfire. Mister Corey was nowhere in sight. Ellen looked toward the wagon. No candle burned inside. It was dark and silent. She glanced over her shoulder. Snoring loudly, Alexandra slumbered on.

On her hands and knees, Ellen slipped out of the tent. She then turned about on her knees and carefully lowered the flap. She rose to her feet, looked cautiously around, only then realizing that she hadn't thought to pick up her house slippers. She made a face, decided it was too risky to go back for them.

She slowly backed away from the tent, the grass soft and dewy beneath her bare feet. The moon was high in the night sky, its radiant beams silvering the mist rising off the river. Crickets croaked at the water's edge, and in the distance a coyote called mournfully to his mate.

Ellen gathered the hem of her nightgown up around her knees and set out toward the falls, which she could hear tumbling and splashing loudly over the rocks.

Her heart in her throat, she nervously rounded the wide bend in the river. The sound of the falls grew stronger and her heartbeat grew louder. She took a few more tentative steps, stopped, slowly turned her head, looked up at the shelf of rock directly beneath the falls and stopped breathing entirely.

Naked, Mister Corey stood beneath the cascading falls with the full moon silvering part of his wet, sleek body, leaving the rest in deep shadow. His feet apart, arms raised, hands in his thick black hair, eyes closed, he was poised like a statue on the ledge six feet above. He was totally unaware of her presence.

So Ellen was given the opportunity to study him without his knowledge. Both fascinated and appalled, she gazed upon his naked body with the embarrassed curiosity of a young, innocent girl. While she had been shockingly intimate with him on the train's observation deck, she hadn't actually seen him, had only felt him.

Intrigued, Ellen let her appraising gaze slide down from his strong sculpted shoulders to his corded ribs to his flat belly.

And lower.

Her face grew hot as she stared at that most masculine part of him. At rest amidst a swirl of curly black hair, his soft male organ looked harmless and totally incapable of giving pleasure.

She knew better.

All at once Mister Corey's eyes opened and his hands came down to his sides. He slowly turned his dark head and looked down at Ellen with no hint of surprise. He made no move to cover his nakedness.

"You came," he said in a low, caressing voice. Then ruined it by adding, "I knew you would."

Instantly insulted, Ellen said, "You did not! I had no idea you were here. I came because I need a bath and…and…"

"I know," he said. "And I'm going to give you one."

"No, you are not. This isn't right. We can't do this. I shouldn't have come here. I…I'm leaving."

"Take off your nightgown and come here," he commanded and his voice was low with a deep resonance that made her shiver.

Ellen hesitated for only a second. So eager to feel his wet flesh against her own she could hardly stand it, she stripped off her gown and dropped it where she stood. Mister Corey bent from the waist and reached out a hand. She took it and, with his help, climbed the slippery rocks up to where he was.

For a long moment they stood facing each other in the moonlight, saying nothing, their bare bodies not quite touching. Then Mister Corey drew her into his close embrace and Ellen felt his wet nakedness against her, felt the fierce animal heat of him enveloping her.

He held her close against his body for only a moment, then released her. He urged her over to stand directly beneath the cascading waterfall and, taking a bar of soap from a small ledge at his elbow, began to lather her neck and throat.

Ellen lifted restless hands, her fingers danced along his rib cage and said, ''Oh, God, you know we shouldn't be doing this.''

''We haven't done anything.''

''But we're going to. You're going to make love to me.''

''If that's what you want to call it,'' he said and her anger instantly flared.

''Whatever it is, it is all I want from you,'' Ellen replied, immediately on the defensive. ''This, and nothing more. Do you understand?''

''What else could I possibly offer you?'' he said, undeterred.

''Nothing. Not a thing and I don't—''

''I know. You don't like me, you don't approve of me.''

''Exactly. I wish we had never—''

''Made love? Had sex?'' he said bluntly. ''But we did. And we will again. Anytime we get the opportunity.''

''No, we won't. Tonight is the last time.'' She tried to sound forceful, decisive. ''After tonight, I want you to leave me alone.''

''Really?'' He raised a dark eyebrow skeptically.

"You should have thought of that before you came here looking for me." She shoved on his slippery chest, made a halfhearted attempt to get away. He held her fast and said, "Calm down, Ellen. You don't have to like me. I don't care whether you do or not. Nobody's looking at forever here." She glared at him, but softened when he said, "Let me give you a nice refreshing bath, then if you change your mind…"

"You…you don't have to," she began, conquered.

"I want to," he said and her breath caught in her throat when he slowly moved the soap down her slippery chest and around her left breast.

"Tell me that doesn't feel good," he said and brushed a kiss to her forehead.

"Yes," she admitted. "Damn you, it does. It feels…good."

"Let me make you feel real good, baby. Better than you've ever felt before. Say yes."

"Yes," she breathed.

The bath beneath the waterfall became a seductive, sensual ritual that left Ellen breathless and aroused. At first it seemed so taboo, so decadent, to have a man bathing her as if she were a helpless child. But the experience quickly became so pleasurable, so erotic, it seemed natural and right and she loved every thrilling minute.

Mister Corey washed her breasts, her belly, her thighs, and knelt before her to lather her long, slender legs.

Continuing to kneel, he took her arm, turned her about so that she was facing away from him. He washed her back, her buttocks, the calves of her legs, her delicate ankles, her small feet. Soapy from throat to toe, Ellen stood there bracing herself against the wall of rock thinking that he had carefully lathered every part of her body.

Except one.

"Turn around," she heard him order, and on weak legs she complied.

He stayed on his knees before her and watched as he rubbed the bar of soap between his hands until they were both well-lathered. He let the soap drop through his fingers and lifted his hands to her.

"Spread your legs a little," he said and she didn't hesitate. She would do anything he asked.

She moved her bare feet apart and then gasped when a soapy, brown hand went between her legs to wash her where once he had loved her. She looked down on him and felt her nipples sting and tingle. The triangle of chestnut curls between her thighs were soon so completely lathered they were stark white. His soapy fingers were between the snowy white curls, washing, cleansing, arousing.

When there was not one single inch of her body that had not been fully lathered, Mister Corey rose to his feet, gave her upturned face a quick kiss, then shifted her slightly to stand directly beneath the most powerful deluge of the falls. He had foamed and frothed her body with the soap, now he rinsed and cleansed the suds away in the rushing, pounding water.

Ellen quickly decided that the rinsing was even better than the soaping. With the water pouring over her and his magical hands sweeping away any residue of clinging suds, she was in heaven. She sighed and smiled and swooned.

What could possibly be more exciting than having this dark, naked man give her a bath in the wilds? Surely nothing could compare. This was, she decided as his lean fingers slid seductively over her clean, slippery flesh, even more exciting than the night on the train.

If they did nothing more than this, if he sent her away after this long, bewitching bath, she wouldn't complain. She would be completely satisfied. She would never again take a bath without thinking of this very special one.

Ellen's eyes opened when Mister Corey's hands finally left her flesh. She looked at him, trying to read his thoughts. It was impossible. Those black, black eyes held no light, no hint of what he was thinking. Snared by his unblinking gaze, Ellen continued to look into his impenetrable eyes as he took her hand in his and put it on him.

Her excitement and confusion instantly escalated. He was quite soft to the touch, not the least bit hard or erect. She wasn't sure what she was supposed to do. So she gently cupped him, held him gently in her hand. Within seconds, to her surprise and delight, he became aroused.

It was, she thought, the strangest, most wonderful feeling, to be holding him, touching him while he literally grew in her hand. It made her feel very feminine, very powerful, very eager to make love with him.

Driven by her own rising desire, Ellen grew bold. She began to stroke the rigid length of him. The hot, heavy feel of him made her extremely curious. She was dying to look down.

"Go ahead. Look at it," she heard him say as if he'd read her thoughts.

Her fingers gently gripping him, Ellen lowered her gaze and stared. She smiled foolishly. What a change from when she'd first spotted him standing under the falls. Now he was huge and hard, jutting out from the dense black hair of his groin, stirring in her hand with hot pulsating life. The tip was velvety smooth and shaped like a mushroom. It looked much too large to fit inside her.

Her eyes reluctantly returned to his face, but her possessive hand remained on him.

"You want it?" he asked.

"Yes," she said excitedly. "I do. Give it to me."

He took her by the shoulders and kissed her hard. And kept on kissing her until she was weak with wanting. He moved her hand from him and drew her arms up around his back. He put a hand beneath her bare bottom and drew her closer against him, lifting her a little, positioning her, letting her feel his hard flesh throb against her bare quivering belly.

For a long, sweet interlude, the eagerly embracing couple stood there naked in the silvery moonlight, letting the warm summer water from the falls splash down over them as they kissed and clung to each other. The cascade struck their shoulders and backs, plastered their hair to their heads and sluiced down their hot pressing bodies.

It was a wonderful sensation to be naked together in the summer moonlight, to hold each other and kiss while the water pelted over them.

Mister Corey finally tore his lips from Ellen's, lowered his hands and clasped her bare bottom. He lifted her up and drew her legs around his back. He locked his wrists beneath her buttocks, urged her a little higher, and began to feast on her bare, wet breasts. His lips kissed and tugged, his teeth nibbled and grazed. Ellen breathed through her mouth, tightened her arms around his neck and threw her head back. He began to suck greedily on a stiff, stinging nipple and Ellen moaned with building pleasure.

So adept was he at making love, Ellen hardly realized that as he suckled her so forcefully, he was positioning her to take him inside her. His lips never leaving her breast, he drew her hand down between them and she knew instinctively what she was to do.

Gazing down at his dark face, she saw that his eyes were closed as his lips tugged on her nipple. Never wanting that marvelous mouth to leave her, Ellen shifted her weight a little, sliding a little higher up his sleek body, until she could successfully take him in her hand and guide him into her hot, yielding flesh. Longing to swallow him up and feel him move inside her, Ellen stayed poised just as she was for a long moment, with just the tip of his erection inside her. Then clinging to his wide shoulders, she slowly slid down his slippery belly, fully impaling herself upon him.

Mister Corey's lips left her diamond-hard nipple. He looked at her for a long, tense moment, then kissed her. And holding both cheeks of her bottom in his spread hands, he began the deep driving movements of lovemaking. Ellen, so hot for him she could hardly control herself, worked with him, tilting her pelvis up, bucking against him. Taking all of him and reveling in the counter-tempo of his invasion and withdrawal into that scorchingly aroused part of her body.

Her arms wrapped around his neck, her head thrown back, she panted as he drove deep inside her again and again. With each hard thrust, Ellen marveled. And just as she had on the train, she wondered if this incredibly sensual man had ever considered making plain old conventional love in the usual, accepted fashion.

As another deep, rolling thrust of his hips drove his hard flesh up inside to fill and stretch her, she hoped that he did not. Who wanted only the kind of lovemaking she had known when they could have this wild, unorthodox coupling?

Ellen opened her eyes and looked up at the moon sailing high overhead, tinting their wet, joined bodies a pale silver. Water from the falls rushed over them as if attempting to tear them apart and cool their raging hot bodies.

But only one thing could do that and Ellen knew

it would soon happen. She couldn't hold back. She felt her release starting and whispered his name.

"Steve."

"Yes, you're coming, I can feel it," he said. "Take me with you. Let me come with you," he murmured huskily.

"Yes, oh yes, come with me!" she gasped.

Seconds later she cried out and he groaned loudly as together they shuddered in a perfectly timed, shared climax.

# *Nineteen*

Three days into their wagon trip, the contingent had reached the canyon country between the Aquarius Plateau on the west and the La Sal Mountains to the east. They now rode south among bloodred arches, slickrock benches and soaring balanced rocks. The farther they advanced into the wild, rugged canyonlands, the more endlessly fascinating the panorama of fins and needles and spires that surrounded them. There were hidden alcoves and huge jutting overhangs and high flat mesas. Buttes and bridges and windows and plateaus. Flaming-red rock sculpted into incredibly unique designs by the wind and the water.

Mister Corey carefully guided his paint gelding among the many arches and benches and soaring spires. His eyes narrowed and focused, he was rigidly alert, constantly watching, searching. It was up to him to choose the right path through this inhospitable country. His responsibility to lead them all safely to their destination.

He generally stayed several yards ahead of the others, looking for passages that would be level and wide enough for the wagon. At times he had to circle back and start over again in a slightly altered direction.

Still, Mister Corey was pleased with their progress. So far there had been no mishaps, no unexpected accidents, and for that he was thankful. While Alexandra Landseer had whined and complained every mile of the way, she was not yet guilty of slowing them down. Padjan was quite good at appeasing the aging heiress. He could make her laugh at herself when no one else could. When she would not be placated, Padjan simply did what the rest of them did.

He ignored her.

If their good luck held, they could be on the Navajo reservation within three or four days. Then on up to the Lost City a couple of days after that and...

A loud commotion and a louder shout instantly snapped Mister Corey out of his musings. A quick jolt of adrenaline rushing through his lanky body, he wheeled the paint around and galloped back toward the others. Well before he reached them, he saw what the problem was.

"Well, I'll be damned," he muttered, his lean face set as he brought the paint to a dead stop and slid down off its back.

"Can you beat this?" said Ricky, shaking his dark head ruefully. "A brand-new wagon and a back wheel already coming loose and falling off."

"Somebody didn't do his job!" snarled Alexandra from her high seat at the wagon's front. "Mister Corey, this is your fault. You should have examined the wagon thoroughly before you took possession. Now just look what's happened."

"Better get down, Miss Landseer, we may be here awhile," was his calm reply.

She made a face at him, but he was unaware. Ricky and Mister Corey unhitched the remounts and pack mules from the wagon's tailgate. Mister Corey led the animals a few yards away and ground-tethered them.

He returned to the wagon, crouched down on his heels and carefully scrutinized the situation. It couldn't have happened in a worse spot. The big wagon was halfway through a narrow slot canyon, the floor of which was the deep sand of an ancient wash.

Padjan, having leaped down like a quick, nimble acrobat the minute the breakdown happened, rubbed his shiny bald head and asked, "You want me to take Summer Dawn out of the wagon?"

Mister Corey nodded. "It might be better for her, Padjan. It's going to take some fierce rocking and pushing to get the wheel back on." He rose to his feet, looked around. He pointed thirty yards ahead to a lone piñon tree that had taken root in a pocket of sand between solid walls of sandstone. "Let's take her up there. That piñon will give her a little shade."

Padjan nodded and swung up into the rear of the wagon. Mister Corey took off his Stetson, tossed it into the wagon and stood at the open tailgate, waiting for Padjan to hand Summer Dawn down to him.

Ellen, having dismounted the moment the wagon wheel came off, was standing a few short feet away when the fragile Indian woman was lowered and placed in Mister Corey's waiting arms. She caught thc look he exchanged with Padjan, saw his expression when he gazed at Summer Dawn.

And just for an instant, she saw the crack in Mister Corey's cool exterior, revealing a love for Padjan and Summer Dawn.

Ellen quickly turned away, blinked and felt her eyes mysteriously sting.

Why, she didn't know.

"Ellen," Ricky said from directly behind. She turned to face him. He smiled and said, "Why don't you go with them? I'll bring Miss Landseer, and the two of you can sit in the shade with Summer Dawn."

Ellen shook her head decisively. "No. I'll help get the wagon up out of the sand."

"Well, if that is what you wish," he said. "I will go—"

"O'Mara, are you *never* going to help me down?" shouted Alexandra.

"Coming, Miss Landseer," said the unflappable Irish-Spaniard.

Ellen took off her straw hat and fanned herself while Mister Corey, Padjan and Ricky got Summer Dawn and Alexandra settled beneath the piñon tree up the canyon. Returning to the wagon, Padjan climbed onto the high seat, ready to coax the harnessed team into helping pull the disabled wagon out of the sand.

At the wagon's rear, Mister Corey gave Ellen a questioning look. She tossed her hat into the wagon as he had done earlier.

"I want to do my part," she announced. "I will help push the—"

"That isn't necessary," he cut her off. "Go on up to—"

"I am helping," she declared and he shrugged.

"Fine, but don't get in the way," he warned. "And don't get hurt."

"I have no intention of getting in the way or getting hurt," she assured him.

He rolled his eyes. "Okay, Padjan," Mister Corey called. "Let's get this thing up and out of here."

Padjan immediately flicked the whip over the team's backs and at the same time Mister Corey, Ricky and Ellen stooped and began trying to lift the rear of the listing wagon up out of the sand.

"Jesus," said Mister Corey, straining under the load. "You'd think we were transporting gold bullion. This wagon weighs a ton."

Bottom lip caught between her teeth, shoving with all her might, Ellen felt as if her arms were being torn from their sockets. But she didn't let on. She continued to heave and push and lift alongside the two strong men, ignoring the pain and the perspiration popping out on her forehead and upper lip.

Axle imbedded in the deep sand, the wagon hardly budged.

"All right," Mister Corey said. "When I count three, everyone let go."

He didn't have to ask twice.

Ellen straightened, put a hand on her drumming heart and fought to get her breath. Ricky, blowing and wiping the sweat from his face, bent over from the waist, placed his hands on his knees and took several long panting breaths. Mister Corey, his throat dust dry, swallowed hard, stripped off his shirt, mopped his chest with it and tossed it aside.

He then stood considering what to do next. He walked from one side of the disabled wagon to the other, shaking his dark head and rubbing his chin.

He said, "We'll lay a rock path directly in front of the mired axle. Once we've done that, we'll cut a strong limb from that piñon tree and lever the wheel hub up onto the rocks."

He turned and walked away to begin gathering large, flat rocks. Ricky and Ellen followed his lead, scattering to search for large, level stones.

Soon Ellen returned to the wagon with a huge rock that was much heavier than she had imagined. Worse, the unwieldy boulder had a rough, jagged edge that was uncomfortably punching her in the stomach through her heavy wool riding skirt. Her knees beginning to buckle under the weight, her arms giving out, she knew that she should drop the big rock where she stood and admit defeat.

But she didn't want the men thinking she was just in the way, nothing but trouble. So she struggled on valiantly and was almost to the wagon when her burden slipped from her gloved hands and banged down her left leg, tearing a long gaping hole in her black skirt and scraping raw flesh from her exposed thigh.

"God in heaven!" Mister Corey shouted and ran to her. "You hurt? You hurt bad?"

"I'm not hurt at all, I just—"

"Let me see," he interrupted, scowling, then when she fidgeted he tersely ordered her to stand still. With no regard for her modesty, he swept the torn skirt out of the way and carefully examined her abraded skin. "Ricky, get that medical kit out of the wagon," he called over his shoulder.

"I wish you wouldn't make such a fuss," she said, embarrassed.

And then was quite sure she had lost her mind entirely when she found herself longing to lean down and run her hands over his straining muscles. She wanted to die when the touch of his lean brown fingers caused a warm throbbing to move up along her inner thighs. She bit the inside of her lip wishing the others would somehow magically disappear. She wished that the two of them were alone as they had been beneath the falls. She wanted to feel his body pressed to hers, his masterful lips covering her own.

"Will you hold still?" Mister Corey ordered and Ellen had no choice but to stand there while he carefully cleaned the long scratch down her thigh with alcohol.

"Need any help?" Padjan shouted.

"Oh, for heaven's sake," Ellen said, mortified. "Must the entire universe know that I—"

"What's wrong down there?" Alexandra shouted from her perch in the shade of piñon tree. "Ellen fall and hurt herself? Wouldn't surprise me, she's always been clumsy and—"

"Ellen's just fine," Ricky assured both Padjan and Alexandra.

"That will do!" Ellen snapped as she anxiously pushed Mister Corey away and attempted to pull her tattered riding skirt together around her leg.

"Stay right here," he said, rising to his feet and walking to his tethered paint gelding. "Easy, boy," he soothed when the paint shuffled and whinnied.

He unbuckled his saddlebags and from them withdrew an article of clothing. He returned, handed the pair of soft chamois trousers to Ellen and said, "Go get changed." He glanced at Ricky, who was several yards away now, picking up a flat boulder. "Ricky and I will take care of the wagon wheel." He stepped in closer and Ellen blushed crimson, knowing he'd read her guilty thoughts when he said, barely above a whisper, "And I'll take care of you the first chance I get."

# *Twenty*

An hour after the breakdown, the wheel was back on the wagon and the gang was ready to continue on their journey. But before they could get under way, another minor mishap occurred.

Alexandra, stubbornly refusing to take Ricky's supporting arm, started toward the wagon, made a misstep on the uneven ground and turned her ankle.

Another half hour was lost as she winced and wailed and made certain everyone knew she was in utter agony. Ellen hurriedly brought down the rubbing liniment and Padjan applied the liquid balm to the heiress's swelling ankle. Ricky then carried the moaning Alexandra to the wagon where Ellen gave her aunt a couple of aspirin. Alexandra insisted that she was in far too much pain to travel.

"Couldn't we just camp here and then tomorrow when I'm feeling better we can go on?"

"No, Miss Landseer, you would be in no less pain if we stayed here," Mister Corey reasoned. "And precious traveling hours would be lost. We're moving out."

Despite Alexandra's angry mutterings and threats, they promptly got back on the trail. The next hour passed somewhat peacefully as they rode through the twisting, turning canyon where juniper and piñon had taken root in pockets of sand between solid rock. Dramatic red sandstone monoliths towered over them as they snaked through the canyon, at times completely shutting out the sun and casting the chasm into deep shadow. In tiny crevices in the soaring rock walls, maidenhair ferns and mosses miraculously grew.

Ellen, entranced by the spectacular scenery, thought they were ascending. It seemed to her that they were moving higher and higher, but she wasn't sure until all at once they exited the canyon and rode out into a lush mountain meadow. They were, she realized, now well into the foothills of the Abajo Mountains. She'd been gazing up at the misty blue range all morning and now they surrounded them.

It was a beautiful place. Baby-blue iris, purple lupines and pink roses bordered a forest of quaking aspen and Douglas fir. Tiny hummingbirds were busy pollinating the colorful wildflowers.

The contrast from steep-sided sandstone canyon to open mountain meadow was dramatic.

It seemed impossible that two such diverse terrains could exist so close together. Ricky, riding alongside Ellen, pointed to a stream at the edge of the conifer forest.

"Look there!" he said excitedly.

She did and her eyes widened in surprise when she spotted a huge black bear lumbering along the banks of the rushing water.

"Is he dangerous?" she asked.

"Only if he catches us," Ricky said with a wink and a smile. Then reassured her, "No, he would only hurt us if he were hungry. He's not. There's plenty of trout in that stream."

Awed by the size of the bear, Ellen was still staring at him when Ricky directed her attention to a half-dozen white-tailed deer grazing languidly in the peaceful meadow. This was, she thought, a glorious, unspoiled wonderland. And riding on level ground for a change was a blessing.

All too soon they were leaving the high, flat meadow behind and starting a sharp descent off the mountain and back into the rugged rocky region below. Shortly, they were once again inside a narrow slot canyon. The lower they dropped, following the bed of a creek that had carved out the chasm, the wider the canyon became.

Red rock walls rose majestically on both sides, opening now and then into little alcoves of intricately sculptured stone. Ferns clustered in the dark wet corners, trickles of water and patches of emerald-green moss splashed down the rocks.

The summer sun was still high overhead, bathing the canyon in its hot white light. It was not quite four o'clock. A long time until sunset.

A half mile into the canyon, it started narrowing slightly.

Mister Corey, riding far ahead of the others, put the paint into a fast gallop and advanced along the creek bed. He turned his head this way, then that, looking around, high and low, carefully examining every square inch of the arroyo.

Huge stacks of rock were scattered along the canyon floor. Harmless pebbles and huge dangerous boulders that had come from the high canyon walls above. The sun-heated stone had cooled during the chilly nights, broken off from the ridges hundreds of feet above and crashed down below.

Tapping the paint's flanks with his booted heels, Mister Corey continued to ride farther into the canyon. He didn't stop until he had ridden completely through it. At the other side was a plateau.

He abruptly pulled up on the paint and turned back. A few yards into the canyon, he drew rein and brought the horse to a complete halt. Forearm resting on the saddle horn, Mister Corey pushed back his Stetson, leaned his head way back and looked straight up at the sky. He nudged the big paint with his knees and the responsive steed slowly turned in a complete circle.

He dismounted, kicked at the ground with the toe of his boot. And was relieved to see that a floor of solid rock lay just beneath a thick covering of sand.

His ebony eyes narrowing, Mister Corey looked up, studied the heavens.

There was not a cloud to be seen anywhere. The sky was a giant blue dome high overhead. The chances of rain were next to none. Mister Corey climbed back into the saddle and sat there atop the paint, considering, weighing the odds, coming to a decision.

Riding through a dry-wash canyon like this one was always risky. Rainstorms could blow up and quickly flood the canyon floor. Mister Corey again studied the sky. No clouds. Not a one.

If he didn't take them through the canyon, he would have to scout out another route. That would take time. A lot of time. And even if he found an alternate route, it could well mean they would have to travel an extra twenty to thirty miles out of the way.

With any luck, he could get them all safely through the narrow canyon in an hour.

Mister Corey returned to the slow-moving caravan. He led them into the three-mile-long canyon where the slickrock walls rose five hundred feet on each side, nearly straight up. But there were, Mister Corey had carefully noted, jutting ridges, deep crevices and craters specking the soaring sandstone walls.

When the contingent had ridden a little more than a mile deeper into the canyon, a small, fluffy white thunderhead moved abruptly into view above the canyon rim.

Mister Corey was the only one who noticed. He felt the fine hair rise on the nape of his neck. Within five minutes the air had become heavy. The big paint pricked up his ears, whinnied nervously. A hawk took flight above, the frantic flapping of its wings echoing in the strange stillness.

Mister Corey ground his teeth.

A storm was coming. He could feel it. If he was right, they could all drown trapped in this narrow canyon by the rushing floodwaters. And it would be his fault. It was too late to turn back, they'd never make it. Nor could they reach the other side.

The sky suddenly darkened ominously.

Mister Corey turned back and, with practiced military precision, gave signals and shouted commands, "Ellen, Ricky, dismount and loosen the cinches of your saddles!" Bewildered, Ellen frowned and stayed in her saddle.

"What's wrong?" she asked Ricky as he hurriedly slid off his black and began loosening the cinch beneath the animal's belly.

"A storm's coming," he said. "Get down now and I'll loosen your saddle cinch."

"But why?"

"Because the horses will have to swim for it," he said, a look of worry crossing his face.

"What about us?" Ellen asked.

"Start climbing," Ricky instructed as a low rumble of thunder echoed through the canyon. "Climb until you can reach a high crater or overhang."

Alarmed, Ellen anxiously dismounted and glanced toward the wagon. She saw Mister Corey hurriedly untying the remounts and burros. Then heard him shouting for Padjan to head for the near wall. Padjan was already lashing the team. Mister Corey ran up ahead of the wagon, wrapped his hand around one of the bridles of the harnessed team. Walking fast, he began pulling and guiding the frightened horses toward a sloping overhang on the canyon's west side.

Padjan was on the high seat, looking frightened and

cracking the whip over the team's backs. Alexandra, inside the wagon, had stopped complaining about her painful ankle long enough to demand to know what was going on. Ellen who was on the opposite side of the canyon, began to head for the wagon to offer her help.

"No!" Ricky stopped her, grabbing her arm and pulling her back. "Don't try crossing the canyon. Start climbing!"

Her heart hammering, Ellen nodded, turned and ran toward the canyon's east wall as the rains pelted her.

The lone thunderhead that Mister Corey had seen earlier had quickly billowed into a gigantic black cloud that completely obliterated the sun. The canyon was thrown into eerie murky shadow. A flash of lightning streaked across the rapidly darkening sky. A tremendous clap of thunder followed.

The storm burst in all its fury.

The heavens opened up and blinding, pounding rain poured into the canyon. Ellen heard the roar of the flood before she could see it. Then came a froth of foam and flotsam down the rushing, muddy river. The flood picked up trees and rocks and swept them downstream.

Ellen, struggling to get a foothold on the slick rock wall, watched until she could no longer see across the canyon. She couldn't make out the wagon. The rains were too heavy. Great sheets of water driven by rising wind obliterated everything.

Trying to remain calm, Ellen anxiously hoisted herself up the canyon's rock face, getting a toehold two feet up and reaching and feeling with her hand for any small crevice she could get her fingers into. She gave a little yelp of triumph when she found, and managed to grip, a handful of maidenhair fern. But she winced in defeat when the fern slipped through her wet hand and she slid back the few inches she'd gained.

She experienced a moment of sheer panic when she felt the water flowing over her feet and ankles. Blinking away the moisture that was blinding her, Ellen looked down and saw that the red, muddy water was rapidly rising. It was roaring through the canyon, sweeping debris with it.

"Oh, dear God," she murmured and redoubled her efforts to climb the canyon wall.

Through the sheets of water pelting her face, she was able to make out the darkened contour of a small alcove some fifteen feet above. If she could just make it to that crater, she would be safe. Survival the only thing on her mind, Ellen Cornelius grunted and groaned and shimmied up the face of the wall, desperately seeking handholds and footholds wherever she could find them.

It took ten minutes to reach the alcove. It seemed like an hour. When her hands were both on the flat lip of the crater rim, she gave a great cry of relief. But it was quickly followed by a sob of despair. How could she pull herself up into the crater? She couldn't. Her arms were not strong enough.

Clinging to the crater's edge with both hands, Ellen kicked her feet around, searching for a foothold. She almost lost her grip, but just then her right foot located a tiny jutting ledge big enough for the toe of her boot. She gingerly stepped onto the tiny ledge.

Ellen was now gasping for breath under the torrent of rain. Her heart was pounding with exertion and fear. She realized it was up to her. No one was there to help her. No one was coming. If she couldn't reach the safety of that crater, she might well die. Drown in the rushing muddy waters swirling through the canyon.

The wind-driven rain was stinging her face, plastering her hair to her head and nearly blinding her. She reasoned that if she carefully used the tentative toehold on which she stood, she could push off, leap up and hopefully crawl into the open crater.

If she missed…

Ellen said a prayer. Then she cautiously moved one of her hands across the alcove's floor to its right side. Just as she'd hoped, she found a firm perpendicular frame that offered a much safer hold. With her fingers tightly gripping the horizontal slab of stone and her toes resting atop the tiny foothold, Ellen told herself that she could do it. She could lunge to safety because she had to.

Wishing she could brush the water from her eyes, knowing that she could not, she took as deep a breath as possible and readied to make her move. The first time had to count. There would be no second chance.

Hardly realizing that she was screaming, Ellen leaped upward with an agility fathered by necessity, and hanging on with all her might, fell forward from the waist into the open crater. Her hips and legs still dangling precariously from the alcove, she gave another firm lunge and crawled fully into the dry, sheltered alcove.

Sighing with relief and exhaustion, Ellen turned over onto her back and lay there on the crater floor, waiting for her heart to stop racing, her breathing to slow.

In seconds she sat up, pushed her soaked hair back from her eyes and immediately began to worry about the others. She blinked and attempted to peer out through the falling rain, but she could see nothing. Had they made it? Was her aunt okay? Padjan, Ricky and Summer Dawn?

Mister Corey?

Ellen's lips fell open in shocked surprise when a wet, brown hand suddenly appeared on the lip of the crater. She knew immediately whose hand. Another appeared and then a dark, wet head and wide shoulders. With seemingly little effort, Mister Corey levered himself up into the crater, rose to his feet, having to duck his head beneath the crater's low rocky ceiling.

He pushed his hair out of his eyes with one hand, looked down at Ellen and said, "Thank God you're okay."

"The others…?"

"Settled and secure atop an incline on the other side of the canyon."

She exhaled heavily. "You're sure they are really safe? You aren't just…?"

"I swear to you that they are all totally safe. Ricky is with them and we managed to get the wagon up onto high ground and well out of harm's way."

She nodded. Then asked, "How did you know where I was?"

"I didn't. I was worried, searching for you, afraid you might not have made it to safety. Then I heard you scream."

Ellen nodded. She had begun to shiver, her teeth were starting to chatter.

"Better get out of those wet clothes," Mister Corey said. "You don't want to catch cold."

Ellen stayed as she was, seated, her knees raised, arms wrapped around them. "What about you?" she countered. "Your clothes are as wet as mine."

"I know and they're coming off," he said as he began unbuttoning his sopping shirt down his dark chest.

# Twenty-One

Mister Corey quickly peeled off his soaked shirt and carelessly tossed it aside. He stood directly above Ellen, bare to the waist, his taut muscles gleaming wet from the rain.

Ellen swallowed with difficulty when he stretched out a hand to her. She knew she shouldn't take it, knew she should keep all her clothes on, no matter how damp they were. But she didn't want to—she didn't want to resist him. She couldn't do it. She knew it was both foolish and sinful, but when she was in his arms, she simply did not care about right or wrong.

She wanted to be naked again with this dark, seductive man who had taught her more about passion and desire in the two incredible nights they had shared than she had learned in a lifetime.

Ellen placed her hand in his.

Mister Corey drew her to her feet before him and, without preamble, began unbuttoning her blouse. She let him. Made no offer to stop him or to help. She stood there in the shadowy shelter of that dry stone alcove with the storm raging outside, the deluge flooding the canyon below, tense, but not with fear or cold.

With sexual anticipation.

She willingly allowed him to strip her to the waist. Then trembled under his gaze when he focused on her wet nipples, which were already peaking into twin points of feeling. He stared at her for a long moment, then drew her into his arms.

The sudden contact of his hot, naked chest against her cold breasts made her stomach flutter and contract sharply. With a long arm wrapped tightly around her waist, Mister Corey placed his hand on her slender back and urged her closer still.

She tingled from head to toe when her sensitive nipples were abruptly pressed into the crisp black hair covering his broad chest. For a time he did nothing more, just held her against his body and looked into her eyes.

Ellen stood there against him with her arms still at her sides, her head thrown back. For the thousandth time since she'd met him, she desperately tried to read his thoughts, but could not. If he really desired her, if he wanted her the way she wanted him, it was impossible to tell by the expression in his eyes. Or rather the lack of expression. His strangely seductive, heavily lashed eyes remained black and lifeless.

Idly, she wondered what it would take to make them light up.

With his arm wrapped firmly around her, Mister Corey lifted a hand, cupped the side of her throat with his fingers, bent and brushed a kiss to her lips. He ran the tip of his tongue along the seam of her lips, teasing her, tasting her. He drew her bottom lip into his mouth and bit it gently, playfully.

And then he began kissing her in earnest.

Turning his head slightly to one side, he slanted his lips over hers and thrust his tongue deep inside her mouth in a forceful, intimate possession. Ellen sighed and her arms finally lifted from her sides. She put them around Mister Corey's neck and locked her wrists behind his head. She willingly accepted and eagerly returned every kind of kiss he offered.

The couple, gleaming wet and naked to their waists, stood locked in a close embrace, kissing, touching, sighing until finally, weak with rising desire, they sank to their knees on the stone floor and continued to kiss and kiss and kiss again.

Their hearts hammering in their bare chests, they finally tore their lips apart, pulled back a little and looked at each other.

"Is there enough time?" she asked.

"All evening," he told her.

"That long?"

"The canyon's already flooded and it's still raining hard. It could rain for hours. But even if it stopped now, it would take time for the floodwaters to recede." As he spoke, he put a hand between their bodies and began unbuttoning her damp chamois trousers.

Ellen sighed and said, "You're sure no one can see us?"

Her sentence was punctuated with a flash of lightning, followed by a clap of loud thunder.

"Look out," he instructed. "What do you see?"

Ellen turned her head, glanced toward the alcove's entrance and could see nothing but driving rain and deepening darkness. "Now, stand up," he said and lifted her to her feet.

Mister Corey stayed on his knees before her and finished unbuttoning her trousers. When they were open down her flat belly, he turned his attention to her feet. She gripped his shoulders while he took her wet boots and stockings off and laid them aside.

Ellen stiffened slightly when he then urged the trousers down over her hips, taking her damp underwear with them. In seconds she was nude and vulnerable before him. She blushed when a bolt of lightning brightly illuminated the alcove and her nakedness. And she shuddered when he impulsively leaned to her and pressed an openmouthed kiss to her bare belly, teasing her with his tongue.

Her weak legs no longer able to support her, she sank to her knees and then sat back on her bare heels while he rose and undressed. Never taking her eyes off him, she found herself wishing it were not so dark. She wanted to see him, to look at him.

And as if the gods of passion had heard her silent wish, a bright bolt of lightning struck just outside in the canyon. The sudden brilliance offered a fleeting look at him in all his naked glory. She trembled at the sight. He stood above her, his feet apart, his bare brown body glistening with moisture. He was, she noted with feminine pride, already fully erect.

Mister Corey bent from the waist, clasped her shoulders and urged her back up onto her knees. Continuing to stand, he drew her close against him and

Ellen almost lost her breath when she found her cheek resting against his flat belly, her face actually touching that awesome power of pulsing masculinity.

His hand cupping the back of her head, he said, "I'm sorry we don't have a blanket to lie down on."

"Doesn't matter," she managed to say, wondering what he would think if she kissed his belly as he had kissed hers. Or if she kissed...

Before she could get up the nerve to do either, he urged her face up away from his body and said, "You won't have to lie on this hard stone floor."

"I won't?" she said, puzzled.

"No, I'll stretch out on my back and you can get on top."

With that he released her, sank to his knees and lay down on his back. Reluctant to admit that she was totally unfamiliar with this way of making love, she hesitated, then eagerly followed his instructions.

"What are you waiting for?" he said. "Climb astride me."

"Oh, yes, of course," she said and did just that.

But she was not in the right position. Far from it. When she sank down onto him, her bare bottom was resting somewhere around his knees.

Mister Corey lifted his head, looked curiously at her and teased, "I'm big, but not that big. Scoot up so we can put it in."

Mortified, Ellen slid up his body until her open thighs were cradling his erection. The second her warmth touched him, his hot hard flesh involuntarily surged against her, thrilling her.

"Isn't that better?" he asked and laid his hands on her pale thighs.

"It is," she admitted, not knowing what to do with her own hands.

"You can put them on me," he said as if he'd read her thoughts. "Choose your spot. Ribs. Shoulders. Belly. Anything you want to touch."

Ellen smiled shyly and fanned a nervous hand across his chest. "You're wet," she said foolishly.

"You are too, but I'm going to make you wetter. Will you let me?"

She looked into his eyes and admitted, "You already have."

"Let me see." He reached a hand between her spread thighs and gently touched her. Pleased, he said, "Ahhhh. Yes, you are wet. Dripping wet and burning hot." He moved his hand away and said, "Lean down here and kiss me, Ellen."

Ellen placed her hands lightly on his shoulders, leaned down and eagerly kissed him. While his mouth mastered hers in a fiery kiss, he lowered both his hands. With one he clasped the twin cheeks of her bare, squirming bottom, the other he placed on his heavy tumescence. He eased her up a little and put the head of his throbbing erection just inside her. She felt it, sighed into his mouth and tore her lips from his.

He sat her up and she bit her bottom lip as she slowly, deliciously impaled herself upon him. When he was fully inside her, he stayed very still for a long moment, not wanting to hurt her. So she stayed still, too.

They lingered there like that, unmoving, as another flash of white lightning filled the alcove, illuminating their little haven and their bodies in a day-bright glow. The roar of the thunder that followed was deafening.

The fury of the tempest only added to their shared sexual excitement and Ellen soon found herself anxiously grinding her hips upon her prostrate lover and moaning with building pleasure as she felt him move and surge inside her.

An innately sensual woman despite her lack of experience, Ellen moved instinctively, provocatively, losing herself in the experience. His touch burned her flesh and inflamed an answering fire in him that kept him throbbingly erect and giving her incredible pleasure. A not-of-this-world pleasure that she wanted to last and last.

"Let's take a long time," she heard herself plead.

"As long as you want," was his low, caressing reply and he instinctively slowed his strokes to prolong the ecstasy.

She sighed with gratitude, sank more fully on him, began to rotate her hips seductively and he felt himself hotly enveloped in a nucleus of writhing, burning flame that ignited his very being.

Mister Corey bit the inside of his jaw to keep from climaxing. He looked away from the small, hard-nippled breasts that were swaying with her movements. He purposely kept his eyes off the spot where a triangle of damp chestnut curls was melded with the jet-black hair of his groin.

He was amazed by her. When she was making

love, she was the exact opposite of her usual caustic, bitter, buttoned-up, timid, cautious self. It was almost impossible to believe this naked wanton mounted on him was that same woman.

She was like a wild thing now, finally let out of her cage, holding back nothing, grabbing for the brass ring. He could tell by her frantic bucking that she couldn't last much longer. But he knew that her first wild climax would not totally satisfy her on this stormy summer afternoon. She was too aroused, too excited, too hot.

She would need more.

Ellen felt herself losing control and was frightened by the intensity of her oncoming release. Already past the point where she wondered or worried about her partner's state of satisfaction, Ellen rode him like a woman possessed. She bucked and thrust and squeezed him with a fury that matched that of the growing tempest.

As the storm escalated, the rain driving hard and lightning exploding and thunder reverberating, a wildly excited Ellen was driving hard against her lover, exploding with ecstasy, her screams of joy echoing as the thunder.

"Steve!" she wailed. "Oh, Steve, Steeeeve!"

Then her screams became a choked cry as she weakly collapsed atop him, her head dropping onto his shoulder. Trembling and jerking, she began to sob, very near to sexual hysteria. He clamped the weeping woman to him and allowed her to cry it out, stroking her hair, murmuring comforting words to her.

At last Ellen began to calm and she was immediately amazed to find that he was still fully distended and pulsating inside her. And she couldn't understand how she could possibly want more after the shattering completeness of her climax—but she did.

Without raising her head, she whispered, "I was hoping I'd find you like this."

"How's that?" he teased.

"Hard and hot inside me," she murmured.

He took hold of her upper arms and gently sat her up. "We've just begun to play," he said and began the subtle lifting and lowering of his hips.

"I'm glad," she said, answering his slow movements with her own swaying, rocking motion. "Let's play as long as the storm lasts."

"I'll do my best," he said, then implanted himself more deeply inside her. She let out a little yelp of pleasure. "Feel me?"

"Mmmm," she breathed.

"Good," he said, then lazily raised his arms and folded his hands beneath his head. "Know what I want?"

"Tell me."

"I want you to make love to me while I do nothing but lie here and watch."

A flash of lightning struck nearby. Thunder roared. Ellen lowered her lips to his, kissed him, licked playfully at his lips and whispered, "I will make love to you. And I'll make you cry out just as I did."

And in time, to her surprised delight, she did.

# Twenty-Two

The thunderstorm continued to rage.

So did the lovestorm.

The hard, driving rain came down in heavy, blinding sheets and the swirling, muddy floodwaters rose dangerously up the canyon walls.

But Ellen and Mister Corey, dry and safe inside the privacy of their refuge, paid no attention to the storm. They paid attention only to each other, were temporarily lost in a world of their own making.

Playing at sex as if it were a harmless game, which for the moment it was. Mister Corey naturally assumed the role of experienced, knowledgeable teacher. Ellen the part of apt, eager pupil.

Patient and forthcoming, the helpful teacher fully acquainted the curious student with the many mysteries of her own body. Explaining exactly what he was doing, he tenderly touched, stroked and aroused various parts of Ellen's bare, responsive body while she watched and listened and stirred to the feel of his hands on her flesh. She was surprised that there were so many places on her body that could excite her when properly caressed.

When the enjoyable lesson of self-discovery had

been fully studied and learned, the wise instructor then turned his pupil's attention to his own body. Fascinated, Ellen watched and nodded as he touched himself in various places, explaining as he did so. It excited her to see him demonstrate, thrilled her to watch his lean hands touch and stroke his own well-toned body. She made a mental note to remember just where and how he touched himself so that when it was her turn, she'd know how to correctly caress and arouse him.

"It's final-quiz time," he said at last, taking her hand in his and placing it on his groin. "I showed you how to best excite me. Do you remember?"

Her soft fingers already toying with the flaccid flesh, she said, "Yes, Professor, I remember."

"Then do it, please. Caress me until I'm rock hard."

Ellen wrapped gentle fingers around him and began the slow, stroking up and down movements just as he had shown her. In seconds she could feel him stiffening to her caressive touch.

She licked her lips and asked, "Once I've made it hard, Professor, will we make love?"

"Yes, we will. It'll be graduation time," he said and kissed her.

Soon they made love again and when the graduation coupling finally ended, the exhausted pair agreed they needed to rest. Get a second breath. Restore energy for the long night of loving ahead.

In minutes both were sound asleep, lying naked in each other's arms. Sleeping soundly, they didn't

know that the rain had stopped falling. Were blissfully unaware that a late-afternoon sun had begun to
shine through the dissipating clouds. Or that the
floodwaters below were rapidly subsiding.

"Steve? Can you hear me, Steve?" Ricky O'Mara
shouted, anxiously scanning the canyon walls. "Ellen? Ellen? Where are you? Answer me!" The shouting finally awakened the sleeping pair.

"Jesus God!" swore Mister Corey under his breath
as he and Ellen exchanged startled looks. "We're
okay, Ricky!" he shouted, thinking fast. "Both safe.
Be right down."

"Where are you? I can't see you," Ricky called
out.

As they scrambled to get dressed, Ellen lamented
miserably, "They'll know, dear Lord, they'll all know
that we…"

"They'll know nothing," Mister Corey calmly said
as he stood and pulled on his faded Levi's. "You get
dressed and I'll stall Ricky."

He yanked up his shirt, stuck his long arms into
the sleeves and shoved the tail down inside his Levi's.
He glanced at Ellen. She was vainly struggling to get
her chamois trousers up over her hips. Her white underwear lay forgotten on the stone floor.

"Coming down from my perch, Ricky," Mister
Corey shouted as he tugged on his boots. "Hurry,"
he whispered to Ellen, then slipped out the alcove's
sunny opening.

Buttoning her pants with shaking fingers, Ellen

heard Ricky say, "You found Ellen? You were with her during the storm?"

"Luckily I did find her," Mister Corey said. "A close call, but she's okay."

The two men discussed the damage they'd likely find, while Ellen finished dressing. One button of her blouse missed, she hurried to the crater's open entrance, looked down, took a deep breath and said, "Ricky, are the others…?"

"Ellen!" he exclaimed with a wide smile. "I was worried sick about you. I'm so glad to know that Steve was here with you through the terrible storm. Are you okay? Did he take good care of you?"

*You have no idea,* was the guilty thought that ran through her mind. "As you can see, we're both fine," she said, then sat down and swung her legs over the lip of the crater.

"Wait!" cautioned Ricky. "I'll climb up and help you down."

"No." She stopped him. "I can manage, thank you." Turning about, she agilely slithered down the slick rock face, snagging handholds and footholds where she could find them. When she dropped to the ground near the two men, she again immediately asked, "Aunt Alexandra and Padjan and Summer Dawn?"

"All are safe and sound," Ricky assured her. "I was with them in the wagon throughout the storm. Why, they didn't even get wet." He eyed her badly wrinkled blouse and damp chamois trousers and added, "Looks like you and Steve did though."

Before she could reply, Mister Corey said, "Ricky, looks like the floodwaters are receding as swiftly as they rose. Let's get a move on and start hunting down the scattered stock. There's not much daylight left."

A half mile up the canyon, Mister Corey's paint stallion, standing stock-still on the rocky canyon floor, was waiting patiently for his master. Unhurt, except for scratches and bruises from the debris in the water, the paint whinnied a loud hello when Steve climbed into the wet leather saddle.

Taking the hand Mister Corey offered, Ricky swung up behind and they set out to find the rest of the animals. Ellen's dun saffron and Ricky's big black had both made it. One of the remounts and both pack burros had drowned in the deluge. The unfortunate burros had been too weighted down with equipment to swim to higher ground. The supplies had broken loose from the packs and washed away in the flood.

Fortunately, the most valuable provisions, the rifles and tools, had been loaded in the wagon and were safe.

With the sun starting to go down, Mister Corey and Ricky rounded up the horses. Mister Corey was determined to take the contingent all the way through the canyon before stopping for the night.

Back near the wagon, he and Ricky hastily dismounted. Ricky tended the horses while Mister Corey climbed the incline to the wagon. Padjan saw him coming, called out to him and jumped down, smiling. Ellen, hearing Padjan shout to Mister Corey, got out of the wagon where she had been trying to soothe her aunt's jangled nerves.

Before Mister Corey reached Padjan, he asked, "Summer Dawn? Is she...?"

"Sleeping like a baby," assured Padjan.

"Good," said Mister Corey.

He had reached the wagon. He stood a few short feet from Ellen, but didn't so much as glance at her. He had only one thing on his mind. Getting the wagon down to the level rocky ground and getting them all through the canyon before nightfall.

"What about me?" Alexandra abruptly stuck her head out of the wagon and directed her question at Mister Corey. "I suppose for all you care I could have drowned."

"I'm glad to see you're safe," said Mister Corey.

"Well, it's no thanks to you! It's a wonder we didn't all drown because you led us into this...this steep-sided death trap! Some guide you've turned out to be."

"I warned you that this journey would be no Sunday stroll in Central Park, Miss Landseer."

Not satisfied with his answer, she continued to blister him with scathing rebukes. He shrugged, ignored her, went directly up ahead to the still-harnessed team. Ellen knew his intention, so she joined him to help coax the horses to back slowly, cautiously down the incline.

When finally the wagon reached level ground and the wheels took purchase on the rocky valley floor, Alexandra, atop the high seat now, was still griping about the fact that she might have perished and that her swollen ankle was killing her.

Nobody listened.

By the time full darkness closed in, the caravan had made it completely out of the canyon. As soon as they exited the steep-sided chasm, they stopped and made camp near a thick grove of maples. A stream, rushing and splashing from the afternoon rains, bordered the bosk.

Within minutes of making camp, the horses had been watered and fed, the canvas tent had been erected, a campfire coaxed to life finally blazed and trout sizzled in the pan. The conversation, as they ate supper, was of the afternoon thunderstorm.

Padjan talked excitedly of how he and Ricky had nervously watched the rise of the water, fearing that any minute the wagon would be washed off the narrow rock incline and swept along in the torrent. The others listened.

"So," Padjan said, warming to his topic, looking from Mister Corey to Ellen, "how did you two manage to find each other in the terrible deluge?"

Ellen immediately stiffened and nervously cleared her throat. Mister Corey, having finished his meal, lighted a cigarette and spoke for them.

"I heard a scream," he said, his voice low, level. "Otherwise I would never have found Ellen."

He went on to explain that he, like they, had been worried for her safety. He'd gone looking for her, but couldn't locate her. As it turned out he had been very near to where she was, but was unaware of her proximity. Then she'd screamed and he knew he'd found her. So he had climbed up to the rock alcove where she'd wisely sought shelter.

As he spoke in low, conversational tones, Ellen stole a long glance at him as he stared into the fire. His lean, dark face was relaxed, yet there was a certain tightness around the mouth that denoted inward tension.

"You were up inside a crater on the canyon wall?" Alexandra asked.

"Yes," he said, "we were."

"Was it a big place or was there barely room for the two of you?"

"Large enough for us to be comfortable," he said, taking a long drag on his cigarette.

Alexandra turned to Ellen. "The deluge lasted for more than two hours. What did you do the whole time?"

"The same thing you did, Aunt Alexandra," she replied, grateful for the darkness that concealed the telltale reddening of her face. "We worried about the floodwaters rising high enough to reach us."

# Twenty-Three

The next day the caravan snaked its slow way through an awesome maze of benches and spires and buttes. The immensity, the changing colors, the contour of rock upon rock was endlessly enchanting to anyone who appreciated stark beauty.

Which meant everyone but Alexandra Landseer.

She saw nothing amazing or magical about the landscape. Besides, it was hot as a furnace in this godforsaken place and she was miserable. Furthermore, her ankle hurt. When were they *ever* going to reach the Lost City?

Around noon they came up on a natural amphitheater. The space had been carved a quarter of a mile into a side canyon through which a rushing creek ran down into the Dirty Devil River. It was a cool and wondrous place shaped like a gigantic band shell, its floor hard-packed sand.

They stopped there for lunch and it was such a comfortable, inviting place, all hated to leave it.

But on they went, winding around swells and reefs of stone, weaving their way through an intricate labyrinth of spires and monoliths. They rode over high natural bridges made of stone that had been created by the carving action of water running through a drainage. Then it was down underneath towering natural arches that were giant windows in the rock formed by frost and wind and water. Narrow slickrock canyons and parklike hollows and yawning chasms that had to be carefully navigated.

At around three in the afternoon the sun was bathing everything in a glowing wash of warmth and the soaring vermilion cliffs blazed fiery red. Ellen, her face burning from the heat radiating off the rocks, suddenly spotted, high up on the canyon wall, a waterfall spilling long ribbons of silver water into a lovely pool surrounded by ferns and tamarisks and willows.

"Ricky, look at that waterfall!"

"That's a hanging basket," he told her. "That's what they're called here. Some are slow-dripping springs, others are gushing cascades. And you can bet that the water in the pool is ice cold."

"Mmm," she murmured, wishing she could find out.

Above the falls, a red-tailed hawk sailed on thermals of air that came off the peaks. And on a ledge halfway to the rim, a majestic mountain lion lay stretched out in the sun, dozing peacefully.

Ellen inhaled the clean, high desert air and sighed. She glanced ahead to where Mister Corey, astride the paint stallion, rode alone, his lanky body in an attitude of easy relaxation. Was he thinking what she was thinking? That she wanted the two of them to strip off all their hot, sticky clothes and play in that glacial pool beneath the silver waterfall?

The thought caused her to inwardly shiver with anticipation. She could hardly wait for night to come. She was certain that once the others were asleep, Mister Corey would make love to her. And that's exactly what she wanted. She had decided to take what pleasure she could for as long as it lasted and when it was over to never look back. She wasn't, she told herself, heading down a trail of hurt and disappointment because she knew in advance what the end would be.

She didn't fool herself. She meant absolutely nothing to Mister Corey. Well, fine, she didn't care, because he meant nothing to her either. She was not a complete dunce. She could certainly never have any deep or lasting feelings for a man who was a charlatan, a thief, a coward and an adulterer. Mister Corey was all of those, yet she was looking eagerly forward to next time she would be in his arms.

Hopefully tonight.

On they rode.

When finally the sun slid behind the canyon's rim, lowering a cool curtain of shade over everything, and the coming evening's light cast long shadows, they stopped for the night.

They made camp at a place called the River Bench where the sand was smooth and clean and was bordered on one side by the river and on the other by a thick stand of cottonwoods.

When bedtime came, Ellen was confused and disappointed that Mister Corey had not seized an opportunity to suggest she meet him somewhere once everyone was asleep. The same thing had happened last night after the storm, but she had told herself then that she was being very silly. The poor man had been exhausted from their afternoon frolic. That was it, of course. He was still tired and so was she.

Tomorrow night they would make up for lost time.

"I hope today's an easier one than yesterday," Ricky said at breakfast the next morning.

"It will be," said a smiling Padjan. "By this afternoon we should be in the Valley of the Gods. The rest of the way to the Navajo reservation will be easy. What could possibly go wrong?"

"Don't tempt fate," said an unsmiling Mister Corey.

"Mister Corey is superstitious," Padjan said to Ellen with a chuckle. "He has a twenty-dollar gold piece his father gave him many years ago. It's his good-luck charm and he's rubbed it so often its face is almost worn smooth." Laughing, Padjan turned to Mister Corey and said, "Show it to her. Show her that gold piece that means so much to you."

Mister Corey's eyes narrowed and his jaw tightened minutely. He said, "It's time to break camp and get on the trail."

He tossed the dregs of his coffee cup into the cold campfire and turned away. Shortly, they all rode out.

The morning passed uneventfully with only one or two small mishaps. Ellen was stung by a bee, but

gritted her teeth and assured everyone it was not painful. One of the remounts broke free of his tether and
had to be chased down and returned. Padjan fell and
skinned his knee while scrambling to get a drink of
water from what the early Spaniards had named a
*tinajas,* a natural tank that was a large bedrock de-
pression filled with summer rain. Like Ellen, he didn't
carry on. Alexandra, of course, was still groaning
about her swollen ankle. If it hadn't been that, it
would have been something else.

By midafternoon everyone was completely silent,
bored and sleepy as they rode out onto a flat, high
desert valley whose floor was sparsely dotted with
prickly pear, yucca and squawbrush. The red sandstone spires and buttes that had been so close together
before were now scattered farther and farther apart.
Pillars in the sky.

Directly in front of the moving caravan, the nearest
needles and mesas and buttes were a good two hundred yards away. Mister Corey, as usual, rode ahead
of the others. Ellen and Ricky rode side by side. Both
were swaying in their saddles, barely able to keep
their eyes open. Ellen decided that if they didn't do
something, they were going to fall asleep.

"Ricky?"

Startled, Ricky's head snapped up and his eyes
widened. "Yes?"

She smiled at him and asked, "You sleepy?"

"Miserably sleepy."

"Want to wake up fast?"

"Sure. How?"

"I'll race you to that big balanced rock that looks like a man's raised fist. It's straight ahead. See the one I mean?" She lifted a hand and pointed.

"I see it," Ricky said and began to smile. "I just hate to break your heart, Ellen. I know my gelding will leave yours in the dust." His boyish grin widened.

"We'll just see about that," she said and she, too, was smiling now. "When I count to three."

He nodded, pulled his hat brim lower, adjusted his scabbarded rifle and wrapped a gloved hand tightly around the long leather reins.

Ellen slid her feet out of the stirrups, placed the heels of her boots lightly against the dun's belly, ready to dig them into his sleek flanks once the race began.

"One," she said, glanced at Ricky and gave him a you-don't-stand-a-chance look. "Two." A long purposeful pause. "Three!"

They were off.

Both steeds bolted forward, their pointed ears lying flat against their heads, their hooves flinging up loose sand. Padjan, on the wagon's high seat, was jolted awake. He blinked, saw what was happening and laughed.

"I'm betting on Ellen!" he shouted.

Mister Corey heard the commotion, turned his paint around and saw the two racing headlong in his direction, laughing as they came.

He didn't laugh. He scowled with displeasure. He called out, told them to stop, to slow down, they were behaving foolishly. Somebody might get hurt. Out of habit he reached into his pocket to rub his twenty-dollar gold piece for luck. Then remembered and made a face.

Ellen and Ricky didn't listen.

Neck and neck they flew past Mister Corey, both leaning low over their mounts' withers, riding hell-bent for leather, the horses' manes and tails streaming straight out.

Ricky's black abruptly pulled up a nose ahead of Ellen's saffron dun and he gave a great whoop of joy. Ellen glanced over, frowned, kicked her gelding more forcefully and pleaded with the beast to run faster. Responding, the creature sprinted forward and Ellen laughed with delight when he sped past the hard gal-loping black.

In a flash she moved a full length ahead of Ricky and was confident she was going to win the race. She could practically taste the victory. She squealed like an excited child, shoved her straw hat off her head and let it bounce off her shoulder blades, held by the drawstrings.

"Oh no you don't!" she heard Ricky call out and blinked in disbelief when he overtook and passed her. "See you later," he shouted, grinning, as the foam-flecked black, giving it everything he had, thundered forward.

Redoubling her efforts, Ellen anxiously slapped the reins back and forth on the dun's shiny neck and drew up even with Ricky and the black. For a few seconds they stayed totally even.

Knee to knee they raced across the burning desert land, the wind billowing their shirts out behind them and making their eyes sting with tears. They were having a high time. Laughing and carefree.

Then, in a heartbeat, the merriment ended.

# Twenty-Four

Suddenly, without warning, Ricky's winded black gelding plunged both feet into a prairie-dog hole that was completely hidden in the sparse underbrush. The big horse went down and Ricky was catapulted over his head, sailing thirty feet through the air before coming to rest on the hard-packed ground.

The bewildered black whinnied and struggled frantically to rise. The sudden, jerky movement hurled Ricky's rifle from its saddle scabbard. The firearm discharged. The wild bullet struck Ricky squarely in the back.

For Ellen, it took a few seconds for the tragedy to register. One moment she and Ricky were riding side by side, the next he wasn't there. At first, she thought she had simply pulled ahead. Laughing, she glanced back over her shoulder.

Ricky was on the ground, lying on his stomach. He was still.

Ellen screamed.

Her hands as cold as ice, her heart hammering with fear, she pulled up hard on the reins, wheeled the dun gelding around and raced back to where Ricky lay unmoving on the ground. In seconds she was at his side. She leaped from her saddle and ran, falling to her knees beside him. A bright blossom of blood, staining his snowy-white shirt, was rapidly spreading.

"Ricky! Ricky!" she called his name and reached a hand out to him.

"No, Ellen! Don't! Don't touch him!"

It was Mister Corey's calm, commanding voice. Ellen looked up to see him dismounting a few feet away. Then he was on his knees beside her, hastily peeling off his suede gloves and carefully laying a thumb against the pulse point in Ricky's tan throat. He felt a slow weak beat.

"He's alive," he told the terrified Ellen, then ripped Ricky's bloodstained shirt apart and examined the fresh wound. Turning to Ellen, he said, "I'm going to lift Ricky just a little. When I do, I want you to check for signs of an exit wound on his stomach, chest or shoulders."

She nodded.

Mister Corey pushed the torn shirt up to Ricky's shoulders. Then, sliding his arms underneath the wounded man, he carefully lifted the unconscious man. Ellen pressed her cheek to the ground and anxiously inspected Ricky's bare chest and stomach. Not a drop of blood. No sign of an injury.

"Nothing," she said, raising her head, not knowing if that was good news or bad.

"Damn it to hell," Mister Corey swore and lowered Ricky back to the ground. "That means the bullet's still in him. It will have to come out."

Expecting her to wring her hands in horror and sob,

Ellen surprised Mister Corey when she said in a level voice, "Yes, it will. And the sooner the better. I'll help in any way I can."

Mister Corey stole a glance at her pale, stricken face, saw her slender shoulders trembling and was tempted to put an arm around her to console her. But there wasn't time.

Instead, he rose to his feet, said, "Here comes Padjan. He'll be here in a minute and he can help us load Ricky onto the wagon. I'll be right back."

Wondering why he would leave her at a time like this, Ellen didn't reply. Just stayed there on her knees beside the unresponsive Ricky, a soothing hand lying lightly on his dark head, a silent prayer on her lips. Mister Corey turned and walked away.

Ellen was swamped with fear and guilt. She was responsible. It was she who had challenged Ricky to the race. How could she have been so thoughtless? So foolish? Mister Corey had warned them, but she hadn't listened. Ellen's teeth began to chatter and she felt as if she couldn't get a breath. Her chest felt as if someone's heavy foot was resting on it.

Wishing Padjan would hurry and get there to help her, Ellen anxiously looked up. She saw the wagon fast approaching, Padjan slapping the reins across the backs of the galloping team, and felt a small measure of relief that he would soon reach her.

She turned her head, searched for Mister Corey. She spotted him several yards away, walking toward the badly injured black gelding. He carried his rifle in his hands. She knew what he was going to do. A wave of nausea assaulted her. She watched, horrified, as Mister Corey approached the frantically whinnying gelding. She saw him reach the poor creature whose right front leg was badly shattered. He took hold of the bridle, urged the black's majestic head down. She saw his lips moving, knew he was speaking to the terrified animal, soothing it.

Tears clogged her already aching throat and she knew that she should look away. But she didn't. She watched as Mister Corey lifted the rifle, placed the barrel squarely against the black's temple and squeezed the trigger. The shocked horse neighed loudly, tossed his head wildly a couple of times, then thrust his velvet muzzle against Mister Corey's chest and made a weak, plaintive sound before crumpling to the ground. He tried, pitifully, to rise. Ellen moaned. Mister Corey took quick aim, fired again.

The gelding was dead.

Ellen swallowed hard and turned her attention back to Ricky. The wagon rolled to a stop at the exact time Mister Corey reached the group. He placed the still-smoking rifle in its scabbard and returned to the fallen Ricky.

Padjan jumped down off the wagon's high seat and rushed forward. "How bad is it? Is he alive?"

"He is, Padjan," said Mister Corey. "But unconscious and the bullet didn't exit."

Padjan shook his bald head. "We better get him into the wagon before we try to take it out."

"I agree," said Mister Corey. "First, we need to get Miss Landseer out of the way."

"Let me handle her," said Padjan as he shot to his feet and hurried off.

Neither Ellen or Mister Corey knew exactly what Padjan said to her, but for once in her life Alexandra Landseer did just as she was told and without complaint. Surprisingly, she seemed genuinely concerned for Ricky. With her out of the wagon and out of their way, they lifted Ricky and carried him toward the wagon.

Although both Mister Corey and Padjan had told Ellen it wasn't necessary that she help, the truth was it took all three of them to lift and carry Ricky's unconscious body. Getting him up inside the wagon was almost more than they could manage.

Out of breath, perspiring and breathing hard, the trio finally laid Ricky gingerly down on his stomach as far away from the sleeping Summer Dawn as possible. Sitting flat down at his side, Ellen began removing his torn, bloody shirt while Padjan built a fire to heat water.

"What's that terrible rasping sound he's making?" Ellen asked Mister Corey.

*The death rattle.* "It's nothing. A good sound really. Means his breathing is strong and regular." They exchanged quick glances. He could tell she didn't believe him. He reached across Ricky, touched her slender shoulder. "He's tough as a boot, Ricky is. Try not to worry."

"This is all my fault," she said sadly, fighting to hold back her tears. "I'm so sorry."

"It's nobody's fault," he assured her. "It was an accident, so don't go blaming yourself."

"But if I hadn't challenged Ricky to a race..."

"He'd have challenged you, so let it go. We have work to do." He rose then, went forward to the front of the wagon and began peeling back the black leather hood, explaining as he did so, "We'll need all the light we can get."

When he had completed the task and bright, hot sunshine spilled down on Ricky, Mister Corey jumped down off the wagon, went directly to Padjan's crackling fire and the pan of water boiling atop it. He scrubbed his hands clean and sterilized his sharp-bladed hunting knife as best he could.

Soon Padjan was back inside the wagon with a fresh pan of boiling water, which he carefully placed near Ricky. He reached beneath the prostrate man, unbuckled his belt, pulled it through the belt loops and laid it aside. He then unbuttoned Ricky's faded Levi's so that there'd be nothing restrictive and tight on his injured body.

Mister Corey returned to find Ellen laying out a large bottle of alcohol, a small bottle of iodine, some clean white bandages, a roll of cotton, a pair of scissors and some tweezers. It was she who painstakingly cleaned the blood-caked wound with alcohol until she was sure it was antiseptic.

"He's ready," she announced and looked from Padjan to Mister Corey.

Mister Corey nodded, took a long, deep breath and, with the gleaming knife held firmly in his right hand, said to the unconscious man, "If I hurt you, old friend, you let me know."

Ellen stole a glance at Mister Corey as, with steady hand, he lowered the knife's gleaming point to Ricky's bleeding back. His lean face was full of strength and determination, but with an unmistakable tightness around the mouth that bespoke tension. He was frightened. This uncaring, detached, complex, enigmatic man was scared, though he would never have admitted it.

Oddly, his very understandable, touchingly human fear infused Ellen with an uncommon courage. He needed her to be strong, dauntless, lest his own fragile control crumble. She rallied to the call, was resolved to remain as calm and as composed as a battlefield surgeon.

While Padjan, seated at Ricky's head, pressed down on his bare shoulders in an effort to keep him totally still, Mister Corey painstakingly probed the wound with the knifepoint, anxiously searching for the imbedded bullet. Ellen knew he was suffering far more than the man who'd been shot. His jaw was rigid, his teeth clamped together and beads of perspiration dotted his forehead.

Mister Corey was in agony.

Ellen picked up a clean white towel, alerted him to what she was going to do, then leaned close and dabbed the perspiration from his shiny forehead. He thanked her and continued to delve into the wound, anguished by Ricky's moans.

"God, I'm hurting him," Mister Corey said, his own face a mask of pain.

"He won't remember," Padjan consoled. "You'll see. When he wakes up, he will have forgotten."

The crude surgery continued and after several excruciatingly frustrating moments, Mister Corey located the deeply imbedded bullet and, with the pair of tweezers Ellen quickly supplied, retrieved it. He dropped the bloody bullet into the tin cup held by Ellen. It made a loud pinging sound when it hit the bottom and all three of them laughed nervously.

"Let me," Ellen said as she began to carefully clean Ricky's wound with the alcohol before Mister Corey closed the gash with crude stitches. Then Ellen liberally slathered iodine over it and all the surrounding flesh before placing a large white piece of gauze on the area. With Mister Corey and Padjan's help, she managed to wrap a long, wide bandage completely around Ricky's body, covering him from waist to shoulder blades.

When she finished, she looked up, asked, "Should we leave him here like this, on his stomach?"

"Yes," Mister Corey said. "I'll get a blanket, cover him. We'll camp here tonight, give him a chance to rest and hopefully awaken."

Unspoken was the shared fear that he might never awaken. Ricky's breathing had grown fainter and more irregular. He was, they all knew, barely alive.

"He'll come around," said Padjan optimistically. He read the doubt and despair in Mister Corey's sharp features, touched the younger man's shoulder and said, "Don't worry, son. We'll get him through this."

"Yes, we will, and I'll take the first watch," Ellen said, looking tenderly down at the unconscious Ricky.

# Twenty-Five

The two men nodded their agreement.

Padjan went to check on Alexandra while Mister Corey began to draw the heavy black leather covering back into place to shut out the burning sun.

When the chore was completed, he came over, crouched down on his heels and said to Ellen, "I'll relieve you come bedtime." She shook her head. He added softly, "If Ricky wakes up, come get me."

"I will," she promised without looking at him.

When he moved away, she glanced up to see him taking down the shovel and immediately knew his intent. He was going out to bury the beautiful black gelding. But she didn't want to think about the poor dead creature, couldn't bear it. If not for her, the black would still be alive.

Ellen turned her full attention on her patient.

For the next couple of hours, Ellen's worried gaze never left Ricky, except for a moment when she turned away to light a coal oil lamp as darkness closed in. Her thumb lightly rubbing the inside of Ricky's wrist, she whispered softly to him, begging him to awaken, to open his eyes, to speak to her, to live.

Mister Corey and Padjan checked periodically to see if there had been any change. But Ellen was alone with Ricky when, around nine-thirty that night, his eyelids fluttered restlessly a time or two, then his eyes slowly opened.

"Ricky?" Ellen said, her heart hammering in her chest. "Oh, Ricky, Ricky, you're awake! Thank God!"

"Who won the race?" he rasped, tried to move and groaned with pain.

Laughing and crying at once, Ellen said, "You did! You won, but you must lie still!"

"Why? What happened?"

"An accident," she said. "I'll explain everything later. You're going to be just fine. Promise me you won't move while I go get Mister Corey."

"I promise."

Ricky was soon in good spirits, despite no small degree of pain. But he bemoaned the fact that he was now as helpless as a baby. He felt badly that someone had to constantly look after him. That he could be of no help to anyone, couldn't even take care of himself.

With Ricky badly injured, Ellen, Padjan and Mister Corey were the only able-bodied of the group. Ricky, like Summer Dawn and Alexandra, had to be continuously watched and tended. It was hard, back-breaking work and a struggle to proceed on the difficult journey while saddled with three totally dependent people. Jealous at all the attention the wounded Ricky was receiving and incensed that he was allowed to lie comfortably stretched out in the wagon while she had to sit on the high, uncomfortable front seat, Alexandra announced that her sprained ankle had gotten worse. Much worse. She simply couldn't walk on it and was in continual pain. She needed more care than she was getting.

She didn't seem to notice—or if she did she didn't care—how pale and tired Ellen was beginning to look from patiently playing nursemaid to three people.

Mister Corey did.

He was watching her change Ricky's bandages when the thought occurred to him that Ellen Cornelius was proving herself to be quite a remarkable woman. Hardships didn't do her in. In the dangerous flood she had never once shown any sign of weakness. She hadn't panicked, she hadn't screamed in terror and ordered someone to carry her to safety. She had done what she had to do to save herself, by herself.

And now—seeing the way, without complaint, she pitched in and again proved her grit—Mister Corey's grudging admiration for her grew. While he found her willingness to kowtow to a disagreeable old woman for that evil of all evils—the love of money—to be less than laudable, he had to admit that she had many commendable qualities. She was no soft, spoiled whiner. She could be counted on to always do her part and then some. She was a strong, resourceful woman who was willing and ready to risk her neck for others.

Curiously, with his growing admiration came nagging contrition. He was beginning to suffer from an unfamiliar guilt, a kind of remorse that was foreign to him.

Because of Ellen.

He was genuinely sorry that he had ever seduced the naive, defenseless Ellen. He was ashamed that he had taken unfair advantage of a lonely, unsophisticated woman who had been disappointed far too many times in her life. She hadn't deserved it; she hadn't deserved him.

He felt like the world's biggest bastard for having casually dishonored her. It was the first time in his life he had regretted bedding a woman. But it was the first time in his life he had carelessly made love to someone as guileless as Ellen Cornelius.

He wished that it had never happened, that he had never touched her. He wished as well that he could tell her how sorry he was, wished that he could make it up to her somehow. But knew that he could not.

The only thing he could do to redeem himself even a little in her eyes—and his own—was to leave her alone. To never again take her into his arms, knowing, as he did, that she was lonely and virtually defenseless.

His resolve firm, Mister Corey began to purposely avoid being alone with Ellen. He didn't think she'd noticed. She was far too busy with her demanding chores. Besides, had he wanted to get her alone, it would have been next to impossible.

Ellen had no idea that there had been a change in Mister Corey. She saw no difference in his demeanor.

The couple had never had much to say to each other when anyone else was present. From the beginning it had been clearly understood between them that neither admired nor respected the other. No matter. Oddly, their elemental dislike of each other made their clandestine encounters all the hotter and more exciting.

Ellen supposed that Mister Corey, like she, was very busy and that the two would be together again once they got the opportunity. She looked forward to being in his arms again and hoped that it wouldn't be too long.

She was counting the days. The hours. The minutes.

It was late afternoon and they were now traveling through a vast valley filled with huge stone monoliths that looked like an armada of giant ships riding a sea of red clay. Padjan had told them that the Navajos called this valley the Temples of the Past. The name suited. It was an awesomely beautiful place that looked untouched by time or man. With the sunlight spilling through the clouds, the colors changed almost before the eye could register them. From gray to lavender to blazing red.

As sunset approached, the stark desert changed in the slanting light from amber and orange and gold. In time it would change to brown and blue and purple.

The slowly sinking sun still bathed the wide valley when Padjan, pulling up on the team, shouted, ''There it is!'' He pointed across sheep pastures and juniper-dotted ridges to the sprawling Navajo village in the near distance. "The Navajo reservation. The Gateway to the Lost City."

Mister Corey turned his paint stallion about, rode back to the wagon. Resting a hand on the saddle horn, he said, "These are your friends, Padjan. Why don't you lead us into the village?"

"You mean it?" Padjan asked, liking the idea very much.

Mister Corey dismounted. "I mean it. You ride the paint in and I'll drive the wagon."

"Oh, for heaven's sake," said Alexandra. "Let's not quibble about who leads who in. Let's just get there. I'm tired and hungry and I need a hot bath."

Padjan smiled and jumped down off the wagon. He eagerly shook Mister Corey's hand as they passed and said, "Thanks, son. They expect me to be the leader."

"And you are," said Mister Corey.

His chest puffed out, his bald pate gleaming in the bright summer sunlight, Padjan climbed astride the big paint stallion and addressed those whom he would lead into the village.

"The Navajo reservation," he said, "encompasses a quarter of the Four Corners country. It is huge. If a Navajo stands at the center of his heart's homeland, he looks to the La Plata Mountains in southwestern Colorado, to Blanca Peak in the Sangre de Cristo Mountains, to Mount Taylor in western New Mexico and to the San Francisco peaks in northern Arizona. And when—"

"Enough of your long drawn-out oratory, Padjan," Alexandra rudely interrupted. "Let's ride on in."

He nodded, but added solemnly, "These people have great respect for me, Alexandra."

"Well, good for you."

"I am suggesting that while you are in their village, as well as when you are in the Lost City, you show me the same respect."

"Oh, relax, I'm not going to embarrass you in front of your people."

"See that you don't," he said and without smiling wheeled the paint about and led the contingent toward the village.

On the outskirts they passed gardens filled with summer beans, corn and squash and corrals where sheep bleated inside the fences. Ahead, small round hogans with smoke curling up from their centers dotted the land as far as the eye could see.

Laughing children immediately ran out to meet them. Barking dogs followed. Women looked up from their chores. Men, talking excitedly in their native tongue, quickly congregated. They were saying Padjan's name as if in awe.

And they were in awe of him.

He had passed through their village before. The Navajos feared and idolized him, believing him to be an Ancient One, perhaps a spirit in the form of man who lived somewhere high above the clouds in the mysterious Lost City.

Padjan pulled up on the paint and raised his hand for the others to halt, when an aged Navajo, his leather-hard face creased by a thousand deep wrinkles, stepped directly into the path of the paint.

"*Ya-ta-hey!*" the old man said, speaking the Navajo hello, and Padjan, swinging down out of the saddle, warmly returned the greeting.

"*Ya-ta-hey,* Johnny Old Chief," he said.

The two embraced and conversed in the Navajo's native tongue. Then the frail Navajo chieftain raised an age-spotted hand, snapped his brittle fingers and at once a half-dozen young men scurried forward to get their visitors settled and tend their horses.

Alexandra winced when a muscular young Navajo swiftly approached the wagon and reached for her. But remembering Padjan's warning to show respect, she said nothing and allowed the boy to lift her down from the wagon.

Alexandra and Ellen were immediately taken to a hogan where they were to stay while in the village. Holding Ellen's arm, Alexandra hobbled along on her sprained ankle, making sure everyone noticed her infirmity. The muscular Navajo followed with their belongings.

A woman, dressed in the traditional long colorful skirts with velvet blouse and silver jewelry, waited just outside the hogan. She smiled at Ellen and Alexandra and, speaking Navajo, indicated that they were to go inside.

She followed them in and stood smiling while they looked around. Alexandra began to frown. She had never seen such a crude dwelling in her life. Two thin mats on the floor were obviously where they were expected to sleep. A couple of wooden straight-back chairs were the dwelling's only furniture. At the center of the hogan was a small rock pit where freshly cut wood was stacked and ready for building a fire. A kettle hung over the cold rock pit and a couple of large pans rested nearby. The hogan's octagonal walls were bare.

There were no beds with nice soft mattresses. No easy chairs or sofas. No lamps, no tables. Worst of all, no bathtub. Alexandra turned and frowned at Ellen and started to speak, but Ellen shot her a silencing glance, so she closed her mouth.

Ellen turned to the waiting Navajo woman and, smiling warmly, said, "Thank you. We'll be most comfortable here."

The young woman looked puzzled, didn't understand a word. So Ellen looked all around, stretched out a hand in a sweeping gesture and nodded approvingly in an attempt to convey her thoughts. At last the woman nodded back and left.

"Well, this is a fine how-do-you-do!" said Alexandra, hands going to her broad hips the minute the woman's long skirts were out the door. "I'm not going to stay in this…this…primitive mud hut. I'll just go tell Mister Corey to put up the tent and—"

Ellen caught her aunt's arm. "Listen to me," she said in a tone that brooked no arguments. "You'll do nothing of the kind. You promised Padjan you'd behave yourself and you will. You will sleep in this hogan and you will eat the food that is put before you and you will be courteous to our hosts. Is that clear?"

Alexandra's eyebrows knitted and, acting as if she was very near to tears, said, "Well, you'll forgive me if I'm just a little disappointed. My ankle hurts and I was hoping to soak it in a nice hot tub."

"Life's full of disappointments," Ellen said. "Here, why don't you sit down—" she steered Alexandra to one of the chairs "—while I see about boiling some water for you."

With a great sigh of resignation, Alexandra dropped onto the chair. Ellen immediately turned away, went directly to the rock pit and sank onto her knees beside it. She rearranged the firewood and was taking the kettle down when Alexandra screamed.

Startled, Ellen dropped the kettle and turned anxiously to her aunt. "What? What is it?"

"There!" Alexandra said, frowning, pointing furiously.

Her hand on her racing heart, Ellen quickly looked toward the hogan's entrance.

She immediately smiled.

In a shaft of sunshine pouring into the shadowy hogan stood a tiny Navajo boy who couldn't have been more than three or four years old. He wore a pair of soft doeskin leggings with fringes down the outside of each short leg, the garment's waistband dipping low beneath his rounded belly. His narrow chest and feet were bare. A bright necklace of silver and turquoise adorned his throat. He was grinning and pointing a short finger at the grimacing, muttering Alexandra.

He was absolutely adorable, and Ellen, smiling, eagerly crossed to him, went down on her knees before him and said, "Ellen," and pointed to herself.

The child giggled, thrust a thumb into his naked chest and said, "Spear."

"Ah, your name is Spear?" said Ellen.

"Spear!" he repeated, bobbing his head and setting his shoulder-length black hair to swaying.

"*Ya-ta-hey,* Spear," Ellen said and, because he was so precious, she couldn't keep herself from giving his small waist a squeeze. He laughed merrily.

"Get him out of here!" shouted Alexandra gruffly.

Surprisingly, her stern tone of voice and scowling countenance did not scare little Spear. Instead, he seemed intrigued by Alexandra. Staring directly at her, he sauntered across the room, not stopping until he reached her chair.

"What do you want?" she snapped. The little boy wrapped his arms around himself, hopped on one bare foot, then the other, and grinned at her. "Your mother is surely looking for you!" Alexandra told him gruffly. "Go home. Go, get out of here."

Spear didn't leave. His short arms unwound and, to Alexandra's shock and dismay, he rose up on tiptoe and reached a small, dirty hand out and touched her face.

"*Idaa'yee,*" he said, grinning at her. "*Idaa'yee!*"

Alexandra shoved his dirty hand away and snarled, "I have no idea what you're trying to say. Get away from me."

"I'll be back shortly," Ellen announced. "I'm going out to get some water."

"Take this child with you!" ordered Alexandra.

But Ellen just smiled and ducked out.

*"Idaa'yee!"* the little boy repeated, his obsidian eyes riveted to Alexandra.

Alexandra Landseer finally softened. She couldn't help herself, she began to smile. She reached out and picked up the little boy. She sat him on her lap and said softly, tapping her chest, "Alexandra."

*"Idaa'yee,"* Spear said again, then snuggled comfortably back against Alexandra as her arms closed around him.

# Twenty-Six

Carrying the large kettle, Ellen went in search of water. Weaving her way in and out among the many hogans, she asked anyone she saw where she could find water. But they didn't understand. Just smiled and nodded.

She was growing frustrated when, up ahead, she caught sight of Mister Corey and Padjan. They were standing in front of a hogan, talking quietly. Before she could reach them, Padjan had turned away and ducked inside. Mister Corey was alone.

Ellen took a deep breath and hurried toward him. Silhouetted against the lavender sky, he was tall and slim and appealing and she had the strongest urge to touch him. To feel his steely muscles tighten under her fingertips. To press herself up against the hard wall of his chest.

Mister Corey slowly turned, saw her coming and appeared to visibly stiffen. Ellen was totally baffled. It was as if he dreaded seeing her, talking to her. Thinking she must surely be mistaken, Ellen proceeded directly to him.

"Mister Corey, I need your help," she said, looking anxiously up at him. "I don't know where to get water."

"I'll get some for you," he said as he reached out and took the kettle from her.

"I'll go with you."

His face tightened noticeably. "There's a well on the west perimeter of the village. It's about a half mile from here. You must be tired, there's no need for you to go. I'll bring the water to your hogan."

"I'm not tired," she lied. "I'll go with you and then next time I'll know where to get the water myself."

He gave no reply, but nodded, and inclined his head in the direction of the well. They fell into step together and made their way out of the village. The wooden well stood deserted in the dying desert light.

Ellen began to tingle with anticipation. It was just the two of them now, alone and apart from the others. The perfect opportunity for Mister Corey to tell her where she was to meet him come midnight.

It never happened.

He said little or nothing to her, but instead busied himself lowering the wooden bucket down into the well and hauling it back up, full of water. Carefully he filled her kettle.

"We better get back, it's getting dark," he said.

"Yes," she responded, wondering what was wrong with him. Had she done something to displease him? Was he angry with her for some reason? He was behaving strangely.

From the beginning, anytime they were alone he

had flirted and teased and tempted her. Or else made love to her. Was he already tired of her? Was she such an inept, unexciting lover that he wanted no more of her, was bored with her?

They walked quietly back to the village with Mister Corey carrying the heavy kettle of water.

"Is Ricky feeling better?" Ellen finally asked, breaking the silence.

"Yes."

"Is he resting now?"

"Yes."

"Does he need me to come by and change his dressings?"

"No."

Ellen gave up. The silent couple walked through the village and straight to the door of Ellen's hogan.

"Want me to carry the water inside?" he asked, saying more than he'd said the entire time.

"Not necessary," she replied and took it from him. "Good night, Mister Corey." She waited, held her breath, looked expectantly at him.

"Good night, Ellen."

But for Ellen it was not a good night.


Sunrise.

Ellen and Alexandra rose early and joined the throng of Navajo people watching aged Johnny Old Chief pray to the White Dawn and to Grandfather Talking God.

Ellen's attention strayed. She looked away from the old chief, searching the sea of faces. She easily spotted Mister Corey. He was taller than the Navajo men. She caught his eye. He quickly looked away. She felt her heart sink and she turned her attention back to the ceremony at hand.

In his native tongue, the chieftain thanked the Holy People for life, for placing them in this land bound by sacred mountains, this land of rivers and deserts and canyons.

He then offered a pinch of cornmeal to each of the six directions. To the east. To the south. To the west. To the north. And to that point in the heavens most distant above, the zenith. And to the point in the earth most distant below, the nadir.

Watching the strange presentation, Alexandra leaned over to Ellen and whispered, "Have you ever heard such nonsense?"

Ellen looked sharply at her aunt. "It isn't nonsense to them! Their customs are sacred, their beliefs strong."

"Maybe, but I still think that…what the…?"

Alexandra abruptly stopped speaking, looked down and saw that Spear was tugging on her long skirt. When he had her attention, he lifted his short arms, wanting her to pick him up. Had there been no one around, she would have done just that. As it was, she said, "You're too young to be up at this hour. Go home."

Spear didn't budge. Bare feet planted firmly on the ground, he crossed his arms and stuck out his lips in a pout.

Ellen smiled at the tiny boy and said, "Good morning, Spear."

"Spear!" he repeated his name, slapping his belly with an open hand.

By now the ceremony was ending and the crowd was beginning to disperse. Padjan came over, greeted Ellen and Alexandra. And when he saw the child, he laughed, lifted him and said to the women, "I see you've met Spear."

"The little cuss walked right into our hogan yesterday," said Alexandra. "Thought I'd never get rid of him."

"That just means he likes you," said Padjan and without asking permission handed the beaming little boy to her. She pretended disgust, but fooled no one. "Come along with me," said Padjan. "We'll take Spear home."

"Do you know where he lives?" asked Alexandra.

"No, but he does," said Padjan, and speaking to the child in his native tongue asked if Spear knew which hogan was his. He did.

They took Spear home and were warmly greeted by a young, slender woman who invited them in, then shook her finger in Spear's face, obviously scolding him for wandering away again. He lunged from Alexandra's to his mother's arms and his mother's ebony eyes immediately flashed with forgiveness and love.

Speaking to Padjan, the woman insisted they stay and enjoy her hospitality, but he declined for them all, saying that they were busy and that they knew she was too.

After they'd gone, Padjan told Ellen and Alexandra that on the day Spear had been born—following timeless tradition—his parents had placed his umbilical cord in the ceiling of the hogan so that he would always remember where he lived.

"That's barbaric," sniffed Alexandra. Padjan and Ellen exchanged glances. She saw them. "Well, it is."

"It is an ancient custom," said Padjan. "And, as you saw, the little boy already remembers where he lives." He smiled.

"Balderdash! It was a lucky guess." As they walked toward their hogan, Alexandra, looking around, commented, "These people are so thin. So poor. They look as if they've never had a square meal."

"Many times they do not have enough to eat," Padjan said. "Especially in the dead of winter when the snow flies and it's bitterly cold here." He shook his head sadly and added, "The United States government's Bureau of Indian Affairs is often late with the rationing of beef, flour and other staples promised the hungry Navajo. These people have come close to starving more than once."

"That's so sad," said Ellen. "I can't bear to think about little Spear and the other children being cold and hungry."

"Let's change the subject," said Alexandra. "How

long are we staying here in this village? You know I'm anxious to get to the Lost City.''

''We'll stay tonight, perhaps tomorrow night, no more,'' said Padjan. ''I want to let Ricky regain a little strength before we start the last difficult leg of the journey.''

''How's he doing?'' Ellen asked. ''I'd like to look in on him, but...''

''Why don't you? He's bored and lonely lying there in the hogan. He'd be happy to see you.''

She smiled. ''Where is he staying? Is it nearby?''

Padjan stopped walking. ''Three hogans down from yours,'' he said, pointing.

''That close? Is he staying there alone?''

''No. Mister Corey shares the hogan. I saw him heading that way. Shall we say hello?''

''Ah, perhaps later today,'' said Ellen. ''We haven't had breakfast yet.''

Alexandra snorted. ''I can just imagine what it's going to be. Probably a hard clump of cornmeal mush and a hunk of rancid bacon.''

Padjan gave her a dark look. ''The Navajo are a proud people, they serve their guests the best they have.''

Alexandra said no more. But since arriving at this barren village and seeing these poor, undernourished people, she was beginning to seriously doubt that there really was such a place as Padjan's Lost City. For the first time, she was afraid the whole thing was a sham, just as Ellen had warned.

If there was actually a lush green paradise where

Magic Waters flowed, a beautiful place that was guarded by this sprawling village, why wouldn't these poor starving people go there themselves? she wondered.

As she looked around at the thin, half-naked children, she frowned and thought of their bleak futures without industry, health facilities or education. But it wasn't her concern, she had her own worries.

"By the way, Padjan," she said, "I've been meaning to ask you, what does...ah...I hope I'm pronouncing this correctly...*idaa'yee*...that's it, I believe. What does *idaa'yee* mean?"

"Why do you ask?" Padjan was curious.

"Just tell me what it means."

"Old," he replied softly. "The old."

Alexandra blanched. That's what Spear had called her. Old. She automatically touched her badly wrinkled face and said, "Get me to those Magic Waters!"

"Soon," Padjan promised. "Very soon."

During that night, as the village slept, Ellen was awakened by the unmistakable sound of Mister Corey's deep, low voice.

"Ellen," he said. "Ellen! Wake up. I need you."

Ellen's eyes opened before he'd finished the sentence and she began to sigh and smile with pleasure. *I need you.* What a welcome wonderful statement. She glanced cautiously at her aunt. Alexandra was asleep. Snoring.

Her heart beating wildly in her chest, Ellen eagerly rose from her sleeping mat and reached for her robe.

"Ellen," he called again from just outside the hogan's door.

"Yes, I'm coming," she whispered, sliding her bare feet into her house slippers and tying the sash of her robe with shaking hands.

Anticipation swiftly building, she wondered where he was going to take her. They couldn't go to his hogan, Ricky was there. Maybe he meant for them to ride out of the village to some romantic, secluded spot. He'd know where to go, he always did. And it really didn't matter to her where they went so long as they could be alone.

Smoothing her sleep-tumbled hair, Ellen crossed the darkened hogan, threw back the covering curtain and stepped out into the moonlight.

"Mister Corey," she said breathlessly.

"It's Ricky," he said, taking her arm and propelling her forward. "He's developed a fever. You must come with me at once!"

# Twenty-Seven

In worried silence the pair hurried through the darkness to the hogan where Ricky O'Mara lay sick and suffering. A lighted candle rested on the floor beside his mat, its tiny flame casting shadows over his shiny ashen face.

Ellen fell quickly to her knees beside him, pressed her cheek to his.

"Dear God, he's burning up with fever," she said. "He needs a doctor."

"I'll get Padjan," said Mister Corey. "He'll know who can help."

He rushed out, and Ellen, hating to make the sick man suffer more than he already was, steeled herself to his moans of pain and pulled the covers down from his naked chest to his waist. His teeth chattering, his entire body racked with terrible trembling, Ricky weakly fought Ellen as she turned him onto his side and peeled the bandage from his back.

Her eyes quickly widened in horror.

The bullet wound had become badly infected. Thick poison pus oozed from the stitched area and streaks of red radiated outward. This was the reason for the high fever. He had developed an infection and that infection was swiftly spreading through his bloodstream.

Biting her bottom lip to keep it from trembling as badly as the sick man before her, Ellen managed to keep Ricky balanced on his side with one firm hand while she reached for the bottle of alcohol with the other.

Hating the thought of tormenting him more, she uncapped the alcohol with her teeth and then looked up gratefully as Mister Corey and Padjan entered.

"Infection has set in," she stated levelly.

"No," exclaimed Padjan.

"Jesus God," muttered Mister Corey.

"A clean cloth," she said. "I need…"

Mister Corey hurried to hand her one from a stack between the two mats. "You'll have to help me hold him still," she said. "We must cleanse the wound, try to sterilize it."

Padjan had already circled the mat and was on his knees across from her, his hands gripping Ricky's waist and hip. Kneeling beside her, Mister Corey clasped Ricky's shoulders. They eased Ricky over onto his stomach and held him as still as possible while Ellen applied the alcohol, carefully cleaning and blotting away the dying skin and flesh.

The feverish Ricky moaned and spasmed in agony. Mister Corey ground his teeth. His chest so tight he could hardly breathe, he stole a glance at Ellen as she continued in her attempt to purge and purify the infected wound. Her thin face was set with fierce determination, but her pale eyes couldn't hide her fear and deep compassion.

When finally the agonizing task was finished and a clean white bandage protected Ricky's wound, they pulled the covers up and tucked them in around his neck and shoulders.

Ellen looked at Mister Corey. "He's shaking more violently than ever, which means, of course, that his fever is still rising."

Mister Corey nodded. He snatched the covers from his own sleeping mat and spread them over Ricky. "I'll build a fire," he said, turning away.

"Padjan, is there a medical doctor on the reservation?" Ellen asked.

"No," he sadly admitted. "Only an old medicine man who heals by using herbs and calling on the spirits."

"Would he do Ricky any good?"

"Truthfully, no. But do not worry," he said brightly, wanting to reassure her. "Once we get Ricky to the Lost City, the Magic Waters will quickly heal him."

The skeptical Ellen was certain that no so-called Magic Waters would help Ricky.

But she simply said, "I don't think he'll live that long. He's very sick and the infection is—"

"Then we must depart immediately," reasoned Padjan. "It is nearing 3:00 a. m. In a couple of hours it will be daylight. We'll leave at dawn." Ellen looked from Padjan to Mister Corey.

Sharing Ellen's skepticism, he nonetheless nodded

and said, "I'll start making the preparations. We can leave at sunup."

"You two go on," Ellen said. "I'll stay here with Ricky while you get everything ready."

When the first streaks of gray lightened the eastern horizon, the caravan was ready to ride out of the Navajo village. The wagon was to be left behind and picked up on the way back. Ricky and Summer Dawn were each strapped onto separate travois, the Indian way of transporting heavy loads.

The two supporting poles of the travois on which Ricky lay trembling and feverish were secured to Mister Corey's paint stallion. The one on which Summer Dawn lay was fastened to the horse Padjan was to ride, a pinto stallion.

Alexandra, with the help of both Padjan and Mister Corey, managed, after numerous failed attempts, to get atop a gentle bay mare. She longed to berate Mister Corey for not buying a side saddle for her, but under the circumstances decided she'd best not make a fuss.

As Ellen swung up onto the saffron dun's back, Padjan walked out to speak with Johnny Old Chief.

In the Navajo's native language, Padjan said, "My friend, we appreciate your warm hospitality. We wish that we could stay longer, but we have two very sick people who badly need to reach my Lost City." The chief nodded his understanding. "We are leaving the wagon here. In three or four weeks Mister Corey and the others will come back for it."

Again the chief nodded.

"We will ride the horses as far as possible, then turn them loose. They will, I believe, eventually wander back this way."

Johnny Old Chief said, "We will round the horses up."

"I hoped you would," said Padjan. "None of your people are to make any attempt to trail us, to follow us."

"No one will follow," assured Johnny Old Chief.

"Then goodbye, old friend," said Padjan before embracing the chief.

"As you leave our village, may Father Sky and Mother Earth safely guide you to your home above the clouds," the Navajo chieftain said solemnly.

Padjan gave no reply. He turned, walked away, mounted the pinto stallion and rode off as the sun began to rise. He was now leading the caravan since he was the only one who knew the way to the Lost City.

Padjan was aware, although he didn't tell the others, that it would take most of the day to reach their destination. The horses were rested and fresh and, given their heads, could have loped or galloped for miles.

But both he and Mister Corey had to hold their mounts to a gentle walk, lest they cause harm or discomfort to Summer Dawn or Ricky. Each rider regularly looked back over his shoulder, anxiously checking the patient he was dragging behind on the travois.

Long hours after leaving the Navajo village, the distant vermilion cliffs toward which they were steadily riding became ablaze in the early-afternoon sun, a purple mist lingering in their clefts. Skirting the scattered totem poles that dotted the desert floor, Padjan led the contingent directly toward the soaring mountains.

The nearer they got to the cliffs, the higher the ridges rose. Ellen threw back her head and looked up, but she couldn't see the summits. The craggy peaks far above were completely enveloped in clouds.

Without explanation, Padjan suddenly drew rein, halted and threw up his hand for the others to stop. And wait. No one questioned him, but all wondered why they had stopped. It had been little more than an hour since their lunch break.

Padjan's ebony eyes were focused on the sheer wall of rock before them. Patiently he waited for the entrance to the Lost City to be revealed to him. There was, he knew well, certain times of the day when the angle of the sun exposed to the trained and expectant eye the hidden portal into the seemingly solid wall of rock.

Five minutes passed.

Ten.

All at once a shaft of bright light from the slow-moving sun struck the entrance, and Padjan, smiling, rode forward. The others followed, but Ellen, staring at the towering wall of solid rock before them, wondered at Padjan's judgment. If he really knew where he was going, why was he leading them straight into what appeared to be a dead end?

The question had no more than passed through her mind when Padjan mysteriously disappeared. One minute he was there, atop the pinto stallion with Summer Dawn on the travois behind him, the next both were gone.

Ellen blinked in confusion and felt the fine hair rise on the back of her neck.

"We've lost Padjan," said Alexandra. "Where did he go?"

"I don't know," said Ellen who was staring in disbelief as Mister Corey, riding a few yards ahead, disappeared just as Padjan had.

Ellen and Alexandra exchanged worried looks and followed. It wasn't until they were a few short feet from the solid rock wall that they saw the well-concealed crevice into which the others had vanished.

"You go in first," said Ellen to her aunt. "I'll follow."

"I'm frightened," said Alexandra.

"Don't be," said Ellen. "Padjan knows what he's doing."

Reluctantly the two women entered the passage and found themselves inside a treacherous, steep-sided sandstone cavern that began, almost at once, to angle upward. After riding less than a half mile, the canyon narrowed. Soon there was barely enough distance between the two towering sides for a man's spread arms.

The sun did not reach down into this slim fracture in the rock. It was dark, shadowy, foreboding. Making the dimly lit trail all the more perilous was the fact that it constantly twisted and turned. It was a perplexing labyrinth where fallen rocks often covered the path and jagged ledges jutted out on each side of the high, close walls.

More than once Mister Corey and Padjan had to dismount and clear pebbles and stones out of the way. Anytime that happened, Ellen also dismounted to check on Ricky and Summer Dawn. She saw no change in the old woman's condition, although when she bent over Summer Dawn, her marble-like ebony eyes opened and Ellen saw in them the strength and intelligence that had once been distributed throughout her now-useless body. Ellen realized that Summer Dawn was aware she was going home.

"Yes, Summer Dawn," Ellen said kindly, "you're going home. You'll be there very soon."

Summer Dawn's bright eyes flashed with thanks and relief. Ellen patted her thin shoulder and turned away to check on Ricky. His fever was still rising and Ellen was terrified he wouldn't live to reach Padjan's Lost City.

"You must hold on, Ricky," she whispered, pushing the damp dark hair off his forehead. He didn't respond. She softly promised, "We'll be there soon and you'll feel better."

She hoped it was true.

But their progress was slow and arduous. The going was extremely difficult with a badly wounded man, a very sick old woman and the whining, com-

plaining Alexandra. Hours passed much faster than
the miles. It was late afternoon and they were still not
to the Lost City.

Ellen was bent on not becoming part of the problem. As usual, she found herself longing to prove to
Mister Corey that while she might well have been a
witless fool in his arms, she was totally capable elsewhere. She wanted him to know that she was willing
and able to do her share, to be a burden to no one.

Her efforts were not in vain. Mister Corey was
once again quietly amazed by her unflagging mettle.
She was tireless and optimistic in the face of adver-
sity. Obstacles did not deter her, trouble did not dis-
courage her, risk did not seem to frighten her.

She was a true gem.

While Ellen was in his thoughts, Mister Corey was
very much on Ellen's mind. She had noticed, more
than once, that he was never in doubt, was always
decisive and showed no strain or fear despite the fact
that they all turned to him for strength and guidance.
She wondered at the puzzling paradox. Knowing him
as she did, it was almost impossible to believe that
the imperturbable Mister Corey was actually guilty of
military cowardice.

It was equally hard—and far more painful—to believe that this man who had made such thrilling love
to her had a beautiful, aristocratic wife whom he was
supposedly "mad about."

But apparently it was true.

Ellen was shaken from her tortured musings when
Padjan pulled up on the pinto, dismounted and an-

nounced, "This is where we leave the horses. We will take them no farther."

"Why?" Alexandra asked. "Are we almost to the Lost City? Are we there?"

"No, Alexandra," Padjan said calmly, "we are not there. But we are not going to punish the horses by attempting to take them through the steep, narrow, ascending corridors ahead."

"Are you saying that they don't even have horses in your Lost City?"

"No," he said, "that's not what I'm saying. There are horses in the Lost City."

"Aha!" she said. "And just how did they get there?"

He gave no reply to her question, instead said calmly, "We will turn the horses loose here and proceed on foot."

"Proceed on foot, *my* foot!" huffed Alexandra. "Perhaps you have forgotten that I have a sprained ankle!"

"It's time you started putting some weight on it," said Padjan, then raised a hand to silence her when Alexandra started to angrily protest. He said, "From here on out we must all be uncommonly alert. The final mile not only twists and turns sharply, but steadily ascends until finally we reach the high mountain valley where the Lost City is located." He paused, pointed over his shoulder and said, "Just ahead the trail falls away on one side, so walk very slowly and do not look down."

Muttering under her breath, Alexandra allowed

Mister Corey to assist her in dismounting. "Ooooh," she moaned when her feet touched the ground. "I tell you my ankle hurts and I can't be expected to walk. I can't, I just can't. I'll never make it!"

"That, Miss Landseer, is solely up to you," said Mister Corey. "There is no one to carry you. Padjan and I will be pulling Summer Dawn and Ricky. Walk or you'll be left behind."

Alexandra glared at his retreating back, knowing he meant what he said. Minutes later they were all— including Alexandra, who had secretly known she could walk without any real pain—carefully traversing the dangerous path between jagged vertical walls that were no more than an armspan apart and beside which a void plummeted to a depth of more than a hundred feet.

Ellen, bringing up the rear, was so tense her hands were clammy and her heart was racing in her chest. She wondered at her aunt's surprising calm. Alexandra remained totally silent as she carefully picked her way up the turning, twisting trail beside the deep, dark chasm. Ellen noted that her aunt took one careful step after another, the limp that had plagued her mysteriously missing.

Ellen heeded Padjan's advice. She did not look down, lest she grow dizzy and fall. She winced in terror when, beneath her boot, a loose rock gave way, knocking it over the side. It seemed like an eternity before the falling stone hit bottom.

Ellen, like the others, gave a great sigh of relief when they left that part of the trail behind them. They stopped for a few minutes and she checked on the patients.

Then the really hard part of the journey began.

It seemed that they were climbing straight up to the clouds. Ellen's legs had begun to ache painfully and she was dangerously short of breath. She had to help the puffing Alexandra every step of the way now, but realized she had it easy compared with Padjan and Mister Corey.

The incline was so steep and the trail so uneven, Ricky and Summer Dawn had to be removed from their conveyances. Which meant they had to be carried. Padjan, carrying Summer Dawn, who weighed less than a hundred pounds, was struggling under the load. It was worse for Mister Corey. Ricky O'Mara was a big strapping man and the slimly built Mister Corey could barely lift him, much less carry him uphill.

But he did it.

There were occasions during the torturous climb that they would reach a cramped, nearly impassable slot in the stone. At such times, Mister Corey would carefully lay Ricky down and help Padjan ease Summer Dawn up through the narrow opening. Once she was up to a wider spot, they would gingerly set her down and go back for Ricky.

Ellen noted how exhausted both men looked. Their faces were shiny with perspiration and their shirts were soaked with sweat. She didn't think either of them could go much farther. On one occasion after they'd lifted Ricky up through a narrow passage, she saw Mister Corey's knees buckle, watched as he sank to the ground, fighting to get his breath.

Touched and worried about him, Ellen acted on impulse. She uncorked her canteen of precious water, stepped forward and emptied it over his head. Gasping with surprise, he raised his hands and spread the water over his hot, flushed face.

"Thanks," he said without looking up.

"You're welcome."

On his feet again he pushed his damp hair back, took a long, deep breath and lifted his burden once more.

Up, up they climbed, tired to the bone, yearning for rest, wondering how much longer they could last.

Then finally they exited a last narrow, darkened passage and walked out onto a flat, cloud-enshrouded plain that Padjan happily declared was Mystery Valley.

All at once the low misty clouds evaporated and a bright alpine sun spread its powerful illumination over the entire valley.

And there before them, directly in the center of the vast plateau called Mystery Valley, shimmering in the bright, blinding sunshine, rose the Lost City of the Anasazi.

# PART THREE

# Twenty-Eight

All stood and stared at the Lost City of the Anasazi, a city that was completely surrounded by mountains.

In the remote valley village they could see many multistory stone structures grouped around courtyards. Some dwellings were built on cliffs high above the valley floor, reached by ladders or handholds and footholds chipped from the rock face. Still others were nestled back in open caves of the rock walls of the canyon.

While Ellen and Mister Corey stared, enchanted by what they saw, Alexandra was already beginning to sneer with bitter disappointment. It was nothing like she had expected! Padjan had led her to believe that his city was a singular paradise floating above the clouds.

She had envisioned emerald-green grass, blossom-filled trees and luxurious quarters with modern conveniences. She saw none of those things here. No eye-soothing blues and greens and lavenders. Nothing but the same old desert tones of sand and brick and red. As far as she could tell, there was little difference between this primitive, impossible-to-get-to place and the Navajo reservation below.

She had, she feared, made a monumental mistake. She had let herself be bamboozled by a persuasive Indian and a fraudulent carnival barker. Ellen was right. This was an expensive wild-goose chase. There couldn't possibly be any such thing as Magic Waters in this godforsaken place.

Ellen viewed the shining city in a much different light. She was amazed by the magnificent location, undoubtedly chosen for its safety, isolation and stark beauty. Unlike Alexandra, Ellen thought that master craftsmen must have surely been responsible for the incredible architecture of the city's varied dwellings. There was only one strange thing about the Lost City. There were no people. The streets appeared to be empty. Was the Lost City deserted?

Staring transfixed, Ellen audibly gasped when she suddenly saw a shandrydan—a hooded chair—being carried forward by four big, bronze-skinned Indians. Automatically supposing that the chair was meant for her, Alexandra started to step forward. Padjan stopped her with a sharp look. The Indians set the hooded chair down directly before Padjan and stepped aside.

An imposing man stepped out of the shandrydan. Tall and muscular, he wore a colorful headdress and a somber expression.

Padjan bowed to him. And then, sweeping his arm about in an encompassing gesture, he formally introduced Natan, Keeper of the Waters.

Nodding to the guests, Natan said to Padjan in flawless English, ''You were expected. We have waited for you. Are you in time?''

Nodding his bald head, Padjan replied, "Summer Dawn still lives."

The Lost City was not deserted.

The People lived there. Happy people. Young people. Vigorous People.

The Anasazi.

The Ancient Ones, the tribe believed to have disappeared from the face of the earth centuries ago.

A swarm of young men immediately appeared. In shandrydans they swiftly whisked Summer Dawn and Ricky O'Mara away after Natan, Keeper of the Waters, instructed them, in a low, commanding voice, to take the sick pair directly to the Magic Waters.

The others were then escorted to their quarters. As if they had been expected.

Each visitor was given his own private chamber in a multistoried, multiroomed masonry pueblo. Alexandra was shown to her quarters first, a spotless, spacious abode decorated with exquisite handmade pottery of black, white and red on orange. Ellen went inside with her, as did Padjan.

Frowning with displeasure the minute she stepped in, Alexandra said, "Well, I guess this will have to do. At least it's on the ground and I won't be expected to climb one of those rickety ladders." She turned quickly and asked, "And where will you be, Ellen?"

Padjan said, "She will be next door."

"Why can't she stay here with me?"

"No need," explained Padjan. "There is plenty of room here for us all to have our own privacy."

Ellen could have kissed him. The prospect of having a room to herself, some space to herself, some time to herself, was pure heaven.

Ellen felt as if she'd been released from prison when she left Alexandra and was taken to a large, pleasant room with a wide, soft-looking sleeping mat placed along the back wall. There was, she noted with pleasure, a fresh bouquet of wildflowers artfully arranged in a black-and-white bowl on a table near the center fire pit.

She smiled as she turned round and round in the room and then finally ventured back to stand for a moment in the open doorway. She looked out on the city. It was a fortified pueblo with many well-constructed square, oval, circular and D-shaped towers. A remote, secure fortress where everyone she'd seen so far looked young and healthy and happy.

That evening Padjan appeared at the dwelling where Alexandra was staying. Smiling, he told her that he was ready to take her to the Magic Waters. She begged off, said she was far too weary to go there tonight.

"Do you suppose Ellen would like to go?"

Alexandra snorted. "Not a chance," she said, shaking her head back and forth. "Ellen is a cynical young woman and she certainly doesn't believe in your Magic Waters."

"All the same, I think I will ask her," said Padjan, smiling as he left the room.

He hurried next door, invited Ellen to visit the

Magic Waters, and was not surprised when she said yes. Uncommonly curious, Ellen eagerly followed Padjan out into the warm twilight. But she hesitated when she saw Mister Corey waiting with a lighted torch. Without a word, he casually took her arm and propelled her forward into the rapidly fading twilight.

The three of them made their way out of the compact city, climbing farther up the valley's northern rocky face. Halfway to the summit of the craggy, oddly shaped peak, Ellen thought she detected a hazy blue light. She blinked and thought she saw the faint light flicker, but wasn't sure. Soon they neared the spot where she thought she had seen the light.

No light was there.

They continued walking.

Mister Corey's torch illuminated their way as total darkness descended. Shortly, Padjan disappeared around a tall spire of rock. Ellen followed with Mister Corey directly behind her, holding the torch high.

Suddenly the torch mysteriously went dark. Ellen winced. Then her lips fell open in shocked surprise when she stepped out into a gigantic room bordered by rock walls.

For a fleeting, blinding second, a bright blue light flared and danced on the walls. A natural fountain, splashing high into the air and falling back in a huge circular pool, was a vivid sapphire blue. The blue phosphorescent light dancing around the fountain grew much brighter, illuminating their faces as they gazed at the waters. Reflections of the blue bubbling waters shimmered on the walls.

"The Magic Waters," Padjan proudly announced.

Ellen and Mister Corey could only nod and stare, astonished by the sight of the brilliant blue waters and the strange, mysterious light. It was a dazzling spectacle to behold, unlike anything either had ever seen. Both stood there hypnotized.

But impressed though they were, neither believed in the waters' magical powers. Neither drank of the waters.

Alexandra desperately wanted to believe.

The next morning the aging heiress made the tiring trek up to the waters, dipped the golden goblet she'd brought along expressly for the momentous occasion and drank deeply of the bubbly blue water.

Old Summer Dawn and Ricky O'Mara had been carried up to the waters as soon as they had arrived in the Lost City. Summer Dawn was given small sips, while the unconscious Ricky's lips had been moistened and his wound carefully bathed in the healing waters.

It promptly became a ritual. Twice daily, Alexandra and Summer Dawn drank of the Magic Waters while the skeptical Ellen and the cynical Mister Corey silently scoffed at such absurdity.

Ricky O'Mara quickly became a believer.

Not thirty-six hours after arriving in the Lost City, Ricky awakened from his feverish coma. He opened his eyes and there standing above him was a woman. A young Anasazi woman. She was tall and slender and her face was oval-shaped with large dark eyes, a small proud nose and wide generous lips. She wore a summer dress with unique geometric designs woven through the hem and the sleeves. Beautifully crafted jewelry adorned each slender wrist and her elegant throat. Her hair, parted in the middle and reaching her waist, was as black and shiny as a raven's wing.

She was the most beautiful creature Ricky O'Mara had ever seen.

"Am I dreaming?" he asked earnestly. "If I touched you, would you evaporate into thin air?"

The lovely woman laughed musically, fell to her knees beside his sleeping mat and said, "I am real. You may touch me if you doubt it." Ricky raised a weak hand and laid it lightly on her forearm. She smiled and said, "My name is Tallas. I was chosen to take care of you. I have been with you since you arrived and I will stay with you until you are completely well."

Ricky grinned boyishly. "In that case, I may never get completely well."

"You will," she said and turned away to get a pan of water—blue water—and a clean cloth. "Already your fever is much lower. And you have awakened. Your friends will be relieved."

She dipped the cloth into the blue water and Ricky's grin turned into a hint of a frown. "What are you going to do?"

"Give you a bath," she said matter-of-factly.

"Ah…wait, no…I…aren't you a little young to be…"

"No," she stated simply. "I am not. I have already given you three baths while you were unconscious."

Ricky's pallid face flushed. "Yes, but…"

"Just relax," said the beautiful Tallas in a low, soothing voice, "and I will make you feel better."

She did just that.

Later that evening Ellen stopped in to check on Ricky. She was delighted to find him awake and astonished by the change in him. His fever was mostly gone and the color was already returning to his face. He was laughing and talking to the lovely young Indian woman who had been selected to tend him during his illness.

From his bed, Ricky introduced the two women and Ellen found Tallas to be as pleasant and sweet as she was beautiful. Ellen left Ricky's quarters wondering at his dramatic recovery. But she never once considered that it had anything to do with the Magic Waters.

She checked with Padjan to see if there'd been any change in Summer Dawn. There had not. And there sure hadn't been any change in Alexandra.

So Ellen remained skeptical, did not believe for a moment that any waters on this earth held the power to restore health and youth. Staunchly refusing to take even one tiny sip, she continued to silently mock the behavior of the others.

Until…one peaceful, lazy summer afternoon when the village was sleeping, Ellen quietly stole up to the Magic Waters. Once there she looked cautiously about and finally, confident she was alone, sank down to her knees, lifted a handful of the bubbling blue water to her lips and drank.

No sooner had she done it than she felt foolish. She vowed that she would never again do such a silly thing. Feeling much like a guilty thief stealing through the night, Ellen skipped back down the rocky trail, hurried up the empty street and ducked anxiously into her quarters.

She was safely in her room when the bored, restless Mister Corey made the solitary trek up to the waters. His black, lifeless eyes focused on the dancing blue waters, he shrugged, crouched down on his heels, cupped both hands in the water and, for the first time, drank. He wiped his mouth on his shirtsleeve.

Then he shook his dark head and laughed at his idiocy.

God, what kind of fool was he?

# Twenty-Nine

When three warm, balmy nights had passed without Mister Corey making any attempt to see her, to catch her alone, Ellen faced the bitter truth. He didn't want to be with her.

Here it was bedtime again—past bedtime, really. Well past midnight. And Ellen was lying alone in bed in her silent quarters, sleepless. Frustrated. Lonely. Hurt.

Mister Corey did not want her, it was as simple as that. He had made his point. He had proved that he could have her with the snap of his fingers.

She had her own private quarters and so did he. He could have come to her, or he could have taken her to his lodgings, had he cared to do so.

But he hadn't.

And he wasn't going to.

He had, she sadly reasoned, quickly tired of her. Just as her husband had quickly tired of her all those years ago. Tears sprang to Ellen's eyes when she realized, with a sobering jolt of despair, that Mister Corey's rejection was far more painful than her husband's.

Ellen turned onto her side, drew her knees up and

lay in a fetal position. She squeezed her eyes tightly shut in an attempt to keep from crying. She deserved to suffer. This whole sordid affair was her fault. She had, of her own free will, given herself to the reckless Mister Corey. He had not forced her, had made no promises, had given her no reason to suppose he cared one whit for her.

And, obviously, he did not.

Ellen's tear-filled eyes opened, she rolled onto her back and gazed through the blur at the ceiling above. She clamped her teeth down tight, set her jaw and told herself she was glad he was no longer interested in her. He'd be doing her a great favor if he never again took her in his arms.

They wouldn't be staying in the Lost City very long. Soon—in a few short weeks—she would be back in New York. And he, she supposed, would be back with his wife. In time she would forget. Memories would fade and die. And her foolish, unreasonable, shameful desire for an unprincipled married man would die as well.

The warm, sunny days in the Lost City glided peacefully by, and Ricky, jealously nursed and tended by the beautiful Tallas, was mending rapidly. Unfortunately, Summer Dawn had not yet rallied.

And Alexandra, griping bitterly to anyone who would listen, including the majestic Natan, Keeper of the Waters, could see and feel no change whatsoever, despite her many treks up to the Magic Waters. She spent hours gazing hopefully into the silver-handled hand mirror she had brought from home, expecting to find a more youthful-looking woman.

She saw only the same jowly, badly wrinkled face she'd been looking at for the past decade. Furious, she would go in search of Padjan and blister him with harsh words of reproach.

"Just exactly when," she wanted to know, "will I become young again?"

The little man grinned, shrugged and calmly replied, "This is up to you, Alexandra. The heart must first believe before it can become young."

"The devil with my heart," she hotly rejoined. "I want my face and body to be young!"

Not for a minute did Ellen actually believe in the wizardry of the waters, but nonetheless she didn't keep the vow she'd made. She *did* return to the Magic Waters. Again and yet again.

She was not the only one.

Mister Corey also found himself returning to the waters. Both took great care not to let anyone see them make the journey and they told no one of those secret visits.

Ellen didn't even tell Tallas, although the two had become friends. The patient, caring Tallas was always at Ricky's bedside when Ellen—or anyone—visited. Tallas was unfailingly warm and agreeable and in no time it seemed as if the two women had known each other all their lives. Soon they were talking up a storm and laughing together like young girls.

Tallas spoke glowingly of her beloved Lost City

and of the vigorous, youthful-looking people who inhabited it. But the information she happily shared with Ellen related only to the present. She never spoke of the past, never revealed the mystery of the Lost City's existence.

She said that Padjan had taught her—and several others—English, but that she, herself, had never been out of the Lost City. And would never be. She would never wander from her sky-high home above the clouds.

Therefore, she was eager to hear about Ellen's very different world in faraway New York. Ellen described the bustling island of Manhattan with its many skyscrapers and large population and her Park Avenue home.

"You can't show me your home, but I can show you mine," Tallas told her new friend one quiet afternoon. And she promised that when the opportunity arose, she would get a couple of horses and show Ellen every part of the Lost City and the cliff palaces above.

So, on a sunny, prearranged morning, Ellen rose rested and eagerly looking forward to the adventure. She hastily dressed, twisted her hair up into its usual knot at the back of her head, drew on her soft chamois trousers and a blouse and hurried through the village to Ricky's quarters where she was to meet Tallas. But she stiffened when she stepped inside and saw Mister Corey lounging lazily near Ricky's bed.

He glanced at her, nodded and said softly, "Good morning, Ellen."

She bobbed her head, quickly looked away and he felt a sharp pang of guilt stab through his chest. She was hurt, he could tell. And he was the thoughtless bastard responsible. Jesus, as if she hadn't been hurt enough in her life.

Tallas stepped forward. "Mister Corey has agreed to stay with Ricky so that you and I may spend the day together," she whispered so as not to disturb her sleeping charge. "Isn't that kind of him?" The tall Anasazi woman smiled warmly at Mister Corey.

"Most considerate," Ellen managed to say, wishing she could hate him. Wishing she had never laid eyes on him. Wishing he didn't look so appealing lolling there with his long legs crossed at the ankles and a wayward lock of thick raven hair falling over his high forehead. "Shall we go?" she anxiously asked Tallas.

"Right away," said Tallas, but instead of crossing to the door, Tallas went to Ricky's sleeping mat, sank down onto her knees, took one of his hands in both of hers and whispered to him in her native language so that neither he, nor Ellen and Mister Corey, could understand.

But the tenderness that shone from her dark eyes as she gazed at the sleeping Ricky was unmistakable.

Tallas gently placed Ricky's hand back on the mat, shot to her feet and addressed Mister Corey. "We may be gone a long time. You don't mind staying until…"

"Not at all," said Mister Corey. "Don't worry, I won't leave him."

"Thank you," said Tallas and then turned to Ellen and said, "Ready?"

It was a most enjoyable and enlightening day for Ellen.

The Anasazi's high mesa pueblo was much larger than she had assumed. It was also a city of remarkable complexity and beauty. Dozens and dozens of multistoried, five-to-twenty-room dwellings covered the vast mesa top, all built to face a large round open space at the very center of the city where the oval, square and circular towers rose high above the other buildings.

On horseback the two women rode through the city and around its outer circumference, Tallas proudly pointing out places of special interest to Ellen. Ellen noted five distinct roads leading from the outer limits directly into the city's core. She wondered at these roads since, as far as she could tell, the Anasazi had no wheeled conveyances.

The roads were forgotten as Ellen admired the design and masonry of the dwellings that were incredibly distinctive. Tallas explained that the craftsmen had patiently pecked rocks to size and built the walls with little mortar or rubble fill. An amazing accomplishment, had it been undertaken in this age, when the twentieth century was about to dawn? But if, as Ellen suspected, these unique dwellings had been constructed hundreds of years ago, the accomplishment was absolutely amazing.

The magnificent multistoried homes were not the

only treasures created by these highly intelligent, talented people. They were the master jewelers and ornament carvers of the Anasazi.

Dismounting and leading their horses, Ellen and Tallas walked among the houses where men and women sat outdoors in the sunlight, weaving sandals, fashioning jewelry and forging pottery. Ellen was awed by the intricately carved bracelets and rings and necklaces of silver and turquoise. And by the exquisite pottery: elaborate black on white and the first polychrome—black, white and red on orange. Rare, priceless urns and pots and water jugs.

She shook her head in embarrassment when one of the women held out a wide silver bracelet to her. Ellen asked Tallas to please explain to the woman that she thought the bracelet beautiful, but that she had no money with which to purchase it.

Tallas laughed her musical laugh and said, "She is giving the bracelet to you as a gift, Ellen. She does not want money. There is no need for money here."

"Oh, I didn't..." Ellen smiled at the woman, took the offered gift and said, "Thank you so much. I shall treasure the bracelet always."

Tallas translated and the woman beamed happily.

By noon Tallas had shown Ellen most of the city that was built below on the huge flat mesa. In the afternoon the two rode out of the sprawling pueblo and almost at once began ascending the slopes of the northern canyon walls. Ellen looked up and knew immediately where they were headed. She saw the many scattered dwellings up in the protected alcoves of the canyon. Built on cliffs high above the valley floor, the upper floors had to be reached by ladders.

Tallas drew rein midway up to the majestic cliff palaces. Ellen quickly halted her own mount as Tallas pointed to a distinct cliff palace that was nestled back into a large open cave in the high rock wall.

"Think you can walk the rest of the way and then climb one of those ladders?" Tallas asked. "My home is on the top story."

"I can do it once," Ellen said with a laugh. "But to live there, one would have to be very young, like you."

Tallas smiled enigmatically and said, "You are younger than I, Ellen."

"No! I am not. Why, I'm thirty-six and—"

"Let's go up," Tallas interrupted, and the subject was dropped.

The two dismounted, tethered their horses and hiked up the canyon wall to the well-protected cliff houses. There they climbed a ladder to the fifth-story dwelling that Tallas called home. Inside it was spacious and cool and quiet. It looked very much like the woman herself, serene, friendly and attractive.

"Make yourself at home, Ellen," said Tallas, "while I fix us something to eat."

Nodding, Ellen moved around the large, comfortable room where colorful woven rugs covered much of the stone floor and arresting artifacts had been carefully arranged in every nook and cranny. A delicate garment, lying across a chair back, immediately caught Ellen's eye.

Tallas looked up from her task and said, "It's a dress I'm making. Pick it up. Look at it, tell me what you think."

Ellen lifted the dress, held it up before her and admired the garment. The dress was white, the fabric a material resembling fine linen. Around the neckline were the woven beginnings of triangles and squares and other interesting geometric patterns. It was a gorgeous, feminine dress and Ellen automatically drew it to her, held it against her slender frame. The neckline was cut daringly low and the full white skirts reached only to her knees.

"You like the dress?" Tallas stood with a plate of hot fried bread in her hands.

"Oh, Tallas, it's absolutely beautiful," said Ellen. "You made it?"

Tallas nodded. "It's not finished." She waved a slender hand toward the dress. "There's all that decorative weaving yet to be done around the bodice and the hem. Will you help?"

Ellen looked up. "Of course I will. Will it be worn for a special occasion?"

"Yes, it will," Tallas said, her dark eyes flashing with merriment. "The dress is for you, Ellen."

"For me? But, I don't—"

"You'll know when to wear it."

# Thirty

Something had changed.

Lately Mister Corey had begun to see Ellen in a new and different light. He noticed things about her that he hadn't noticed before.

In this relatively small pueblo he saw her every day, several times a day. He studied her when she was unaware of his scrutiny and he wondered, had her eyes always been such an incredible shade of dark luminous green? Had her lips always been so incredibly full, so temptingly luscious? Had her hair always been such a unique shade of warm golden chestnut?

Was it possible that she had gained a few pounds? Her thin face looked fuller and her slender frame appeared to be more supple, almost lissome. As he watched her go about the Lost City, it seemed to him she carried herself with a newfound confidence and grace. She moved lithely with an appealingly feminine stride, poised, sure of herself, in charge.

Totally different from the awkward, reticent woman he'd met in London at the street fair that balmy night last spring.

Perversely, now that it was too late, now that he had hurt and humiliated her, Mister Corey found himself strongly attracted to Ellen. He wanted her as he'd never wanted her before. Each time he saw her, his desire grew. The sway of her skirts, the sunlight shimmering like Midas's gold in her hair, the regal arch of her throat; all these things made him weak in the knees.

The sound of her laughter carrying on the thin, clear air, the sparkling of her beautiful eyes, her blatant neglect of him—she now pointedly ignored him—made his body ache with the overwhelming impact of his desire.

Had she always been so breathtakingly beautiful?

The tables had definitely been turned.

Or so he thought.

In truth, Ellen was more wistfully aware of Mister Corey than she'd ever been. She avoided any and all eye contact with him, but she stole enough covert glances to notice subtle changes in him.

Was it her imagination or had some of the hardness gone out of his sharply cut profile? Had his lean, strongly contoured face softened so that there was a hint of the appealing boyishness of his youth? Had the long white scar slicing down his right cheek darkened in the sun until it was hardly noticeable? Was there the slightest glimmer of soft, warm light radiating from those midnight eyes? Had his too-thin body added a small degree of well-honed muscle?

Had he always been so devastatingly handsome?

Despite all of her best efforts, Ellen's innate dislike and distrust of Mister Corey had begun to fade. Only the powerful attraction remained. The mystery of such fierce physical magnetism had heretofore been unknown to the unworldly Ellen Cornelius.

From the very beginning she had been unnerved by his strong, undeniable maleness. The aura of mystery surrounding him, the danger he represented to a woman like her was truly tantalizing.

And, ironically, now that he was no longer interested in her, she found him more irresistible than ever. She wanted him desperately with all her heart, body and soul.

She couldn't have him, she knew that. He belonged to another. But she would never forget him. She would remember him—would miss him—for the rest of her life.

The pattern was set, had been set years ago. She would always be alone. She saw her loveless life stretch out before her like a long, dusty road across a barren plain, going on endlessly toward the sunset of her days.

Alexandra awoke at sunrise. The silver-handled mirror lay nearby, but for the first time since arriving in the Lost City, she didn't reach for it, didn't pick it up.

She didn't need to look into it. She knew that there had been no change in her appearance and that there was not going to be no matter how many gallons of the Magic Waters she consumed.

Oddly, it no longer mattered that much. She had other things on her mind now. She was, she realized, very lonely. She missed Ellen's calming, constant presence. She realized with some surprise that she had taken Ellen for granted all these years, content in the knowledge that she could always count on Ellen to be there. To do her bidding. To run her household. To keep her company.

Here in the Lost City Ellen had her own private quarters and as much as it hurt Alexandra to admit it, it was obvious that her only niece chose to spend time with others rather than with her aged aunt. Ellen had taken up with the Indian woman who tended O'Mara and the two of them seemed as close as sisters. Alexandra couldn't help being a bit envious of their friendship.

Her forehead knitted as she pondered her situation.

Perhaps it was her own fault that Ellen stayed away from her. Admittedly, she had been demanding with Ellen, had expected a great deal of her, had never encouraged her to have a life of her own. She had been unforgivably selfish, preferring to have Ellen there at her beck and call, never really considering how Ellen might have felt.

Alexandra sighed wearily, plagued by unfamiliar twinges of guilt. She shook her head and allowed her thoughts, as they had quite often of late, to return to the precious little boy back down in the Navajo village. The impudent child who had called her "old." With a smile of pleasure, Alexandra fondly recalled the way the tiny boy named Spear had climbed up onto her lap and snuggled close as if she were his beloved grandmother.

Alexandra's aging heart contracted at the pleasant memory.

Her smile began to fade as she considered Spear's bleak future. It was evident that life on the huge Navajo reservation was far from easy. The people seemed happy, but they were poor and underfed. There were no schools where the children could learn or hospitals where the sick could be healed. The little children like Spear would spend their lives as their parents and grandparents before them, futilely fighting hunger and cold and hopelessness.

Sad, so very sad.

A loud rap on the door abruptly snapped Alexandra out of her reverie. She hurried to answer it, thinking it would be Ellen.

A smiling Padjan stood in the portal. "Good morning, Alexandra," he said cheerfully. "Natan is watching Summer Dawn. Would you like to come along with me on an outing? There's a special place I want to show you."

Eager for company, Alexandra didn't need her arm to be twisted. "Let me get my cane," she said with enthusiasm.

The two walked in and out of morning shadows until finally, outside of the village, they stood on the slickrock in the full sunlight.

"This is the special place?" Alexandra asked as she looked around, seeing nothing particularly special about it.

"No, we're not quite there yet. You will have to climb a little to reach it, think you can manage?"

"What exactly is *it?*"

"A kiva," he said solemnly. "A sacred ceremonial place in which no white person has ever been allowed to enter."

"And you're taking me there?" Alexandra said, puzzled. "Why?"

"Come," he replied and guided her directly upward as he carefully searched the canyon's rocky face, hunting for that certain alcove that contained the kiva.

Just then, a raven flew out of the rocks above.

"Ah, yes, there it is!" said Padjan.

The pair began to climb to where the raven flew. Impatient to see this secret Anasazi chamber, Alexandra, on her hands and knees the last part of the way, crawled through the sandstone scree.

Finally, breathless, she sighed with relief when she heard Padjan say, "We're here."

He helped her to her feet and Alexandra stood, leaning on her cane, gaping in wonder. They had entered an open-sided hallway of stone. Pink stone. There were figures with broad shoulders and wild eyes staring at them from inside the rock. Petroglyphs. Animals with bear bodies and deer heads danced on the overhang.

Walls made of dry-laid stone divided the ledge. No mortar had been used, just the very careful placement of stone against stone. Inside this ancient dwelling, slabs of sandstone framed the entrance to the kiva, which appeared as a dark square on the stone floor.

A juniper ladder with rungs of willow led down to the mysterious underworld.

"Can you climb down the ladder?" Padjan asked.

As curious as a child, Alexandra bobbed her head. "Yes, I can." And then, laying her cane aside, proved it.

Clinging to the ladder, she soon reached the bottom. She stood there unmoving in the kiva that was round like the earth. Hidden in the earth. It took a few minutes for her eyes to adjust. Then she looked around at the logs and pilasters. Walls bricked, then plastered, created the red circumference of the sacred ceremonial chamber. Four shelves were cut into the walls. Each was lined with juniper and berries.

Two full moons, one white and one green, faced each other on the east and west walls. A green serpent moved on the north wall, west to east, connecting the circle.

Neither Padjan nor Alexandra spoke much. Each was lost in his own thoughts. An angle of light poured through the hole in the ceiling. They quietly sat down on the floor to meditate and to allow the hallowed place to work its magic.

There was a hearth in the center of the kiva and a smoke vent. But both Alexandra and Padjan were focused on the *sipapu*—the small hole in the floor that, according to Padjan, symbolized the opening through which mankind entered the world.

The two sat in the kiva for a full half hour. Padjan with his eyes closed, his thoughts on the spirit world above and on the sick Summer Dawn back down in the city.

Alexandra, eyes wide open, stared at her sacred surroundings, let her thoughts flow free and soon felt a great measure of peace washing over her.

It was while she sat there in the ancient kiva that the idea first came to her. Padjan had said that mankind entered the world through the *sipapu.* Well, she didn't know about that, but she did know how she could help some of mankind with their struggles. And she realized, with delight, that for the first time in her life, she wanted to help someone other than herself. It felt very good.

Why hadn't she thought of it before? It was the thing to do and no doubt about it. A wonderful sense of well-being warmly enveloping her, Alexandra began to smile as she considered her great idea. It quickly became concrete.

Brimming over with excitement, Alexandra whispered, "Padjan, may I speak in this ceremonial kiva?"

His eyes opened and he slowly returned from that far-off place where he had been. "You may, if it is important."

"Oh, it is, it is!" she assured him and then excitedly told him exactly what she intended to do.

Alexandra Landseer spoke and Padjan listened with great interest, then smiled happily, his ebony eyes twinkling with pleasure before he said, "Look into your silver-handled mirror when you get back, Alexandra."

# *Thirty-One*

For the next full week Ellen and Tallas spent each long, hot afternoon painstakingly weaving sunbursts, stars and intricate geometric patterns on the white dress, Tallas working on the skirt, Ellen on the blouse. They labored in Ricky's quarters, each clucking over him and chattering companionably. Ricky enjoyed the afternoons almost as much as the women.

His convalescence had been so pleasant he was almost reluctant to get well. The hours Tallas had spent patiently ministering to him had been pure heaven. No one had ever cared for him the way she had. The amazing Anasazi woman was not only physically beautiful, she was beautiful inside as well, the kindest, the sweetest, the most thoughtful woman he'd ever known. The sight of her perfect face, the gentle touch of her hands, the pleasing sound of her voice, all gave him unmeasured pleasure.

He was, he knew, falling in love with Tallas, but he was afraid to tell her, afraid she might be offended, might stop coming to stay with him. The risk was too great. He couldn't reveal his love for her. He would have to content himself with having her in his life for however long it lasted. And when he left the Lost

City, he would take the sweet memories of her with him.

These were Ricky's thoughts as he drifted toward slumber on a hot, still afternoon.

The last sound he heard was Tallas saying, "Can you believe it? We're finished, Ellen. The dress is finally finished!"

Ellen nodded and admired the lovely white blouse and skirt with its intricate woven designs edging the low-cut bodice and the full skirt's hem. While she carefully examined the garment, Tallas rose, went across the room and came back carrying a pair of delicately woven sandals. She held them out to Ellen.

"To go with the dress," she explained.

Ellen took the sandals and said, "The sandals, the dress—they're absolutely beautiful. Thank you so much."

"You're very welcome," said Tallas.

She reached out, took both the sandals and dress from Ellen and laid them aside. Then, without asking permission, she took the pins from Ellen's knotted-up hair and said, "I think it's time you had a magical shampoo."

Ellen laughed. "What exactly is a magical shampoo?"

"I'll show you," said Tallas, turning away. Shortly she was back. She carried a round earthen pan and a large matching pitcher, both of which she placed on the stone floor. "Take off your blouse," she instructed.

Ellen glanced at Ricky, saw that he had fallen

asleep and complied. Tallas poured from the pitcher and Ellen saw that the water was a deep indigo hue. She looked up at Tallas. Tallas nodded. Together they laughed.

On her knees, Ellen leaned over and dunked her head into the pan of blue water. When her hair was fully saturated, Tallas poured a few drops of home-made liquid soap on Ellen's scalp and began to scrub, her long nails almost punishing in their vigorous scouring.

When the shampoo was completed and all the soap had been rinsed away, Tallas towel-dried Ellen's long chestnut tresses. When she took the towel away, Ellen immediately started twisting the clean hair into the usual knot at the back of her head.

Tallas said, "Ellen, have you ever considered wearing your hair down?"

Ellen made a face. "This horrible hair? Not on your life. I'm not fortunate like you, Tallas. Your hair is thick and beautiful, while mine..." She shrugged slender shoulders.

Tallas said, "When you leave, you are going home to try on the new dress and sandals, aren't you?"

Ellen smiled. "You know I am."

"I thought so," Tallas said. "When you get the dress on, let your hair down and take a good long look at yourself in your aunt's hand mirror."

"I will," said Ellen, having no intention of doing any such thing. She put on her blouse and rose to her feet. She snagged the sandals with her fingers, placed the white dress over her arm and said, "Thank you so much for everything. You're the best friend I've ever had.''

Pleased, Tallas said, "Promise me one thing, my friend."

"Name it."

"After you have all left the Lost City," she said, and her voice seemed to fracture slightly, "look after my...look after Ricky."

The two women stood facing each other. Ellen saw the pain in Tallas's dark eyes and realized that the beautiful Anasazi was in love with Ricky.

"Oh, Tallas," she said, reaching out to touch her shoulder. "I had no idea."

"Nor does he, and he must never know," Tallas said. "Now go along, I'm feeling drowsy. I think I'll lie down and rest until Ricky awakens."

Ellen nodded, hugged her friend and left.

She was in no hurry to get back to her private quarters. While Tallas supposed that she couldn't wait to get home and try on the dress, Ellen was in no hurry to do so. She knew in her heart there would never be a special occasion to which she would wear the stunning white dress.

But she hadn't told this to Tallas. She wouldn't dare tell her kind, good friend that the lovely dress on which she had labored so many hours would very likely never be worn.

Ellen reached her apartment. She went inside, carefully laid out the dress and sandals on the bed. She turned away, wandered aimlessly around the hot, still room. Restless, bored, she decided she'd look in on her aunt. She felt guilty that she had spent so little time with Alexandra since arriving in the Lost City. At the same time, she dreaded the visit. She knew she'd have to hear her aunt's bitter complaints that the Magic Waters had not altered her appearance.

When Ellen stepped inside her aunt's roomy dwelling, she was glad to see that Padjan was there. And she was surprised. Alexandra wasn't chastising Padjan because she was not yet young. The two seemed to be relaxed and companionable, each enjoying the other's company. Alexandra, especially, appeared to be in an uncommonly good mood.

Both Alexandra and Padjan warmly welcomed her, and Ellen, greeting the two, gaped at her aunt in shocked surprise. Alexandra was smiling easily, her eyes glowing with an inner warmth. Such a rarity. Ellen could count on her fingers the times she'd seen her irascible aunt look so pleased with the world. And what a difference it made in her appearance.

"Aunt Alexandra," Ellen said, truly astonished, "I do believe the Magic Waters are working. You look younger!"

Alexandra laughed merrily and further shocked her niece by saying, "Not really, dear, but I feel younger and that's what matters. Sit down, Ellen, and visit with us. I've missed you."

Ellen sat down, turned to Padjan and inquired, "How is Summer Dawn today?"

His eyes clouded and he shook his head. "Not well. I am afraid that she—" his words trailed away and he swallowed hard.

"I'm so sorry," said Ellen.

He brightened a little and said, "But at least she is still with us."

"I'll drop by to see her tomorrow."

"Summer Dawn would like that," he said. "Alexandra visited her this morning."

Again Ellen was flabbergasted. Her Aunt Alexandra visiting the sick old Indian woman? Would wonders never cease? Quietly studying her aunt, Ellen wondered what had happened, what was going on.

"…and so I'm genuinely worried about him." Padjan was speaking.

"Who?" Ellen asked, turning her full attention on Padjan. "Sorry, my mind was wandering and I—"

"Mister Corey," said Padjan. "He's not the man I have known lo these many years. He has always been a loner, but I don't know, he's…" Padjan's words trailed away.

"What are you talking about?" asked Ellen. "Why are you worried about him?"

"Something's wrong," said Padjan. "He seems so melancholy, so…lonely."

"Oh, really?" Ellen said sarcastically, a smug expression on her face. "Perhaps the poor man misses his beautiful wife. Maybe he should send for her."

"Wife?" Padjan said, staring at Ellen. "Mister Corey has no wife."

"Oh yes he does," Ellen quickly corrected him. "When we were in Grand Junction, Colonel Lord told us that Mister Corey is married to a beautiful southern aristocrat."

Padjan sighed heavily. "Obviously, the good Colonel has been out of touch for some time."

"What are you saying?" asked Ellen, her well-arched eyebrows lifting.

"It is true that long ago Mister Corey was once wed," Padjan replied. "The marriage ended a decade ago."

Stunned, Ellen was speechless for a long moment. Then, struggling to keep the excitement from her voice, said, "You mean, he's not...he isn't...?"

"His wife divorced him," said Padjan. "As soon as she was free, she sailed to Europe and within a year she was wed to a titled nobleman."

Ellen's eyes were wide, her lips were open and her heart was beating wildly in her chest. "Are you sure about this, Padjan? Mister Corey is not...he isn't still married?" She was already rising to her feet.

"He is *not* a married man and this I know for certain," stated Padjan. "You see, when Summer Dawn and I—"

"I must go," Ellen said, interrupting.

"Why are you so interested in Mister Corey's marital status?" Alexandra asked, seeing the high color in her niece's cheeks. "Does this man mean something to you?"

Ellen gave no reply, but started for the door. She stopped abruptly, turned back and asked, "Aunt Alexandra, may I borrow your hand mirror?"

"Yes, you know where it is. Take it. But where are you going? Has this something to do with Mister Corey?"

Ellen didn't hesitate to admit it. "It has everything to do with Mister Corey!"

"Now, Ellen, I wouldn't go looking for..." Alexandra began, but Padjan silenced her with a sharp look.

"Well, I would!" said a happy Ellen and left them both staring after her.

The mirror gripped tightly in her hand, Ellen flew to her quarters as if she had wings on her feet. As soon as she was inside, she laid the mirror down and began stripping off her clothes. She poured water from a decorative jug into a pan and sponged her warm flesh until it was as clean as her freshly shampooed hair.

Hurriedly donning fresh underwear, she then drew on the beautiful white blouse and matching skirt. She sat down and put on the delicate sandals, then stood and reached for the mirror.

She looked at herself appraisingly and remembered what Tallas had said. *When you try on the dress, let your hair down and take a look at yourself.* Ellen laid the mirror aside, reached up and took the pins from her hair.

The tresses spilled down around her shoulders. She took up her hairbrush and pulled it vigorously through the long locks several times. When she again looked into the mirror, she could hardly believe it was really her, the shy, stuffy, plain Ellen Cornelius smiling back.

The woman in the mirror was...dare she think...pretty! Sparkling green eyes, rosy cheeks, full lips and shimmering chestnut hair. And, incredibly, there was a subtle hint of playful sensuality about her. The kind of innate allure that attracted men. She wasn't imagining it. She actually was an attractive, enticing woman.

Ellen smiled at her pleasing reflection, held the mirror out as far away as possible and admired the beautiful dress she wore. It fit her perfectly. She gave the right side of the low-cut bodice a gentle tug. It fell over her shoulder and slipped down her arm. She liked the effect. It was saucy and seductive. And so was she.

She raised the mirror back up to her face, bit her lips to give them more color and took a deep, slow breath, purposely pressing her breasts against the dress's gathered bodice.

She laid the mirror aside and headed for the door.

Ellen hesitated, nervously swept her hair back over her shoulders and smoothed the gathers of her full white skirts.

And very nearly lost her nerve. She had never done anything like this. She'd never set out to charm and captivate a man. She had no idea how to go about it. She had never learned how to flirt and play the coquette. She wasn't sure she was capable of enchanting any man, much less this one.

Ellen took a calming breath and reminded herself that she was pretty. She smiled and confidently stepped out into the brilliant afternoon sun shining down on the Lost City.

# Thirty-Two

On this placid, sunny afternoon, a pensive Mister Corey rode horseback alone above the city, drinking in the beauty of his surroundings. The isolation suited his somber mood—isolation that was suddenly broken by the sound of hoofbeats.

Startled, he looked up in time to see Ellen ride quickly by him—laughing delightedly. As she passed him, she waved gaily. Mister Corey's face automatically broke into a grin and, compelled to follow her, he wheeled the gray stallion around and gave chase.

He followed in determined pursuit, feeling as if he *had* to catch her, to be with her. But despite closing in on Ellen, she was lost from sight when she disappeared behind a bend in the soaring sandstone rocks.

He reined the stallion around in a circle several times, puzzled, squinting in the strong sunlight, unable to find her. Frowning now, finally giving up, he began to wonder if he had simply imagined seeing her. Had it just been an illusion?

And then the silence was broken by the sound of her enchanting laughter. He looked anxiously around and finally spotted her.

High on a summit of the rocky ramparts, Ellen, astride a big roan mare was waving and laughing. But the minute she caught his attention, she turned her horse away and again disappeared.

Intensely intrigued, Mister Corey went after her, determined to catch her. When finally he reached her, his heart skipped several beats.

Dismounted now, she was sitting on a huge flat rock. A pair of sandals rested beside her. She was barefoot. She wore an incredibly feminine white dress with colorful patterns of sunbursts and stars and geometric designs decorating the borders of the bodice and hem. One side of the blouse had fallen down her arm, exposing the pleasing roundness of her shoulder. She had one knee raised, a forearm resting atop it, giving him a provocative glimpse of her pale thigh beneath the full skirts of the dress.

Her hair, long and glistening, was loose and flying wildly about in the soft summer wind. An openly brazen smile was on her lips and her emerald eyes were dancing with mischief.

She was utterly irresistible.

Mister Corey dropped the leather reins, dismounted and approached her. His heart now hammering in his chest, he paused for a long uncertain moment, gazing at her.

His first base urge was to go directly to her and take her without a word or a kiss.

His better self checked the animalistic urge.

It was then that Mister Corey realized fully, with no small degree of surprise, that he now wanted more than just this lovely woman's body. He wanted her pure heart as well.

He smiled and put out his hand to Ellen. Laughing, she took it and allowed him to draw her to her feet. Mister Corey stopped smiling. Ellen stopped laughing. Her lovely face was turned up to his. He had the ardent desire to kiss her. Their gazes locked, he saw a similar impulse in her.

They looked into each other's eyes for several tension-filled seconds. Then Mister Corey released her and stepped back. Ellen followed him, hypnotized.

He said, his voice rough, "I shouldn't have followed you."

"I meant for you to follow me," she told him, looking him straight in the eye with a fearless sort of self-assurance.

"You did?"

"I did," she said as she spread her hand across his chest. "I know about you now. Padjan told me about your wife."

"My wife? I have no wife, Ellen."

"I know, that's what he told me." She smiled at him.

Twin pinpoints of light appeared in Mister Corey's dark eyes and he smiled back at her, his harshly planed face softening. "All this time you thought that I was married?" She nodded. "Ah, Ellen, I've been divorced for more than nine years. My wife left me, married another man."

Ellen laughed girlishly and said, "Then she was a fool and you're better off without her."

"And you are better off without me," he said, although he was pleased with her statement. Soberly, he added, "Ellen, I owe you an apology. Many apologies. I'm genuinely sorry for the way I've treated you, mistreated you really. I should never have taken advantage of you, never have made love to you. It was wrong and—"

"Shh." She put fingers over his lips. "No, it wasn't, because I wanted it. I wanted you. I still do." She searched the depths of his eyes when she added, "But you've stopped wanting me."

"No, no I haven't," he said, gently moving her hand from his face. "That's not it. I want you more than ever."

"Then why...?"

"Because I came to genuinely care for you, Ellen," he said truthfully. "And I started feeling guilty about what I had done to you."

"You stopped making love to me because you care for me?"

"Yes."

"Men are fools," Ellen declared.

"It's the truth, I swear it," he said. "Listen to me, Ellen, you judged me correctly from the beginning. You had my number from the first night you saw me at the street carnival in London. Everything you have accused me of is true. All of it. I have nothing to offer you. I'm a drifter with a tarnished past and absolutely no future."

"I don't care," she stated simply.

"Of course you care," he corrected her. "And you

should care. I'd give anything if I could right the wrongs I've done you, but I can't. You shouldn't be here with me now, I can only hurt and disappoint you." He swallowed hard and said, "There's still time for you to run. To turn your back on me. That's exactly what you should do. Go, Ellen. Go while you have the chance. For your own good, stay away from me."

Ellen shook her head, setting her unbound hair to dancing. "No, I will not go. I will not stay away from you. I don't care what you've done, I don't want to leave you. We no longer reside in that harsh, judgmental world below." She moved a step closer, put her arms around his trim waist. "We are together here in this remote city where nothing and no one can touch us. Neither our pasts nor our future in the world below make any difference here." Realizing that Summer Dawn was dying and that the day would soon come when they would have to go back, Ellen said with touching honesty, "Mister Corey, I don't ask for undying devotion for an eternity. But for as long as we are here in the Lost City, I want to be with you."

He finally smiled, lifted his hands and tenderly cupped her upturned face. "I want the same thing, sweetheart. Oh, God, I've been such a cold, cruel bastard. I've said and done such terrible things to you. I'm so sorry." His eyes clouded with regret.

"We start anew today. Right now, this minute," she said brightly. "A new beginning for us both. I don't want to know about your past. Tell me nothing, please. The present is all I care about. The present here with you. I want to forget the past—yours and mine—and enjoy the time we have left here.''

''Then that's what we will do,'' he assured her. ''But I promise I'll try and make up for the injustices I've done you.'' He smiled then and told her, ''From this moment forward, Ellen Cornelius, I'll treat you the way you should be treated.'' He drew her closer into his embrace and said, ''If you'll let me, I'll show you just how sweet love can be.''

At hearing the word *love* on his lips, Ellen's heart swelled with happiness. ''Oh, Steve,'' she sighed, ''I can't wait.''

''And I can't wait to show you,'' he said as his dark head began to lower. When his lips were only an inch from hers, he asked, ''More than anything in this world, I want to kiss you. But only if you want me to.'' His breath was warm on her face.

''I've never wanted anything more,'' she said.

He kissed her.

It was as if they had never kissed before. His lips were soft and gentle on hers, totally undemanding, brushing lightly back and forth. The kiss lasted for only a few short seconds, but a dazzled Ellen knew that she would remember the kiss forever.

A romantic courtship had begun.

Feeling very much like a gallant young suitor with his first real sweetheart, Steve Corey skillfully, carefully drew Ellen into the magical kind of man-woman relationship he sensed was foreign to her.

He no longer rushed her. No longer took advantage of her. Made no attempt to force his will on her. Was no longer the amoral seducer.

Ellen loved it.

She blossomed like a flower in the springtime. No man had ever before held her hand, gazed into her eyes and stroked her hair as he spoke to her in low, gentle tones.

No beau had ever kissed her with such heart-stopping tenderness. No lover had ever drawn her gently into his strong arms and held her in his protective embrace.

So this was what it was like? This dizzy, world-off-its-axis feeling. She had fallen in love with this paradoxical man who had changed so completely.

Gone was the callous scamp whose overpowering sexuality and reckless lovemaking had caused her such pain and guilt. In his place was a caring, gentle man who was as conscious of her fragile heart as he was of her yielding body.

Glorious sunlit days went by with the two spending as much time together as possible. They took long walks in the village. They went for horseback rides. They had picnics high up in the canyons. They sat in front of Ellen's quarters at night and counted the stars in the heavens.

Steve was the thoughtful suitor, always seeking permission before he called on Ellen. He picked wildflowers and presented them to her. He told her repeatedly how beautiful she was and he treated her with devotion and respect. He held his burning passion in constant check, resolved to wait until the time was right.

Ellen had never been half so happy in her life.

And it showed.

Tallas, Padjan, Ricky and even Alexandra commented on how youthful and pretty she looked of late. Padjan had even asked if she'd been slipping up to the Magic Waters.

Wondering at her aunt's unusual lack of probing curiosity and unfailing censure, Ellen made no reply to these casual inquiries. Just smiled enigmatically and sighed with contentment. And dreamed of the hour when she and her beloved would finally come together completely.

Since this new beginning, Steve had made no real attempt to make love to her. He had held her in his arms, murmured exciting words of desire, kissed her until she was weak and trembling, but it had gone no further. Which made her want him all the more. There were times when she felt she could stand it no longer. Her skin felt as if it was on fire and her whole body yearned to be conquered by his.

When he kissed her good-night and left her, she would lie awake for hours longing for him, craving what he alone could give her. Here in this high mountain redoubt, the summer days were blistering hot, but at sunset the temperature dropped and the nights were pleasantly cool.

Not so for Ellen.

She was burning up. She lay hot and miserable in her bed each night, the flames of desire licking at her sensitive flesh, the agony of unsatisfied lust over-whelming her. She suffered from her growing obses-sion, yet at the same time enjoyed the delay, the con-stantly building anticipation.

The waiting was sweet torture.

Counting the minutes, the hours until at last that longed-for release was somehow exciting. So incred-ibly exciting she hoped they could hold out for weeks.

And felt as if she couldn't possibly make it for one more hour.

Midnight.

One more night without sleeping.

Steve, tossing, turning, longing to hold Ellen in his arms, knew exactly what she was feeling because he was feeling it, too. He had carefully planned it that way. He wanted her to be totally secure in his genuine adoration before they made love.

But it wasn't easy for him to keep his hands off her. It seemed that every day she got a little prettier, a little sweeter, a lot harder to resist. She had become a masterful flirt and knew how to tease and tempt him. It was as if she'd become the world's most skilled courtesan.

The many hours they spent together were a mixture of lighthearted fun and unfulfilled passion. They'd be laughing at something and then all at once they'd be in each other's arms, kissing hungrily.

It was the first time in his life he had ever waited. He had always bedded a woman as soon as he wanted her, never seeing the reason to postpone the inevita-

ble. But this time it was different. Love had made it
so. When next he made love to Ellen, he wanted it to
be as perfect as possible. He wanted to know that he
had won her total and lasting trust. He wanted to
make sure that she knew just how much he loved her.

He would know when the time was right.

Until then, he would suffer in silence. And he did
suffer. It got more difficult each night to leave her, to
go alone to his quarters. He wanted her with him,
wanted to have her lying beside him when the moon
climbed into the night sky. He wanted to feel her flesh
pressed against his own. He wanted to touch her and
excite her and make her his own.

So Steve lay restless and perspiring on his bed,
thinking of Ellen. Over and over he envisioned her
silently slipping into his room in the darkness to tell
him she couldn't stand to spend another moment out
of his arms. He could almost see her undressing in
the shadows before walking naked and enticing to his
bed. He could almost hear her softly whisper, "Let's
make love, Steve."

# Thirty-Three

The sun had not yet risen when Tallas stepped quietly into Ricky's private quarters. She hadn't told him, but today was to be her last day tending him. He was now completely recovered and no longer needed her care.

He no longer needed her.

Which made Tallas very sad.

She was, of course, glad that he was no longer suffering, but she was going to miss spending her days with him. She had come to love him dearly and the prospect of not being with him made her incredibly unhappy.

She knew that soon he and the others would be leaving the Lost City and that she would never see Ricky again. She knew that she would spend the rest of her life missing him.

Squinting in the deep shadows as she tiptoed across the silent room, the wistful Anasazi woman began to smile with pleasure as she gazed fondly on the dear man asleep on his pallet.

His muscular arms were thrown up over his head and his dark hair was badly tousled. His head was turned to the side, his nose and mouth buried in the pillow. He was smiling in his slumber and that made Tallas's smile broaden. He looked like a little boy who was having a wonderful dream. She hoped that he was.

Longing to reach out and touch Ricky, not daring to do so, Tallas sank to her knees beside him and contented herself by just watching him. She studied everything about him. From the way his dark eyebrows grew into devilish arches to the shape of his arrogant nose. His lips, slightly open, white teeth gleaming, were full and very soft-looking. She touched her own lips as she looked at his and wondered how it would feel to kiss him.

The minute the thought passed through her mind, Tallas scolded herself. She was being foolish and she was far too old and wise to be thinking of such silly things as kissing and...

Ricky's eyes suddenly opened and he was looking at her. He smiled, reached out and laid a hand on her forearm.

He said, his voice heavy with sleep, "I had the most wonderful dream."

She smiled back at him. "Tell me about it."

His hand slid down her arm, captured her slender fingers and held them in a gentle grip. "I dreamed that you came here this morning to tell me that you love me and can't live without me."

Tallas's face quickly reddened. Trying to make light of it, she said, "Dreams are strange and—"

"There was nothing strange about this dream," he replied. "It was beautiful. So beautiful." He paused, squeezed her hand and said, "I want my dream to come true. I want you to love me, Tallas."

Caught off guard, Tallas didn't know what to do or say. She swallowed hard and finally said, attempting to laugh, "Dreams are just that, Ricky. Dreams. They don't come true."

Continuing to hold her hand, Ricky rolled up into a sitting position to face her. "This dream *can* come true," he said softly. "You can make it come true. It's up to you. I love you, darling." He shook his head as if mystified and admitted, "I never thought I'd fall in love. Ask Ellen, she'll tell you about me. I've never loved just one woman, but I love you. I love you and no other. I'm in love with you, Tallas."

Tallas tried to calm the racing of her heart as she reasoned, "No, Ricky, you don't love me. You've become dependent on me. That's very different. It's common for someone who has been badly hurt or very sick to grow close to the one who takes care of him."

Ricky dropped Tallas's hand and gently cupped her shoulders. "If I had been totally able-bodied when we met, I would have still fallen in love with you."

Tallas bowed her head, exhaled heavily. "Ricky, please, don't…"

"Why not?" he asked. "Look at me and tell me why I can't love you."

Tallas slowly raised her eyes to meet his. "Ricky, shall I tell you how old I am?"

"No," he was quick to reply. "I don't care how old you are. I don't want to know."

"But you should know. I'm much older than you and—"

"It makes no difference to me," he assured her. "You're a vibrant, beautiful woman."

She tried again. "Ricky, you do know, don't you, the ancient laws are firm. I can never leave the Lost City."

"I can stay here with you."

Her lips parted and her eyes widened with surprise and happiness. "You'd do that? You'd stay here when the others leave?"

"I would," he said. "I will."

"But you'd be lonely, you'd miss your friends."

"Never. You're all I need. Yours is the face I want to see every morning and every night for the rest of my life."

Tears sprang to Tallas's eyes and she said, "Ricky, I want you to be happy and I..."

"Well, darlin', you're the only one who can make me happy," he said, then smiled and added, "You can make me very happy right now, Tallas."

"How?" she asked, her face radiant.

"There are two things I want and the first one is for you to say you love me."

Tallas laid her hand on his cheek. "I love you, Ricky. I will love you for as long as I live. And the second?"

He drew her hand to his lips, kissed the warm palm and said, "Make love to me as the sun rises this morning and then again tonight as it sets."

"My love," she murmured, rose to her feet, lifted her dress up over her head and dropped it to the floor.

Naked, she stood above, allowing him the opportunity to look at her. She didn't need to ask if she pleased him. His breath was labored and the expression on his face was one of awe and adoration. He fell over onto his back and continued to admire her.

Finally he raised a trembling hand and said, "Come here to me and promise you'll never go away."

Tallas lay down beside him. "I promise."

Ellen was cheerfully astounded by her aunt's recent uncharacteristic behavior. For the past two weeks, Alexandra had not said an unkind word to her. Which was shocking because it was clear her aunt knew everything that was going on. Alexandra, like everyone else in the Lost City, was fully aware that Ellen and Steve were spending a great deal of time together.

Ellen had expected to receive the full brunt of Alexandra's wrath once her aunt found out about the relationship with Steve. She had been ready for the onslaught. Loaded for bear. She had rehearsed in her mind exactly how it would go, what she would say.

She imagined that Alexandra would begin by stating the obvious, "Ellen, I've noticed that since we've been here in the Lost City you have been spending a great deal of your time with Mister Corey."

"Guilty as charged!" Ellen intended to firmly reply.

And her aunt would frown and warn, "I don't think it's wise for you to…"

"I don't care if it's wise or not," would be Ellen's jabbing rejoinder.

"How can you say such a foolish thing?" an angry Alexandra would demand to know. "Don't you care about propriety? Have you no consideration for your son? And what about me?"

"What about you?" Ellen would bite out the words as she crossed her arms over her chest.

"You know I don't approve of Mister Corey!"

"Really? Well, please correct me if I'm wrong. Aren't you the one who hired him to bring us here?"

"Well, yes, but I never intended for my own niece to…to…fraternize with his sort. I want you to stay away from him. Tell me you will."

"I will do no such thing," Ellen could hear herself declare. "Let me get this straight, you are concerned that Steve might hurt me? Is that it?"

"Why, yes, I don't want to see you hurt and—"

"Since when have you been sensitive to my feelings? Or to anyone else's?"

"I suppose I deserve that, but—"

"No buts, Aunt Alexandra. Think what you like, I don't care. As for Christopher, he wants me to be happy. And I am happy. For the first time in my life I know exactly what I want and I'm reaching out and taking it. And I don't give a tinker's damn whether you approve or if I'm being silly and irresponsible. I don't even care if I get hurt in the end. It wouldn't be the first time and no one should know that better than you! You haven't exactly shown me any affection all these years, now, have you?''

But nothing of the kind ever happened. The unpleasant confrontation never took place.

Alexandra never said a malicious word to Ellen about Steve. In fact, her aunt was beginning to act like a caring human being.

It was downright puzzling.

Ellen had noticed that Alexandra no longer ordered everyone about as if they were her own personal slaves. She no longer stuck her nose into other people's business and gave her opinion whether it was wanted or not. She no longer sat around with an ugly frown frozen on her face.

She had changed so much, Ellen hardly recognized her aunt. The new Alexandra was pleasant and thoughtful and she openly complimented Ellen, commenting on how youthful and lovely Ellen looked.

It was a first.

Alexandra Landseer had *never* before told her niece that she was attractive.

Ellen began to like this stranger, this kind elderly woman who smiled easily, rarely complained and talked often and with fondness about Spear, the little boy they'd met in the Navajo village.

''Isn't Spear the most adorable child?'' Alexandra said late one afternoon as she and Ellen sat visiting.

''He certainly is,'' Ellen said, smiling.

Alexandra sighed. ''I worry about him though. Spear and all the other sweet little children on that big, barren reservation.''

"I know," Ellen agreed. "Theirs is not an easy life."

"No. No, it isn't," Alexandra mused, then decided that this was the perfect opportunity to tell Ellen of her plans and see if her niece would approve. "Ellen, I've been thinking…"

Ellen abruptly rose, her eyes suddenly widening, a flushed look on her face. "Tell me later, Auntie," she managed to say and hurried toward the door.

"Where are you going, dear?" Alexandra was baffled. "Is something wrong? What is it, Ellen?"

At the door, Ellen turned and smiled. "Nothing's wrong. It's time, that's all."

"Time? Time for what? It's not even four o'clock yet."

But Ellen was already gone.

# *Thirty-Four*

His pulse suddenly began to hammer and Steve knew instinctively that the time was right.

This was the afternoon.

He knew it as well as he knew his own name. He knew that neither he nor Ellen could, would wait another day. So as the hour of four o'clock rapidly approached, he lathered his face and shaved. Then shaved again. He'd had a cold, invigorating bath high up in the canyon not an hour ago.

He donned fresh clothes and brushed his hair with his fingers. He grabbed the blanket off his bed, folded it, tossed it over his arm and crossed hurriedly to the door.

Just before he stepped outside, he paused, snapped his fingers, grinned and turned back. He went directly to his saddle bags, which were stored on a low shelf by the bed. From the leather bags, he took a brown paper sack with the words Wagonwheel Emporium, Denver, Colorado, printed across it. He opened the bag, peered inside at the contents and nodded, pleased with himself.

Steve closed the sack, tucked it into the crook of his arm and, whistling, left his quarters. He didn't go for a horse. He decided he'd rather walk. It would be quicker. Once he was out of the village and started climbing the canyon wall, it was less than a mile to the top of Enchanted Mesa. He could be there in fifteen minutes.

As he climbed, he wondered if Ellen might already be there, waiting for him. Would she, like he, know instinctively that this was the day they would finally make love. He was counting on it. He was counting on her.

The possibility that she was already there, waiting for him, made him climb faster.

Relaxed, half-lethargic, Ellen had been visiting with her aunt when all at once her pulse had begun to pound. Immediately she had known the reason.

The time had come.

Steve was waiting for her up on Enchanted Mesa. She knew he was. There was no doubt in her mind.

Now as she hurried to get ready for the rendezvous, she hummed happily. The treasured dress was freshly laundered and ready for her to put on. Thank goodness she had bathed and shampooed her hair not an hour ago.

Anxiously Ellen dressed and strapped on her sandals. She hurried to the door, but stopped there. She turned back, took some fresh wildflowers from a pottery vase and carefully wove them into her unbound hair. Satisfied with her appearance, she left.

Outside, she hurried through the village.

When she began to climb the canyon wall to the secluded Enchanted Mesa, she wondered if Steve was already there, waiting for her. The probability made her climb faster.

She looked up, but couldn't see the mesa's summit. Fully enveloped in white billowy clouds, the lofty flat top was invisible. He was there, she knew he was.

On legs as strong and tireless as a young girl's, Ellen climbed high, high up through the clouds until she reached the level crest of the starkly beautiful Enchanted Mesa.

There on the very summit, Steve stepped out of the cool, enveloping mists and, smiling, wordlessly took Ellen's hand. Entranced, she gazed at him. He was impeccably groomed, freshly shaven and was wearing a snowy-white shirt with snugly fitting dark trousers. Those penetrating mysterious eyes, dark as midnight, looking into hers, were hypnotic.

She would, she knew as they stood there together in the mists, do anything he wanted her to do. Go anywhere he wanted her to go. She knew as well that this hunger, this intense yearning, was more than just physical. This deep feeling for him was a longing of the heart, not just the body.

As she gazed up at him, Steve leisurely caressed her with his eyes. She had let her hair down, literally, and woven flowers into the lush chestnut tresses. The total effect was erotic. She was a lovely, alluring woman, a rare combination of intelligence, emotional depth and sensuality that was hidden beneath a lady-like facade. Every man's dream girl. Incredibly appealing.

He intensely desired her, but the desire was more

than just physical. The profound passion he felt for her was a yearning of the heart, not just the body.

"You'll spend the rest of the evening with me?" he spoke at last.

"I will," she said.

And had an almost frightening response when his lips caressed hers in a kiss.

When he lifted his head, he smiled at her and said, "Want to go exploring?"

"I'd love to," she said, and meant it.

He took her hand in his and told her, "I stumbled upon a secret cave one day that I believe you'll find most interesting."

"Oh? Is it near?"

He inclined his dark head toward the back edge of the mesa. "Across the mesa and down its northern face a few yards."

The mist continued to swirl around them as they crossed the flat tableland to the far side. With Steve holding Ellen's hand and leading the way, they descended the stony slopes and stepped into the bright sunshine. Blinking, they carefully picked their way over scattered boulders until they reached the wide shadowy mouth of a cave.

They had to duck to clear the low entrance. But once inside there was ample room to stand. For a time they stood unmoving, side by side, holding hands, waiting for their vision to adjust to the dimness of the cavern.

When Ellen could see clearly, she abruptly dropped Steve's hand and moved toward a high rock wall that was covered with a large spiral petroglyph. From a crater in the rocks above, a dagger of slanting light sliced through the center of the spiral.

Ellen stared in awe and listened enraptured as Steve explained the carving.

"It's a sun calendar." His voice was low, level. "These calendars mark the solstice and equinox. We are now in the summer solstice."

"Have the calendars been here long?" she asked.

"Yes. They are hundreds of years old. The Anasazi have always used them to time the planting of their crops."

Nodding, Ellen continued to gaze at the giant sun calendar, before finally moving farther into the cave to explore the remaining petroglyphs. To her delight, she also discovered many colorful pictographs.

Fascinated, Ellen carefully examined the wonderfully mysterious paintings, amazed by the talent of those who had created them. In silence she moved along the walls, smiling and admiring the work, until all at once she stopped abruptly, as if she had bumped into the stone wall. Her eyes widened, her hand went to her throat and she stared in stunned disbelief.

A large petroglyph, directly before her, depicted a creature-man with a heavy pack on his back, a flute in his mouth and an erection that was nearly as long as the flute. He seemed to be dancing as he leaned toward the coiled figure of a horned rattlesnake and played an eternal piping.

Ellen gasped, blushed and automatically turned to glance nervously at Steve. He laughed and stepping up directly behind her, wrapped his arms around her.

"He's the god the Indians call Kokopelli. It is said

that Kokopelli would travel from village to village with a heavy sack of corn seed on his back, teaching the people how to plant and nurture the corn. When the crop was planted, he would dance through the fields playing his flute all night and in the morning the corn would have sprouted." His arms tightened around Ellen's slender waist and he said against her fragrant hair, "It was not only the corn seed that got planted during the long desert night."

"Don't tell me, let me guess," said Ellen, her face hot.

He chuckled and continued, "It seems that same morning, most of the young women in the village would find themselves mysteriously pregnant."

"Lord, no wonder," said Ellen, unable to take her eyes off the figure's giant erection. She shivered and said, "Let's go, I think I've seen enough for one afternoon."

Steve laughed again and gave her a gentle squeeze.

Outside, both squinted in the harsh sunlight, then carefully made their way back to the mesa's cloud-encased summit.

Once they'd caught their breaths, Steve said, "I have something for you." The vision of a huge phallus still dancing through her mind, Ellen's well-arched eyebrows lifted skeptically. But he smiled and said, "No, not that. At least not this very minute."

"What then?"

"I bought a present for you."

"A present?" she said, pleasantly surprised. "Something from the village?"

"No. Just wait, you'll see," he said, grinning mischievously as he led her directly to a rock-rimmed spot at the west edge of the mesa's summit.

There a blanket had been spread. Ellen glanced at him, then sat down on the blanket, carefully arranging her skirts as she did so. Steve crouched beside her, gave her a quick kiss and said, "Don't move. I'll be right back."

He left and Ellen watched as he disappeared into the mist. In seconds he was back carrying a brown paper sack. He came down on his knees atop the blanket and said, behaving very much like a young schoolboy, "Now you have to close your eyes so it will be a surprise."

Smiling, Ellen closed her eyes. She heard the faint rustle of paper. Then nothing. Long seconds passed.

Finally, he said, "Open your eyes, sweetheart."

Ellen's eyes opened and immediately widened. Resting on the blanket directly in front of her was the exquisite black porcelain cat she had so admired at the Wagonwheel Emporium back in Denver. Her lips fell open and she was, for a long moment, speechless. She looked at the shimmering cat and she looked at the pleased-with-himself Steve.

Finally reaching out to pick up the delicate figurine, she drew it to her breasts, looked at him with eyes now swimming in tears and asked, "How on earth did you know that I so desperately wanted this beautiful porcelain cat?" She shook her head and added, "I had no money, so I asked Aunt Alexandra to buy it for me. But she refused." A tear slipped down her cheek.

"I know," he said soothingly, raising a hand to

wipe the tear away. "I was there that night in the emporium and saw you admiring the ceramic cat." He smiled and explained, "Since your aunt refused to let you have it, I bought it for you."

"You actually bought this for me? But why? You didn't even like me then and…"

"Maybe I did like you then and didn't know it," he said, shrugging wide shoulders. "I must have, I used my lucky twenty-dollar gold piece to buy the—"

"Oh no, you didn't," she lamented. "The gold piece that your father gave you? Padjan told me how much it meant to you."

"That's the one."

Ellen swallowed hard, clutched the precious treasure and said with appealing honestly, "Well, I just want you to know that I have never received a gift that meant more to me than this one. Thank you, Steve. Thank you so much."

"You're very welcome, Ellen," he said, then really made her heart sing with joy when he added, "When we get back to civilization, I'm going to get you a real live cat. Cats. As many cats as you want."

Ellen laughed delightedly, but admitted, "I'd love to have a house cat, but Aunt Alexandra would never allow it."

He said nothing, just smiled enigmatically, took the ceramic cat and carefully set it aside, and then eased Ellen back onto the blanket. He brushed a kiss to her open lips, then stretched out on his back beside her.

He yawned and told her, "I got very little sleep last night. I couldn't stop thinking about you. Couldn't stop wanting you."

She turned her head, gazed adoringly at him. "I had the same problem."

He slipped a long arm underneath to support her head, drew her close against his long body, kissed her forehead and said, "I believe we've tortured each other long enough, don't you?"

"Yes," she said, and sighed contentedly. "I do."

Again he yawned, then declared, "You're the one to determine exactly when we are to make love, sweetheart." He rolled up onto one shoulder, gazed down at her and said, "Before this day has ended, before the sun we cannot see sets, I want to hear you say, 'Let's make love, Steve.'"

She laid a hand on his arm and promised, "And so you will." Then she smiled seductively and said, "But not just yet. Let's see just how much longer we can wait. Minutes? Hours?"

"Hours?" He groaned and again fell over onto his back, closing his eyes. "You're a cruel woman, Ellen Cornelius."

"Not really," she replied. "I doubt seriously that I can last until sunset."

He laughed with delight and the sound warmed Ellen's heart. She couldn't recall ever hearing him laugh like this before. As if he was genuinely happy. As happy as she.

She raised up onto an elbow. "Do you know that we've never *slept* together."

He cocked an eye open. "Now, darlin', I may not be the stud old Kokopelli is, but I can't believe you'd forget that we—"

"No, not that!" she interrupted and gave him a

playful punch to the belly. "I mean we have never slumbered together, side by side, in the same bed or place."

"No, we never have," he said thoughtfully.

"Shall we try it now? We're both quite tired from the lack of sleep. Why don't we take a restful little nap together?"

"Sounds like a good idea to me," he murmured, exhaling deeply and again closing both eyes.

"It does, doesn't it," she whispered as she snuggled close against him.

His free arm slid possessively across her waist and he drew her head back down on his shoulder.

"Sweet dreams," he said against her temple.

"You, too," she replied with a sigh.

Seconds passed.

Minutes.

Neither could seem to get comfortable. Both squirmed and wiggled and fidgeted. They continued to lie there together, their taut bodies brushing and pressing, their hearts beating as one.

It was no use.

Their need for each was too potent, too powerful.

Steve finally gave up. He opened his eyes and saw that Ellen was looking at him.

"I can't sleep with you lying here in my arms," he said.

"I can't either." She gave him a dazzling smile and then said the words he was longing to hear, "Let's make love, Steve."

# Thirty-Five

"I thought you'd never ask," he said softly, smiling at her. "Ellen, I want you so much. I can't remember ever wanting anyone the way I want you." He looked into her eyes and solemnly told her, "This is not like those other times. This will be the first time we've ever made love, sweetheart."

"I know," she said, gazing at him. "I know and I want to please you, Steve. Teach me how. Show me what to do to make you happy. I'll do anything you want."

"God, you're so sweet. All I want is for you to let me love you the way you should be loved," he said and his handsome face wore an ardent expression, his eyes were shining with a new hot light. "I want to love you so tenderly and completely that once it's over, you'll know no shame, will feel only contentment."

At his stirring words and his expression, Ellen suddenly became frightened by the intensity of her feelings. She wanted him too much. Cared too much. Loved too much.

As if he'd read her thoughts, he said, "Don't be

afraid, Ellen. I've hurt you before, but I never will again, I promise.''

She smiled then, relaxed a little, lifted a hand and placed the tip of her forefinger on the scar going down his right cheek. She gently traced its downward path thinking that when first they'd met she had thought the imperfection gave him a sinister appearance. Not anymore. Now it was simply a part of him and didn't mar his dark good looks. Someday she would ask him how he got the scar.

''As long as your arms are around me,'' she said, ''I won't be afraid.''

Touched, longing to keep her safe and protected in his arms forever, Steve drew her more fully into his close embrace and kissed her softly, lightly. He kept on kissing her over and over again and at the same time he began to deftly undress her before shedding his own clothing.

Ellen was so completely lost in his stirring kisses, she didn't realize what he was doing until suddenly both were naked to the waist, skin against skin. She drew in a quick intake of air as she felt her sensitive nipples brush against the heat and hardness of his chest.

''Feels good, doesn't it?'' he said.

''Yes, oh, yes.''

In seconds the rest of her clothes, and his, seemed to have melted away and they were gloriously naked. At that moment a strong southern breeze quickly dissipated the misty clouds enveloping the level summit of Enchanted Mesa. All at once a fading summer sun washed over their bare bodies, bathing them in an ethereal golden glow.

They weren't concerned by the loss of the cloud cover. A rocky redoubt shielded the mesa's level top and guaranteed privacy and seclusion.

Neither was plagued by modesty. Both knew that they were alone, in no danger of being seen, free to enjoy each other to the fullest. For the first time, the couple was allowed to gaze appraisingly and unhurriedly on the naked form of the other.

Ellen, staring at Steve with a mixture of curiosity and wonder, was certain that a more beautiful man did not exist. His body was sheer perfection. Once, not too long ago, he had been too thin. Not anymore. Somewhere along the way he had gained needed pounds.

The wide shoulders, the deep chest, the corded ribs. The long, muscular arms and legs, the slim hips, the tight buttocks, the flat belly. And, that most masculine part of him, at rest now amidst a swirl of dense raven curls. She blushed as she gazed at it, realizing instinctively that he was very well-endowed. Presently it looked soft and harmless, but she knew how quickly it could change, recalled how huge it could become. She tingled with the sure knowledge that it would soon spring to life and then all that awesome power would throb deep inside her.

If she found him beautiful, the assessment was mutual. Steve Corey gazed on the slender woman beside him and thought her the loveliest creature he'd ever seen. He couldn't believe she was the same person who had been so plain and skinny and shy when they'd met in London.

Here she was, willingly lying naked with him, unashamed and seemingly at total ease. And beautiful. God, she was beautiful. Her lustrous hair swirled around her head on the blanket, shining in the sunlight like a shimmering silken fan. Some of the flowers she'd woven into the tresses had fallen out and rested beside her. A few blossoms still adorned her temples and above her left ear.

She had lovely ivory shoulders and a regal throat. Her breasts, though small, were perfectly shaped, softly rounded and firm. The nipples were small with a tempting wine-colored hue.

She had, he knew, been married and given birth to a child, yet there was an appealing innocence about her body, as if she were a young girl. She was pleasingly long-waisted and long-legged. Her legs were shapely, her ankles small, her knees cutely dimpled. Her delicate ribs showed slightly through her flawless flesh and her stomach was so flat it was almost concave. Between her pale thighs a thick triangle of chestnut curls—pinkened now by the dying sun—protected that most sensitive part of her soft woman's body.

''I'm sorry I'm not prettier,'' Steve heard Ellen say apologetically.

At once he stopped staring at her body and raised his eyes to meet hers. ''Sweetheart, you are beautiful,'' he assured her. ''Don't ever forget that. You're a very beautiful woman and I could lie here and look at you like this forever.''

"You mean it?" she asked, still skeptical. No man had ever told her she was pretty, much less beautiful.

"I do and I will tell you every day for the rest of our lives." He lowered his face, kissed her lips and said against them, "Let me show you just how beautiful you are to me."

Giving her no opportunity to reply, he kissed her again. This time a long, hot, penetrating kiss, and when their lips parted, he took both her hands in his and raised her arms above her head. He released her hands and she let her arms fall to the blanket. Then she sighed with bliss when he began to press worshipful kisses to her throat, her shoulders, her breasts.

As if in a dream—a lovely dream that she knew would end all too soon—Ellen lay there naked beneath her handsome lover, and watched the sinking sun play on his shoulders as he bent to her and adored her with his hands and mouth.

Sighing with joy, Ellen slowly turned her head and her glance fell on the shimmering black porcelain cat that Steve had bought for her. She reached out a hand and touched the figurine's smooth surface with her fingertips as Steve's face settled on her stomach.

With his tongue he painted her prominent hipbones, then moved dead center on her fluttering belly, put out the tip of his tongue and began to lick the baby-fine line of hair going down from her navel.

The black porcelain cat was promptly forgotten.

Although she had never been loved in such a forbidden, unique manner, Ellen knew instinctively what Steve's intention was. She trembled and wondered if she should make him stop.

She didn't.

Almost giddy with desire, she parted her legs a little more widely as he slowly, surely kissed his way downward to where she was on fire for him.

Ellen was breathing through her mouth now, panting really, as she raised her head from the blanket to nervously watch him. Her heart tried to pound its way out of her chest as she took in the shockingly intimate vision of the two of them making love beneath the setting sun.

Steve lay on his stomach between her open thighs, his dark head bent to her. His hands were on the insides of her thighs, gently urging them wider apart.

He looked as if he were going to literally devour her and she was so highly aroused she was perfectly willing for him to do so. Her whole body was now tensed and waiting anxiously for his loving mouth to move to its ultimate target and warmly enclose that pulsing, burning flesh that ached for him.

Steve's nose was nuzzled in the chestnut coils and his breath was hot on her. She shivered from head to toe and was so excited she could hardly lie still. She felt like shouting at him, "Please! I can't stand it any longer! Kiss me! Kiss me there!"

She said nothing, just bit her lip, held her breath and waited impatiently. Steve brushed one last teasing kiss to her lower belly, raised his head and looked directly into her eyes.

"I want to love you in every way a man can love a woman, sweetheart," he said huskily. "I want to kiss you right here," he said, touching the tip of his finger to her wet pulsing flesh. "I want your scent in my nostrils, your taste in my mouth. I want to kiss you and make you my own. Say you'll let me. Let me, sweetheart.''

Ellen couldn't answer. She was far too unnerved and excited. But she didn't have to reply. Steve knew that she wanted the same thing he wanted. So he lowered his face and pressed a soft kiss to her burning flesh.

''Steeeeve,'' she murmured a strangled cry. ''Oh, Steve.''

''Mmm,'' he breathed, opened his mouth and began to pleasure her as she'd never been pleasured before.

At first he tenderly kissed that tiny button of flesh and heard her moan with shocked joy. He put out his tongue and began to lick and circle until her bare bottom was lifting off the blanket in an attempt to get ever closer to the promised deliverance of his talented tongue.

Steve knew that Ellen had never been loved in this fashion, so he was extra careful and purposely patient. He took his time, slowly guiding her upward toward a climax that he knew would be new to her.

Ellen was wild with elation, frantic with burning lust, almost out of her mind with escalating carnal delight. Never had she felt anything so incredibly pleasurable. She tossed her head back and forth and ground her hips against Steve's hot face and prayed that he would never take his loving mouth from her. She'd surely die if he did. He *had* to keep on kissing her this way forever and ever.

His face buried in her, Steve could easily read the

frenzied movements of her fiery body, knew the tortured thoughts racing through her fevered brain. He managed to let her know, without his lips ever leaving her flesh, that he wouldn't desert her, wouldn't leave her suspended. He would, if need be, stay right there between her legs for hours and hours if she wanted.

The unspoken message reached the near-hysteric Ellen and she silently gave thanks. Then she parted her legs even wider, reached down and put her hands into the thick raven hair at the sides of his head and clasped it tightly. It was a signal that he instantly understood.

He deepened his kiss and his tongue stroked more rapidly. He put his hands beneath her writhing bottom, lifted her a little and then licked and lashed and loved her until she was on her way to climax.

In seconds Ellen was spiraling into a frightening release. Astounded by the intensity of her ecstasy, she screamed and bucked and spasmed as wave after wave of incredible sensation buffeted her entire body. Steve stayed with her, his mouth fused on her until, unable to stand one more second of such incredible pleasure, Ellen frantically pushed him away.

Pleased with himself, Steve slid up beside her, gathered her into his arms and kissed her. He smiled when she made a face, tasting herself on his mouth. He held her as she trembled and her heart pounded and she clung desperately to him. She was deliriously happy, yet felt as if she was going to start crying uncontrollably.

Steve understood.

He held her and calmed her and soothed her with

sweet words of love and affection. He stroked her slender back and gently rocked her until she began to calm. When finally she sighed heavily and went totally limp against him, he tilted her chin up and smiled devilishly at her.

She raised a well-arched eyebrow and whispered, "You're a very bad boy, Steve Corey." She grinned and added, "And I'm so glad you are."

He laughed and kissed her.

Then he very gently laid her down on the blanket. Ellen, smiling foolishly, sighed again, stretched and yawned. She was totally gratified and wonderfully tired. Spent. Weak. Fulfilled.

But she was aware that her experienced lover was still fully erect and unsatisfied. She didn't know how to tell him, but she was certain she couldn't possibly make love again anytime soon. She felt bad for his sake. She had, she realized now, been unforgivably selfish.

She murmured apologetically, "Steve, I...I'm sorry, I can't...I know that you...I...I'm so..."

"I know," he said, remarkably understanding. "It's all right, sweetheart. Don't worry about it. Just lie here with me and rest."

She gave him a grateful smile and closed her eyes. Steve smiled as well, stretched out beside her and put his arms around her. She exhaled and snuggled close. His strong arms felt good around her, his warm body right against hers. He did nothing more than hold her. He didn't kiss her. He didn't stroke her. Just held her pressed against his aroused male body until the fire that still burned within him began to warm and re-awaken her.

Without saying a word or opening her eyes, Ellen began to kiss Steve's tanned throat as she ran her hand slowly over his chest and belly. He lay still and tensed, so aroused he was in agony, but determined he wouldn't rush her.

Ellen raised her head and began to press kisses to the width of his chest. Gritting his teeth, Steve felt her soft lips teasing his tingling flesh, her tongue circling his nipples. Then he felt her hand slide down to his waist, pause there and move cautiously southward.

His breath was now ragged and his heart was pounding heavily. Her shining chestnut hair was spilling over his chest, tickling him, exciting him.

Steve groaned aloud when Ellen abruptly raised her head, gave him a naughty look, then wrapped her slender fingers around his throbbing erection and studied his face for reaction. She saw his heavy lashes sweep down over his beautiful eyes and his jaw tighten.

"Look at me, Steve," she ordered, her hand gently but possessively enclosing his hard, jerking flesh. Steve opened his eyes and looked at her, but his hands were clenched into fists at his sides. Ellen said brazenly, "When are you going to put this in me, darling?"

He exhaled heavily, agilely rolled up into a sitting position, cupped her shoulders, kissed her hard on the lips, then covered her hand with his as she continued to enfold him.

He said, "Just as soon as you let go of it."

She laughed, a sexual, throaty laugh, released him, lay down on her back and eagerly parted her legs. He immediately came between, pressed his pelvis against her, letting her feel the heavy hardness of his erection. He kissed her, stroked her breasts, then slipped his caressing fingers between her legs where he found her growing wet once again beneath his gentle exploring.

With his knee he urged her thighs farther apart and, raising up onto a stiffened arm, he said, "Look at me, Ellen. Tell me you want me inside you."

Ellen looked directly into his eyes and said, "I want you inside me, Steve, now and forever."

As he entered her, she gasped and her hips responded immediately to his rhythm. They made sweet, unhurried love as the sun finally slipped beneath the horizon, leaving only a rose-orange afterglow. Steve slowly measured his thrusts, driving deeply into Ellen, then withdrawing until only the shiny tip was inside her.

They looked steadily into each other's eyes as they moved together, and Ellen, clutching at his bulging biceps, said, "Do you realize that this is the first time we have ever made love like this. Lying down, facing each other?"

Steve drove slowly into her and replied, "I like it this way. I like to look at your face while I'm making love to you."

For a long, lovely time they continued to move slowly, seductively together, teasing each other, prolonging the pleasure. But in time both were so aroused they automatically changed their rhythm. Ellen began to arch her back and buck impatiently against Steve, wanting more, wanting all he had.

He gave it to her. He put his hands underneath her knees, lifted them up atop his shoulders, took the twin cheeks of her bottom in his spread hands and began to move faster, drive deeper, thrust more forcefully.

It was heaven for them both.

They gasped and sighed and urged each other on, murmuring shocking endearments as they soared toward release. Perspiring now, they took their carnal mating to a level that delivered supreme ecstasy to them both.

Ellen felt the incredible heat rising up in her and was far past the point of stopping it. But there was no need. He was coming with her, she could feel him coming. She experienced an incredible joy and knew that their hearts were fused as well as their bodies. She was joined with him in a way she had never been joined with anyone else. She belonged to him body and soul.

Ellen screamed as she reached the peak and at the same time Steve groaned loudly in his own wrenching orgasm.

Both finally came back to earth and Steve sagged against Ellen. He attempted to move, but she wouldn't let him.

"No," she whispered, her arms wrapped around him. "Don't move. Don't leave me. Stay inside me for just a while longer."

"For as long as you want, sweetheart."

# Thirty-Six

Later that night, when she was back in her quarters, alone in bed, Ellen sighed and smiled and happily relived the evening's glorious lovemaking. Vividly she recalled each look, each kiss, each touch, and told herself, as she had before, that there was no past, no future. There was only now. Here and now with Steve, the only man she had ever loved.

Ellen was so deeply in love, she had convinced herself it didn't really matter that the man she adored was a coward and a swindler. It might be cause for concern in New York City, but what difference did it make in the Lost City?

She forced nagging doubts to the back of her mind, did not want to think about them. She was, she assured herself, perfectly content to live only in the present with the dark lover of her dreams.

But that wasn't quite true.

Despite the character flaws, Ellen was hopelessly in love with this man who had shown her the beautiful mystery of passion. She felt alive as she never had before and it was all because of him. He was, for now, the center of her universe. Nothing else mattered.

Just Steve.

Only Steve.

Yet much as she tried to push away the disturbing thought of it, already she was dreading the moment when they would part. And they would part, she knew they would. They would go back to civilization and reality would set in. Steve would leave her without a backward glance. That's the kind of man he was. Hadn't he warned her that he was a drifter with no future and nothing to offer?

Suddenly Ellen, who had been so incredibly happy all night, was swamped with despair. She felt a deep loneliness wash over her and her eyes began to sting. She turned onto her side, drew her knees up, folded her hands beneath her cheek and exhaled wearily, her heart now aching dully.

Only this afternoon Alexandra had mentioned that it was time for them to think about returning home. Which meant, if she knew her aunt, that they might leave any day now. And that, of course, meant her precious, fleeting interval with Steve was rapidly coming to an end.

Ellen sighed again, rolled onto her back and tossed her head back and forth on the pillow.

She wouldn't think about it. She wouldn't face it until it happened. Until then, she would pretend that nothing was ever going to change. That she and Steve would be together in this high mountain retreat forever.

*She was running after Steve, telling him she loved him, begging him not to leave her. He turned abruptly and his face was hard and cruel, the slashing scar on his right cheek standing out in bold relief. He looked at her as if she repulsed him, as if he despised her.*

*She reached for him, gripped frantically at his shirtfront. Roughly he pushed her away. She stumbled, fell and hurt her knee. She couldn't stand on her injured leg. She sobbed and crawled after him, pleading with him.*

*He laughed demonically and announced, "I don't need you anymore, I got what I wanted!"*

*"I thought you wanted me," she wept.*

*"Money!" he stated coldly. "The Landseer fortune was all I ever wanted." He laughed again and bragged, "I took your aunt for everything she had, the vain old fool."*

*"No," she sobbed. "No, no, no."*

Ellen awakened with a start and bolted upright in bed, tears streaming down her cheeks. She trembled and told herself that it had only been a dream. A bad dream that meant nothing.

Shaken by the terrible nightmare, Ellen knew she wouldn't be able to go back to sleep. She rose from her bed, crossed the room and peered out. Dawn was breaking. She dressed and left her quarters while the village slept.

She made her way up to the Magic Waters. It was quiet and peaceful here at this early hour. No one was around. The bubbling blue waters were somehow soothing to look upon.

The troubled Ellen was drinking from the Magic Waters when Padjan, looking unusually sober, suddenly appeared.

Ellen looked up, saw him approaching, and felt like a child who had been caught in a naughty act.

"I was only, I...I...don't know why I..."

But Padjan smiled and shook his head, silencing her. "I have," he said, standing on the rocks just above, "known that you have been drinking from the waters all along."

"You have?" she said sheepishly.

"Yes," he said. "Mister Corey has been drinking regularly from the Magic Waters as well."

"Mister Corey? Steve has been...?" Ellen blinked at Padjan in disbelief.

He nodded. "It seems to me," said Padjan, his eyes beginning to twinkle, "that the waters must have worked their wizardry. You both look and feel younger. Is this not true?"

Ellen blushed hotly, knowing there was another explanation.

Padjan surprised her when he echoed her guilty thoughts. "Or is it love that has put the bloom of the rose back into your pale cheeks?" His eyebrows lifted and he grinned mischievously. "No matter. It's magic, nonetheless."

"Yes," she said thoughtfully, "I suppose it is."

"So you are willing to admit your love for Mister Corey?"

Ellen hesitated. But what good would it do to deny it? "Yes, unfortunately, I am in love with Steve Corey."

"Perhaps it's not so unfortunate," he said and nimbly sat down cross-legged beside Ellen. Without preamble, he stated, "Since you are in love with him, there are some things you should know about Mister Corey.''

Ellen turned away, bowed her head. "No. Don't bother telling me. I already know," she said.

"No, you do not," he corrected her. "There are many things about him you don't know." Ellen's head snapped up. She looked at him, frowned and held her breath, fearing she was about to learn more negative things about the man she so foolishly adored.

"I will tell you what the discreet Mister Corey will not," Padjan announced grandly. He looked her straight in the eye and began his story. "In the winter of 1890, my beloved wife and I were visiting her people, the Sioux."

"Your wife isn't Anasazi?"

"No, she isn't. Please do not interrupt me, Ellen. You'll make me lose my train of thought." Without pausing he continued. "It was a bitter December that year. My wife and I were with her people where they were camped in the Badlands south of the Cheyenne River. I recall so well the sound of the waters gurgling under a thick coating of ice and the crunching whiteness that covered everything." Padjan's dark eyes clouded as they looked back into the past. "It was cold, so terribly cold. On December 29, eight troops of the Seventh U.S. Cavalry suddenly surrounded the Hunkpapa village there on Wounded Knee Creek." He paused, drew a slow, long breath.

"I've heard of the Battle of Wounded Knee," Ellen softly offered. "And you were there when it happened?"

"We were. The bluecoats wanted to herd us all

back to the Standing Rock Agency. The Sioux chief, Big Foot, was far too ill with pneumonia to be herded anywhere or to be a threat to anyone. But five hundred armed troopers rode into camp that day, heavily outnumbering the Sioux.''

Eyes wide, Ellen nodded, engrossed.

''The cavalry commander trained his rapid-firing cannon onto the village and ordered a shakedown in a search for weapons.'' Padjan shook his head sorrowfully. ''The Sioux had no guns, but from somewhere a shot rang out and within seconds the cavalry's big Hotchkiss guns were pouring fragmentation shells into the village. Tepees disintegrated, bursting into flames. We all scattered, but had nowhere to run.''

He closed his eyes, opened them, ''Men, women and children fell before a barrage of fire, some managing to run a mile or two before being overtaken and clubbed or shot to death.''

''Dear God in heaven,'' Ellen murmured, horrified, her hands going to her mouth.

''My wife and I were running, trying to escape, when we saw a young cavalry captain, his sidearm holstered, refusing to take part in the slaughter. The right side of the captain's face was streaming blood, a Sioux brave had lunged up in a surprise attack and sliced his cheek from eye to jaw.''

At once Ellen thought of the long scar going down the side of Steve's face and her stomach clenched spasmodically. She said nothing. Just waited, tense, eager to hear the rest of Padjan's tale.

Padjan continued. ''The young captain was commanded to shoot down women and children, but he disobeyed orders. He and his brave first sergeant saved my wife and me from the murdering soldiers. The captain spotted the two of us—unarmed—in the middle of the melee. He rode straight to us, pulled my wife up onto the horse before him, then leaned down and drew me up behind the saddle. With the sergeant protecting our flank, the captain carried us to safety." Padjan paused, then added solemnly, "He saved our lives, but ruined his own." He turned and looked directly at Ellen. "Do you know who that young captain was? The sergeant?"

Ellen swallowed with difficulty. "I think so," she said softly, the pulse pounding in her throat.

"Captain Steven J. Corey and Sergeant Enrique O'Mara."

Feeling as if she was going to laugh and cry at once, Ellen said, "Then Steve, though he was forced to leave the army in seeming disgrace, is not a coward, he is—"

"The bravest man I've ever known," said Padjan. "In saving us, a couple of frightened Indians, he ended his brilliant military career. He was cashiered out of the army for cowardice in the face of the enemy." Padjan rubbed a hand over his eyes and sighed. "The military was everything to him. He loved the army, graduated from the Citadel at the top of his class."

"My poor Steve," Ellen murmured, her heart hurting for the man she loved. "It must have been devastating for him to be branded a coward."

"There's more. His wife immediately divorced

him. She was a beautiful, spoiled aristocrat who had married a dashing southern officer. When he lost his commission, he lost her as well. She went abroad to join some rich, distant cousins in Europe. She later married a nobleman.''

"How cruel of her," Ellen thought aloud. "How could she leave him when he needed her most! The whole sad affair must have broken his heart," Ellen stated softly.

"I would imagine, but he kept his pain to himself. That's the kind of man Mister Corey is. He takes his lumps without complaint and soldiers on." Nodding, Ellen started to speak, but Padjan silenced her. "I lost track of Mister Corey shortly after that. Years passed and then our paths crossed again last spring when Mister Corey and Ricky, down on their luck, joined a traveling Wild West show in which I was a star performer. Soon after, the show was taken abroad and the entire troupe went along.

"We were in London when the show went bankrupt, leaving us stranded. My wife became very ill. I knew I had to get her home...back here to the Lost City. Mister Corey once again helped us in our hour of need."

"And so he saved you twice," she said with pride.

"He did. I don't know what we would have done without him. Another thing, Ellen, contrary to what you may believe, we did *not* take money from your wealthy aunt. In return for guiding her here to the Magic Waters, we asked only for transportation costs and expenses. Nothing more. Mister Corey never took one red cent from Alexandra.''

He fixed Ellen with his shiny obsidian eyes and assured her, "Mister Corey is no greedy opportunist. He would *never* swindle anyone. Never, no matter how down and out he was. Mister Corey is a fine gentleman. A brave, good, modest man."

Struggling to swallow the lump in her throat, Ellen said, "Thank you, Padjan, for telling me all this. I love him so much and I..."

"If you do, then remember this, child, you are not the only one who has been hurt in the past. He was hurt as well. You must learn to trust again, and so must he. Teach him. Show him you'll be there no matter what. Don't let him get away."

"I won't," she said with a happy smile. Her heart bursting with joy, she said, "I'm confused. You said you wanted to bring your wife home, but..."

Padjan nodded, replied stoically, "It was too late. Summer Dawn died an hour ago." Ellen was speechless as he calmly explained that Summer Dawn was his beloved wife. "She was Sioux, not Anasazi," he said. "She did not believe, refused for years to drink of the Magic Waters. And now she has passed away in her eighty-eighth year."

Stunned, Ellen exclaimed, "But...but you are so young and...?"

"I am older than Summer Dawn," he declared proudly. Then he sighed suddenly and added, "That is long enough to live, I think."

# Thirty-Seven

Ellen remained at the waters.

She mulled over all Padjan had told her. She would, she decided, go to Steve right now and confess she loved him with all her heart and could not live without him. She wouldn't let him get away, even if it meant sacrificing her pride.

Her mind made up, Ellen sprang to her feet and started down to the village. Halfway there she met Steve coming up. When they were several yards apart, Steve stopped.

Ellen didn't.

She ran straight to him, threw her arms around his neck and said, "I have lied to you, Steve."

"You have?" he said, a worried expression on his face.

She pulled back, smiled up at him and said, "Yes. I said I wanted to be with you for as long as we are here in the Lost City. That was a lie. I want to be with you for the rest of my life."

His handsome face broke into a broad smile and, relieved, he told her, "I want the same thing, sweetheart. Marry me, Ellen Cornelius. Marry me. I'm not much of a bargain, but I do own some coastal land in South Carolina that my father left me and I have a small bankroll I won at cards on the ship's crossing. It's enough for a start and we could—''

"You own property in South Carolina?" she said, jubilant. "Oh, Steve, I've always wanted to live there! It's so beautiful and I could see my son at the—''

"Your son won't approve of me, Ellen," he interrupted. "I'm a Citadel graduate myself. After the Battle of Wounded Knee, I was cashiered out of the army, disgraced and removed from the academy's hall of honor.''

"Once he knows the truth, he'll think you a hero, just as I do." Her arms tightened around him and she admitted, "Padjan told me what really happened at Wounded Knee.''

"Padjan talks too much," Steve said.

"I'm glad he does," she said, smiling. "You would never have told me yourself. Oh, darling, forgive me for doubting you.''

"You're forgiven," he said, his arms tightening around her. "Now tell me, will you marry me? But be very sure, Ellen. If you become my wife, it could mean losing your inheritance. Your son's inheritance.''

"I don't care for myself," she told him truthfully. "And Christopher has said many times that the money doesn't matter to him. Let Aunt Alexandra try and take the fortune with her when she dies. I no longer care.''

"You're a remarkable woman, Ellen, and I'm a lucky man." He grinned and repeated, "Will you marry me?''

"I will! Yes, oh, yes.''

\* \* \*

"Aunt Alexandra, I need to talk to you."

"And I need to talk to you, Ellen."

The two women stood facing each other in Alexandra's room. After convincing Steve that it would be better if she spoke with her aunt alone, Ellen had gone straight there to tell Alexandra she was going to marry Steve Corey.

"You first," Alexandra invited.

"Yes, all right." Ellen took a deep breath. "Auntie, I'm in love with Steve Corey," she stated firmly. "We're going to be married and live together on a piece of land he owns in South Carolina."

Alexandra displayed no surprise or censure. She smiled warmly. "Why, Ellen, dear, that's wonderful."

"It is?" Ellen said, stunned by her aunt's response.

"Yes, it is. I'm happy for you both," said Alexandra, beaming at her niece even as tears filled her eyes. "I have to confess something to you. I warned Mister Corey that I would cut you off without a cent if you married him."

"Oh, Auntie," Ellen said, shaking her head.

"To which he replied, 'It is Ellen I want, not her inheritance.' You're a very fortunate woman," Alexandra added wistfully. "He loves you very much, and without love, life is meaningless. No one knows that better than I."

"I'm sorry that you never…"

"It was my own fault. Nobody else's. I should have done more. I did too little of everything. Always kept people at arm's length. I never gave love a chance, I was always afraid that any gentleman caller was only trying to get his hands on my money. I kept such a close grip on the Landseer fortune, I had time for nothing else. It ruined my life, left me a bitter old maid.''

"That's very sad, Auntie," said Ellen. "You underestimated your own self-worth."

"Oh, I don't know, dear. Look at me. I was never pretty. Nor, as you well know, was I lovable.''

"Don't say that."

"Why not? It's true and we both know it. I've been mean and stingy, particularly with you and Chris. Shut you both out, refused to show either of you any love and affection. I hope that one day you'll both be able to forgive me." Ellen started to speak, but Alexandra raised a hand and silenced her. "Ellen, I'm sure you know that I am a very, very wealthy old woman.''

"Yes, I know."

"Well, don't think I've forgotten that half of the vast Landseer fortune would rightfully have been yours all these years, had my dear brother…''

Ellen nodded, speechless.

"When we get back home, I will have my business managers show you the ledgers and books, make you aware of exactly how much money there is and where it is being held and in what investments and real-estate holdings. I want you to know where every penny is.''

Ellen couldn't believe her ears. She said, "You don't have to do that."

"I want to. I'm a changed woman, Ellen, even if it doesn't show on the outside. Maybe the Magic Waters worked, who knows? I just know that I desperately want to make up for all the years I was so cruel and miserly."

Ellen smiled affectionately at the woman who remained as badly wrinkled as ever.

While the Magic Waters Alexandra had consumed had done little to alter her outward appearance, they had apparently worked their magic on her heart. She had finally realized, with regret, that hers had been a life lived in total selfishness and that it had made her, and everyone around her, miserable. Alexandra told Ellen she had been wrong about so many things and that she was truly sorry.

"I didn't mean it when I told Mister Corey I would disinherit you," Alexandra assured Ellen. "I want you and Christopher to have the bulk of the fortune. There is so much money you both couldn't possibly spend it all in a hundred lifetimes." She smiled sheepishly and said, "So here's what I've been wanting to talk about with you. There is something I'd like to do with a portion of the fortune. That is, if you agree. It will be as much your decision as mine and I've been dying to tell you about it."

"I am listening."

Alexandra brightened and said, "You remember how I fell in love with that little boy named Spear down on the Navajo reservation."

"I remember."

"Well, I've been thinking a lot about him and wondering how his life could be made better. There's a way we can help that precious child and the others like him.'' Her eyes began to gleam as she revealed her well-thought-out plans. "We'll build schools, hospitals and housing for the Navajo people and—"

"That's a wonderful idea," Ellen cut in, genuinely enthusiastic. "They will greatly benefit from your kindness, and they will love you for it. Little Spear already loves you."

"You think so?" Alexandra said, wanting to believe it. "You know, maybe I could even travel out West once a year to visit. The journey isn't really that difficult."

After burying his beloved Summer Dawn, Padjan told his friends that they could remain in the Lost City as long as they wished.

Ricky O'Mara had chosen to stay. He had fallen in love with Tallas. She could not leave the Lost City and he refused to go without her. Tallas promised him that if he stayed with her, he, too, would remain forever young.

Ellen and Steve chose to go home. The happy lovers eagerly prepared to escort the transformed Alexandra down out of the Lost City.

The sun was shining brightly on the morning the trio were to depart. The people of the village, led by Natan, Keeper of the Waters, gathered to say goodbye. Ellen spotted the woman who had given her the silver bracelet and raised her wrist so the woman could see that she was wearing the treasured gift.

Tallas and Ricky were there to see them off. Ellen and Tallas hugged warmly and whispered to each other, sharing secrets. Ricky and Steve firmly shook hands.

"I'll miss you," Steve said to his old buddy.

*"Como siempre, amigo,"* Ricky replied and his dark eyes shone with affection.

Padjan walked the trio out of the village. At the city's edge, they stopped and said a last goodbye.

"Thank you so much for bringing me here to your Lost City," said Alexandra before she hugged Padjan. "The Magic Waters have transformed me, don't you think?"

"Indeed," Padjan replied with a wink. "Why, you look years younger."

She laughed, knowing he was teasing her, and said, "Should you ever get lonely or restless, come to New York to see me."

He smiled and said that he would.

But both knew they would never see each other again.

"We better go," said Steve. "We want to get down off the mountain before dark."

They agreed and immediately started the journey down toward the treacherous trail. At the city's far perimeter, they turned, looked back and waved at the suddenly old-looking Padjan. The stooped little man, now bent with age, weakly lifted a hand in return.

Then he turned and slowly walked away.

Needing no fountain of youth or magic clock to keep their love brand-new, the much-in-love soul mates, with a spry, uncomplaining Alexandra in tow, left the Lost City behind. The sky-high village disappeared in the clouds.

The trio was silent.

Each was wondering what was responsible for the changes in their lives. Was it the Magic Waters? Or the magic of love?

Did it really matter?

"Sure you want to go, Steve?" Ellen asked, looking up at him.

He smiled down at her. "Afraid you'll tire of me if we go home to South Carolina?"

"Perhaps," she replied as he hugged her to him. "But not for at least a hundred years."

# EMMA DARCY

## THE SECRETS WITHIN

A mother's lust for power...a daughter's desire for revenge

Published May 17th 2002

MIRA®

# GWEN HUNTER

# DELAYED
## DIAGNOSIS
### CONSPIRACY IN THE EMERGENCY ROOM

Published 17th May 2002

From out of the ashes arises an
old and deadly secret...

# TAYLOR
# SMITH
## DEADLY GRACE

Published 21st June 2002

M257

# Robyn CARR

# The Wedding Party

EVERYONE'S IN THE MOOD FOR ROMANCE...EXCEPT THE BRIDE

Published 21st June 2002

MIRA®

M258

# MEG O'BRIEN

## CRASHING DOWN

*When everything you believe
is not what it seems . . .*

From the bestselling author of GATHERING LIES

Published 21st June 2002

# Contents

# Introduction

*Thanks to sensational tales in the tabloid press and being the butt of jokes in 80s sitcoms, the word 'Majorca' used to conjure up none-too-flattering images of sunburned flesh and grey concrete. These days, however, that older British spelling is frowned upon by the island's authorities, and 21st-century Mallorca has become one of Europe's most desirable hotspots.*

Writers, artists and celebrities have long been attracted by the island's climate and beauty. In days gone by, composer Frédéric Chopin, artist Joan Miró and writer Robert Graves were all beguiled by Mallorca's charms. Now, Catherine Zeta Jones and Michael Douglas, Claudia Schiffer, Andrew Lloyd Webber and Sir Richard Branson all own homes here. But its most famous inhabitant is tennis player Rafael Nadal, who was born and bred in Manacor.

However, you don't need to be a millionaire to enjoy Mallorca. As a well-established Mediterranean destination, the island has everything you would expect: miles of sandy beaches, guaranteed summer sunshine, safe water for swimming and a wide range of accommodation to suit all tastes and budgets.

Whether you like age-old mountain villages or picture-perfect harbours, water sports or golf courses, getting back to nature or lying on the beach, gourmet meals or fast food – they're all here.

And there is a lot more besides. Palma, the capital, has a dramatic seafront cathedral, a vibrant cultural life, designer shopping and an atmospheric old town filled with history. Elsewhere, there are breathtaking underground caves, isolated hilltop monasteries, lush gardens and imposing mountain ranges as well as nature reserves and offshore islands that attract birdwatchers from around the globe. In summer, you'll never be far from a lively festival.

Families are spoilt for choice. If you don't want to spend all day on one of the Mallorca's 40 or so Blue Flag beaches, there's plenty to keep the tribe occupied: playing at pirates in the ruins of an old castle, watching the dolphins and sea lions at Marineland, hurtling down a water chute at a hydro-park or taking the scenic old tram from Sóller to Port de Sóller.

# Mallorca

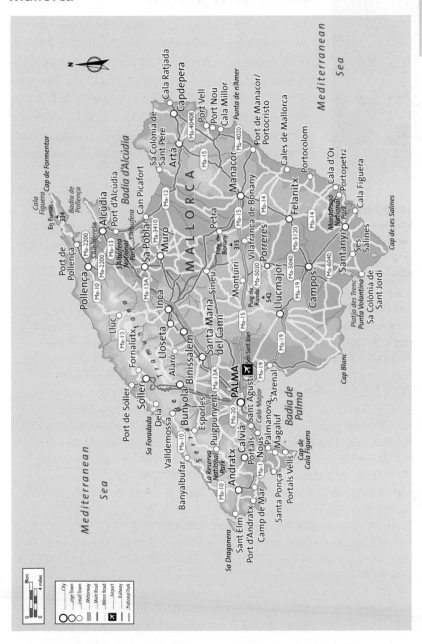

# Land and people

*The Balearic Islands lie 82km (51 miles) east of the Spanish mainland in the Mediterranean Sea. Mallorca is the largest island, roughly 100km (62 miles) from east to west. Menorca, only a fifth of Mallorca's size, lies 40km (25 miles) to its east, while the even smaller island of Ibiza, also known as Eivissa, is 85km (53 miles) to the southwest. Formentera, hanging close to Ibiza's southern coast, completes an archipelago attended by another hundred or so tiny islands.*

## Landscape

A range of dominating mountains, the Serra de Tramuntana, runs the length of Mallorca's northwest coast. The highest peaks gather in the centre around the island's summit, Puig Major (1,445m/4,740ft). A second, lower mountain range, the Serra de Llevant, runs like an echo across the southeast of the island. Its highest point, Puig de Sant Salvador, rises to 510m (1,673ft) and is capped by a religious sanctuary. Between these mountains lies Es Pla, a flat, cultivated plain dotted with windmills and small agricultural towns.

Mallorca's coastline stretches for some 555km (345 miles). In the north, high cliffs fall abruptly to the sea, while the east coast is indented with *calas* (coves). Two great sandy bays gnaw into the island: Badia d'Alcúdia in the northeast and Badia de Palma in the west, home to the island's capital, Palma. The small uninhabited island of Sa Dragonera, now a Natural Park, lies just off the island's western tip, and

18km (11 miles) south of Mallorca is Cabrera, the largest in a cluster of tiny islands that now form a national land-sea park.

## Geology

The mountains of Mallorca are part of the Baetic Cordillera, a range of peaks that runs southwest through Ibiza to southern Andalucía and Cádiz.

The island is predominantly limestone, and in places severe erosion has created deep canyons and extraordinary caves that have become major tourist attractions. The rich soil in the central plain gets its striking reddish-brown colour from iron-oxide deposits.

## Climate

Mallorca enjoys a Mediterranean climate with mild winters and hot, dry summers. The Serra de Tramuntana attracts the greatest rainfall, and the mountains are sometimes capped with snow in winter. The range acts as a buffer against winds from the north, while sea breezes temper the heat of the summer months.

## Population

The population of Mallorca is almost 814,300 of whom 383,000 live in Palma. In addition, over 13 million tourists visited the island in 2008, attracting an influx of seasonal staff to serve them. An idea of the lopsided effect tourism has on the island's character can be gauged from the fact that the resort of Cales de Mallorca has a resident population of only 250, but accommodation for 8,500 visitors.

Vegetables, salad crops and fruit are cultivated in the fertile soil around Sa Pobla

## Economy

A favourite topic of conversation among Mallorcans is the death of the island's agriculture. As a result of the tourist boom, two-thirds of the island's working population are now employed in the service sector. The fruit growing so picturesquely in fields, orchards and olive groves is often never picked, and staircases of abandoned terraces are a frequent and poignant sight in the more remote parts of the island. Agriculture is still commercially viable on the central plain, helped by modern methods and irrigation, and grants are given to landowners to keep their property in shape – which usually means employing sheep as lawnmowers. In urban areas, the construction industry and factories manufacturing shoes, garments and costume jewellery provide employment, but tourism is the overwhelming mainstay of the island's economy.

Steep-sloping, pine-forested cliffs run the length of Mallorca's northwest coast

## Wildlife

The star character of Mallorcan wildlife has long been extinct. Six million years ago, Myotragus stalked the Balearic Islands, a peculiarly shaped antelope with eyes at the front of its head and buck teeth that functioned like a pickaxe. In comparison, the creatures currently scurrying around Mallorca appear unexciting: four types of snake (all non-poisonous), a rarely seen spotted civet cat, goats, hares and rabbits, frogs, toads and various insects. Only on the island of Cabrera, a protected wilderness, do a few endemic species of lizard arouse the visitor's curiosity.

Look skyward though and it's a different picture. Mallorca is of great interest to birdwatchers, and flocks of binocular-addicts regularly descend on the island in April and May during the migration season. Hoopoes, Eleonora's falcons, black vultures, red kites and several types of eagle cause particular excitement. Diverse habitats that include wetlands, saltpans, rocky cliffs and offshore islets, as well as the woods and forests of Mallorca's mountains, enhance the appeal of the island to both birds and their admirers.

Hunting remains popular with a powerful section of the community: wild goats, rabbits, quail, turtle doves, wood pigeon, partridges, mallards and coots are some of the targets. The wholesale slaughter of migrating thrushes, using purpose-made nets known as *filats de coll,* is also permitted.

The hoopoe, frequently seen in Mallorca

Land and people

Farmers consider the olive-loving birds a pest, while cooks see them as a country delicacy. Restrictions were recently introduced to promote more responsible hunting – a heavy fine has been imposed on the killing of black vultures, which were once in danger of extinction here.

As in so many parts of the Mediterranean, wildlife and the natural landscape are under threat from development. Fortunately, through the efforts of the environmental group **Grup Balear d'Ornitologia** (in Catalan; Grupo Ornitologia Balear in Spanish; *www.gobmallorca.com*) and the local authorities, almost a third of the island is now under protection.

# Talayot culture

The Balearic Islands were originally settled by an industrious and well-organised people who left enigmatic visiting cards around Mallorca known as *talayots*. These megalithic monuments get their name from *atalaya*, the Arab word for a watchtower, and have become eponymous symbols of the talented civilisation that flourished here during the Bronze Age.

The Talayot Period came in three waves. Pre-Talayot culture started around 2000 BC and was principally cave-based. By 1500 BC *navetes* (burial chambers that resemble upturned boats) were being constructed: there are abundant

Talayot de Ses Païsses, dating back to 1300 BC

Talayot de S'Illot

examples on Menorca. The most creative phase, the Talaiotic, lasted from 1300 BC until about 800 BC and coincided with the emergence of a more violent and hierarchical society. A third stage, Late Talayot, is characterised by the construction of *taulas*, colossal table-like stone structures that are well preserved on Menorca. By the 6th century BC, Talayot culture was on the wane as the islands came under the influence of the Greeks and Phoenicians.

Archaeological research and evidence from similar cultures in Sardinia and Corsica suggest that life in Talayot times was surprisingly sophisticated. The islanders kept sheep, pigs and cattle, constructed ingenious wells, and made delicate, decorated pottery.

Talayots were built to both circular and quadrangular plans, and were most likely constructed as main residences and observation posts in the islands' fortified settlements. On Mallorca, the best opportunities to inspect them are at Capocorb Vell and Ses Païsses.

Archaeological finds from the period, including ceramics, weapons, tools and jewellery, can be seen in the Museu de Mallorca in Palma and the Museu Regional in Artà.

# History

**5000 BC**    Remains found in caves near Sóller and Valldemossa indicate the presence of humans on the island.

**1300–800 BC**    Talayot culture flourishes in Mallorca and Menorca, leaving behind enigmatic stone towers and ruined dwellings at sites such as Capocorb Vell and Ses Païsses.

**1000–123 BC**    Phoenician, Greek and Carthaginian traders visit the Balearics: the name probably derives from the Greek verb *ballein*, which means 'to throw' – a reference to the leather slings used as deadly weapons by the islanders.

**123 BC–AD 425**    Roman commander Quintus Cecilius Metullus conquers Mallorca. The island is called Balearis Major (hence its modern name) with the capital in Pollentia, now Alcúdia, site of a surviving Roman theatre. Christianity takes hold during the 2nd century AD.

**425–707**    With the decline of the Roman Empire, Mallorca comes under Vandal and Byzantine rule.

**707–1229**    Raids by the Moors accompany their conquest of mainland Iberia – by 902 Mallorca is part of the Emirate of Córdoba. The Moors build mosques, Arab baths, palaces and gardens, and introduce sophisticated agricultural methods using windmills and waterwheels.

**1229–1492**    During the *Reconquista*, the Reconquest of Spain by the Christians, Jaume I of Aragón lands at Santa Ponça and takes the island. Subsequently, under his son, Jaume II, Mallorca enjoys a Golden Age that produces the Castell de Bellver and the polymath Ramón Llull. Mallorca's brief spell as an independent kingdom, however, ends in 1349 with the defeat of Jaume III at Llucmajor. By 1492, the island becomes a part of Spain.

| | |
|---|---|
| **16th–18th centuries** | The island's fortunes decline as Spain turns its attention to the New World. Watchtowers and fortified churches are built in response to repeated attacks from pirates. Mallorca backs the losing side in the War of the Spanish Succession (1701–14), and receives an influx of refugees after the French Revolution. |
| **19th– early 20th century** | Frédéric Chopin and George Sand stay in the monastery at Valldemossa in 1838–9. A regular steamship service links Mallorca to the mainland and in 1875 the island's first railway line opens. |
| **1936–9** | Spanish Civil War. Quickly seized by the Nationalists, Mallorca becomes a base for assaults on the mainland. |
| **1939–75** | Dictatorship of General Franco. By the early 1960s Mallorca is at the forefront of Spain's tourist boom. After Franco's death, monarchy returns with King Juan Carlos I. |
| **1983** | The Balearic Islands become an autonomous region of Spain. |
| **1986** | Spain joins the European Community. |
| **1992** | The summer Olympics in Barcelona and Expo '92 in Seville. |
| **2003–7** | The Mallorcan government invests heavily in road-building across the island. |
| **2006** | A museum dedicated to the life of British writer Robert Graves opens in Deià. |
| **2007** | Britain's cycling, swimming and sailing teams train on Mallorca prior to the Beijing Olympics. |
| **2008** | The government announces an investment of €660 million to improve and upgrade the island's rail network over a four-year period. |
| **2009** | Palma Airport is voted best airport in the 10–25 million passenger category by Airports Council International. |
| **2010** | Mallorca celebrates the bicentenary of the birth of Frédéric Chopin, who stayed on the island during the winter of 1838–9. |

# Politics

*The Balearic Islands have been an autonomous region of Spain since 1983. While language issues and the effects of tourism give rise to much debate, Mallorca is a stable and deeply conservative island.*

Spain is a constitutional monarchy and the regular summer visits of King Juan Carlos I and the royal family to Mallorca bring pride and prestige to the island. The king, who was member of Spain's sailing team at the 1972 Munich Olympics, has a summer residence near Cala Mayor and often moors his yacht at the exclusive port of Portals Nous.

As the largest and most influential island in the archipelago, Mallorca is the seat of the Govern Balear (Balearic Government). The Balearic Islands are one of Spain's 17 autonomous communities and their regional government is responsible for their day-to-day running.

The regional parliament meets in the Círculo Mallorquín building (one-time HQ of Mallorcan high society) close to Palma Cathedral. Out of a total of 59 seats, Mallorca has 33, Menorca 13, Ibiza 12 and Formentera 1. Since the 2007 regional elections, a centre-left coalition government – popularly known as the 'rainbow coalition' – made up of the *Unió Mallorquina* (liberals), the PSOE (Spanish Socialist Party), *Eivissa pel Canvi* (Ibizan coalition) and *Bloc Per Mallorca* (left-wing coalition) has governed the islands.

The *Consell de Mallorca* was set up in 1979 and looks after the island's roads, railways, environment, culture and general administration. Mallorca is split into 54 municipalities, the largest being Llucmajor in the south, east of Palma, which covers 326sq km (126sq miles) and has around 300,000 inhabitants.

## Official Language

Catalan and Castilian have dual official status on the Balearic Islands. Catalan, one of the group of Romance languages which evolved from Latin, is spoken by around nine million people in Catalonia, Valencia and the Balearics as well as parts of France and Italy. After decades of repression by Franco, the preservation of Catalan is seen by most islanders as the cornerstone of their identity. Although Catalan is its official name, islanders prefer to call their language Mallorqui. Today, Catalan predominates in most of the island's public life including politics, the Church and education.

The former Círculo Mallorquín building, seat of the Balearic government

# Culture

*Mallorca's long-standing tag as the* Isla de la Calma *(Island of Calm) might seem absurd amid the disco frenzy of Magaluf or the beaches with gently-roasting bodies at Cala Millor, but prior to the arrival of mass tourism the island was a bastion of tranquillity and tradition.*

## The Mallorcans

'Caution and reserve are the ruling trends of the Mallorcan character,' George Sand declared in her notorious travel book *A Winter in Majorca*. Mallorcans add a muted strand to the Spanish national character: they might not have the flamboyance of the Sevillians or the cosmopolitan buzz of citizens of Madrid or Barcelona, but they do possess the appealing virtues of politeness, placidity and prudence found in many other Mediterranean communities – and small islands in general.

## Religion

The Christians raised new churches on the site of Moorish mosques after the Reconquest in even the most obscure corners of the island. Since the death of Franco, the influence of the Church has declined, though Mallorca remains a traditional society moulded by Church, family and school. Every year some 50,000 islanders make a pilgrimage to the monastery at Lluc, home of Mallorca's patron saint, La Moreneta. Even a little-known sanctuary such as the Ermita de Sant Blai outside Campos del Port will attract a saint's-day procession of more than 2,000 walkers and cyclists.

## Folklore

Mallorca's folklore, darkened with medieval fatalism and superstition, reflects the insularity of its history. Author Robert Graves claimed that witches were still practising on the island when he arrived in 1929. They are said to have favoured abandoned *talayot* sites for their occult assemblies, and a favourite piece of Mallorcan witchcraft involved using a bull's horn anointed with olive oil to curse victims.

Island folklore as presented to tourists appears sanitised in comparison, focusing on coy courtship dances in colourful costume. Catch some of the island's religious celebrations, though, such as *Semana Santa* (Easter) with its processions of hooded penitents, or the more anarchic moments in the village *festa* when the firework-brandishing devils take over, and you will get an inkling of the historic fears and impulses that still underpin Mallorcan culture.

## Education

Cultural life on Mallorca benefits from the presence of the island's Universitat des Illes Baleares, a university founded in 1978 which now has some 15,000 students. In the state-run schools, all lessons are in Catalan. English, American, French and Swedish international schools follow the curriculum of their home country.

## Art

Boosted by the profits from tourism, Mallorca has developed a reputation as an island that nurtures artists. Children are encouraged to attend art classes and exhibitions from an early age, and many wealthy islanders and visitors from the mainland have started collecting art. The population of Pollença is only 13,000, yet it has at least a dozen art galleries. Inspired by the famous light and landscape of Mallorca, and the aesthetic achievements of the late Joan Miró and the Felanitx-born painter Miquel Barceló, many young Mallorcans are entering the arts.

At the same time, new exhibition spaces are being opened in Palma's historic buildings, and there is a revival of interest in the island's flamboyant *Modernista* (Spanish Art Nouveau) architecture.

Life in the slow lane: in the country they still like to take things easy

# Dancing with the Devil

The Spanish are addicted to fiestas: in Spanish, the word is *fiesta* (singular) or *fiestas* (plural); in Catalan, the words are *festa* and *festes*. In Mallorca, scarcely a week goes by without a celebration of some kind. The inspiration for most festivities is religious, but rural traditions and historic events on the island make their mark too. Animals, fish, grapes, sausages and even melons are all cause for a *festa* here, while heroic resistance against invading Turkish pirates in the mid-16th century is still remembered in Sóller and Pollença with mock battles between Moors and Christians.

*Dimonis* (devils) are among the most eye-catching characters that dance through Mallorcan *festes*. Once banned by the Church, devils now appear at many *festes*, hurling firecrackers and lewdly tempting saints and spectators alike. One of the island's oldest rituals, played out annually by dancers at Montuïri,

*El ball del cossiers* in Montuïri during *la festa de Sant Bartomeu*

Carnival costumes are varied and fanciful

features a shabbily dressed devil with horns and a cowbell being danced into submission by a woman, who concludes her conquest by placing a triumphant foot on the defeated embodiment of evil. In a *festa* at Santa Margalida anarchic devils infiltrate a procession of villagers dressed in rural costume, snatching their *gerres* (pitchers) which are then smashed at the feet of Mallorca's own saint, Santa Catalina Thomás.

Some *festes* begin on the *revelta* (eve) of a local saint's day, when ceremonial *foguerons* (bonfires) are lit. At Sa Pobla, where the Revelta de Sant Antoni dates back to 1365, the celebrants tuck into specially made eel and spinach pie and dance to traditional music played on bagpipe, flute and drum. In Pollença, the local braves bring a pine tree down from the mountains and make it into a soapy pole for the townsfolk to climb.

The *festa* calendar is fullest between June and September. For the non-religious visitor, country fairs and the more theatrical *festes* will be the most rewarding events to track down. Instead of standing around waiting for the parade to begin (it is bound to be late), go to a bar, have a few drinks, and ask the waiter which is the best place to stand – and when. Then have a devil of a good time.

# Festivals

*There is always something going on in Mallorca. Every town and village has its own Festa Major, with traditional parades and activities in honour of the local patron saint. Many of the island's festivals have endured for centuries: some, like Sóller's re-creations of the battles between Moors and Christians, commemorate historical events, whereas others, like Benissalem's wine festival, celebrate the grape harvest or other seasonal happenings. Perhaps the biggest and wildest* festa *on the island's calendar is Palma's wonderful week-long* Festa de Sant Sebastià *in January.*

## January

**Cabalgata de los Reyes Magos** (Cavalcade of the Three Kings) (5th): In Palma, the Kings arrive by boat, and proceed through the town accompanied by toy-laden lorries.

**Festa de Sant Sebastià** (patron saint of Palma and Alcúdia) (20th): Celebrated with music and bonfires.

## February

February is Carnival month. In Palma, it is known as **Sa Rúa**. Montuïri's **Darrer Dies** (Last Days) is celebrated with fancy dress, stalls, wine, food and bonfires.

## March/April

**Semana Santa** (Easter) is a serious religious occasion. Masked penitents in pointed hoods march along Palma's streets carrying torches and holy relics. The processions in Sineu and Pollença are very dramatic.

**Festa de l'Àngel** (18 April): In the forest around Castell de Bellver.

## May/June

**Ses Valentes Dones** (The Valiant Women) (13 May): Commemorates the defeat of Turkish pirates in 1561, an encounter in which two local women were outstandingly brave. A battle between Christians and Moors is re-enacted in Port de Sóller and later in the evening in Sóller town.

**Corpus Christi**: Religious celebration in honour of the Blessed Sacrament, especially in Pollença and Palma.

**Festes de Sant Joan**: Celebrations involving bonfires, fireworks and demons across the island; bullfights in Muro.

**Festes de Sant Pere** (28–29 June): Port d'Alcúdia pays homage to St Peter, patron saint of fishermen.

## July

**Mare de Deu de la Victòria** (2nd): Pilgrimage from Alcúdia to Ermita de la Victoria.

**Festes de la Verge del Carme** (16th): Local *festes* in Port d'Andratx, Cala

Ratjada, Port de Pollença and Port de Sóller.

**La Beata** (27th–28th): In Valldemossa, a bull is led through the streets as part of the cult of Santa Catalina Thomás.

## August

**Festa de Nostra Senyora de los Àngels** (2nd): Pollença's *festa* includes a mock fight between Christians and Moors.

**Sant Bartomeu** (24th): Devil dances in Montuïri.

**Sant Agustí** (28th): Dancing and horsey antics in Felanitx.

**Sant Joan** (29th): Sant Joan celebrates its patron with dancing and Balearic singing. Pilgrimage from Palma to Lluc.

## September

Devils-versus-saints procession in Santa Margalida (first Sunday).

**Diada de Mallorca** (12th): Festivities in commemoration of the day on which Jaume I's troops landed on Mallorca.

**Festa de Sant Mateu** (21st): *Festa* in Bunyola.

**Festa des Vermar** (last week in Sept): Binissalem's grape and wine festival; country fairs in Montuïri and Artà.

## October

**La Beata** (16th): Costumed procession in Palma.

**Festa des Botifarró** (third Sunday): *Botifarró* sausage festival in Sant Joan.

## November

**Dijous Bò** (third Thursday): Major agricultural show in Inca.

**Festa de Sant Andreu** (30th): *Festa* in Santanyí.

## December

**Navidad** (25th): Mallorcan Christmas with carol concerts and Nativity scenes.

**Festa de l'Estendard** (31st): Palma remembers Jaume I's capture of the city in 1229.

*Ask at a tourist office for up-to-date information, as dates sometimes change.*

Festivals

Costumed figures re-enact festive life in Mallorca

# Impressions

*Mallorca presents few problems to visitors, though services and facilities can get strained at peak season. To get the best out of Mallorca, spend time picking the right resort and accommodation for your needs, then use this as a base for forays to other parts of the island.*

## When to go

Mallorca is very much a summer holiday resort, with the season running between April and October. July and August are the peak months. If you pay a visit outside of these times be prepared for poor weather. Many of the hotels close for at least part of the winter, and the choice of excursions, restaurants and shops, and the opening hours of sights are all considerably reduced. Great efforts are currently being made to make it an attractive destination all year round for holidaymakers.

However, Palma never really closes, and if lying on a sun-scorched beach is not your main objective, Mallorca can be very rewarding to visit in either spring or late autumn, when things are less hectic.

Rural Mallorca shows a different facet of the island

Try a tour of Palma by horse and carriage – Sunday is best, as there is less traffic

## Where to stay

Most visitors to Mallorca stay in pre-booked accommodation. Pick somewhere as close as possible to your preferred holiday option, whether the seafront in Palma, or rural isolation in a mountain farmhouse, or round-the-clock partying at resorts such as Palma Nova and S'Arenal.

Bear in mind that most resorts, though superficially international, are often favoured by one or two nationalities in particular. For example, you will find Germans mostly in S'Arenal, Scandinavians in Cala Major, the French in Port de Sóller and the British in Magaluf and Port de Pollença. Whether it is best to stay with or without your compatriots is another tough decision.

For the types of accommodation available, *see pp170–73.*

## Getting around

Wherever you stay on Mallorca, any other part of the island can be reached within a day trip. In recent years the roads have greatly improved; if you enjoy driving and like to get out into the peace of the mountains or visit the quieter beaches, it is worth hiring a car for two or three days.

While it is possible to zoom around the island in a day, the sightseeing is better taken at a leisurely pace. Four drives – covering the best of Mallorca – are included in this guide. Each one can be done in around five hours, but you should really make a day of it.

Public transport on the island is good. If you are staying outside Palma, consider taking a bus into the capital rather than paying for a car you will hardly use. Buses get to most corners of (*Cont. on p26*)

# Beaches and coves

One of the nicest jobs on Mallorca must be counting its beaches. The last official tally was 76, of which more than half are awarded Blue Flags by the European Union for being safe, clean and well kept. Beaches are crucial to the success of tourism on the island, and the Mallorcans work hard to maintain standards in the resorts; the seafronts in Palma Nova, Magaluf and S'Arenal were recently given a facelift.

If you come in summer, don't waste time trying to find that undiscovered, blissfully deserted beach. It is possible to get away from (most of) it all, but you will need to park your rented car and take a long, long walk. Until recently, Platja des Trenc in the south of the island fulfilled most people's isolationist dreams, but now even that has a car park and attendant at one end. There are no developments here, though, and it is a popular spot for

A peaceful cove at Cala Llombards

The beach is easy to access at Platja de Canyamel

nude sunbathing and swimming. Nearer Palma, the tiny Platja Mago (off the road to Portals Vells) attracts a similar nudist crowd.

However, the majority of visitors are happy to join the seething, sun-wallowing masses in the resorts. The most popular beaches are those around Badia de Palma, Badia d'Alcúdia and Badia de Pollença. On the east coast the tourist centres are Cala Bona, Cala d'Or, Cala Millor and Sa Coma. *Calas* (coves) offer an enjoyable and quieter alternative to these well-known hot spots. High, deeply eroded cliffs often shelter the sands at the end of these small inlets. The water tends to be invitingly clear – ideal for snorkelling, diving from the rocks, and for strong swimmers who feel frustrated by the shallow waters in the larger bays. Try Cala Pi (south of Llucmajor), Cala Llombards and Cala Santanyí (both east of Santanyí), or the larger beaches at Cala Agulla and Cala Mesquida (both north of Capdepera).

the island, and the service is generally reliable. Tourist offices can give you a free timetable. Mallorca has two railway lines, too: a historic line running from Palma through the Serra de Tramuntana to Sóller, and a half-hour run east to Inca. The line has now been extended to Sa Pobla and Manacor.

## The Mallorcan day

Organise your sightseeing around the fact that almost everything closes for lunch and a siesta between 1.30pm and 4.30pm. A notable exception is La Seu, Palma's cathedral, which stays open through the lunch hour in summer. Most smaller museums and art galleries close on Saturday afternoon and Sunday. In the evening, the hotter the weather, the later the locals eat. Most Mallorcans wouldn't think of eating before 9pm in summer.

The resorts live by their own laws: if there are people about and if there is money to be made, the shops and bars will stay open.

### FINDING THE SIGHTS

This guide divides Mallorca into five sections, with the sights arranged alphabetically in each. If your time is limited, you should try to spend a few hours in Palma, and make a trip by car, train or bus into the mountains of the Serra de Tramuntana. The following sights of the island are recommended.

### Palma

La Seu, Palma's seafront cathedral, is the island's star sight, but find time to also

---

### THOMAS COOK'S MALLORCA

Cook's first advertised Mallorca as part of a conducted tour to the Balearics in the winter of 1903. Potential visitors were informed that 'the climate of Palma rivals that of Málaga and Algiers' and that they could visit the Cathedral, La Llotja (Lonja), bullring, casino and quaint 16th-century houses. In 1905, the island was promoted as one of the best places to view the eclipse of the sun, due to take place on 30 August that year. It was popular as a 'Winter Paradise' destination before the advent of the package holiday.

---

visit La Llotja nearby, once the city's maritime trading exchange. A walk along the seafront and Passeig des Born, the city's promenade, is the statutory introduction to the Mallorcan capital, but don't miss Es Baluard, its museum of contemporary art.

### West of Palma

Well-developed resorts run all along the coast west of Palma. Get into the mountains behind them to visit the country house of La Granja, and the tailor-made nature reserve, La Reserva. To see Mallorca in a different light, visit Porto Portals, an elite marina for the waterborne jet set, and the Fundació Pilar i Joan Miró, the studio of the late surrealist painter, Joan Miró.

### The northwest

This is the most accessible part of the Serra de Tramuntana. Take the Palma–Sóller train and the tram ride on to Port de Sóller for an insight into island life at the start of the 20th century. The former Carthusian monastery at Valldemossa, where George Sand and Frédéric Chopin stayed during their visit of 1838–9, is an essential Mallorcan sight. The Moorish gardens at Alfàbia, the spectacular descent down the northern cliffs to Sa Calobra, and the revered monastery at Lluc are all of interest.

### The northeast

Try to savour the atmosphere of at least a couple of Mallorca's ancient towns, such as Alcúdia, Artà, Petra or Pollença.

Here the scenic draws are the Cap de Formentor peninsula, the illuminated subterranean caves at Artà and the great sandy sweep of the Badia d'Alcúdia. Nature-lovers should make for the Bóquer Valley and S'Albufera wetlands.

### The south

Crossing Es Pla, Mallorca's inland plain, is as crucial to understanding the island as touring its mountains. Drive up to the religious sanctuaries on Puig de Randa for an overview of this area, then relax in the quieter *calas* (coves) of the east

Olive trees and a backdrop of mountains: a classic Mallorcan landscape near Andratx

coast. There are large caves at Drac and Hams, prehistoric ruins at Capocorb Vell, and artificial pearl and glass factories along the Palma–Manacor road. If all this sounds too much, escape on a boat to the island of Cabrera.

## Language

Catalan is the favoured language of the Balearic Islands, with each island claiming that its version is the oldest and purest one! Although many elderly people in the villages still do not speak Castilian Spanish, let alone write it, there is no need to learn Catalan before visiting Mallorca, but if you do make the slightest effort to learn even the smallest phrase, you will be better received.

A friendly 'Bon dia' (good day) to passers-by in the streets or a 'Moltes gracies' (thanks very much) in the bar or shop will do wonders. And, like people all over the world, Mallorcans are only too happy to discuss the weather – a few expressive gestures in response to the warm sun beating down on you will encourage an immediate response.

Otherwise, the language creates few problems for visitors. In Palma and in the holiday resorts, most people speak English and enjoy practising it. However, if you know any Castilian Spanish, the language remains useful. (In this book, all place names and streets are in Catalan.)

## Excursions

Organised coach and minibus excursions are a popular way of seeing the island. If you don't mind travelling at group pace to a preordained itinerary, they are an easy way to catch the well-known sights. The choice of routes increases in the summer, when some excursions are combined with a boat trip, for instance from Port de Sóller to Sa Calobra.

Most companies offer set excursions on certain days of the week: they can be booked through your hotel, holiday representative or travel agent. Itineraries do vary, so it pays to shop around. Lunch is sometimes included in the price, but it is rarely anything to get excited about and can devour a lot of sightseeing time. Hotels can provide packed lunches, or you can simply go to a supermarket and create your own picnic.

Favourite destinations for coach tours are Valldemossa, Sa Calobra, the Coves del Drac, the pearl factories at Manacor and the country house of La Granja. Trips advertised as an 'Island Tour' are rarely that comprehensive. As a rough guide, excursions venturing into the Serra de Tramuntana or out to Cap de Formentor are the most visually rewarding. It is worth remembering that you can travel under your own steam: Valldemossa is only half an hour's drive or bus ride from Palma, and to travel on the scenic Palma–Sóller train all you need to do is go to the station and buy a ticket. If you would like all the arrangements taken care of for you, a good travel agency to contact is **Viajes Marsans** (*Passeig des Born 6, Palma. Tel: (902) 30 60 90. www.marsans.es*).

Mountain scene from the Palma–Sóller wooden train

# Palma

*Palma, sometimes referred to simply as Ciutat (City), is the key to Mallorca. Stroll down its leafy promenades, behold the triumphant cathedral, savour the severe façades of its churches and the joie de vivre in its Art Nouveau buildings and you will appreciate the richness of an island that has always been far more than a developers' playground.*

Walking is the best way to discover Palma as its essential sights are arranged compactly around a central north–south pedestrian thoroughfare, Passeig des Born.

Just take a look at any map and you will see the zigzag shape of the old city walls, now a defensive stream of traffic. Apart from a seafront walk and trips to the Poble Espanyol and Castell de Bellver, there is very little need to stray outside these ancient boundaries.

## The growth of Palma

The story of present-day Palma begins with the Christian reconquest of the island in 1229. Vestiges of the Moorish presence survive in the Banys Àrabs (Arab Baths), but it is the great seafront cathedral, begun in 1230, a year after Jaume I and his troops had taken the island, that puts Palma on the map. A wealth of churches and convents was later added; there are 27 churches within the city walls today, their

Fishing boats moored along the seafront, watched over by La Seu, Palma's Gothic cathedral

# Palma city centre (*see pp48–9 for route*)

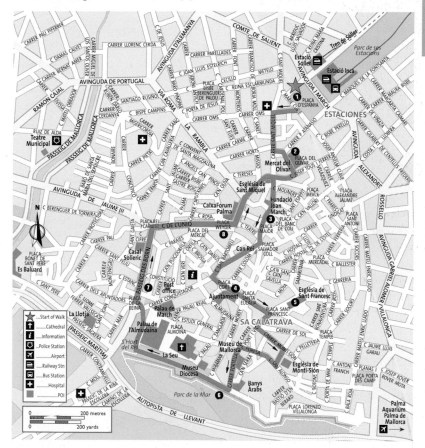

restrained exteriors complemented by stalwart palaces built by the Mallorcan aristocracy in the 17th and 18th centuries.

By 1900, when Palma's population was some 64,000, the city's outer walls had been demolished and two tree-lined promenades, Passeig de la Rambla and Passeig des Born, built above the original course of Palma's river, La Riera. Today, as part of the Mallorcans'

growing respect for their architectural heritage, many of the great turn-of-the-century buildings in the city centre are being restored. The flagship of this renaissance is the spectacular contemporary art museum, Es Baluard, built into a bastion in the old city walls. Palma's population is more than 383,000, almost half that of the island, but at heart it remains a place of peace and civility.

# Palma city plan (*see pp50–51 for route*)

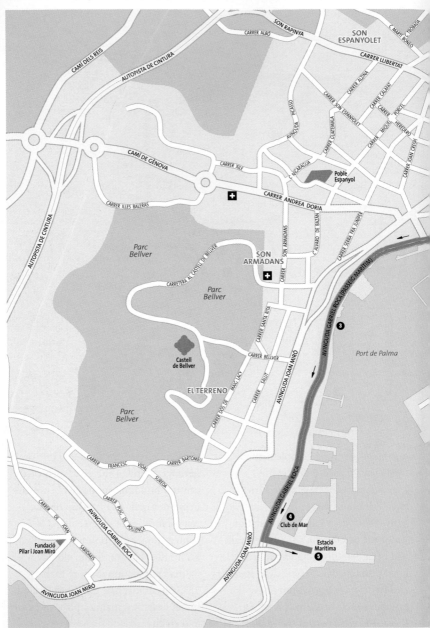

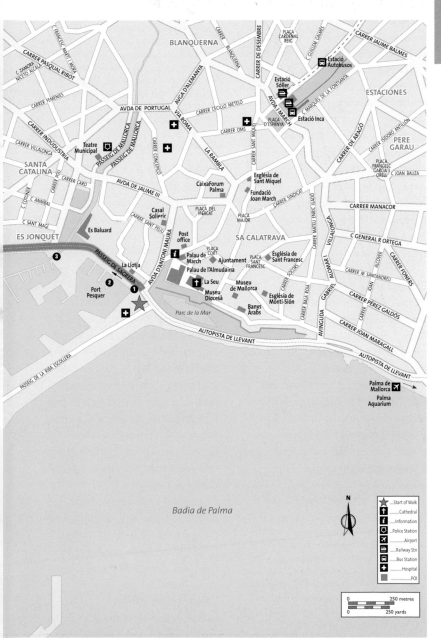

BLANQUERNA

CARRER PASQUAL RIBOT
C FRANCESC MARTÍ MORA
CARRER ZAMORA
NICETO ALCALÁ

CARRER FEMENÍES

CARRER INDÚSTRIA

CARRER VILLALONGA

SANTA
CATALINA

C COTONER
C POU
CARRER CARO
C ANNÍBAL
C SANT MAGÍ

ES JONQUET

Teatre
Municipal

PASSEIG DE MALLORCA
PASSEIG DE MALLORCA

AVDA DE PORTUGAL
AVGDA D'ALEMANYA
VIA ROMA
CARRER CECILIO METELO
CARRER OMS

CARRER CONCEPCÍO

LA RAMBLA
CARRER SANT MIQUEL

AVDA DE JAUME III

CaixaForum
Palma

Casal
Solleric
CARRER SANT FELIU

Es Baluard

PLAÇA DEL
MERCAT

PLAÇA
MAJOR

Església de
Sant Miquel

Fundació
Joan March
CARRER SINDICAT

SA CALATRAVA

CARRER DE DESEMBRE

PLAÇA
CARDENAL
REIG

C GUILLEM GALMÉS

AVDA MARCH
PLAÇA
D'ESPANYA

CARRER JAUME BALMES

Estació
Autobusos

Estació
Sóller

Estació Inca

ESTACIONES

C MARQUÉS DE LA FONTSANTA

CARRER DE ARAGÓ
CARRER ISIDORO ANTILLÓN

PERE
GARAU

PLAÇA
FRANCESC
GARCIA I
ORELL
C JOAN BAUZA

CARRER MANACOR

C GENERAL R ORTEGA

La Llotja

Port
Pesquer

PASSEIG DE SAGRERA

AVDA D'ANTONI MAURA

Post
office

Palau de
March
Palau de l'Almudaina

La Seu

Museu
Diocesà

Ajuntament

PLAÇA
CORT

PLAÇA
SANT
FRANCESC

Museu
de Mallorca

Banys
Arabs

Església de
Sant Francesc

Església de
Montí-Sión

CARRER SOCORS

CARRER MATEU ENRIC LLADÓ

CARRER BALA ROJA

VILLALONGA

ALOMAR I

GABRIEL

AVINGUDA

CARRER M. SANTANDREU

CARRER PÉREZ GALDÓS

CARRER JOAN MARAGALL

CARRER JOAN

CARRER PONERS

AUTOPISTA DE LLEVANT

AUTOPISTA DE LLEVANT

PASSEIG DE LA RIBA ESCOLERA

Parc de la Mar

Palma de
Mallorca

Palma
Aquarium

Badia de Palma

N

Start of Walk
Cathedral
Information
Police Station
Airport
Railway Stn
Bus Station
Hospital
POI

0          250 metres

0          250 yards

## Ajuntament (Town Hall)

Palma's 17th-century town hall is showy and grand, but also charming and clearly citizen-friendly. A long stone bench lines its exterior, where the locals sit looking like an identity parade for the Mallorcan character. Be sure to look up at the long-suffering caryatids and telamons carved in the eaves, and go inside if you happen to be passing when the great doors are open. To the left are a couple of rustic giants used in the city's *festes*, and another jolly-faced pair with musical instruments by the central stairs.
*Plaça Cort. Tel: (971) 22 59 00. www.a-palma.es*

## Es Baluard

Palma's superb museum of modern and contemporary art, Es Baluard, is housed in a striking building which ingeniously incorporates a Renaissance bastion into its sleekly modern lines. The permanent collection includes 19th-century Mallorcan landscapes, and works by Joan Miró and Miquel Barceló. Temporary exhibitions are usually cutting-edge and reliably good. There's a great gift shop and the

### TOURIST OFFICES

The two major tourist offices are located at the Plaça d'Espanya (*tel: (902) 10 23 65*) and at the Plaça de la Reina 2 (*tel: (971) 71 22 16*). There are additional offices located for convenience – Casal Solleric Office at Passeig des Born 27 (*tel: (902) 10 23 65*), Palma Beach Plaça Meravelles s/n, Platja de Palma (*tel: (971) 26 45 32*), and the Airport Information Office (*tel: (971) 78 95 56*).

rooftop terrace with café offers some of the best views in town.
*Plaça Porta Santa Catalina 10.
Tel: (971) 90 82 00. www.esbaluard.org.
Open: 1 Oct–15 Jun Tue–Sun
10am–8pm; 16 Jun–30 Sept Tue–Sun
10am–9pm. Admission charge.*

## Banys Àrabs (Arab Baths)

Palma's Arab Baths are a souvenir of Medina Mayurqa, the Moorish city that once existed here from the 8th to the 13th century. The baths date from the 10th century: the domed colander-like roof, originally pierced with 25 small skylights, is supported by 12 slender columns. Bathers used to move between two chambers, the hot steamy *caldarium* and the cooler *tepidarium*.
*Carrer de Can Serra 3–7. Tel: (971) 72 15 49. Follow the signs from the cathedral. Open: daily 9.30am–7.30pm (summer); 9.30am–6pm (winter). Closed: as it pleases, so ringing ahead is a good idea. Admission charge.*

## CaixaForum Palma

Palma's Gran Hotel, the city's first quality hotel, opened in 1902. Designed

Built to a rare circular design, Castell de Bellver crowns a hill to the west of Palma

by the Catalan architect Lluis Domènech i Montaner, it was the first of several Modernista (Spanish Art Nouveau) buildings to grace the city. In 1993, after careful restoration by the Fundació La Caixa, it was unveiled as a stunning cultural centre staging exhibitions and musical events. Spectacularly lit up at night, it has a popular ground-floor bar/café.

*Plaça Weyler 3. Tel: (971) 17 85 00. Open: Mon–Sat 10am–9pm, Sun 10am–2pm. Admission charge for special events, otherwise free.*

### Castell de Bellver (Bellver Castle)

Even today, this great castle, begun in 1309, can easily be seen from Palma's seafront. Framed by thick pinewoods, it stood as a signal to all-comers that the island's rulers were firmly in control. If you do not have a car, consider taking a taxi up, then walking back through the woods – look for the path opposite the entrance, which leads down via a chapel to Carrer de Bellver and Avinguda de Joan Miró.

Bellver means 'good view', and the opportunity to stand on its roof and survey Palma and its bay should not be missed. The castle is remarkable for its circular shape. Four round towers stand at the compass points, with the largest, the Tower of Homage, connected by an arch to the centre. A deep moat, which you can walk right around, completes the defences.

The mighty façade of the Església de Sant Francesc

Restful cloisters lie within the Església de Sant Francesc

The castle was used as a summer residence by the Mallorcan kings, and served for many centuries as a political prison: graffiti carved by French prisoners-of-war can still be seen on its stones. Today the atmosphere is rather sterile, but the central arcaded courtyard and sweeping stone roof above (carefully designed to feed every raindrop into a central cistern) are aesthetic marvels. Archaeological finds from around Mallorca are exhibited in some of the lower rooms. The castle is home to the Despuìg classical sculpture collection, displayed on the upper level, and is used as a popular venue for concerts in the summer, and for government receptions.

*West of Avinguda Joan Miró. Tel: (971) 73 06 57. Open: Apr–Sept daily 8am–8pm; Oct–Mar 8am–7pm. Sun & holidays 10am–7pm. Museums closed on Sun. Admission charge to museums.*

## Església de Sant Francesc (St Francis Church)

A statue of Junípero Serra, California's founding friar (*see pp40–41*), greets visitors to this mighty church. Behind him rises a sober, sunbaked façade, with an impressively ornate portal added in 1700. Foundations for the church and monastery of St Francis were laid in 1281, but the original ensemble was remodelled following a strike by lightning in 1580. The cloisters are an example of the many tranquil oases that lie hidden behind the high walls of Old Palma. Lemon trees, a central well and arcades of slim Gothic pillars create

The main entrance to La Llotja

### Església de Sant Miquel (St Michael Church)

The Church of Sant Miquel is one of the most popular in the city. Its plain façade dates from the 14th century. Built on the site of a mosque, it was here that Jaume I celebrated Mass after capturing the city in the name of Christianity.
*Carrer de Sant Miquel 2.*
*Tel: (971) 71 54 55. Open: Mon–Sat 5–7pm; on Sun, as services permit. Free admission.*

### Fundació Joan March (March Foundation)

The Mallorcan banker, Joan March, who financed Franco's uprising and became one of the world's wealthiest men, amassed a substantial modern art collection. Among the large and colourful works of Spanish contemporary art displayed are pieces by the famous, including Picasso, Miró, Dalí and the Mallorca-born Miquel Barceló.
*Carrer de Sant Miquel 11.*
*Tel: (971) 71 35 15. www.march.es.*
*Open: Mon–Fri 10am–6.30pm, Sat 10.30am–2pm. Closed: Sun. Free admission.*

### La Llotja (The Exchange)

Close to the seafront, La Llotja and its adjacent *plaça* (square) and garden are testimony to the maritime might that underpinned Palma's prosperity. Built between 1426 and 1456 to designs by Guillem Sagrera, La Llotja served as a meeting place for shipping merchants

a meditative ambience. In comparison, the interior of the church, with its vaulted ceiling, Baroque altar and intensely decorated side chapels, seems pompous and overblown. A focal point of interest is the spotlit tomb of the 13th-century Mallorcan writer Ramón Llull, which is behind the altar in the first chapel on the left. His effigy rests high up in the wall, adorned by an inverted crescent symbolising his missionary work in North Africa.
*Plaça Sant Francesc 6–7.*
*Tel: (971) 71 26 95. Open: Mon–Fri 3–6pm. Admission charge.*

and commercial traders. A kindly guardian angel hovers over the entrance, but once you are within it is not hard to imagine a cut-throat atmosphere with insider deals being struck on the stone benches and hard-done-by merchants gazing up in despair at the palm-like pillars supporting the vaulted roof. When Palma's seafaring fortunes declined, La Llotja became a granary and is now used as a venue for cultural exhibitions. *Plaça Llotja. Palma Tourist Office. Tel: (971) 71 17 05. Open: check before visiting. Free admission.*

## Palma Aquarium

Explore the world's seas and oceans, from the Mediterranean to the Pacific, at Palma's brand-new aquarium, a favourite with families. The faithfully re-created habitats are

(*Cont. on p42*)

Once a hotel, CaixaForum Palma is now the flagship of Palma's architectural renaissance

# Local heroes

Mallorca's two best-known sons both gained fame and beatification through their work as missionaries.

Ramón Llull, whose flowing-bearded statue enjoys a commanding position on Palma's seafront, was born in 1235 of noble parentage. His sudden conversion to the religious cause is alleged to have been the result of a grotesque incident near Palma's Santa Eulalia church. During a hot-blooded courtship of a married woman, he rode his horse into the church where she was praying, then pursued her down the street. Unable to deter his ardour, his quarry suddenly pulled up her blouse to reveal breasts riddled with cancerous growths.

Duly chastened, the 40-year-old Llull embarked on a career of scholarly devotion that took him to medieval centres of learning around the Mediterranean. A prolific author who wrote in Latin, Catalan and Arabic on subjects ranging from metaphysics to gastronomy, Llull founded a religious sanctuary that still stands on top of Puig de Randa. He is said to have been stoned to death by an infidel mob while spreading the word in Tunisia at the age of 80, and is now buried in the Església de Sant Francesc in Palma.

## PUNISHED FOR PUNS

Two witty heroes of Mallorcan history are portrayed in the Sant Sebastià chapel in La Seu. During the siege of Castell d'Alaró (*see p70*) by Alfonsó III in 1285, the soldiers Cabrit and Bassa deliberately mistook the hostile king's name, Alfonsó, for *anfós*, a local fish. 'We like our *anfós* grilled!' they yelled in defiance. After Alfonsó took the castle, he asked what their names were. Then he roasted Cabrit and Bassa alive on a spit – just like *cabritos* (kid goats).

Four centuries later, Junípero Serra (1713–84) was born into a humble family in the country town of Petra in the east of the island. At the age of 17 he joined the Franciscan order and in 1749 sailed to Mexico as a missionary to convert its natives to Catholicism.

When he was 54 years of age, Serra embarked on a bold colonising crusade, backed by the Spanish Crown, to establish missionary stations in what is now the state of California in the USA. The first was built at San Diego in 1769 and, by the time of Junípero Serra's death 15 years later, a line of nine missions stretched north to San Francisco. Twelve more were completed after his death, linked by El Camino Real (The Royal Road).

Homage to Junípero Serra in Palma

home to everything from stingrays to sea horses, but the slow journey through the gigantic shark tank remains the biggest draw.

*Carrer Manuela de los Herreros I Sorà 21, Platja de Palma. Tel: (971) 26 42 75. www.palmaaquarium.com. Open: daily 10am–6pm. Admission charge (expensive).*

## Museu Diocesà (Diocesan Museum)

Tucked round the back of the cathedral in the Episcopal Palace is one of the most engaging museums in Palma. More like an antiques shop than a museum, its displays are a wide-ranging mixture of religious and historical *objets trouvés* from around the island, including Roman *amphorae*, Moorish pottery and painted tiles, Mallorcan coins, bibles, missals and paintings and statues of pious and suffering saints. Highlights include a 13th-century Mudéjar pulpit, a portrait of Sant Jordi (St George) with medieval Palma in the background, and an 18th-century jasper sepulchre for Jaume II. Best of all, you get a rare chance to stare into the eyes of some jovial and anguished religious statues which are not, as is normal, set on high.

*Carrer de Mirador 5. Tel: (971) 72 38 60. Open: Mon–Sat 10am–2pm. Admission charge.*

## Museu de Mallorca (Museum of Mallorca)

Mallorca's leading historical museum occupies a 17th-century mansion known as Casa de la Gran Cristiana, in one of the most evocative corners of old Palma. To the right as you enter are rooms devoted to the Moorish occupation of Mallorca, with exhibits that include bowls, jars and pottery oil lamps. The mansion was in fact built on the site of one of the island's earliest Arab houses. In the main building, several rooms are devoted to the Talayot period (*see pp10–11*), with ceramics, Bronze Age tools and weapons, and jewellery. Upstairs, overseen by an attractive angel, are poorly displayed religious paintings rescued from the island's churches and monasteries. There are also painted tiles and crockery from the 18th and 19th centuries as well as a section of Modernist furniture. Changing exhibitions on themes like Mallorcan cartography and writers increase the museum's appeal.

*Carrer de Portella 5. Tel: (971) 71 75 40. Open: Tue–Sat 10am–7pm, Sun 10am–2pm. Closed: Mon. Admission charge.*

## Palau de l'Almudaina (Almudaina Palace)

*Almudaina* is the Arab word for 'citadel', and Palma's Royal Palace evolved from the Moorish *alcázar* (fortress) that once commanded the Badia de Palma. Originally used by the kings of Mallorca, the royal functions of the palace have been revived with the reinstatement of the Spanish monarchy.

Self-guided tours (using an audioguide) now include the offices used by King Juan Carlos I and Queen Sofía when they visit the island in the summer. Part of the building is still occupied by the military, who permit photography only in certain directions. Tours start in the central courtyard, and proceed through a series of Gothic reception rooms and chambers decorated with antique furniture and tapestries; in some parts original 17th-century frescoes have been revealed. After walking on the terrace, which offers a kingly view of Palma, visitors return to the courtyard. On the west side is the Capilla de Santa Ana, the Royal Chapel, which has a marbled Romanesque portal and Gothic nave.

*Carrer de Palau Reial. Tel: (971) 21 41 34.*
*www.patrimonionacianal.es. Open:*
*Apr–Sept, Mon–Fri 10am–5.30pm;*
*Oct–Mar 10am–1.15pm & 4–5.15pm,*
*Sat 10am–1.15pm. Closed: Sun.*
*Admission charge.*

## Palma sightseeing bus

A handy way to see the major sights and get a sense of where things are in the city is to hop aboard a double-decker, open-topped sightseeing bus. The service runs frequently and you can board at Parc de la Mar, Bellver Castle or Plaça d'Espanya and 12 other stops and listen to a narration in

Castell de Belver offers remarkable views of Mallorca

your own language on the provided headset. The entire circuit takes an hour and 20 minutes and you can leave the bus to visit a sight and rejoin it later.

*Tel: (902) 10 10 81. www.citysightseeing.com. Buses leave daily every 20 minutes, year-round. Please consult staff for exact times. There are 15 stops on the circuit.*

## Parc de la Mar

Created in the mid-1980s, Parc de la Mar is an extensive, multi-level public space bordering the south side of the cathedral. It is worth exploring for the changing vistas it provides of the bay and La Seu, and there are several cafés where you can take a break from the city bustle.

Parc de la Mar is a welcome break from Palma and home to modern sculptures

Modern sculpture in the park includes a tiled mural by Miró. A large lake has been specifically created to reflect the cathedral. Nearby is Ses Voltes, a series of vaults that are now an exhibition and concert space. Further west, on the ramparts and close to a children's playground, is the Arc de la Drassana Musulmana, looping over a lake with black swans. The arch dates from the Moorish presence in Palma and was once the gateway to the royal docks.

## Passeig des Born

Like Barcelona's Las Ramblas, Palma's Passeig des Born is where city life struts and loiters. In Moorish times it was a moat guarding the walled city, and in Franco's day it was, inevitably, renamed Paseo de Generalíssimo Franco. Everyone still calls it El Born though, a name derived from its days as a jousting ground.

You will not have 'done' Palma until you have walked 'The Born' or argued with its newspaper-sellers, who are famous for getting upset if you attempt to read a paper before deciding to buy it. Bordered by plane trees, benches and floral urns, and mysteriously guarded by pairs of sphinxes, this pedestrian promenade still functions as a spine dividing the city. At its southern end is Plaça de la Reina. At the north is Plaça Rei Joan Carles I, where a bizarre obelisk is supported by four minute tortoises. To the west is the elegant Can Sollerich, a restored 18th-century palace with an exhibition space and popular café. On the opposite side, Bar Bosch is a focus of city life.

## Plaça del Mercat

Walk along Carrer de l'Unió to find a popular square that presents a scene typical of traditional Palma. Beneath its venerable rubber tree is a statue of Mallorca's most famous politician, Antoni Maura, a conservative prime minister of Spain several times over at the start of the 20th century. Behind him rises the belfry of the church of Sant Nicolau. To the left are two vivacious Modernista buildings, the Pensió Menorquina, and, next door, the rippling Can Casasayas, now a clothes shop. Further along is the Palau de Justícia, Palma's courthouse. It was once a private palace called Can Berga. Walk into the courtyard to appreciate the capacious plan on which it was built.

## Poble Espanyol (Spanish Village)

Spain in a nutshell is the objective of this architectural theme park-cum-conference facility in the west of Palma. Reproduced attractions include the Patio de los Arrayanes and Arab Baths from Granada's Alhambra, Toledo's mammoth Puerta de Bisagra and Casa de El Greco, a Canary Islands house and an *ayuntamiento* (town hall) from Guipúzcoa. Spain's most popular architectural showpieces are replicated in miniature and sold as artefacts in craft workshops and souvenir shops.

Spanish architecture's greatest hits are paraded in the Poble Espanyol

*Carrer de Poble Espanyol 39. Tel: (971) 73 70 75. www.poble-espanyol.com. Open: daily from 9am, closing times vary. Shops closed: Sat afternoon & Sun. Admission charge. Bus: 5.*

## La Seu

Built right on the water's edge for all to see, Palma's cathedral is an expression of political power rather than religious fervour. Like the towering Palau de l'Almudaina and the mighty Castell de Bellver, La Seu was a declaration to the world that the island's Christian colonists were here to stay. It is particularly beautiful when seen from the sea, as intended, but like all great buildings it constantly surprises its onlookers. By day the sun burnishes the soft-toned sandstone of its south front; come nightfall its bony skeleton is illuminated like a rocket ship departing for the heavens.

## Exterior

Work began on La Seu (the Catalan word for a bishop's see) in 1230, but it was not until 1601 that the cathedral was completed. In 1851 the west front was damaged in an earthquake. During the restoration two turrets were added, and the side rose windows and doors blocked up. The cathedral saves its best profile for the sea: a stroll along the south front provides good views of the line of pinnacled buttresses that support the central nave. The Portal del Mirador here dates from 1389 and includes a *Last Supper* in the tympanum and five statues on either side of the door by the Mallorcan sculptor, Guillem Sagrera.

## Treasury

The cathedral is entered on its north side through the Portal del Almoina where alms were dispensed to the poor. This leads into the Treasury, where vast numbers of manuscripts, silverware, monstrances, processional props and holy relics are displayed. A pair of early 18th-century man-high candelabra gives a clue to the past wealth enjoyed by the Catholic Church in Mallorca.

## Interior

Stand with your back to the west front's rarely opened Portal Mayor, and you

Detail from the Portal del Mirador

will appreciate the size and rhythm of the cathedral's three naves. Supported by 14 slender octagonal pillars, the central nave soars 44m (144ft) high, and the east rose window, with a diameter of 13.3m (43½ft), is among the largest in the world. The glass was damaged during an air raid at the start of the Spanish Civil War. In 1902 Antoni Gaudí, architect of Barcelona's dazzling Sagrada Família church, was invited to restore the cathedral to its 14th-century glory. His reforms remain controversial: some visitors will gain spiritual uplift from the illuminated Crown of Thorns now suspended over the altar, others may feel it looks like an accident at a funfair.

Among the 14 side chapels, Nostra Senyora de la Corona (on the south side, second in from the east) has four athletic angels brought from the Carthusian monastery in Valldemossa. The most striking chapel is the Chapel of Sant Pere 'El Santisimo', created by Mallorcan artist Miguel Baneló and inaugurated in early 2007. The walls seem to undulate, echoing the sea, and the images recall the biblical story of the feeding of the five thousand with loaves and fishes. Other points of interest are the Plateresque stone pulpit to the north of the altar and the 110 walnut choir stalls carved in 1328. The oldest part of the cathedral, the Trinity Chapel, is behind the altar but not accessible. Inside are the tombs of Jaume II and Jaume III: times have changed since George Sand visited in 1838, when guides would open up their marble sarcophagi so that visitors could behold the mummified corpses. The exit from the cathedral leads through its neglected cloisters. Look up and you can see La Seu's 47m (154ft) high belltower. When its largest bell, which weighs over four tonnes, was rung in 1857 as a storm warning it shattered most of the cathedral's stained glass.

*Carrer de Palau Reial 29. Tel: (902) 02 24 45. www.catedraldemallorca.org. Open: Jun–Sept Mon–Fri 10am– 6.15pm, Sat 10am–2.15pm; Apr, May & Oct Mon–Fri 10am–5.15pm, Sat 10am–2.15pm; Nov–Mar Mon–Fri 10am–3.15pm, Sat 10am–2.15pm.*

The cathedral's south front once stood right at the water's edge

# Walk: Historic Palma

*The charm of modern Palma, which was once an ancient Mediterranean port city, comes from its architectural blend of Gothic, Moorish and Renaissance monuments. This walk should preferably be taken before 1pm when markets and churches are open.* (See map on p31 for route.)

*Allow 2 hours, excluding stops at sights and bars.*

*Start at Plaça d'Espanya.*

### 1 Plaça d'Espanya

In the centre of this transport hub of Mallorca is the equestrian statue of Jaume I, Conquistador of Mallorca. *Walk west via Plaça de la Porta Pintada to Carrer de Sant Miquel. Turn south, past the church of Santa Catalina and the Hospital Militar on the opposite corner.*

### 2 Mercat del Olivar

Veer left into Plaça del Olivar, the city's most enjoyable market: see spectacular displays in the *peixateria* (fish market). *Take Carrer de Josep Tous I Ferrer back to Carrer de Sant Miquel.*

### 3 Plaça Major

Look in the Church of Sant Miquel (*see p38*), then follow the pedestrianised Carrer de Sant Miquel past the Fundació March (*see p38*) to the enclosed, arcaded Plaça Major, with its street entertainers and artisans' stalls.

Leave by the opposite arch. Look up to the right to admire two Modernista buildings, L'Àguila and Can Forteza Rei. *Walk down Carrer de Jaume II.*

### 4 Plaça Cort

Carrer de Jaume II is typical of the lively pedestrian shopping streets that lie east of Passeig des Born. At the bottom, turn left past the blushing

The wonderfully decorated Església de Sant Miquel

edifice of Can Corbella for Plaça Cort. The square, with its wizened olive tree, is dominated by the Ajuntament (*see p34*).
*Cross to take Carrer del Convent de Sant Francesc.*

### 5 Plaça de Sant Francesc

Passing the restored 13th-century Church of Santa Eulalia, you reach the Església de Sant Francesc (*see pp37–8*). The narrow streets here, with their high-walled, solid-door buildings, are filled with the introspective spirit of old Palma. Turn back down Carrer del Pare Nadal, then left into Carrer de Monti-Sión to reach the Jesuit Església de Monti-Sión with its glorious and grimy Baroque façade.
*Take the adjacent Carrer de Vent, turn right into Carrer de Sant Alonso and Carrer de la Puresa, then go left down Carrer de la Portella. After passing the Museu de Mallorca (see p42), note the sneering faces adorning the Hostal Isabel II as you leave the old city.*

### 6 Parc de la Mar

Sunlight returns as you emerge by the city ramparts. Just before the arching Porta de la Portella, turn right up an incline to walk beside the south front of the cathedral, with views over the Parc de la Mar.

At the end, descend some steps and turn right into S'Hort del Rei, the shady gardens with fountains situated in front of the Moorish Palau de l'Almudaina (*see* Honderos *box, p34*).

*Modernista* decor in Carrer de Jaume II

*At the end of the gardens walk through an arch and cross the small garden in Plaça de la Reina.*

### 7 Passeig des Born

Walk the length of this historic avenue (*see pp44–5*).
*Turn right into Carrer de l'Unió.*

### 8 Plaça Weyler

Passing the shabby bulk of the Círculo de Bellas Artes on your left, and the leafy world of Plaça del Mercat (*see p45*) on the right, you reach Plaça Weyler and the Modernista grandeur of the CaixaForum Palma (*see pp34–5*). Follow the curve of the road, passing the Teatre Principal, to reach the tree-lined avenue of La Rambla, which was once a river but is today awash with flower stalls.
*Climb up Costa de la Pols, by the Libreria Fondevilas bookshop, to return to Carrer de Sant Miquel.*

# Walk: Maritime Palma

*Palma embraces the sea, and a stroll along its waterfront provides ample proof that this long-standing love affair is far from over. This easy walk follows the curve of the bay from the city centre to its passenger ship terminal, and is particularly enjoyable in the early evening. It can also be done in reverse – just take a taxi, a number 1 bus, or a horse-drawn carriage out to the Estació Marítima, and walk back. (See map on pp32–3 for route).*

*Allow 1½ hours one way.*

*The walk starts in Passeig de Sagrera, just west of the roundabout and statue of Ramón Llull at the southern end of Avinguda d'Antoni Maura.*

### 1 Passeig de Sagrera

Lined with tall palms, this pedestrian avenue is flanked to the north by historic buildings recalling Palma's maritime past. An ancient gate to the port, Porta Vella del Moll, has been reconstructed to the left of the 15th-century Exchange, La Llotja (*see pp38–9*). Next door is the galleried Consulat del Mar, built in the 17th century as a court to resolve trading disputes. Decorated with flags and cannons, it is now used by the Balearic Islands' government.

Two statues can be seen at either end of Passeig de Sagrera. To the east is the bearded medieval sage Ramón Llull, apparently making notes of traffic violations with pen and quill. To the west is the Nicaraguan writer and modernist poet Rubén Dario.

*Cross Avinguda Gabriel Roca by the yellow traffic lights and walk west along the seafront.*

### 2 Port Pesquer

Lines of vivid blue nets strung along the quayside mark the entrance to Palma's fishing port, where fishermen paint boats and mend nets. The monumental pair of sundials nearby offers a brainteasing explanation of how to convert True Time into Legal Time.

*Continue walking west, passing through a small garden.*

### 3 Passeig Marítim

Though bordered by a busy road, this waterside promenade allows walkers to progress peacefully round the harbour. A 4.5km (2¾-mile) cycle track from Portixol west to Sa Pedrera runs alongside. On the left you pass Palma's Reial Club Nautic (Royal Yacht Club), while across the road rise the mighty bastions that once protected Palma. One of these now contains the contemporary arts museum, Es Baluard, with a fabulous rooftop café which commands superb sea views. The remains of five windmills dominate the skyline. On the horizon ahead you can see the imposing silhouette of Castell de Bellver. Further along you reach a tree-lined jetty where excursion boats offer tours of the harbour, and a monument celebrates Palma's 15th-century cartographers.

*Continue southwest along the seafront.*

### 4  Club de Mar

This walk is really a social climb through Palma's seafaring classes. Hardworking fishing vessels give way to hobby boats and weekend craft, rust buckets and tourist galleons are overshadowed by gin palaces and Mediterranean cruise ships. The Club de Mar is where many of these pleasure boats moor – a captivating sight for anyone drawn to the romance of the sea. Spare a moment to look back across the bay at Palma cathedral.

*Follow the pavement east, passing under a bridge.*

### 5  Estació Marítima

Naval ships, cruise liners, ferries from mainland Spain and the other Balearic islands all call here at various times of the year. Walk as far as the large anchor set on a lawn, and you can see two more signs of Palma's maritime

prowess: the 15th-century Torre Paraires, like a chess-piece castle, and beyond it the medieval lighthouse at Porto Pi.

*Take a taxi or number 1 bus back from the Estació Marítima.*

Working fishing boats add a note of salty realism to the leisured ambience of Palma's seafront

# West of Palma

*The western corner of Mallorca was one of the first areas to be settled by the Spanish in the 13th century – a cross at Santa Ponça commemorates the spot where Jaume I and his troops landed on 12 September 1229. Today a ribbon of resorts decorates the south coast all the way to Sant Elm, the port closest to the dramatic, lizard-shaped island of Sa Dragonera. Inland, and along the precipitous north coast, you can tour some of the most enjoyable mountain scenery on the island.*

### Andratx

Known to the Romans as *Andrachium*, Andratx was built inland from its harbour (Port d'Andratx) as a precaution against pirate attack, a measure that has also saved it from the tourism developments now ravaging this coast. Framed by orange groves, the town appears still to be on the defensive, with sturdy buildings lining its narrow streets, its few shops hiding their minimal wares behind opaque doors and curtained windows. Andratx is dominated by the hulking 13th-century church of Santa Maria, which

was rebuilt in the 1720s, and – further up the valley – the castellated 16th-century mansion of Son Mas.
*32km (20 miles) west of Palma on the Ma-10. Tourist Office: Avenida de la Cúria 1. Tel: (971) 62 80 19.*

### Cala Major

The Badia de Palma is fringed with a string of tourist developments, of which Cala Major is the closest to Palma. The resort is a mixture of high-class residences now somewhat swamped by mass-market complexes. There is a small sandy beach, but parking can be

Scene on the Victory Cross at Santa Ponça

difficult. Further west are two more resorts, **Sant Agustí** and **Ses Illetes**, with similar facilities. The latter has a less frantic atmosphere, with swimming possible off the rocks. The three resorts are fast becoming one, though who is devouring whom is uncertain.

The coastline here is dominated by the closely guarded summer residence of the Spanish royal family at Marivent, where the monarchs indulge in their favourite pastimes of sailing and entertaining.

*6km (4 miles) southwest of Palma.*

### CASTELL DE BENDINAT

The outline of this 13th-century castle can easily be seen 8km (5 miles) southwest of Palma, near the turn-off for Bendinat when you are driving along the Palma–Andratx road. Enlarged in the 18th century, Castell de Bendinat is now a conference hall and not open to the public, but nevertheless makes a majestic sight with its battlements, fortified towers and surrounding pinewoods. According to an oft-told story, its name derives from an after-dinner remark uttered by a contented Jaume I after the king and his retinue had dined on the site in 1229. *'Havem ben dinat'* ('We have eaten well'), the monarch is said to have declared.

## West of Palma (*see pp64–5 for route*)

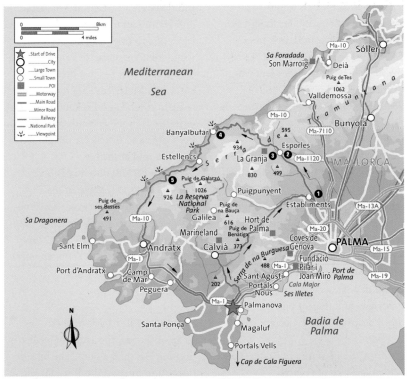

## Calvià

On the southern edge of the Serra de Tramuntana, Calvià appears to be just another attractive country town where nothing much happens. But as the administrative centre for the district of Calvià, its municipal offices rule over a great swathe of pulsating resorts stretching west from Ses Illetes to Santa Ponça. Despite the profits and problems this brings, the town remains endearingly tranquil, with rustic bars and Mallorcan-cuisine restaurants where you can escape the madness of the coast. Calvià's unmissable landmark is its church, begun in 1245. The small square beside it offers extensive views over the neighbouring farms and fields flecked with olive and carob trees. Don't miss the lively pictorial history of the town displayed in tiles on the wall of the nearby library.

*18km (11 miles) west of Palma, take the road to Establiments.*

## Camp de Mar

In a secluded bay surrounded by high cliffs, this holiday village has a small sandy beach with swimming off the rocks. Just offshore is a tiny islet reached by a frail bridge, where there is a restaurant. An enjoyable 5km (3-mile) walk leads uphill from Camp de Mar, west along a coast of fine views and fragant pines, and down again to Port d'Andratx (*see p60*).

*25km (15½ miles) west of Palma, 4km (2½ miles) west of Peguera.*

### MUSHROOMS

In the Mallorcan countryside you may see signs declaring '*Se Prohibe Buscar Setas*' (Do Not Pick the Mushrooms). The warnings are worth heeding, not because you might be pinching an islander's breakfast, but because it is hard for the untrained eye to tell the difference between the edible and the poisonous. Some 700 species are found on Mallorca, including four or five that can be deadly. Wild mushrooms are generally picked in the autumn – look for the trumpet-shaped *girgola* variety sold in markets.

## Coves de Gènova

If you don't have the time or inclination to see the great multicoloured caverns at Artà, Drac and Hams (*see p99, p121 & p124*), these caves offer a brief insight into the wonderland of stalactites and stalagmites that lies just below the surface of Mallorca. They are located close to several good restaurants – the entrance is in the grounds of restaurant Les Coves and tickets for the guided tour are sold at the bar.

*5km (3 miles) southwest of Palma. Look for signs to Gènova off the Palma–Andratx motorway, then climb up a steep hill to the Coves. Carrer de Barranc 45. Tel: (971) 40 23 87. Open: daily 10am–1.30pm, 4–7pm (summer); 10am–1pm, 4–6pm (winter). Admission charge. Bus: 4.*

## Fundació Pilar i Joan Miró

In Spanish eyes, the artist Joan Miró is nothing less than a saint. The hillside house and purpose-built studio where the painter lived and worked from 1956 has now been proclaimed 'Miró Territory'. Galleries have been built in bleached stone to exhibit some of the 5,000 works he left behind, and you can peep into the studio where he worked, left much as it was at the time of his death in 1983. The adjacent garden, with its trees, stones and old cartwheel, gives clues to the way Miró drew inspiration from the Mallorcan landscape. As his friend Joan Prats put it: 'When I pick up a rock, it's a rock; when Miró picks it up, it's a Miró.'

*4km (2½ miles) southwest of Palma. Carrer de Joan de Saridakis 29, Cala Major. Tel: (971) 70 14 20. http://miro.palmademallorca.es. Open: mid-May–mid-Sept, Tue–Sat 10am–7pm; mid-Sept–mid-May, Tue–Sat 10am–6pm, Sun 10am–3pm year round. Admission charge. Bus: 3 & 46.*

The story of Calvià's agriculture is recorded in tiles on the walls of the town library

## Galilea

If you get the urge to jump into a hire car and swap the concrete mayhem of the Badia de Palma for tranquil rural scenery and the mountain air, Galilea is a worthwhile destination. You can get to this isolated village via Calvià (*see p54*) or Puigpunyent (*see p62*), following winding but generally quiet roads through delightful scenery. To the north rises the mighty peak of Puig de Galatzó.

Surrounded by cultivated hills with almond and carob trees and the odd picturesque windmill, Galilea has developed into an artists' colony. Steep roads lead up to the parish church in Plaça Pio XII, from where there are terrific views down the island to the sea. There are also two cafés which make a visit here complete.

*25km (15¹/₂ miles) west of Palma, 13km (8 miles) north of Calvià.*

## La Granja

A grand Mallorcan country house set on a large estate in a wooded valley,

La Granja was originally a Cistercian monastery. A natural spring here still spouts water some 9m (30ft) into the air, and the site has been occupied since Moorish times. It has been owned by a succession of noble families since the 15th century, and its present owners, the Segui family, take an active interest in running the estate.

La Granja is an engrossing window on Mallorca's past (although it's best out of season, when it isn't clogged with coach tours). A vast collection of antiques, furniture, ceramics and art adorns the house, and everyday life on the estate is recalled with displays of tools and household equipment in its kitchens, cellars and workshops. Visitors can watch wool being spun and lace and candles being made, sip Mallorcan wine and herbal liqueurs, and sample traditional homemade cakes and sweets. The bar-restaurant serves tasty Mallorcan dishes. After your meal, you can walk in extensive grounds that include ornamental

The mansion of La Granja

shrubs, medicinal plants and a 1.2km ($^3$/$_4$-mile) signposted walk in the company of roaming pigs and goats.
*15km (9 miles) northwest of Palma, 1.5km (1 mile) west of Esporles. Tel: (971) 61 00 32. www.lagranja.net. Open: daily 10am–7pm in summer; 10am–6pm in winter. Folk music, dance and games are staged every Wed & Fri 3.30–5pm. Admission charge.*

### Hort de Palma (Garden of Palma)
On the northwestern outskirts of Palma is the fertile countryside called Hort de Palma. This cultivated landscape, with its small villages and undulating roads, is only 5km (3 miles) from the centre of the capital and makes a refreshing change from the resorts below. Several old estates and mansions have been turned into high-class hotels and restaurants.

The Hotel Son Vida, a converted castle, and the newer Arabella Golf Hotel, with gardens and golf courses, are two luxury hotels. Open to non-residents, they make a refined venue for a drink or meal.
*From the Palma–Andratx motorway or the Via Cintura ring road, follow the signs north for Son Vida, passing through the busy shopping district of Sa Vileta.*

### Marineland
The resort of Calvià is home to one of the island's best-known family attractions. The stars of Marineland are its performing dolphins and sea

Palmanova is a favourite resort with package holiday operators

lions, whose regular displays of ball-balancing, hoop-jumping, synchronised leaping and zealous aquabatics attract appreciative crowds. In the Parrot Circus, trained macaws exhibit their skill at arithmetic and ride a comic cavalcade of bicycles, jeeps and roller skates.

Marineland boasts one of the largest collections of sharks in Europe, and has bred its own sea lions and dolphins. An aquarium, reptile zoo and pearl-diving show are other attractions.
*10km (6 miles) southwest of Palma off the Palma–Andratx motorway. Tel: (971) 67 51 25. www.marineland.es. Open: daily mid-Mar–mid-Nov 9.30am–6pm. Admission charge.*

### Palmanova/Magaluf
The gaudy, throbbing heart of mass tourism on the island, Palmanova offers
(*Cont. on p60*)

# Flora

One of the most memorable sights in Mallorca is the pinky-white haze of its almond trees in blossom. Come at the end of January or early in February and the fields of the central plain appear covered with snow. By then the many lemon and orange trees are bejewelled with mature fruit, and Mallorca seems an island of Eden-like plenty.

In March and April wild flowers appear in the banks and verges – tiny orange field marigolds (*Calendula arvenis*) and the tall white-flowered umbellifers and cow parsley known to the British as Queen Anne's lace. On the roadsides you will see shepherd's purse (*Capsella bursa-pastoris*), common fennel (*Foeniculum vulgare*), bright yellow oxalis and the white

Endless orange tree orchards are a feast for the eyes

Spring flowers in a country garden

flowers of the tall, spiky asphodel. Walkers will enjoy the blue-flowered rosemary and vivid yellow broom that illuminate the hills.

The shiny-leaved strawberry trees (*Arbutus unedo*), with fruits that turn red in October, always draw the attention – there are plenty on the road between Can Picafort and Artà. Carob trees, holm oaks, dwarf palms and Aleppo pines are ubiquitous, as are silvery-leaved olive trees. Some of these are over 1,000 years old, with fantastically contorted trunks to prove it. At dusk, as George Sand noted, they resemble fairy-tale monsters 'which one expects every moment to break into prophetic voice'.

With such natural abundance, the Mallorcans are understandably fond of flowers. Take a walk through the flower stalls on Palma's La Rambla and you can see the serious contemplation that invariably precedes a purchase. Like their Moorish predecessors, the islanders value gardens as places of beauty and refuge from the summer heat. Their balconies and patios are often full of ferns, carnations and geraniums and, in the resorts, garish modern architecture is tempered by the presence of date palms, cacti, honeysuckle and bougainvillaea.

the archetypal package holiday experience. The beach here is good, with fine white sands somewhere under the rows of bronzing bodies, and shallow, child-safe water nearby. Behind this lies a dense grid of high-rise apartment blocks and hotels with plenty of bars, restaurants and souvenir shops. A five-minute walk inland, in Carrer de Tenis, is the family amusement Golf Fantasia.

To the west, Palmanova merges into Magaluf, creating a continuous resort, sometimes referred to as Maganova. Magaluf was among Mallorca's earliest tourist developments and is synonymous with the cheap 'n' cheerful sun 'n' sea holidays that brought the island to the world's attention – though not always for the right reasons. Magaluf is still a concrete jungle, attracting a raucous element. Both resorts have been given a long-overdue facelift, widening the seafront promenade and creating new boulevards, gardens and green spaces.

*14km (8½ miles) southwest of Palma, off the Palma–Andratx motorway. Tourist Office: Passeig de la Mar 13, Palmanova. Tel: (971) 68 23 65.*

## Peguera

Peguera is a well-established package holiday centre with two sandy beaches, Platja de Palmira and the smaller Platja de Tora. Several of its hotels stay open through the winter, and the

### LA JET-SET

Mallorca's reputation as an island of sun, sea and celebrities is well earned. The Spanish and British royal families often holiday here, heading a VIP guest list that stretches from Errol Flynn and Charlie Chaplin, to Jack Nicholson and Claudia Schiffer. Some arrive in luxury yachts and cruisers, others stay at top hotels such as the Son Vida and La Residencia, or rent dream-size villas in the mountains. A few even buy property: for instance, film star Michael Douglas purchased a house once owned by Archduke Luis Salvador of Austria. Douglas started a centre (subsequently bought by the local government), the Centro Cultural Costa Nord, to protect and promote the treasures of the Serra de Tramuntana: its landscape, its people and their history.

resort is particularly popular with German visitors.
*21km (13 miles) southwest of Palma on the Ma-1. Tourist Office: Carrer Ratoli 1. Tel: (971) 68 70 83.*

## Port d'Andratx

Exploiting a deep natural harbour, Port d'Andratx is a classic example of a pretty fishing port turned upmarket holiday resort. The old harbour on the east side of the bay has charm and agreeable fish restaurants, while further east lie Camp de Mar and a parade of luxury villas climbing up the hillside.
The port is a favourite haunt of the yachting fraternity. In summer, boat excursions run to the nearby island of Sa Dragonera (*see p141*).
*35km (22 miles) southwest of Palma, 5km (3 miles) south of Andratx.*

## Portals Nous

Portals Nous is an upmarket tourist complex with a small sandy beach, and swimming off the rocks. At its eastern end is Porto Portals, a top-notch marina opened in 1987 that attracts fabulously expensive yachts and cruisers. If you like mixing with the well-tanned well-off, and enjoy promenading past ships' chandlers and boutiques selling designer nautical gear, this is the place for you. There is a good choice of ritzy restaurants, with cuisines ranging from *nouvelle* to Chinese. Behind this opulent shore, high-walled villas sit among the pines, and barking dogs warn that you are on moneyed ground.

*10km (6 miles) southwest of Palma off the Ma-1.*

Porto Portals, where the rich moor up

## Portals Vells

A left turn off the Palma–Andratx road, signposted Cala Figuera, leads south past a golf course and thick pinewoods to the western horn of the Badia de Palma. A turning left down a dusty side road can take you to the tiny but official nudist beach at Platja Mago, where there is a small beach bar.

Continuing south, you reach the small bay of Cala de Portals Vells. Walk along the south side of the cliffs and you will reach the Cove de la Mare de Déu, a rock church with two altars and elaborate rock carvings. Legend has it that Genoese fishermen sheltering from a storm placed a statue of the Virgin from their ship in the caves as a thanks-offering for their survival. In 1866 the statue was taken to the chapel on the seafront in Portals Nous.

In the 13th and 14th centuries the caves were quarried to supply stone for Palma cathedral. The peninsula is also used by the military.
*24km (15 miles) southwest of Palma.*

## Puigpunyent

Tucked into a valley, Puigpunyent is a pretty village you will inevitably pass through if you are touring the interior of the western Serra de Tramuntana. Nearby are the historic country house La Granja (*see pp56–7*), the splendid nature reserve La Reserva (*see pp138–9*) and the epic road to Galilea (*see p56*).

Two kilometres (1¼ miles) along the road north to Esporles is the 17th-century mansion house Son Fortesa,

---

### THE CONQUEST OF MALLORCA

Jaume I's original plan was to land his troops in the Badia de Pollença, but a storm forced his fleet along the island's north coast to Sant Elm. He came well armed, with 150 ships carrying 16,000 troops and 1,500 horses. The Moors fled to the mountains, and Palma was besieged for three months before its surrender on 31 December 1229. By the following March, the king was rewarding his conquistadores with huge estates.

---

a typical Mallorcan country estate with waterfalls and citrus orchards. Prince Charles spent a holiday sketching here in 1991.

The Gran Hotel Son Net and L'Orangerie Restaurant offer sheer elegance and luxury.
*15km (9 miles) northwest of Palma, 8km (5 miles) west of Establiments.*

## La Reserva

*See pp138–9.*

## Santa Ponça

Just west of the Badia de Palma, this sheltered resort is on an attractive site, with pinewoods and a large sandy beach washed by clear, shallow water. Often used by British tour operators, it is packed in summer, but never attains the brash atmosphere of nearby Magaluf. A marina, golf course and water sports are part of its wide-ranging facilities.

### Caleta de Santa Ponça

From the marina, a road signposted Sa Caleta leads south to the rocky headland of Es Malgrat. En route you will reach a superb vantage point, Caleta de Santa Ponça, site of a large white Victory Cross, a memorial erected in 1929 to mark the 700th anniversary of the landing on Mallorca of Jaume I of Aragón on 12 September 1229 and the beginning of the *Reconquista* of the island from the Moors. In the battle that morning some 1,500 Moors were killed. Sculpted scenes depict the bravery of the Christian troops.

Further along the same road, after passing many substantial villas, is a spot from where you can look back towards Santa Ponça, enjoying the sea air and a panoramic view. You will also see fishermen who appear to like sitting perilously on the cliff-edge with their long rods.

Out at sea lie the craggy islands of Illa Malgrat and Illa na Fordada, and further west the headlands of Cap Andritxol and Cap des Llamp.

*Santa Ponça is 20km (12½ miles) southwest of Palma on the Ma-1. Tourist Office: Via Puig de Galatzó. Tel: (971) 69 17 12.*

Santa Ponça's marina

# Tour: West of Palma

*You do not have to drive far from Palma or its neighbouring resorts to enjoy the peace of Mallorca's countryside. This 86km (53-mile) circular trip guides you round the mountains to the northwest of Palma, climbing along winding rural roads to reach the spectacular cliffs and sea views of the north coast. (See map on p53 for route.)*

*Allow 5 hours.*

*The tour begins at Palmanova, 5km (3 miles) southwest of Palma on the Ma-1 motorway.*

## 1 Establiments

Take the Ma-1015 north, following signs to Calvià. The high-rise buildings of the coast are soon replaced by woods and well-tended farmland, and the twin spires of Calvià's church can be seen in the distance. In the centre of this town (*see p54*), turn right at a T-junction in the direction of Establiments. Climbing steadily, you pass several grand country houses with wrought-iron gates guarding their entrances. The small village of Establiments is where George Sand and Chopin first stayed during their visit of 1838–9, amid a landscape she considered worthy of Poussin's paintbrush.

*From Establiments, take the left turn to Esporles.*

## 2 Esporles

Sheltered by high mountain ridges, this pretty town of tree-lined streets makes

Terrace view: working the fields in Banyalbufar

a pleasant place to stop for a drink or lunch. Apples, pears, oranges and figs, grown on the terraces surrounding Esporles, are sold in its shops.
*Continue west following the signs to Banyalbufar and La Granja.*

### 3 La Granja

La Granja (*see pp56–7*) offers a rare chance to enter one of the highly covetable *fincas* (country houses) that adorn the interior of Mallorca. Today it is a folk museum.
*Continue north to join the Ma-10, turning left for Banyalbufar.*

### 4 Banyalbufar

The sinuous drive along this coast provides magnificent views of mountains, terraced slopes, high cliffs and the sea far below. Clinging perilously to a narrow ridge is the small village of Banyalbufar. Some of the buildings lining its narrow main street are supported by stilts. A few shops and hotels cater to visitors seeking an away-from-it-all holiday. A steep, winding road leads down to the tiny port.
*Continue southwest through Estellencs.*

### 5 Miradores

The steep terraces along here, which support thriving crops of tomatoes, grapes and flowers, were originally constructed by the Moors and are still worked mostly by hand. Several viewpoints (*miradores*) provide a chance to stop and take in the impressive coastline. At the first,

Coastal watchtower at the Mirador de Ses Ànimes, just south of Banyalbufar

**Mirador de Ses Ànimes**, is a restored watchtower built on a high rock beside the cliffs (which can be climbed). If this is crowded, you can continue on through Estellencs to a second *mirador* at **Coll des Pi**, where you will find refreshments and a petrol station, and a good view inland to **Puig de Galatzó** (1,026m/3,366ft).

The parish church at **Estellencs** dates from 1422, and a tortuous road leads down to a small cove with a rocky beach. Further southwest are more viewpoints: **Mirador de Ricardo Roca**, which has a large restaurant, and **Mirador de Ses Ortigues**.
*The road descends comfortably through fields studded with olives to the stately old town of Andratx (see p52). A 5km (3-mile) detour can be made from here down to Port d'Andratx (see p60), where there is a good choice of harbourside restaurants. From Andratx it is a simple 13km (8-mile) drive east along the fast Ma-10 and Ma-1 to Palmanova.*

# Walk: Sa Trapa

*Hidden away in the cliffs north of Sant Elm is the abandoned Trappist monastery of Sa Trapa: it will linger long in your memory if you make the effort to get there. The best route provides superb views over the island of Sa Dragonera, but involves some scrambling up steep rocks. If you prefer, you can get there and return by an inland cart track, as the monks surely did. The track is well signposted. Take a light picnic.*

*Allow 3 hours return, excluding time at Sa Trapa.*

The small resort of Sant Elm lies 8km (5 miles) west of Andratx and is connected by bus to Palma via Peguera. There is a frequent service to Andratx, and you can take a taxi to Sant Elm from the rank beside the Teatro Argentino there. If you are driving, park by the start of the walk at the northern end of Sant Elm in Plaça de Mosser Sebastià Grau – where there is a blue and white windmill.

## 1  Sant Elm

Follow the shore along Avinguda Jaume I and Carrer Cala en Basset, bearing right into Plaça de Mosser Sebastià Grau. Take Avinguda de la Trapa inland; it becomes a country track through pinewoods to the Can Tomeví farmhouse. Here a sign directs you right for Sa Trapa, passing behind the house. At the next sign, Sa Font des Moros, you have a choice – turn left for a steep ascent of the cliffs, or continue straight on to follow the easier but longer inland track up to Sa Trapa (380m/1,250ft), also the return route.

## 2  The ascent

Turning left, walk through the woods until you reach a pair of small concrete gateposts. Turn right here, marked on a nearby stone by the first of many small intermittent black paint arrows that lead the way. The path narrows as it climbs through the trees, crossing several walls and passing the stone ruins of a limekiln. Eventually you ascend above the pines, with ever-improving views of craggy Sa Dragonera just offshore. After a short scramble up through dwarf palms and over steep, bare rocks, you will meet a well-established path that makes an ascending run north through the trees.

Passing a '280' in blue paint, you reach a clifftop viewpoint – a good place to take a breather and admire the coastline below. Continue to follow the path as marked, taking care on the final ascent which nears the cliff-edge – heed the warning crosses and veer right. Suddenly you are on top of the promontory, and can see the romantic buildings of Sa Trapa in the valley ahead.

### 3  Sa Trapa

Follow the path to the monastery, a formidable ensemble, where you can wander around the ruined chapel, kitchen and living quarters. Almond trees continue to blossom on its perfectly built terraces, the mill still has its ancient machinery, and you can easily make out the wide sweep of the threshing floor, now punctured by pines that have grown up since the monastery's closure in the late 18th century. A memorial stone nearby is a sad reminder to keep away from the cliff-edge here.

### 4  The descent

Sa Trapa is now being restored and conserved by the Grupo Ornithologia Balear (GOB, Grup Ornitòlogic Balear in Catalan), and the track used by its vehicles offers an easy descent. This leads inland from behind the monastery, climbs over a pass, then winds patiently down the mountainside, providing ample time to dwell upon the life of this isolated Trappist community. At the bottom the track crosses a bridge, curves through a farm and – forking right – leads down to the house at Can Tomeví.

A view of Sant Elm from the cliffs

# The northwest

*Served by Mallorca's two railway lines, this is both the most accessible part of the island and the best place to get a taste of Mallorca as it was before the resorts arrived. Besides being a spectacular mountain range, the Serra de Tramuntana is full of secrets. Take the slow train up to Sóller, make the hairy descent to Sa Calobra, pay a visit to the monasteries at Valldemossa and Lluc, and you will have a completely different image of Mallorca.*

## Alfabia

The gardens of Alfabia are a delightful memento of when Mallorca was under Moorish rule. Then the estate was known as Al-Fabi ('jar of olives' in Arabic), a lofty residence fit for viziers (high-ranking officials) where the Arab talent for irrigation, garden design and horticulture flourished. The estate is an inviting oasis where you can spend a dreamy morning or afternoon in the shade of swaying palms and fragrant flowers.

An avenue of magisterial plane trees guides visitors to the stone archway marking the entrance. Follow the directions to walk to the left of the house and up steps to the gardens. Cobbled paths lead past a huge cistern and water channels to a long pergola wreathed with a colourful mix of begonia, bougainvillaea, wisteria and honeysuckle. Lavender, sage and box form low hedges, while tall date palms and exotic shrubs provide shaded walks accompanied by the soothing tune of

The house and gardens at Alfabia, a retreat from the summer heat since Moorish times

# The northwest (*see pp86–7 for orange tour, pp88–9 for purple tour*)

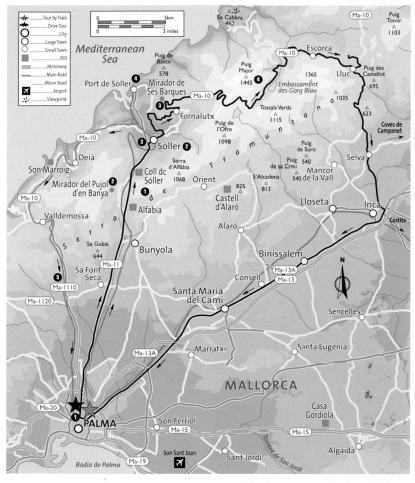

flowing water. At a lower level there are ponds with lilies and fish, bamboos, twining subtropical plants and groves of lemon and orange trees in side gardens. The house, though somewhat run-down, is a fascinating relic of bygone days, with faded wall panels and antique furniture – look out for the

14th-century carved wooden chair, and an ancient cradle.

*14km (8½ miles) north of Palma on the Ma-11. Tel: (971) 61 31 23. www.jardinesdealfabia.com. Open: Apr–Oct Mon–Sat 9.30am–6.30pm; Nov–Mar Mon–Fri 9.30am–5.30pm, Sat 9.30am–1pm. Admission charge.*

## Binissalem

Binissalem is the centre of Mallorca's wine-making industry. Viticulture was introduced to the islands by the Romans and survived the Moorish occupation (Binissalem means 'House of Salem' in Arabic). Production reached a peak in the late 19th century when blight struck the French vineyards. Then there were 30,000 hectares under vines; today, that's down to 400, but the reputation of Mallorcan wines is growing with the help of modern technology and grape varieties exclusive to the island. Wine can be bought from the **Bodega José Ferrer** (*www.vinosferrer.com*). For the El Foro

Binissalem's vineyards produce Mallorca's best wine

de Mallorca wax museum, *see p157.* *22km (13½ miles) northeast of Palma on the Ma-13 motorway or the Ma-13A.*

## Castell d'Alaró

There is little reason to linger in the village of Alaró, except on a Friday afternoon when you might buy picnic provisions in the market prior to ascending to the nearby Castell d'Alaró (817m/2,680ft). To reach this romantically-sited castle, drive northeast on the Ma-2100 towards Orient. At km18, a turning left leads on to a narrow road bordered by stone walls and fields of olives and almond trees. This degenerates into a rough dirt track full of potholes, best suited to four-wheel-drive vehicles or hikers with sturdy footwear.

An alternative approach is to continue skirting right round Puig d'Alaró, park near km11, then follow a path up through the terraces. Either way, you eventually reach a high plateau where your perseverance is rewarded with fantastic views, and Es Verger, a rustic bar-restaurant that serves delicious roast lamb cooked in a clay oven. From here, you must walk (30 minutes) up steep and winding stone steps to see the ruins of the 15th-century castle. A small chapel, **Mare de Déu del Refugi**, has stood here since 1622 and a hostelry still offers sanctuary to pilgrims and visitors. *29km (18 miles) northeast of Palma, 6km (4 miles) north of Alaró.*

## Costitx

Typical of the many small towns in the interior of Mallorca, Costitx was the main centre of population on the island in prehistoric times, and the area has proved a rich source of archaeological treasures. The 14th-century image of the Virgin in its parish church is said to have been found by children in an apple tree.

### Museu de Ciències Naturals

This modern building lies on the south side of the main road from Costitx to Sencelles, signposted Casa Cultura. It exhibits stuffed and preserved examples of the fauna of the Balearic Islands, including wild birds, fish and butterflies. There is a bar-restaurant and library, and a good view of the surrounding agricultural plains.
*Can Font. Tel: (971) 87 60 70. Open: Tue–Sat 9.30am–1pm. Closed: Mon & 1st & 3rd Sun of the month. Admission charge.*

*Costitx is 24km (15 miles) northeast of Palma, 4.5km (2³/₄ miles) east of Sencelles.*

## Coves de Campanet

Campanet is a quiet old town, devoid of tourism and peaceful even on market day. Just 3km (2 miles) to the north, though, the Coves de Campanet are a magnet for sightseers and excursion coaches. Discovered in 1945, the caves are not as spectacular as those at Artà, Drac or Hams (*see p99, p121 & p124*), but neither are they as crowded

The landscaped entrance to the subterranean caves at Campanet

with visitors. The well-signposted entrance is through a colourful garden dripping with bougainvillaea and other flamboyant plants, and a large terrace provides a rewarding opportunity to sit with a drink and survey the charming rural scenery in the Sant Miquel Valley.

Conducted tours lead visitors into a subterranean maze that winds for some 1,300m (1,400yd) past colourfully illuminated stalactites and stalagmites and 'The Enchanted Town'.
*41km (25½ miles) northeast of Palma, 12km (7½ miles) northeast of Inca off the Palma–Port d'Alcúdia motorway. Tel: (971) 51 61 30. www.covesdecampanet.com. Open: Apr–Sept daily 10am–7pm; Oct–Mar daily 10am–6pm. Admission charge.*

Deià: a Mediterranean dream village where the writer Robert Graves set up home in 1929

## Deià

Lodged amid the mountains of the north coast, Deià will be forever associated with the English writer, Robert Graves, who came to live here in 1929 and developed a deep affection for Mallorca and its people. He is buried in the cemetery beside the parish church at the top of the town, and his house Ca n'Alluny is now open to the public (*Carretera de Sóller. Tel: (971) 63 61 85. www.fundaciorobertgraves.com. Open: Mon–Fri 10am–5pm; Sat 10am–3pm. Admission charge*). Graves strove hard to stop Deià being ruined by the encroaching tourist developments: the town's unified and natural appearance is its greatest attraction. There are several restaurants, a couple of art galleries and a narrow, twisting road that leads down to the sea at Cala de Deià.

Many foreign residents now live in and around Deià, and rising property prices have changed its atmosphere. Today, the town lives in thrall to La Residencia, an idyllic mansion-turned-hotel that was formerly owned by British entrepreneur Sir Richard Branson and attracts the very rich and famous from around the world. As author Robert Elms put it, 'Everything in Deià is taken slowly, except your money.'
*30km (18½ miles) north of Palma, 4km (2½ miles) south of Lluc-Alcari.*

## Fornalutx

This is a truly pretty mountain village with a narrow cobbled high street that twists round to a tiny square. The church dates from 1680. Several cafés and inviting restaurants, such as the Santa Marta with its terrace views, make Fornalutx a welcome goal if you are walking from Sóller. Follow the rural road east via Biniaraix, through a valley graced with orange and lemon groves.
*40km (25 miles) north of Palma, 8km (5 miles) northeast of Sóller via the Ma-10 to Lluc or 5km (3 miles) via Biniaraix.*

## Inca

On the railway line from Palma, this modern industrial town is heavily promoted as a place all tourists should visit, although really its only attraction is shopping. Excursions are arranged to the Thursday outdoor market, which spreads around the streets bordering the covered daily market, and usually include a visit to one of the town's several leather factories or their retail outlets along Avinguda General Luque and Gran Via de Colon. Prices are not so low as to merit a special trip, but there is plenty of choice.

Pursuers of Mallorcan cuisine will appreciate the *celler* restaurants in the town centre, where the wine is extracted from mammoth vats, and you can join the locals devouring local specialities such as *caracoles* (*cargols* in Catalan, snails) and roast suckling pig. **Can Amer** in Carrer den Miquel Durán is a famous example. In the shops you may see *concos d'Inca* (Inca bachelors) for sale, a type of cake made by the nuns of Monasterio de las Jerónimas. The island's top agricultural show is held here on the third Thursday in November and is known as *Dijous Bò* – Good Thursday.

## ROBERT GRAVES

English poet and novelist Robert Graves (1895–1985) is well known for his two bestsellers: *Goodbye to All That*, an autobiographical account of his experiences in World War I, and *I, Claudius*, a historical novel that brings to life ancient Rome. Money made from the first book enabled him to move to Mallorca with his muse, mistress and fellow poet Laura Riding. After World War II he settled permanently on the island, writing fiction, poetry and books on mythology.

### Ermita de Santa Magdalena

A turning right off the Inca-Alcúdia road leads up to Puig d'Inca (304m/ 997ft) and a small sanctuary looking over the countryside and mountains. There is a small chapel and a café. A pilgrimage, said to have been followed for 800 years, is made every year to the *ermita* on the first Sunday after Easter.

*Inca is 30km (18½ miles) northeast of Palma on the Ma-13 motorway.*

The peaceful central square in Fornalutx, a mountain village surrounded by citrus groves

# Creative Mallorca

Mallorca has stimulated the creativity of many visiting writers, musicians and artists. George Sand was convinced that the sublimity of Chopin's *Preludes*, composed or completed during their stay at Valldemossa in 1838–9, was a direct response to an environment enriched by deceased monks, birds singing in wet trees and the twang of far-off guitars. To her mind, raindrops falling on the Charterhouse roof were transformed by Chopin's 'imagination and singing gift into tears falling on the heart'. Chopin denied that his art was achieved by a puerile imitation of the external, but critics agree that he emerged from his Mallorcan sojourn a more mature composer.

Painter and sculptor Joan Miró, whose mother and wife came from Mallorca, was more candid about the direct influence of the island on his vibrantly coloured work. 'As a child,' he recalled, 'I loved to watch the always-changing Mallorcan sky. At night I would get carried away by the writing in the sky of the shooting stars, and the lights of the fireflies. The sea, day and night, was always blue. It was here that I received the first creative seeds which became my work.' Miró's studio on the outskirts of Palma is a testimony to the way the artist found inspiration in nature's little works – a piece of driftwood, an almond stone, a dry-stone wall 'carved by real masters'.

The minutiae of island life also absorbed the writer and long-term Deià resident Robert Graves, whose *Majorcan Stories* chronicle tragicomic vicissitudes befalling both locals and visitors, such as the bicycle theft or a farcical christening.

Joan Miró, whose studio on the outskirts of Palma can be visited

Robert Graves's house, Ca n'Alluny

The greatest and most diligent creative response to Mallorca, however, must be the work of the indefatigable Archduke Lluís Salvador. Arriving on the island in 1867 at the age of 19, he sank his fortune into researching his beloved island, sponsoring investigations of its caves and archaeological sites and producing a comprehensive six-volume study of the Balearic Islands, *Die Balearen*, which is still valued to this day.

The monastery at Lluc has grown from humble 13th-century origins into a monumental complex

## Lluc

A revered place of pilgrimage since its founding in 1250, the monastery is a testimony to the Mallorcans' continuing religious conviction. Legend has it that a shepherd boy discovered an image of a dark-skinned Virgin in the forest here and took it to the local priest. The Virgin was placed in the village church at Escorca, but disappeared three times, always being found in the same spot in the forest. Taking this as a divine command, the priest ordered the construction of a chapel to house the peripatetic Virgin.

Today, Lluc is a colossal ensemble that includes a church, choir school, the old Augustinian monastery, a small museum, accommodation for pilgrims and a restaurant and souvenir shop for visitors. To reach the church, enter the main building by the front portal, following a short passage past a patio with a magnificent magnolia to a courtyard. To the right is the Baroque façade of the church. Inside, steps lead up behind the altar to a chapel and the jewel-adorned image of La Moreneta, (the Little Dark One), who is Mallorca's patron saint. You can hear the choirboys – known as Els Blauets (The Blues) for the colour of their cassocks – Mon–Fri 11.15am and 4.45pm. The museum, on the first floor, contains a miscellany of thanksgiving gifts, archaeological finds, coins, costumes and paintings. To the left of the monastery buildings is a path leading to a Way of the Cross, with good views of the quiet countryside. The sculptures, depicting the Mysteries of the Rosary, are the work of the Modernista architects Antoni Gaudí and Joan Rubió, who undertook modernisation of the church at Lluc. Several mountain walks start from here.

*47km (29 miles) northeast of Palma, 16km (10 miles) north of Inca. Tel: (971) 87 15 25. www.lluc.net.*
*Garden open: daily 10am–1pm & 3–6pm. Museum open: daily 10am– 1.30pm & 2.30–5pm. Admission charge for museum.*

### Orient

Claiming to be the smallest village on the island, and once a classic example of 'hidden Mallorca', Orient is now being discovered. The official population at the last census was 26, but at weekends this can swell to 300 when trippers from Palma come up for an away-from-it-all lunch in the countryside. Take the road (PM210) northeast from Bunyola, a twisting, taxing drive with a fine view at every bend. Inaccessibility keeps Orient free of tourist coaches, and its cluster of white houses snuggles beside the mountains of the Serra d'Alfàbia in

picture-book style. The village now has a handful of hostelries including a luxury hotel in the country seat of a 17th-century Spanish Duke, and a *hostal* offering accommodation and food for the many walkers who pass through. You can climb up to Castell d'Alaró from here (*see p70*).
*25km (15½ miles) north of Palma on the Bunyola–Alaró road.*

### Port de Sóller

A quiet and sheltered resort popular with French visitors, Port de Sóller was once the main outlet for produce grown in the valleys and terraces around Sóller. A long, curving seafront bordered by shops and restaurants caters to the daily influx of trippers arriving on the historic tram that connects Palma to the port via Sóller (*see pp79–80*). There is a small sandy beach to the south of the bay that allows swimming. Other attractions are the boat trips along the north coast, particularly to Sa Calobra (*see below*), and the walk up to the lighthouse and Punta de Sóller (*see p91*).
*40km (25 miles) north of Palma, 5km (3 miles) north of Sóller. Tourist Office: Carrer Canonge Oliver 1. Tel: (971) 63 30 42.*

### Sa Calobra

Eavesdrop on the didn't-we-do-well conversations of holidaymakers returning from Mallorca, and it is not long before someone mentions Sa Calobra. Previously remote and only accessible by boat, Sa Calobra is a tiny, once-idyllic cove at the bottom of sheer cliffs near Escorca. It can now be reached by a snaking road that is at least as interesting as the cove itself: there are countless hairy hairpin bends, a looping flourish of road that engineers know as Nus de la Corbeta (Knotted Tie), and plenty of chances to inspect the dramatically eroded limestone cliffs, home to disdainful seabirds and tenacious alpine flowers.

Near the end of the road is a new holiday development, **Cala Tuent**, and down by the sea a car park and bars where dazed visitors can recover. The next challenge is to walk through a set of dimly lit tunnels cut in the rock, with some stooping required, to reach the **Torrent de Pareis**. Formed over thousands of years by water rushing down from the Serra de Tramuntana, this gorge culminates in a small sandy beach. The gorge has two splendid waterfalls and is only 30m (98ft) wide, with walls rising up to 608m (1,995ft). The guides cannot resist saying 'Welcome to Mallorca's Grand Canyon', but be warned: because of flash floods it is extremely unsafe to walk in the canyon, except at the height of summer.

*67km (42 miles) north of Palma, 16km (10 miles) northwest of Escorca.*

Negotiate the twists on the road down to Sa Calobra, or take a boat trip from Port de Sóller

## Santa Maria del Camí

Santa Maria is a historic market town with some notable old buildings. In Plaça Caidos stands the 18th-century church of Santa Maria with its bell-tower decorated with deep blue tiles. Inside is a painting of the Madonna and baby Jesus, who is holding a goldfinch. Signposts direct visitors to the mighty 17th-century **Convent dels Mínims** on the Ma-13A, with its attractive cloisters and gardens.

There is a private historical museum, **Can Conrado** (*tel: (971) 14 02 03. Open: 4–7pm. Admission charge*). Visits by appointment only.

A visit to the large and very popular Sunday-morning market in the neighbouring town of Consell, a short car ride away, can be combined with a visit to the church. The market is famous for its immense boot sale. *14km (8½ miles) northeast of Palma.*

## Sóller

Whether you approach Sóller by road, crossing the mountain pass at Coll de Sóller, or arrive on the old-world train from Palma (*see pp86–7*), this affable town makes a memorable impression. Sprinkled across the broad, fertile **Valle de los Naranjos** (Valley of the Oranges), Sóller is still redolent of the turn-of-the-century days when its citizens grew prosperous from the citrus fruit trade.

### Casa de Cultura

This is in a private house on three floors packed with antiques and relics

Small-town style: the *modernista* Banco de Sóller in Sóller's Plaça Constitució

of old Sóller. In the courtyard are agricultural tools and a wine press, and upstairs religious statues and ornaments, an old-style bedroom, shell-encrusted amphorae, souvenirs of emigrants to Puerto Rico and, incongruously, masks from Papua New Guinea.
*Carrer del Mar 9. Tel: (971) 63 46 93. Open: Mon–Fri 11am–4.30pm, Sat 11am–1pm. Admission charge.*

### Museu Balear de Ciències Naturals (Natural Science Museum) and Jardí Botànic (Botanical Gardens)

A manor house dating from the early 20th century is now home to Mallorca's Museum of Natural Sciences, opened in 1992. Its enthusiastic staff look after a cherished collection of fossils, animal skulls, bones and rocks dating back millions of years. The surrounding grounds contain the terraced Botanical Gardens of Sóller, with plots devoted to Balearic Islands shrubs, and herbal, aromatic and culinary plants. Both museum and gardens are worthwhile places to spend a pleasant hour.

*Camp d'en Prohom. Signposted on the east side of the Sóller to Port de Sóller road at km30. To walk from Plaça Constitució follow signs to the Correus (post office) down Carrer de Rauza Rector, turn right into Carrer de Quadrado, then right again into Carrer de Capitan Angelats. Tel: (971) 63 40 14. www.jardibotanicdesoller.org. Open: Tue–Sat 10am–6pm, Sun 10am–2pm. Closed: Mon. Admission charge.*

**Plaça Constitució**

Take a seat in Sóller's central square, with its venerable trees and fountains, and it is not hard to imagine the excitement and pride which must have

Sa Foradada extends into the sea below Son Marroig

## THE ARCHDUKE

Archduke Lluís Salvador (1847–1915) was a wealthy member of the Austrian imperial family who first set eyes on Mallorca while yachting round the Mediterranean. An ardent naturalist, he spent a great part of his life on the island and owned several estates on the northwest coast in addition to Son Marroig. Stories of his scholastic endeavour are frequently spiced with gossip about his affair with a local girl stricken by leprosy, and every islander has an Archduke story to tell. One recalls how a farmer, unaware of who he was dealing with, gave him a few coins in reward for helping him shift some barrels. 'That is the first money I have earned in my life,' quipped the Archduke.

greeted the opening of the railway line to Palma in 1912, and of the rickety tram line down to Port de Sóller the following year. Look up at the ostentatious Modernista façades of the Banco de Sóller and Església de Sant Bartomeu next door, and you see the strange results of the vagaries of the fruit business. In the 1860s the orange groves were struck by blight, and many of Sóller's residents were forced to seek their fortunes elsewhere. Those that succeeded returned home with new, fanciful ideas from abroad. Examples are these buildings by Joan Rubió, a pupil of Gaudí, who also created a fluid Art Nouveau mansion, Can Prunera, at Carrer de Sa Lluna 104.

*Sóller is 35km (22 miles) north of Palma on the Ma-11. Tourist Office: Placa d'Espanya (opposite railway station). Tel: (971) 63 80 08.*

La Església de Sant Bartomeu in Sóller is a typical example of *modernista* architecture

## Son Marroig

The stately mansion that once belonged to Archduke Luis Salvador is now a shrine to Mallorca's greatest admirer. Even without its associations with this enlightened aristocrat, Son Marroig would be worth visiting simply for its millionaire setting overlooking the coastline of northwest Mallorca.

Only a part of the ground floor and one room of the first are open to the public, but you can see a wealth of memorabilia, including collections of photographs, paintings owned by the Archduke, and his large library. In the garden, a short walk leads to a graceful Greek temple in white

marble where the Archduke would sit and contemplate the sea and the mountains.

The rocky headland below, called Sa Foradada, is pierced by an 18m (60ft) wide hole. You can walk down to the landing stage, built so that the Archduke and his guests could moor their yachts and swim off the rocks. Ask for permission from the house before you set off.

*33km (20½ miles) north of Palma, 4km (2½ miles) west of Deià on the Ma-10. Tel: (971) 63 91 58. Open: Apr–Oct daily 9.30am–2pm & 3–7.30pm; Nov–Mar daily 9.30am–2pm & 3–5.30pm. Admission charge.*

# 'A Winter in Majorca'

Mallorca is still reeling from the visit paid to the island in 1838 by the French literary celebrity George Sand and her lover, Polish-born composer Frédéric Chopin. Sand, the *nom de plume* of Baroness Amandine Aurore Lucie Dupin (1804–76), was also accompanied by her 14-year-old son, Maurice, and 8-year-old daughter, Solange.

In those days there was little accommodation for foreigners available on the island. The party stayed first in a villa in Establiments, but were forced to move out when rumours spread among the villagers that Chopin had tuberculosis, a disease from which he eventually died in 1849. A new home was found in three cells in the former Carthusian monastery at Valldemossa, just three years after its monks had been expelled. Their stay here was far from idyllic, characterised by poor food, 'lugubrious rain', Chopin's declining health and ostracism by the locals.

A free-thinking, cigarette-smoking, trouser-wearing pioneer feminist, Sand later commented how different things might have been had they bothered to attend Mass.

Mallorca has never forgiven Sand for the opinionated account of her travels given in *Un Hiver à Majorque* (*A Winter in Majorca*), published in 1842. While references to the islanders as thieves, monkeys and Polynesian savages are distasteful, her book is appreciative of the Mallorcan countryside and provides a memorable glimpse of the island just 160 years ago. Somewhat ironically, Sand and Chopin's visit has contributed to the image of Mallorca as an island of romance and cultural pedigree, and her book is now sold in several languages in Valldemossa. The English translation by Robert Graves includes his own idiosyncratic annotations. As he observed, the whole episode was a fascinating clash of the classical and romantic worlds.

## REIAL CARTOIXA CHOPIN FESTIVAL

Each August (and occasionally during the rest of the year) a festival celebrates the visit of Frédéric Chopin with a series of Sunday concerts featuring his music. Performed by well-known and rising musicians, these are held in the Carthusian monastery at Valldemossa, where Chopin stayed with George Sand. During the festival the monastery also has exhibits on the period and its art and philosophy.
*Tel: (971) 61 23 51.*
*www.festivalchopin.com*

Valldemossa is one of the most attractive villages on Mallorca

## Valldemossa

Valldemossa is associated with two women utterly different from one another. One is George Sand, the writer-feminist who spent the 1838–9 winter with lover Frédéric Chopin (*see p82*) in a Carthusian monastery, Reial Cartoixa, which looms over the pretty hillside town. The other is Santa Catalina Thomás, Mallorca's 16th-century saint, revered in every Valldemossa home.

Walk down the hill to the parish church, though, and you will discover that Valldemossa is more concerned with remembering Santa Catalina Thomás. There is scarcely a house without a painted tile beside the front door asking for her protection. Take Carrer de Rectoria to the left of the church to see the tiny dwelling where she was born, now restored as a shrine.

### Palau del Rei Sanç
### (King Sancho's Palace)

Next door to the monastery, this palace was originally built in 1311 as an inland hunting lodge for the asthmatic King Sancho. It was donated to the Carthusians in 1399, who lived here until 1767 when the new monastery was occupied. Today, it is stuffed with a miscellany of antiques, furniture, books, utensils and religious finds, including a grim array of ever-suffering saints.

### Reial Cartoixa
### (Royal Carthusian Monastery)

The monastery (La Cartoixa in Catalan) at Valldemossa developed from a royal palace given to the Carthusian order in 1399. Most of the buildings date from the 18th century when the community was at its most wealthy. Visitors enter through the gloomy neoclassical church, begun in 1751 and decorated with frescoes by Bayeu, Goya's brother-in-law. You walk into huge whitewashed cloisters, where signs point out a circuit of the rooms and cells where the monks lived. Their quarters seem luxurious compared to the popular conception of monastic life, with individual prayer rooms, fireplaces and vegetable gardens overlooking the valley.

The monks prepared and dispensed medicine in the Pharmacy; after their expulsion in 1835, one remained to continue treating the villagers. Their cells were auctioned off one by one, and some are still used as private summer residences. The head of the monastery resided in the Prior's Cell, where you can see memorabilia associated with the library of Santa Catalina Thomás, and some of the instruments of flagellation used in penitential moments.

### SANTA CATALINA THOMÁS

Mallorca's own saint was born in Valldemossa in 1531. A humble peasant, Catalina spent most of her 43 years in Palma's Santa Magdalena convent, where she is buried. Her life was truly exemplary – she even mixed sand with her soup as a precaution against gluttony. Canonised in 1627, Santa Catalina is now a revered presence in many of the island's churches.

Take a wander through the well-kept narrow streets of Valldemossa, always full of plants

Cells 2 and 4 recreate the rooms occupied by Sand and Chopin, and contain the manuscript of *A Winter in Majorca* and the two pianos used by the composer. A Pleyel piano sent from France took so long at customs that it arrived only 20 days before Chopin left.

Cells 6 to 9 contain a 16th-century printing press, books and paintings belonging to Archduke Luis Salvador, and 19th- and 20th-century landscape paintings inspired by the Serra de Tramuntana. Upstairs is a museum of contemporary art with works by Miró, Picasso and Henry Moore.

*Palace and Monastery open: Mar–Oct Mon–Sat 9.30am–6.30pm, Sun 10am–1pm; Nov–Feb Mon–Sat 9.30am–4.30pm. Tel: (971) 61 21 06. Admission charge.*

*Valldemossa is 15km (9 miles) north of Palma, 16km (10 miles) southwest of Sóller. Tourist Office: Avenida de Palma 7. Tel: (971) 61 20 19.*

# By train: Palma to Port de Sóller

*An evocative survivor from a bygone Mallorca, this train with its vintage carriages is now a part of the island's tourist appeal, but the line is still used by commuters. (See p69 for route map, with orange numbers.)*

*Although the timetables allow for a shorter trip, it is best to devote a day for this journey.*

*This itinerary is based on weekday timetables only. If you intend to return to Palma by the last bus, tram or train of the day, check that they are running.*

## 1 Palma

The train leaves from the Sóller station on Eusebio Estada street (opposite Plaça d'Espanya). There are up to seven departures a day, but only some trains (the 10.10am, the 10.50am and the 12.15pm in high season) make a special photo-opportunity stop during the hour-long, 27km (17-mile) journey. The train passes through Palma's poorer suburbs, then rattles along to the village of Bunyola. After this stop, the train goes through a series of 13 tunnels to negotiate the mountains. The longest, Túnel Major, runs for 3km (2 miles).

## 2 Mirador del Pujol d'en Banya

The purpose-built viewing stop overlooks the houses of Sóller. The train pauses during playtime at the school far below, and children's cries ring around the valley.

## 3 Sóller

The 10.10am train arrives at Sóller at about 11.10am. The tram to Port de Sóller leaves from just below the station every half hour, and takes 30 minutes, but do not join the rush to board it. Instead, take a walk down the hill to enjoy the sedate delights of Sóller (*see pp79–80*). There is time to visit its two museums before they close, and to relax and have a drink or lunch in one of the handy cafés.

Some of the wooden, orange-fronted tram carriages are now over 90 years old. In the summer more modern open-sided carriages are also used. A loop in the line allows the upcoming tram to pass.
*Return to the railway station to catch the tram.*

## 4 Port de Sóller

By 1917 Mallorca's railway system was at its most extensive, and you could have travelled by train from Palma to

Inca, Manacor, Artà, Felanitx and Santanyí. The line to Sóller, audaciously cut through the Serra de Tramuntana, opened in 1912 and was quickly followed by a connecting tram service to Port de Sóller (*see p77*). Have a lazy lunch, a refreshing swim, walk round the seafront or up to the lighthouse at Punta Grossa (*see p91*).

## 5 Return to Palma

The most scenic way to get back to Palma is by bus from Port de Sóller. Buses go at 4pm or 5.30pm from a quayside stand close to the tram terminus. The bus takes an epic route up around the coast via Deià (*see p72*) and Valldemossa (*see pp84–5*). The journey takes 90 minutes and terminates by Bar La Granja in Carrer de Arxiduc Lluís Salvador, which is a short walk north of Plaça d'Espanya.

*The last train back to Palma leaves Sóller at 6.30pm (Mon–Fri), 7pm (Sat–Sun & hols).*
*Tel: (971) 75 20 51, (971) 75 20 28.*
*www.trendesoller.com*

Vintage trains on the Palma–Sóller railway provide a window to Mallorca's past

# Tour: Serra de Tramuntana

*This exhilarating drive takes you from Palma to the peaks and pines of the Serra de Tramuntana, passing the highest point of the island, Puig Major, and returning across the central plain via Inca. The round trip of 110km (68 miles) incorporates numerous steep roads and hairpins, and will appeal to confident drivers with a good head for heights. (See p69 for map, with the route marked in purple.)*

*Allow 5 hours.*

*Leave (or bypass) Palma by the Via Cintura ring road, taking the exit marked Sóller (Ma-11). The city's industrial estates are soon left behind as the road makes a beeline north towards the mountains. A sharp bend heralds the start of the dizzying climb up to Coll de Sóller – on the right you pass the Moorish gardens at Alfabia (see pp68–9), and the entrance to the toll tunnel through the mountains to Sóller.*

## 1 Coll de Sóller

A traditional mountain pass, Coll de Sóller (496m/1,627ft) offers the first of many panoramic views of the island and its peaks along this route.

*Descend into the Sóller Valley, which has neat orchards and olive groves.*

## 2 Sóller

If you intend to stop in this prosperous market town (*see pp79–80*) continue through the congested inner streets to the northern outskirts, where there is a car park.

*Follow the signs to Lluc, joining the Ma-10 as it climbs east through fragrant pinewoods. A turning to the right offers a short detour to the pretty village of Fornalutx (see p72).*

## 3 Mirador de Ses Barques

This stunning viewpoint overlooks the Badia de Sóller, and is a convenient place to pause for refreshments. The bar-restaurant is famous for its freshly-squeezed orange juice, made with fruit from the prolific valleys below. From the terrace you can look down to the well-protected harbour at Port de Sóller. To the west is the Cap Gros lighthouse, and to the east the headland of Punta Grossa with the old watchtower of Torre Picada.

*Continue east, climbing to a starker landscape overshadowed by craggy peaks, and Puig Major to the north.*

## 4 Puig Major and Gorg Blau

Even though radar installations cap the top of Mallorca's highest peak

(1,445m/4,741ft), and military use prevents close access by the public, Puig Major makes a formidable sight. The road skirts the mountain, burrowing through two tunnels and passing two reservoirs. The mainstay of the island's water supply, these stretches of water are surrounded by a nature reserve. The first reservoir is enlivened by a group of black donkeys, while Gorg Blau is a good spot for a walk or picnic.

*When leaving Gorg Blau, look out for a sharp bend to the left, sometimes obscured by parked cars, which leads into a tunnel. This is the turning to Sa Calobra (a two-hour detour, see pp77–8). Continue along the Ma-10 through Escorca, reaching a junction where you turn right on to a minor road signposted to Caimari. The road makes a gentle descent through stone-walled fields to this village and Selva to reach Inca (see pp72–3). From here drive southwest to Binissalem and on to Palma, taking the new fast motorway or the older highway via Santa Maria del Camí (see p79).*

Port de Sóller seen from the Mirador de Ses Barques

# Walk: Badia de Sóller

*This walk follows the curve of the Badia de Sóller, along a narrow road that climbs up to the lighthouse overlooking the charming little fishing village of Port de Sóller. If you have taken the train and tram ride from Palma (see pp86–7) it is a pleasant way to stretch the legs before your return journey. Keen walkers with strong footwear can continue across the cliffs, with some scrambling involved, to enjoy the views from Punta de Sóller.*

*Allow 90 minutes to the lighthouse and back, 3 hours if you include Punta de Sóller.*

*The walk begins next to the Restaurant Marisol at the tram terminus on the seafront.*

## 1 Port de Sóller

Walk south along the seafront road, passing the Hotel Miramar. On the cliffs overlooking the bay you will see the white, salt-cellar-shaped lighthouse you are aiming for, the Faro de Punta

Grossa. Turn right by Bar Pepe, crossing the tramlines and a blue-railed bridge to follow the curve of the shore. This easy stroll provides changing perspectives of the wide, virtually enclosed bay. Though Port de Sóller is still used by fishermen and the military, new egg-box developments scaling the hillsides for a sea view are proof that it is a popular holiday resort.

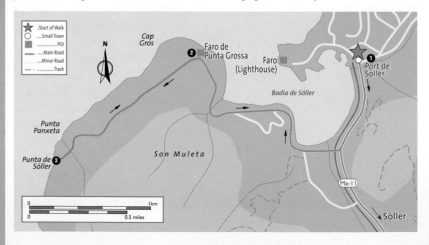

The seafront at Port de Sóller, guarded by the mountains of the Serra de Tramuntana

## 2  Faro de Punta Grossa

The road now makes a steady climb that twists up the side of the cliffs, passing through pinewoods and a variety of well-placed villas owned by foreign residents. From the euphorbia-covered hills, which sparkle with small yellow flowers in early spring, you can look down to the turquoise waters of the bay below. Fishing boats heading off to work or pleasure cruisers taking trippers round to Sa Calobra usually catch the eye.

In the valley below one hairpin bend, you can see the stony ruins of what was either a watchtower or a *forn de calç* (limekiln), built to make the whitewash with which the islanders once painted their houses. A little further on is a memorial to a soldier killed here in the opening days of the Spanish Civil War. When you reach the lighthouse (closed to the public) there are fine views back across the port and the mountains behind, including the island's highest peak, Puig Major, with its crown of communications antennae.

## 3  Punta de Sóller

To continue to Punta de Sóller, take the track to the left of the lighthouse, ducking through two chains. When the wall on your left ends, continue downhill as the path curls around the lonely cliffs. The route is well trodden but overgrown in places – look for the small piles of cairn stones that mark the path at key points. Fragrant pines and wild rosemary enhance the journey, and you will meet more ruined limekilns before the path descends to a river valley. Crossing a stone wall, you then scramble up the bare rocks, keeping away from the cliff-edge and passing a '67' painted on the rocks in red paint. From the summit there are rewarding views south along the coast towards Lluc-Alcari, and back to Cap Gros. To return, retrace your steps to the lighthouse and Port de Sóller.

# The northeast

*Two great bays fringed with fine sand and shallow water bite deep into Mallorca's northeastern corner. The resorts here are among the most relaxed on the island, and there is plenty to discover nearby: the illuminated caves of Artà, the wetlands of S'Albufera, sea views from the Cap de Formentor peninsula and the historic towns of Pollença, Alcúdia and Artà.*

## Alcúdia

Alcúdia is strategically situated at the neck of a peninsula separating the Badia de Pollença and Badia d'Alcúdia, and neatly illustrates the accreted layers of Mallorcan history. Originally a Phoenician settlement, the town was built inland from its port (today Port d'Alcúdia) as a defence against pirates and invaders. It was taken over by the Greeks, then in the 2nd century AD became Pollentia (meaning 'power'), the Roman capital of Balearis Major. Sacked by the Vandals in the 5th century, it was rebuilt by the Moors as Al-Kudia (meaning 'on the hill'). With the conquest of Mallorca by Jaume I in 1229, it again came under Christian rule.

Today Alcúdia's buildings and monuments have been fully restored. The town is boxed in by fort walls, and it is best to park outside these.
*Tourist Office: Carrer Major 17. Tel: (971) 89 71 00.*

The Porta del Moll gate in the walled town of Alcúdia, once the island's capital

# The northeast (*see pp112–13 for tour*)

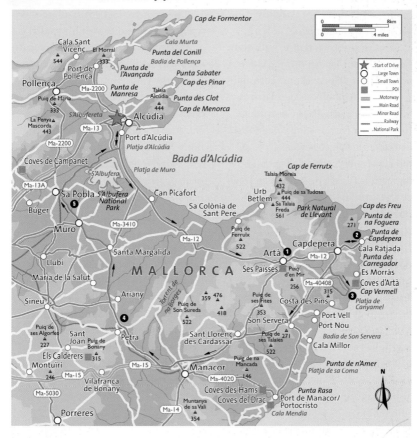

**Museu Monogràfic and Pollentià**

A small museum next to the church of Sant Jaume is devoted to the history of Roman Pollentia. The ticket includes admission to the scanty ruins of the Roman settlement.

*Museum: Carrer de Sant Jaume 30. Tel: (971) 54 70 04. Ruins of Pollentia across the road. Both open: Jul–Sept Tue–Fri 9.30am–8.30pm, Sat–Sun 9.30am–2.30pm; Oct–Jun Tue–Fri 10am–3.30pm, Sat–Sun 10.30am–*

*1.30pm. Admission charge (includes entry to both sites).*

**Old Town**

Take the entrance to the Old Town next to the church of Sant Jaume, which stands at its southwestern corner. Before walking through, you can inspect some remnants of Roman houses lying just across the road behind a row of cypresses. The church of Sant Jaume dates from the 13th century, but the present building is mostly 19th century. On Sundays, it is tightly packed with worshippers.

To reach the town centre, walk along Carrer de Sant Jaume, turning left down Carrer dels Albellons. Turn right past Alcúdia's pompous neoclassical town hall to reach Plaça Constitució. Leave by the narrow shop-lined Carrer de Moll, which brings you to the massive Porta del Moll gate. To the right is Passeig de la Mare de Déu de La Victoria, where the town's market takes place on Tuesdays and Sundays (*9am–1.30pm*).

## Alcúdia environs
### Ermita de la Victoria
The peninsula northeast of Alcúdia can be visited by taking the road towards Es Mal Pas. Leave by the northern gate, Port Roja (near the bullring), and drive through the smart villas of Bonaire toward Cap des Pinar. A watchtower, Torre Major, was constructed on its summit (451m/1,480ft) by Philip II in 1599. En route you will pass a turning to the right, which leads up to a fortress-like hermitage. Inside is a 15th-century wooden statue honouring Victoria, Alcúdia's patroness. Although the road to Cap des Pinar concludes in a military zone, much of this scenic headland is a nature reserve and a rewarding venue for walks, picnics or a cycle ride, offering attractive views.
*55km (34 miles) northeast of Palma on the Ma-13, 11km (7 miles) east of Pollença.*

### Oratori de Sant Anna
Half a kilometre (550yd) south of the town, on the road to Port d'Alcúdia, is a tiny chapel worth a visit purely for its simplicity and peaceful atmosphere. The oratory was built in the early 13th century and is believed to be Mallorca's oldest surviving church. Above the entrance is a carved statue of the Virgin Bona Nova.
*The chapel is on the north side of the road, opposite a cemetery. Open: mornings only.*

### Teatre Romà
A Roman amphitheatre stands 1.5km (1 mile) southwest of the town, on the right-hand side of the road to Port d'Alcúdia. It has the distinction of being the smallest Roman theatre in Spain, but all the same its tiered seats and stubby pillars carry a historic aura.
*Open: at all times. Free admission.*

## Artà
The spires and battlements of this medieval hilltop town can be seen from afar, and although Artà now has a bypass it is well worth a visit. Known to the Moors as Jartan, Artà has an atmosphere of great antiquity that clearly emanates from its principal attraction, the Santuari de Sant Salvador. To reach this, follow signs to the centre of the town, then on and up to the sanctuary: this involves narrow streets, not always one-way. If you prefer a stiff, soul-enhancing climb, you

can take the long, cypress-lined stone stairway that leads from the town centre up past the parish church of the Transfiguració del Senyor.
*Tourist Office: Costa i Llobera, s/n (Antigua Estación de Tren).*
*Tel: (971) 83 69 81.*

### Museu Regional d'Artà
The museum displays archaeological finds such as ceramics, jewellery and bronzes from the nearby site of Ses Països (*see p110*) and elsewhere on the island.
*Carrer d'Estrella 4. Tel: (971) 83 61 57.*
*Open: Tue–Fri 10am–1.30pm;*
*Sat 11am–1pm. Closed: Sun & Mon.*
*Free admission.*

### Santuari de Sant Salvador
The sanctuary occupies the site of a Moorish fortress. The chapel and its castellated walls were built between 1825 and 1832, the previous hermitage having been knocked down as a countermeasure against the spread of a devastating plague. The views from its courtyard over Artà's terracotta roofs and the hazy countryside beyond are engrossing – take a bag of almonds and all your unwritten postcards.
*Tel: (971) 82 72 82. Free admission to see grounds.*

*Artà is 71km (44 miles) northeast of Palma on the Ma-15.*

The amphitheatre at Alcúdia provides tangible evidence of the Roman presence on the island

Cala Sant Vicenç, a quiet resort protected by mountains and popular with artists

## Cala Millor

Cala Millor is the epicentre of recent tourist-wooing developments along Mallorca's east coast. From Cap des Pinar south to Sa Coma, every little bay and cove appears to have sprouted a holiday complex. **Cap des Pinar**, named after the pines growing on this headland, endeavours to remain an upmarket enclave with luxury hotels and private villas. To the south in the Badia d'Artà is **Cala Bona**. Its role as a fishing port has long been superseded with the addition of three man-made beaches and it is now a good spot for water sports, with several seafood restaurants.

Cala Millor is the largest and brashest resort, the coastline stacked with high-rise hotels and apartment blocks. Here the entertainment, like the beer, just keeps on coming – expect one long crowded party in summer. The beach has clean white sand and a wide promenade, with a good range of sports activities that include windsurfing, karting, bowling and riding. If you fancy a return to normality, walk into Son Servera for the Friday-morning market.

An obstacle to the developers' projects is the protected headland at Punta de n'Amer. Just south is **Sa Coma**, another full-blown resort (although it is quieter than Cala Millor) with a great beach and tidy seafront. The roads here are reasonably flat and in good condition, making Sa Coma

a good choice for an easy bike ride.
*71km (44 miles) northeast of Palma,*
*15km (10 miles) south of Artà.*
*Tourist Offices in Cala Millor: Passeig*
*Maritim, s/n. Tel: (971) 58 58 64; Sa*
*Coma: Avinguda les Palmeres.*
*Tel: (971) 81 08 92.*

## Cala Ratjada

Another popular holiday resort that has
evolved from a quiet fishing village,
Cala Ratjada possesses all the seaside
amenities its international clientele
expects, yet still retains some native
Mallorcan charm. A one-way system
leads visitors to the small harbour,
where there is parking and a long
promenade with shops and restaurants.
The beaches close to the town are
nothing special, but there are appealing
sandy bays further north at Cala Guya,
Cala Agulla and Cala Mesquida, and at
Platja Son Moll to the south.

A 2km (1¼-mile) walk uphill
from the port, signposted *Faro*, leads
through woodland to the breezy
headland of Punta de Capdepera
and its lighthouse.

The beautiful sculpture-filled gardens
of **Casa March**, a private estate owned
by the wealthy art-loving March family,
were destroyed by storms a few years
ago but have been restored. Visits by
appointment only through the local
tourist office.

*Cala Ratjada is 80km (50 miles)*
*northeast of Palma, 3km (2 miles) east of*
*Capdepera. Tourist Office: Plaça dels Pins.*
*Tel: (971) 81 94 67.*

## Cala Sant Vicenç

This secluded resort is tucked away in
the northeast corner of the island. Its
two sandy bays, sheltered by the Serra
de Cornavaques to the west, and Serra
de Cavall Bernat to the east, are divided
by the San Pedro hotel, with a jumble
of other hotels, restaurants and shops
following the shoreline. Inland there are
impressive villas with profusely
flowering gardens. Cala Sant Vicenç,
with its easy-going atmosphere and
rugged cliff scenery, has always been an
artists' haven: a statue on its promenade
pays tribute to one local painter,
Llorenc Cerda Bisbal.

*56km (35 miles) northeast of Palma,*
*5km (3 miles) northeast of Pollença.*
*Tourist Office: Plaça Cala Sant Vicenç,*
*s/n. Tel: (971) 53 32 64.*

## Can Picafort

In the centre of the Badia d'Alcúdia,
this fishing port turned resort has a
good family beach fringed with low
pines. A copious supply of restaurants,
supermarkets and souvenir shops meets
the needs of visitors of all ages, who are
mainly package holidaymakers staying
in the high-rise hotels. Those who
prefer quieter beaches and more
solitude should head north to Platja
de Muro.

*64km (40 miles) northeast of Palma,*
*11km (7 miles) southeast of Port*
*d'Alcúdia.*
*Tourist Office: Plaça Gabriel Roca 6.*
*Tel: (971) 85 03 10.*
*Open: Apr/May–Oct/Nov.*

The Cap de Formentor peninsula offers clifftop viewpoints

### Cap de Formentor

The peninsula of Cap de Formentor boasts some of Mallorca's most dramatic scenery, made accessible by a steep and winding road. Leaving Port de Pollença, the road (Ma-2210) climbs steadily with good views over the Badia de Pollença. Be sure to stop after 6km (4 miles) at the Mirador des Colomer, a breathtaking viewpoint above the sea-pounded cliffs. A small, rocky islet, Illot des Colomer, lies offshore and is a sanctuary for nesting seabirds.

From here the road narrows, with sharp bends where monster coaches love to hide. Two more small viewpoints offer breathtaking views, then the road drops down, passing a turning right for Platja de Formentor. Continue east along the spine of the peninsula for another 11km (7 miles), passing through the En Fumat mountain to reach the lighthouse. This was built in 1860 and is closed to the public. Like many 'Land's Ends' around the world, Cap de Formentor can get ludicrously crowded, but few will dispute the magnificence of the sea views, which in good weather stretch to Menorca.

On the return trip, you might stop at Platja de Formentor, a beach visited by boat excursions from Port de Pollença in the summer, or call into the Hotel Formentor for a drink (suitable dress required). Tucked into the sheltered south coast of Cap de Formentor, the hotel was built in 1926 by the wealthy Argentinian Adan Dielh and helped put Mallorca on the luxury holiday map.

*84km (52 miles) northeast of Palma, 20km (12½ miles) northeast of Port de Pollença.*

### Capdepera

Capdepera and its hilltop castle at the eastern tip of the island can be seen from afar as you drive from Artà. The town is the centre of Mallorca's basketmaking industry, and in the nearby hills you can see the dwarf fan palms that provide the raw material. Try to park in the main square, Plaça de l'Orient, then walk up the steps that lead to the ruins of Castell de Capdepera. There are views back to the tightly packed roofs of the town below.

*8km (5 miles) east of Artà.*

### Castell de Capdepera

Constructed during the 14th century, the castle occupies a commanding site overlooking the island's east coast. You can walk round the well-preserved battlements and visit a small chapel, Nostra Senyora de la Esperança. A local legend recounts how, when the town was besieged by the Moors, the citizens of Capdepera hid within the castle walls. An image of Our Lady of Hope was placed on the battlements, and the townsfolk prayed for deliverance. At once a great fog descended, and the Moors fled. The miracle is remembered every year on 18 December, when Capdepera holds its Fiesta de Nostra Senyora d'Esperança.

*Freely accessible.*

### Coves d'Artà (Artà Caves)

Perhaps the grandest of Mallorca's subterranean wonders, these caves are signposted off the Capdepera–Son Servera road. A country lane passes the Canyamel golf course and winds alongside a high cliff to reach the entrance, a dramatic gaping hole 46m (151ft) above the sea. The limestone caves were explored by Édouard Martel in 1896. Steep steps lead up to the entrance where guides take visitors down to the vividly illuminated halls of stalactites and stalagmites, including a 22m (72ft) high column known as 'The Queen'. At the lowest level, organ music by Bach sets the scene for *The Inferno.*

*82km (51 miles) northeast of Palma, 7km (4 miles) southeast of Artà. Tel: (971) 84 12 93. www.cuevasdearta.com. Open: daily Nov–Apr 10am–5pm; May–Oct 10am–6pm. Admission charge.*

# Mallorcan mansions

Luxury housing has always been a feature of the Mallorcan landscape, from the fortified *fincas* (country houses) built by Jaume I's *conquistadores* and their descendants to the aloof, security-screened villas in the hills favoured by the celebrities and *nouveaux riches* of today.

In the past, the Spanish aristocracy were exempted from all taxes, and property made a recession-proof investment. Many of the great palaces in Palma were built in the 17th and 18th centuries by noble dynasties. Today, property and land are still passed down the generations in

Palatial houses such as Els Calderers, Sant Joan ...

… and Rudolf Valentino's house are typical of the style of Mallorcan mansions

Mallorca, and many families now own second homes.

Getting behind the monumental façades of Mallorca's historic mansions is a haphazard affair. Some have been turned into hotels or offices, others are open by private arrangement only or have closed their doors because too many visitors were pouring in.

In the Serra de Tramuntana, the Alfàbia gardens, Son Marroig and La Granja all give clues to life in the island's stately homes.

The best place to visit, however, is Els Calderers, open to the public since 1993. In the heart of the island, this huge 18th-century manor house,

framed by level fields and farm buildings, still has an authentic, lived-in feel, as if the owners had just popped out for a minute. In the winter, log fires blaze, and a black *ca de bestair*, the large smooth-coated dog native to the island, greets visitors with a wary eye.

It is easy to imagine the noble residents of the house receiving their guests, attending Mass in the private chapel, sewing, or listening to music – and their servants at work downstairs in the kitchen, laundry and ironing room. As the adverts put it, this really is *la otra* (the other) Mallorca. (For details of access, *see p102*.)

## Els Calderers

Sumptuous furnishings, family portraits and photographs, collections of fans, hunting weapons and toys in the 20 rooms of this manor house help to recreate the lifestyle of a traditional Mallorcan noble family. (*See also pp100–101.*)

*40km (25 miles) east of Palma on the Ma-15 to Manacor, near Sant Joan. Turn north at km37. Tel: (971) 52 60 69. www.elscalderers.com. Open: daily 10am–5pm (summer), 10am–6pm (winter). Admission charge.*

## Montuïri

Close to the Palma–Manacor road, Montuïri rests on a ridge, its old stone windmills set against the sky. The town has a church dating from the 13th century and is liveliest on Mondays when the weekly market takes place.

A stone windmill by Montuïri

**Ermita de Sant Miquel**, 2km (1¼ miles) to the east, a 19th-century chapel, crowns the top of a small hill and offers grand panoramic views over Mallorca's central plains.

*30km (18 miles) east of Palma on the Ma-15.*

## Muro

Few tourists venture into the heart of this likeable town. Its centrepiece is the Catalan-Gothic church, rebuilt in the 16th century, which has a colourful rose window above the west door and a 46m (151ft) long nave. In Plaça de José Antonio Primo de Rivera stand the Convent dels Mínims and the Church of Santa Ana, outside which is a fountain and a statue of a peasant woman holding a jar of water. Fights between bulls and dogs were once staged between the ancient arcades and cloisters. Bullfights are still occasionally held in Muro's impressive Plaça de Toros, which holds 6,000 spectators. It was built in 1910 within the quarry that provided its white stone.

## Museu Mallorca

The former town house of the Alomar family is now a museum devoted to Mallorcan traditions. There are comprehensive displays of rural furniture, local costume, agricultural tools and island crafts, including many examples of the Mallorcans' curious clay whistle known as the *siurell*.

*Carrer Major 15. Tel: (971) 71 75 40. Open: Tue–Sat 10am–6.30pm; Sun*

Local history: Muro's ethnological museum

*10am–1.30pm. Closed: Mon.*
*Admission charge.*
*Muro is 42km (26 miles) northeast of*
*Palma, 13km (8 miles) east of Inca.*
*Tourist Office: Avinguda Albufera 33.*
*Tel: (971) 89 10 13.*

## Petra

Most visitors to this remote inland town
are American, for Petra is the birthplace
of Junípero Serra (1713–84), founder of
the Spanish Missions that grew into the
State of California (*see pp40–41*). With
its tall old buildings and a maze of
narrow streets, the town seems hardly to
have changed since his day. Fortunately,
there are signs directing you to the
sights associated with its famous son,
who was beatified in 1988.

At the eastern end of the town is the
parish church of Sant Pere, which has a
lovely large, stained-glass rose window.
For an overview of the area, visit the
nearby Ermita de Bonany (*see p111*).

### Convent de Sant Bernat
Across from the entrance of Museu y
Casa Natal Fray Junípero Serra, a short
lane leads to the mighty 17th-century
church with a monument to the friar
outside. Painted tiles framed with
wrought iron depict the missions
Serra founded – a gift from the people
of California.
*Carrer Barracar Alt 6–8. Tel: (971) 56 11*
*49. Visitors by appointment only.*

### Museu y Casa Natal Fray
### Junípero Serra
Small but well laid out, the museum
brings home the epic achievements of
the Franciscan friar who left the island
for Mexico in 1749. Beautifully made
wooden models show the missions he
founded in California, growing ever
larger and more ornate over the years.
Nine were established between San
Diego and San Francisco from 1769 and
1782, and another 12 after his death.

In the same street is the simple
house where Serra was born, with a
tiny loft-like bedroom and a minute
garden at the rear.
*Carrer Barracar 6, 8 & 10.*
*Tel: (971) 56 11 49.*

*Petra is 50km (31 miles) east of Palma,*
*10km (6 miles) northwest of Manacor.*

## Pollença

Reached by a fast road from Palma (Ma-13), Pollença rests in foothills at the eastern end of the Serra de Tramuntana. This attractive town is a haven of sleepy Mallorcan traditions, where café life and the siesta roll on as if package holidaymakers had never been invented. The somewhat austere buildings lining the dusty streets, with their ochre roofs, sun-baked walls and faded wooden shutters, could be virtually anywhere in Spain – as could the street-choking traffic. Do not be deterred by Pollença's parking problems. Leave your vehicle in one of the car parks on the south side of town and walk in to the Plaça Major.

Pollença was put on the map by the Romans, and a Pont Romá still spans the Torrente de Sant Jordi River to the north of the town (just off the Ma-10

Pollença town and the steep staircase to the calvary seen from Puig de Maria

## PROBLEM AT POLLENSA BAY

The Badia de Pollença is the setting for a short story by English crime writer Agatha Christie. *Problem at Pollensa Bay* describes the elaborate strategy of a son to break free from his over-protective mother and find love with a modern girl. Ending with a characteristic twist to the plot, the tale evokes a pre-war world when well-spoken English holidaymakers with 'excellent hotel manners' (as Christie describes them) came to Mallorca on the steamer from Barcelona. They would take a taxi to the new hotels around Port de Pollença, then relax with games of piquet and cocktails on the terrace.

to Lluc). After the Spanish conquest of 1229, Pollença came under the control of the Knights Templar, who built the parish church, Nostra Senyora dels Àngels.

The expulsion of the Moors and resistance against pirates is celebrated every August with a mock battle, Moros i Cristians, that rages around town during the local *festa*.

Pollença's lively market takes place on Sunday mornings, with fruit, flowers and vegetables in the Plaça Major. Local cheeses and roasted almonds are good buys.

*Tourist Office: Carrer Sant Domingo 2. Tel: (971) 53 50 77.*

### Calvari (Calvary)

Just north of Plaça Major, the Convent de Monti-Sión, built by the Jesuits in 1738, has been appropriated by the Ajuntament (Town Hall). From here, heralded by a fountain adorned with a cockerel, a flight of 365 steps,

bordered with cypresses that provide welcome shade in summer, leads up to a hilltop pilgrimage chapel, where the views justify the exertion – of course, you could drive up instead.

Inside the chapel, built in 1794, is a wooden cross said to date from the 13th century. It was placed on the site by grateful mariners who survived a shipwreck off Cala Sant Vicenç.

### Ermita de la Mare de Déu del Puig

About 3km (2 miles) southeast of the town (take the PM-220), a side road leads up to Puig de Maria (320m/1,050ft) and a small hermitage founded by nuns in the 14th century.

### Museu de Municipal Pollença

South of Plaça Major, the 17th-century monastery of Santo Domingo has beautiful cloisters that are the principal venue for an acclaimed international music festival every summer. Inside is a small museum where winning entries from an annual international art competition are exhibited.

*Claustre de Santo Domingo, Carrer Santo Domingo. Tel: (971) 53 11 66. Open: Jul & Sept Tue–Sat 10am–1pm & 5.30–8.30pm, Sun 10am–1pm; Aug Tue–Sat 10am–1pm & 5.30pm–midnight; Oct–Jun Tue–Sun 11am–1pm. Admission charge.*

*Pollença is 55km (34 miles) northeast of Palma, 11km (7 miles) northwest of Alcúdia.*

# Watchtowers and windmills

More than 40 watchtowers or fortified positions, mostly along the north coast – meant to protect the island – are marked on a 1683 map of Mallorca displayed in Palma's Museu Diocesà.

Watchtowers have been a feature of the Mallorcan landscape since Talayot times (*see pp10–11*). Normally seen as defensive lookouts, the strategic position of watchtowers could be used to aggressive ends too: the early Mallorcans were pirates, as well as the victims of piracy.

Watchtowers still punctuate the skyline, for instance at the Mirador de

A watchtower near Estellencs

Ses Animes near Banyalbufar on the northwest coast, and at Punta de n'Amer on the east. But more common now, and sometimes similarly shaped, are the windmills – as much part of the archetypal image of Mallorca as *ensaimadas* (a sugar-dusted pastry) or the Sóller railway line. Windmills are often the first thing visitors notice on arrival at Son Sant Joan airport; there are clusters around Sa Pobla and Llucmajor.

Windmills were constructed to either grind corn or draw underground water. Originally they would all have had cloth sails, which were later replaced by wooden slats and the metal fans of today. Many have fallen idle, some converted into restaurants, houses and discos, some used as unconventional advertising hoardings and colourful declarations of patriotic and football allegiances.

Admirers of these handsome structures and connoisseurs of urban incongruities could seek out Carrer de Indústria in the west of Palma, where, in the middle of a street bordered by featureless housing, stands a defiant row of five windmills – sentinels from another age.

A windmill at Sa Pobla, Carrer de Indùstria, Palma

## Port d'Alcúdia

At the northern end of the Badia d'Alcúdia, Port d'Alcúdia has many functions. The harbour is home to a naval base and a busy fishing fleet, a modern marina caters to the many yachts and pleasure craft cruising the coast, and a daily car ferry service operates between here and the Menorcan port of Ciutadella. If you are interested in fishing trips or sea excursions to Cap des Pinar and Formentor, this is the place to come.

Port d'Alcúdia is also a lively resort, with a long sandy beach and a variety of available sports, including water skiing, water scooters, dinghies and floodlit tennis courts. If you need to buy souvenirs or presents to take home but are not mad about shopping, Port d'Alcúdia could solve a few problems. The souvenir shops along Passeig de Vicealmirante Moreno (Passeig Marítim) sell anything that can be loosely described as Mallorcan. Leather jackets, pottery, jewellery and olive wood products are worth considering. On Sunday mornings, there is a market in Avinguda José Prado Suarez.
*Tourist Office: Carretera Artà 68.*
*Tel: (971) 89 26 15.*

### Platja de Muro

A long sweep of sand curls round from Port d'Alcúdia south to Platja de Muro, 9km (5½ miles) northeast of Muro. The dunes here are fringed with umbrella pines and the bathing is good.
*Port d'Alcúdia is 55km (34 miles)*
*northeast of Palma, 3km (2 miles) south of Alcúdia.*

## Port de Pollença

Set in a splendid horseshoe bay, Port de Pollença is a comparatively quiet resort popular with British visitors. Long, palm-lined promenades extend either side of the harbour – a colourful mêlée of fishing boats, yachts and pleasure cruisers offering trips to the Formentor peninsula and Badia d'Alcúdia. Its sandy beaches are narrow and divided by breakwaters, with shallow water well suited to young children.

Go to the southern end of the bay for water sports, as well as tennis, riding and bowling. In the backstreets and squares behind the seafront there is a range of 'pick-a-fish' restaurants and others serving *típico* Mallorcan cuisine.

Port de Pollença has a relaxed, distinguished air with no nightclubs or blaring discos, though you will find plenty of music and entertainment in restaurants and hotels. The admirable Spanish institution known as the evening *paseo* (promenade) thrives here, with plenty of recruits from the resort's sizeable community of foreign residents and retired visitors taking a long winter break. For the elderly or people with disabilities, Port de Pollença is one of the most congenial destinations on the island.
*57km (35 miles) northeast of Palma, 6km (4 miles) northeast of Pollença.*
*Tourist Office: Paseo de Saralegui. Tel: (971) 86 54 67.*

Port de Pollença is a quieter resort

catamaran trip to Cala San Vicenç. A quiet resort with three separate bays, it is home to the Coves of l'Alzinaret (although usually signposted as Necròpolis de Cala Sant Vicenç). This ancient burial site, one of the most important in the Mediterranean, is at the edge of the resort area, in Los Encinares park.

*Boats: tel: (971) 86 40 14. Purchase tickets opposite the Brisa Marina.*

### S'Albufera

*See pp139–40.*

### Sa Colònia de Sant Pere

At the southern end of Badia d'Alcúdia, this quiet fishing village is slowly developing into a resort. Behind it rises Puig d'en Ferrutx and the mountains of the Serra d'Artà, with the nearby countryside rich with vines, almond and apricot trees, and olive groves decorated with fat, woolly sheep. There is a tiny harbour, a beach that is part rock, part sand, a Club Nàutic, a few shops and simple fish restaurants.

The campsite at the western end of the village makes a quiet base for budget travellers, with good walks around Ermita de Betlem (*see p138*) and Puig de Morei.

*83km (51½ miles) northeast of Palma, 13km (8 miles) northwest of Artà. Take the Ma-12 from Artà or Can Picafort and turn north (Ma-3331), forking left after 5km (3 miles) for the village.*

### Excursions in the bay

During the summer months, the Port de Pollença area is the centre for sightseeing excursions and glass-bottomed boat trips to see the shoreline and the undersea life, and the beaches and other sights around the bay. Boats to Formentor Point run most days but dates and times are subject to change. There is also a daily ferry to Formentor Beach and a weekly

Sheep grazing near Sa Colònia de Sant Pere

## Ses Païsses

The ruins of this Talayot (*see p10*) settlement are an evocative legacy of the inhabitants of Mallorca between 1000 and 800 BC. The impressive portal and most of the perimeter walls are still in place. Some of the blocks used to build this settlement weigh up to eight tonnes.

The site was probably occupied during Roman times. It is not difficult to picture the halls and dwellings, and the lookout tower that would have warned of approaching ships.

Today, Ses Païsses is surrounded by fields covered with almond and carob trees, and the area makes a pleasant picnic spot.

*Open: Apr–Oct Mon–Sat 10am–1pm & 2.30–6.30pm. Tel: 619 070 010.*
*68km (42 miles) northeast of Palma, 2km (1¼ miles) south of Artà. Turn left*
*off the Ma-15 to Capdepera, down a signposted track. Admission charge.*

## Sineu

Sineu is the geographical bull's eye of Mallorca. Jaume II built a royal residence here in the 13th century, which is now a convent where the nuns are known as *monges del palau* (the palace nuns). Outside the massive church in Plaça de Sant Marc is a popular statue of a winged lion, erected in honour of the town's patron, St Mark.

On Wednesday mornings, Sineu's streets and squares are a stage for one of the best village markets on the island – particularly good if you have urgent need of a rabbit or some sheep. The village was once on the railway line between Inca and Artà, and the old station on its eastern side has been converted into an art gallery, S'Estació.

Sineu is also known for its wine-cellar bar-restaurants, which serve typical Mallorcan cuisine.

*30km (18½ miles) northeast of Palma, 12km (7½ miles) north of Montuïri.*

## Vilafranca de Bonany

Stop here to buy strings of red and green peppers, sun-dried tomatoes, garlic, aubergines and sweetcorn. This is also the melon capital of the island in summer. Colourful local produce hangs from many of the walls in the village's main street, while roadside stalls sell intriguing bite-sized doughnuts known as *bunyols.*

### Ermita de Bonany

Crowning the Puig de Bonany (317m/ 1,040ft), this sanctuary lies 5km (3 miles) southwest of Petra. The entrance to the church is through an imposing gate overseen by St Paul and St Anthony with his piglet, depicted on tiles. Inside the dark chapel is a Bethlehem Grotto with a rural Nativity scene, though the real attraction of this *ermita* is the view over the central plains.

*Vilafranca de Bonany is 38km (23½ miles) east of Palma on the Ma-15 to Manacor, 9km (5½ miles) east of Montuïri.*

This statue of a winged lion honours St Mark at Sineu's Plaça de Sant Marc

# Tour: Badia d'Alcúdia

*Following the curve of the Badia d'Alcúdia, this leisurely 120km (75-mile) round trip runs southeast from Port d'Alcúdia to the uplands of the Serra d'Artà, then to Mallorca's easternmost promontory, Punta de Capdepera. Turning south, the drive continues inland to Manacor, then follows mainly quiet country roads back to the northeast coast. (See map p93 for route.)*

*Allow 5 hours.*

*From Port d'Alcúdia you have to take the main road south (Ma-12), following signs to Artà. The road is a scenic one that follows the pines and dunes of the coast with the S'Albufera nature reserve inland (see pp139–40). Passing the resort of Can Picafort (see p97), the road continues east into the green hills of the Serra d'Artà.*

## 1 Artà

This medieval hilltop town dominated by the Santuari de Sant Salvador, Artà (*see pp94–5*) also has an archaeological museum with finds from the nearby Talayot site at Ses Païsses (*see p110*).
*Continuing east for 8km (5 miles), you reach the Capdepera ring road. Follow the signs to Cala Ratjada.*

## 2 Cala Ratjada

A fishing port-cum-resort with fine beaches nearby, Cala Ratjada (or Platja de Canyamel) would make a good place to stop for lunch or for a swim. Follow

the one-way system through the town to the harbour, where you can park (*see p97*).
*Follow signs to the left in the direction of Canyamel and Son Servera. Turn left after 8km (5 miles), following signs to the Coves d'Artà (see p99), driving past the Canyamel golf course to turn right at a junction for Platja de Canyamel.*

## 3 Platja de Canyamel

Now well developed as a holiday resort, Platja de Canyamel enjoys a sheltered position with a beach of fine, white sand served by an arcade of shops and bars. When you leave, following signs for Son Servera, you pass the impressive fortress of Torre de Canyamel built as a lookout for pirates – now partly converted into a restaurant serving Mallorcan dishes (*see p168*, under Canyamel).
*After passing through the sedate old towns of Son Servera and Sant Llorenç des Cardassar, take the Ma-15 to*

*Manacor (see pp125–6). Follow the signs for Palma, but after 2km (1¼ miles) turn right for Petra.*

## 4  Manacor to Sa Pobla

The road now crosses the flat, alluring landscape so characteristic of central Mallorca. Vines, aubergines, tomatoes and melons grow in the dusty soil, and the silhouettes of windmills and village churches are etched sharply on the horizon.

*Bypassing Petra and Santa Margalida, follow the one-way system through Muro's maze of narrow streets (see pp102–3), and continue to Sa Pobla.*

## 5  Sa Pobla

Much of the land surrounding this agricultural town is reclaimed from swamps. New potatoes in the UK at Christmas time come from Sa Pobla. The UK is its biggest market for potatoes. The fields have rich fertile soil where strawberries, artichokes and salad crops are grown. You can park in the northeast of the town and walk back to the central square, which has some fine old houses and a 17th-century church.

*Narrow twisting lanes lead past farms and an electrical power station to the main road (Ma-12). Turn left for Port d'Alcúdia.*

Fields of artichokes around Sa Pobla

# Walk: Bóquer valley

*This easy 6km (4-mile) walk starts in Port de Pollença and follows the course of the Bóquer valley down to the sea. The valley is a popular place for birdwatching, particularly in the migrating seasons (from April to May, and September to October). Stout shoes, binoculars and a drink or picnic lunch are recommended.*

*Allow 2½ hours return. No right-of-way problems.*

*From the roundabout on the seafront in Port de Pollença follow the signs to Formentor, which involves going inland*

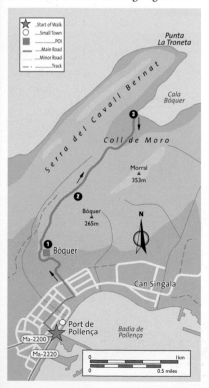

*and turning right by the Hotel Mar Calma. When the houses on the left-hand side peter out, turn left to pass the Oro Playa apartments. If you are driving, park on the rough ground at the end of the tarmac road.*

## 1 Bóquer farm

A pair of stone pillars marks the entrance to a tree-lined lane, which leads to a ridge and a large farmhouse. Do not be surprised if a chained dog serenades your arrival. As you pass, look over the stone wall to the left for a good view across gardens and orchards to the town below.

*Go through a gate and uphill along a stony track to the start of the Bóquer valley.*

## 2 Bóquer valley

You will soon go into a steep-sided cleft in the rocks. The track across the valley is well-worn, weaving through a sparse landscape dotted with wild flowers, small shrubs and windswept pines.

## ELEONORA'S FALCONS

The Bóquer valley and Formentor peninsula are an annual port of call for the endangered Eleonora's falcon. This dark, long-tailed bird of prey gets its name from a 14th-century Sardinian princess who is said to have introduced legislation to protect nesting hawks and falcons. The birds winter in Madagascar, arriving in Mallorca in late April. Their nests are built among the cliffs along Mallorca's northern coast, but breeding does not take place until late summer. By September, other birds are already migrating south, providing easy meat for the young falcons.

Quite likely you will hear the bleating of the wild tan-coloured goats that roam the rocks above. Resident birds you might spot include black vultures, ravens and peregrines, and in spring and summer, Eleonora's falcons, ospreys and even a booted eagle soaring overhead. Stonechats and numerous goldfinches flit around the grass. You may hear red-legged partridges, and keep an eye out for the rare rock sparrow.

*After you pass through a gap in a stone wall, the sea comes into view.*

### 3 Cala Bóquer

Just offshore is the Es Colomer rock and to the left is the high ridge of the Serra del Cavall Bernat. In one place erosion has created a dramatic window in the cliffs; if you are feeling energetic, you can climb up for a closer look.

The track continues down a sharp incline, passing a lazy freshwater spring that runs into a trough, to reach the small rock and shingle beach of Cala Bóquer. Sturdy footwear is recommended.

*When you have had a rest and enjoyed the solitude, retrace your steps to Port de Pollença. It is surprising how different the vistas seem on the way back.*

The Bóquer valley shows a less well-known side of Mallorca

# The south

*Southern Mallorca is predominantly flat and agricultural, a beguiling landscape of dusty towns, windmills, saltpans and relatively undeveloped beaches. In the southeast, the inland plain (Es Pla) ends abruptly in the mountainous Serra de Llevant, capped with a castle and religious sanctuaries. Beyond this, the island's east coast is indented with calas (coves), now fringed with resorts.*

### Algaida

Since the most interesting shops and restaurants are along the main Palma–Manacor road (Ma-15) to the north, visitors usually come across this quiet old town only if they are en route to Puig de Randa (*see pp127–8*). Two ancient stone crosses stand at each end of the town, which is a muddle of narrow streets.

### Botanicactus

Said to be the largest botanical garden in Europe, the still-expanding Botanicactus is a convincing desert landscape with 12,000 cacti of 400 different species, including a 300-year-old Carnegie Giant from Arizona. Those who dismiss cacti as prickly things fit only for cowboy films and suburban windowsills will be amazed by the extraordinary shapes, sizes and exotic blooms here.

Stone walls have been built to protect the cacti from sea breezes, and a third of the gardens is given over to wetland plants, including a bamboo plantation and artificial lake, palms, pines, fruit trees and a Mallorcan garden.

At the eastern end, tropical plants are for sale at the nursery.

*54km (33 miles) southeast of Palma on the road between Ses Salines and Santanyí. The entrance is marked by a windmill with green and white sails. Tel: (971) 64 94 94. www.botanicactus.com. Open: daily, summer 9am–7pm; winter 9am–5.30pm, until 4.30pm in Nov, Dec and Jan. Admission charge.*

Botanicactus will tell you everything you ever wanted to know about cacti

# The south *(see pp132–3 for route)*

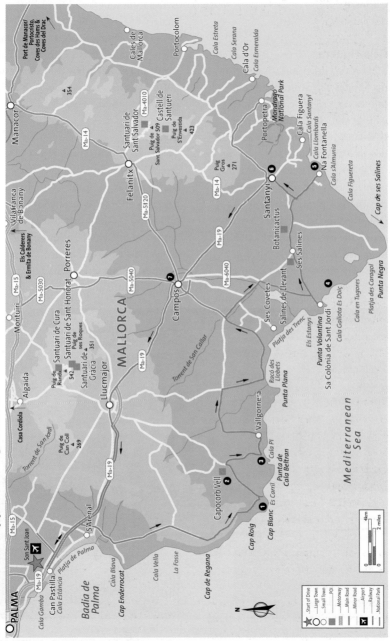

**Map labels:**

PALMA · Cala Gamba · Can Pastilla · Cala Estància · S'Arenal · Platja de Palma · Cala Blava · Cala Vella · La Fosse · Cap Enderrocat · Cap de Regana · Cap Roig · Cap Blanc · Es Carril · Punta de Cala Beltran · Cala Pi · Capocorb Vell · Vallgornera · Punta Plana · Racó des Llobets · Torrent de San Callar · Ses Coves · Salines de Llevant · Platja des Trenc · Els Estanys · Punta Volantina · Sa Colònia de Sant Jordi · Cala Gallota Es Dolç · Cala en Tugores · Platja des Carragol · Punta Negra · Cap de ses Salines · Cala Figuereta · Cala s'Almunia · Na Fontanella · Cala Llombards · Cala Santanyí · Cala Figuera · Mondragó National Park · Portopetra · Cala Esmeralda · Cala d'Or · Cala Serana · Cala Estreta · Portocolom · Cales de Mallorca · Port de Manacor/ Portcristo, Coves des Hams & Coves del Drac

Botanicactus · Ses Salines · Santanyí · Puig Gros 271 · Puig de Sant Salvador 509 · Castell de Santueri · Puig de S'Envestida 423 · Sant Salvador · Santuari de Sant Salvador · Felanitx · Porreres · Campos · Llucmajor · Santuari de Gràcia · Santuari de Sant Honorat · Puig de ses Roques 351 · Santuari de Cura · Puig de Randa 542 · Algaida · Casa Cordiola · Puig de Can Coll 269 · Torrent de San Jordi · Montuïri · Vilafranca de Bonany · Els Calderers & Ermita de Bonany · Manacor · 354

MALLORCA · Mediterranean Sea · Badia de Palma

Roads: Ma-19, Ma-15, Ma-14, Ma-5120, Ma-5040, Ma-5030, Ma-6040, Ma-4010

Son Sant Joan

**Legend:**
- ★ Start of Drive
- ◯ ● Large Town / Small Town
- ■ POI
- Motorway
- Main Road
- Minor Road
- ✈ Airport
- Railway
- National Park

0 — 4km
0 — 2 miles

N

## Cabrera

*See pp140–41.*

## Cala Figuera

Mallorca's 'Little Venice' is a narrow, deep water inlet with fishermen's houses built right up to the water's edge. If you are driving, it is best to park at the top of the port and walk down to the harbour. Here you can find idyllic postcard scenes with brightly painted boats and villagers mending their nets or playing cards.

By the time most tourist coaches arrive, the previous night's catch, unloaded at dawn and rushed away by lorry, will already be on sale in Palma's fish market.

The calm waters and fjord-like scenery of Cala Figuera make it a favoured anchorage for luxury yachts. There is little accommodation, and, surprisingly, only a few fish restaurants. *69km (43 miles) southeast of Palma, 5km (3 miles) from Santanyí.*

## Cala d'Or

This large, tourist-boom resort is built around a series of small bays. Its centrepiece is an Ibizan-style complex, begun in 1932, with low white buildings, spacious courtyards, and an appealing range of boutiques, craft shops, bars and restaurants. The sandy beaches of Cala Gran, Cala Longa and Platja d'Or are lined with low pine

Postcard Mallorca: fishermen's houses line the waterfront at Cala Figuera

trees, but can get very crowded in high season. Things have changed a bit from the conservative days when the beach at Cala Gran was reserved exclusively for men – and the smaller Cala d'Or for women.

A tourist train runs from the town centre along to the marina. Packed with luxury yachts and pleasure boats, this is a favourite spot for a waterfront meal. Cala d'Or is a popular venue for sporting holidays, with good facilities for sailing, diving and tennis; or you can take a lazy boat trip along the coast to Cala Figuera.

*63km (39 miles) southeast of Palma. Turn east at Calonge on the Santanyí–Portocristo road. Tourist Office: Carrer Perico Pomar 10. Tel: (971) 65 74 63.*

## Cales de Mallorca

Between Cala Magraner and Cala Murada, Cales de Mallorca (Coves of Mallorca) is a purpose-built, self-contained resort mixing high-rise hotels, villas and apartments with shops and restaurants. **Cala Murada** is relatively quiet, with a small sand and shingle beach, while **Sa Romaguera** is the most appealing inlet, with bars and cafés close to the sea. Most of the nightlife is in the hotels.

## Can Pastilla

On the east side of the Badia de Palma, Can Pastilla's hotels and apartment complexes stretch inland almost as far as the airport. The resort is a mecca for fun-loving families and the young-at-heart looking for a beach holiday with plenty to do in the evenings.

A palm-lined promenade follows the shore, particularly enjoyable at night when the lights of Palma can be seen across the water. By day the main attraction is the beach, which runs south to S'Arenal and is known as Platja de Palma. It is ideal for children, with clean white sand, shallow water, sun umbrellas, playgrounds and abundant opportunity to indulge in ice creams.

At night, Can Pastilla erupts in a blaze of neon and the ceaseless pounding of discos. The streets leading off the seafront, and along the main road leading east to Las Maravillas and S'Arenal, are crammed with souvenir shops, amusement arcades, predominantly English and German bars, and restaurants serving international cuisine.

*7km (4½ miles) south of Palma. Bus: 15 from Plaça d'Espanya.*

## Capocorb Vell

Capocorb Vell is the site of a Bronze Age settlement dating back to at least 1000 BC. Concrete paths now lead among the ruins of the ancient dwellings, which still have enough of their sturdy walls, doorways, pillars, winding passages and stone floors to make a thought-provoking ghost town.

Beyond the main group of buildings the remains of five Talayots (*see pp10–11*) are spread among the fields.

From the stone tower near the entrance you can sometimes see Cabrera island. *37km (23 miles) southeast of Palma. Take the road from S'Arenal to Cap Blanc, or from Llucmajor towards Cala Pi, then follow signs to the site. Tel: (971) 18 01 55. Open: Fri–Wed 10am–5pm. Closed: Thur. Admission charge. Access may be difficult for visitors with disabilities.*

### Casa Gordiola

On the Ma-15, 2km (1¼ miles) northwest of Algaida, is a mock-medieval castle (1969) containing one of Mallorca's most popular tourist attractions: this is where you can watch craftsmen blowing and fashioning glass, which has been made on the island by the Gordiola family since 1719.

Next door to the workshop is a series of showrooms with a huge choice of beautiful, hand-crafted glass, ceramics and souvenirs displayed for sale. Be sure to make your way upstairs to the museum. This lovely space exhibits glass from various countries, as well as furniture and paintings that have been in the Gordiola family for generations. *19km (12 miles) east of Palma at km19 on the road to Manacor. Tel: (971) 66 50 46. **Glassworks:** open Mon–Sat 9am–1.30pm & 3–6pm, Sun 9am–noon.*

Enigmatic ruins of a settlement at Capocorb Vell, probably 3,000 years old

*Shop and museum: open Mon–Sat 9am–7pm, Sun 9am–1.30pm. Free admission.*

## Castell de Santueri

Castell de Santueri is strategically sited at the summit of a 408m (1,338ft) peak in the Serra de Llevant. Protected by steep cliffs, it was rebuilt in the 14th century above the ruins of a Moorish stronghold. Only parts of the outer walls and ramparts remain. It used to be possible for visitors to explore the vast interior, but access has been temporarily closed while potential restoration programmes are considered. Nonetheless, the views and wild flowers still make a visit to the hilltop ruins very worthwhile.

Casa Gordiola: a glass-making workshop

*57km (35½ miles) southeast of Palma, 6.5km (4 miles) southeast of Felanitx. Take the road for Santanyí, turning left after 2km (1¼ miles) on to a country road that runs through fields and orchards, then climbs up to the castle.*

## Coves del Drac (Dragon Caves)

The Coves del Drac (Dragon Caves) were first explored in 1896 by a French geologist, Édouard Martel, and now attract thousands of visitors every year. The entrance to the caves is down a steep flight of steps, followed by a walk along narrow, but well-lit, underground passages and platforms (not for the claustrophobic).

The labyrinth of tunnels and caves is estimated to run for about 2km (1¼ miles) in total, and fanciful names have been given to many of its physical features. Visitors are guided to the delights of Diana's Bath and the Fairies' Theatre, passing through a fairyland of radiant pools, and stalactites and stalagmites dramatically illuminated by concealed lights in various colours. The tour culminates in the vast Lago Martel and a cavernous auditorium that can hold over a thousand spectators. The show features a torchlight procession with musicians and singers gliding across the water in boats.

*66km (41 miles) east of Palma, 1.5km (1 mile) south of Portocristo. Tel: (971) 82 07 53. www.cuevasdeldrach.com. Open: Apr–Oct daily with tours on the hour from 10am to 5pm; rest of the year 10.45am–noon, 2.30pm & 3.30pm. Visit without concert at 4.30pm. Admission charge.*

# Caves

The caves that formed naturally in Mallorca's limestone rocks have always been useful to its islanders. They provided shelter for the Pre-Talayot settlers (*see pp10–11*) who set up home here around 2000 BC, and are a common thread through the island's social history. Caves served as dank homes for mythical beasts, provided refuge from slave-raiders and lairs for pirates, and were used as smugglers' dens as well as religious sanctuaries. Rediscovered in the late 19th century, the largest and strangest are now technicolour tourist attractions for hordes of sightseers.

Marine caves are created by the quarrying action of the waves. Inland, caves are created as water containing carbon dioxide circulates through the joints and faults in the calcareous rock. In time, the passages and channels formed become caverns which are revealed when the water table drops. This process can create extraordinary deposits, including stalagmites (spikes rising from the ground), stalactites (like icicles hanging from above), draperies (like curtains), and knobbly clusters known as cave coral.

The caves at Artà (*see p99*), probably the best on the island, are said to have inspired Jules Verne's book, *Journey to the Centre of the Earth*. The phantasmagoric rock shapes continue to stimulate the imagination. Once likened to pious subjects such as the Virgin, a cathedral, or grottoes fit for classical deities, these drip-fed rock blobs are now more often seen to resemble human towers, monstrous hairy nostrils, the Leaning Tower of Pisa, eggs and bacon, or vegetables in a great subterranean supermarket.

Awesome formations of stalagmites and stalactites inside a cave

Caves (*coves*) can be visited at Drac (*p121*), Hams (*p124*), Artà (*p99*), Campanet (*p71*) and Gènova (*p54*). Since the temperature inside is constant all year round (about 20°C/68°F), you do not need a coat, but as the ground can be wet and slippery, wear suitable shoes.

The gaping entrance at Artà

## Coves dels Hams

The Coves dels Hams get their name from the similarity of stalactites hanging in some caves to *hams*, a Mallorcan word for fish-hooks. Though the caves are not as extensive as the nearby Coves del Drac (*see p121*), their underground formations, which were only discovered in 1906, are an impressive natural sight, made easily accessible by guided tour. Highlights include the 'Lake of Venice' and rock formations that resemble everything from saints and petrified cities to a herd of elephants. Coloured lights and a *concierto* (concert) enhance the occasion.

*60km (37 miles) east of Palma, 2km (1¼ miles) west of Portocristo. Tel: (971) 82 09 88. www.cuevas-hams.com. Open: Mar–Oct daily 10am–6pm; Nov–Feb 10.30am–5pm. Admission charge.*

## Felanitx

Felanitx is a traditional market town on the west flank of the Serra de Llevant. Its name is thought to be derived, rather poetically, from *fiel a nit* ('faithful to the night'). Seven roads converge on the town, which can make parking in the narrow streets leading to its market square something of an endurance test.

The square is dominated by the 13th-century Church of Sant Miquel, a large, warm-stoned edifice with broad steps leading up to the Renaissance doorway. The Baroque façade includes a memorial plaque to 414 victims killed

The Church of Sant Miquel, Felanitx: Baroque flourishes on a plain canvas

when a wall in the town collapsed in 1844. Sunday morning is a good time to visit Felanitx, when the lively open-air market is in full swing and local pottery is often displayed on the church steps.

*51km (31 miles) southeast of Palma, 13km (8 miles) south of Manacor.*

## Llucmajor

Once the dominant town in the south of the island, Llucmajor is surrounded by flat agricultural land planted with dilapidated windmills. Many of the islanders in this area work in the dried-fruit trade or in shoe factories.

Llucmajor is best known as the battlefield where, in 1349, the forces of Pedro IV of Aragón defeated Jaume III, so bringing an end to the short-lived independent kingdom of Mallorca. Llucmajor is at its liveliest on the local market days of Wednesdays and Sundays.

*25km (15 miles) southeast of Palma,*
*13km (8 miles) northwest of Campos.*

## Manacor

The largest town in Mallorca after
Palma, Manacor is the centre of the
island's artificial pearl industry. It has
always been associated with crafts, and
the local shopping emporia bulge with
dark Mallorcan pottery, painted
ceramics and items carved from olive
wood. The town is also known for its
local sweets, enchantingly known as
*sospiros* (sighs) and for being the home
of tennis player Rafael Nadal.
*Tourist Office: Plaça Ramón Llull.*
*Tel: (971) 84 72 41.*

Manacor's Església dels Dolors, with its eye-
catching tower reminiscent of a minaret

### JAUME II

The present-day shape of Mallorca owes a lot
to the enlightened King Jaume II, who
reigned between 1291 and 1327. He
established 11 new towns to encourage
economic growth in the interior: Algaida,
Binissalem, Selva, Sant Joan, Sa Pobla,
Llucmajor, Manacor, Porreres, Campos,
Felanitx and Santuari. The monarch also built
new churches, bridges and reservoirs, minted
a Mallorcan coinage, and introduced a
programme of weekly markets.

### Església dels Dolors
### (Church of the Virgin of Sorrows)

A notable town landmark, the Church
of the Virgin of the Sorrows is worth
the considerable effort required to track
down a parking space in Manacor.
Built on the site of a mosque, the
church has great atmosphere, with
mighty wooden doors, a huge domed
ceiling, and a slender minaret-like
clock tower. Among its treasures
is an image of Christ on the Cross
with long straggly hair and a short
white skirt.
*Plaça del Rector Rubí. Open: Mon–Sat*
*8.30am–12.30pm & 5–7.30pm; Sun, as*
*services permit. Tel: (971) 55 43 48.*

### Hipódrom de Manacor (racecourse)

For an authentic slice of Mallorcan life,
join the locals at the trotting races.
There's a café and restaurant if you
want to make a night of it.
*Carretera Palma–Arta Km48.*
*Tel: (971) 55 00 23.*
*Races: Sat 9pm (summer);*
*4pm (winter).*

## Pearl factories

Artificial pearls have been made in Manacor since 1890. There are several factories you can visit with an excursion or independently: follow the well-marked directions to the free parking and shops. You can see the various painstaking stages in the birth of an artificial pearl, from glassed-in viewing corridors. The exact ingredients are a closely guarded secret, but if you murmur, 'Ah yes, finely ground fish scales mixed with resin', that will impress your companions, and not be too far off the mark. Artificial pearls are not cheap; their lustre lasts forever. (For shops, *see p149.*)

*Majorica Pearl Factory open: Jul–Sept Mon–Sat 9am–8pm, Sun 10am–7pm; May–Jun & Oct Mon–Fri 9am–7pm, Sat–Sun 10am–1pm; Nov–Apr Mon–Fri 9am–6pm, Sat–Sun 10am–1pm. Free admission.*

*Manacor is 47km (29 miles) east of Palma, 15km (9 miles) north of Felanitx.*

## Platja des Trenc

Many visitors say this is the finest beach in Mallorca. Mostly undeveloped, with low pines, wild flowers, gently rolling dunes and a fine, white-sand shore that stretches for 7km (4½ miles), Platja des Trenc is now a designated nature reserve. Because of its remote location, it is popular with nudists.

Parking can be a problem, especially during summer weekends – the arrival of a few sun umbrellas and a small bar is proof that, despite the beach's protected status, the tide of tourism is relentless. Most of the year the water is calm and clear, but storms can cover the beach with seaweed.

At the western end of Platja des Trenc, close to Sa Ràpita, is Ses Covetes, a tiny village with a couple of bar-restaurants. To get to the village, drive along narrow lanes bordered by dusty fields and farmhouses with ancient windmills. Turn left when the road reaches the coast, bearing right on to a sandy track that leads to a rocky headland and white sand dunes.
*56km (35 miles) southeast of Palma, 14km (8½ miles) south of Campos. Take the road to Sa Colònia de Sant Jordi, then follow signs to the beach. Admission charge.*

## Porreres

This quiet market town is embedded in the heart of the island. Its 17th-century church, Nostra Senyora de Consolació, is decorated with painted tiles. About 3km (2 miles) southwest of the town is the road that climbs up to the **Santuari de Monti-Siòn**, notable for its well-preserved irregular cloisters.
*37km (23 miles) east of Palma, 7km (4½ miles) south of Montuïri.*

## Portocolom

One of the many villages in the Mediterranean that claims to be the birthplace of Christopher Columbus, Portocolom served as the port for the

Traditional fishermen's houses at Portocolom

nearby town of Felanitx and is now a holiday resort. The tiny harbour still has colourful old fishermen's houses and sheds, now complemented by a few souvenir shops, fish restaurants and other tourist amenities.
*63km (39 miles) southeast of Palma, 13km (8 miles) southeast of Felanitx.*

### Portocristo
Being close to the Coves del Drac and Coves dels Hams, Portocristo attracts coachloads of visitors who stop to enjoy its restaurants and souvenir shops. The harbour lies at the end of a long, sheltered inlet, and is still an important fishing centre. It has a small sandy beach.
*63km (39 miles) east of Palma, 13km (8 miles) east of Manacor. Tourist Office: Carrer Moll, s/n. Tel: (971) 81 51 03.*

### Portopetra
Despite some stark high-rise apartments, this simple port has managed to retain its charm. Yachts and fishing boats dot its palm-shaded

harbour, and a few unpretentious restaurants serve fresh fish by weight. Cala Mondragó, to the south, has a pleasant sandy beach.
*69km (43 miles) southeast of Palma. Turn east at S'Alqueria Blanca on the Santanyí–Portocristo road.*

### Puig de Randa
A striking and revered island landmark, Puig de Randa (542m/ 1,778ft) rises sharply from the agricultural plains of central Mallorca. A traditional focus for pilgrimages and religious festivals, its slopes are graced by three monasteries. To reach them, drive through the village of Randa, passing the Celler de Randa bar-restaurant, and follow the signs up to Santuari de Cura (Ma-5017).

The road climbs along a series of hairpin bends to reach a gateway to the right, where a driveway leads to the 15th-century church and medieval hostelry of **Santuari de Gràcia**. From here there are fine views over the south of the island.

### Santuari de Cura

On the summit of Puig de Randa, despite the competing presence of a radio mast, the sacred aura of Santuari de Cura lives on – its terraces offer magical views of much of the island. Founded by the theologian Ramón Llull in the 13th century (most of the present building dates from the early 19th century), the monastery has a cool, gracious courtyard and an ancient library with some of Llull's prayer books and manuscripts (ask for admission if it is not open). The stained-glass windows of the church tell the story of the founder's life (*see p40*). *Tel: (971) 12 02 60. www.santuaridecura.com*

### Santuari de Sant Honorat

A short drive further uphill from Puig de Randa, on the right, this is a 14th-century hermitage with venerable trees in its courtyard. To the left of the monastery, a passage leading to the church is lined with painted tiles recalling the sanctuary's history.

## BREAD AND STONES

One day Jesus and the Apostles were out walking. 'Pick up a stone and follow me,' Jesus said. Seeing that they were about to climb a mountain, St Peter picked up the smallest stone he could find. When they were halfway up, Jesus stopped and blessed each of the stones they had been carrying.

At once the stones turned to bread, which the Apostles ate eagerly. St Peter swallowed his measly piece in one bite, but said nothing about the hunger that still gnawed at his stomach.

'Pick up another stone and follow me,' Jesus said. This time St Peter picked up a great boulder, and struggled and sweated all the way to carry it to the top of the mountain.

'These stones will make good seats,' said Jesus. St Peter let out a silent scream, and tried to admire the view.

MALLORCAN FOLK TALE

*Puig de Randa is 26km (16 miles) east of Palma and 5km (3 miles) south of Algaida. For Randa village, turn east off the Algaida–Llucmajor road.*

### S'Arenal

This pulsating tourist mecca has a long, white-sand beach, merging into Platja de Palma, that attracts foreign

Santuari de Cura, a Franciscan monastery

holidaymakers as well as locals eager to escape the urban jungle of Palma. A continuous line of high-rise hotels and apartment complexes follows the shoreline, fronted by a long promenade (recently rebuilt) that hosts an endless, infinitely watchable parade of vendors and fun-in-the-sun addicts. The beach is usually packed, which is how everyone likes it, and there are *balnearios* (bathing stations) and playgrounds for children.

In the summer, a tourist train runs along the 7km (4-mile) seafront between S'Arenal and Can Pastilla, to the north. At night this strip turns to neon and noise as bars, restaurants, discos and strip joints compete for the holidaymaker's custom. The resort is mainly popular with German holidaymakers.

*Tourist Office: Plaza de las Meravelles. Tel: (902) 10 23 65.*

The popular beach at S'Arenal

### Aqualand El Arenal

Advertising itself as the world's largest water funfair, Aqualand makes exuberant efforts to keep everyone in the family happy. Among its many thrills and attractions are landscaped swimming pools, kamikaze water slides, a Hawaiian wave pool, a mini zoo and farm, parrot show, shops, restaurants – even an antique typewriter museum.

*At the southern end of the motorway from Palma, take Salida 13 (Exit 13), signposted to S'Arenal and Cap Blanc. There are special Aqualand buses from Palma and many of the resorts. The No. 23 city bus from Palma also goes to Aqualand.*
*Tel: (971) 44 00 00. www.aqualand.es.*
*Open: daily May–Jun & Sept 10am–5pm; Jul & Aug 10am–6pm. Admission charge.*

*S'Arenal is 11km (7 miles) southeast of Palma.*

### Sa Colònia de Sant Jordi

This is one of Mallorca's quieter seaside resorts, with sprawling modern buildings that rather mar the charms of its small harbour, Port de Campos. Once the haunt of smugglers from the North African coast, its waters are now popular with boats offering excursions along the coast and south of Cabrera.
*52km (32 miles) southeast of Palma, 15km (9 miles) south of Campos.*

## Salines de Llevant

These were saltpans, in use at least since Roman times, an essential commodity for trading ships plying the Mediterranean. The area is now a paradise for birdwatchers.

*Take the Ma-19 from Campos to Santanyí, and just outside the town turn right to Sa Colònia de Sant Jordi. When you reach the crossroads, continue ahead for another 1km (²/₃ mile). Turn right onto the access road to the Banys, and park at the end of the road. Then go along a track down to the saltpans.*

## Santanyí

Santanyí is famous for producing the warm-toned sandstone that adorns many of the island's important edifices, including Palma's cathedral and Castell de Bellver. A gateway in Plaça Port is a reminder that the town was fortified in medieval times. The dominant sight, though, is the church of Sant Andreu, with its enormous Rococo organ rescued from the Dominican convent in Palma.

## Cala Santanyí

This wide sandy cove lies 7km (4 miles) to the south off the road to Cala Figuera (*see p118*). There is a beach bar and amusements, and to the south there is Es Pontás, a dramatically eroded rock bridge close to the cliffs.

## Santuari de la Consolació

Five kilometres (3 miles) northeast of the town, a country road leads left, passing a quarry, winding up to the little-visited Santuari de la Consolació. Here a 15th-century hilltop chapel houses a gentle-faced Madonna, and

Es Pontás, a natural rock bridge near the relaxed cove of Cala Santanyí

A stone cross encourages pilgrims up the winding ascent to Santuari de Sant Salvador

there are extended views of the surrounding countryside.

Take away the modern eyesores along the coast, and it will be easy to imagine the days when devout pilgrims climbed the stone steps in search of tranquillity and consolation. Ironically, the sanctuary dedicated to the patron saint of rain, Saint Scholastica, is located here, in Mallorca's driest spot. According to legend, Santa Escolástica, a nun, was so happy when her brother visited her that she prayed to God to let them be together longer. Obligingly, it started to rain, and her brother had to stay for longer.

*Tourist Office: Carrer Perico Pomar 10. Tel: (971) 65 74 63.*

*Santanyí is 55km (34 miles) southeast of Palma on the Ma-19.*

## Santuari de Sant Salvador

A physical and spiritual high point of the island, the Santuari de Sant Salvador is approached by a convoluted series of bends that climb up Puig de Sant Salvador (509m/1,670ft), the summit of the Serra de Llevant. During the ascent you pass a small chapel, the 12 Stations of the Cross, a large stone cross and a 37m (121ft) high statue of Christ the King.

A well with ladle greets thirsty visitors to the monastery. Inside the huge gatehouse is a Gothic depiction of the Last Supper and offerings left by pilgrims that include pictures of local cyclists and their jerseys. The 18th-century church has a Bethlehem Grotto (a Nativity scene viewed through magnifying windows), and a revered Virgin.

As photographs, crutches, toys and notes left in the small room by the entrance testify, the Ermita continues to represent a crucial source of spiritual aid. There is a simple restaurant.

*57km (35½ miles) southeast of Palma, 4km (2½ miles) southeast of Felanitx. Take the road to Portocolom, turning right after 2km (1¼ miles) on to a country road.*

# Tour: The tranquil south

*This circular, 123km (76-mile) tour leaves behind the frenzy of the Badia de Palma and offers an easy-going drive around the cliffs, coves and sandy beaches of Mallorca's southern coast. The route then heads inland, returning through a fertile countryside of farms, windmills and historic towns.* (See p117 for route map.)

*Allow 5 hours.*

*Start from Can Pastilla, taking the coastal dual carriageway east. Drive through S'Arenal and uphill to a roundabout. Turn right, following signs to Cap Blanc, and passing Aqualand (see p129) on the left and Cala Blava to the right. Follow the coast south on the Ma-6014 to Cap Blanc.*

## 1  Cap Blanc

A remote, rocky headland punctuated by a lighthouse, Cap Blanc offers clifftop walks and sea views across to the island of Cabrera.
*Continue northeast for 5km (3 miles) to Capocorb Vell.*

## 2  Capocorb Vell

This is one of the most important prehistoric sites in Mallorca, with five Talayots and Bronze Age dwellings dating from around 1000 BC (*see pp119–20*).
*Drive south for 4km (2½ miles) to reach Cala Pi.*

## 3  Cala Pi

Once an island secret, this tiny *cala* lies tucked away beneath thick pine woods. Developers are now building luxury villas and apartments around the inlet, but you can still climb down steep steps to the sandy beach and enjoy the clear turquoise waters. Beside the restored watchtower is a viewpoint with parking and a bar-restaurant.
*Follow the signs for Vallgornera, then drive inland and turn right in the direction of Campos and Sa Colònia de Sant Jordi.*

## 4  Sa Colònia de Sant Jordi

Along the way, rural roads lead south to the small resorts of S'Estanyol de Migjorn and Sa Ràpita, and the splendid beaches at Ses Covetes and Platja des Trenc (*see p126*). Turn right after 14km (8½ miles), passing salt lakes, the Salines de Llevant, on the way, to reach the resort of Sa Colònia de Sant Jordi (*see p129*). A range of bars and restaurants makes this a convenient place to stop for a drink or lunch.

*Continue east towards Santanyí. Turn right 3km (2 miles) outside the town, passing through low pines to reach Cala Llombards. A steep road leads down to the beach.*

### 5  Cala Llombards

The sandy beach in this small resort is sheltered by wooded cliffs, and has shallow waters suitable for young children. A short, rocky walk by the sea provides a good view over the cove.

*Return to the main road and turn right for Santanyí.*

### 6  Santanyí

This old Mallorcan town, like Campos further on, is a world away from the island's brash tourist resorts. Sturdy buildings line its narrow streets, constructed with the local honey-coloured stone that graces many of Mallorca's great buildings (*see pp130–31*).

*Take the Ma-19 northwest to Campos.*

### 7  Campos

Founded by the Romans, Campos has a mighty 16th-century church which boasts a work attributed to Murillo, *El Santo Cristo de la Paciencia* (The Christ of Patience), which hangs to the right of the altar.

Across the road is the recently restored *ajuntament* (town hall), with its balustrades and coat of arms – a monument to the civic pride of this sleepy agricultural town.

*Follow the fast Ma-19 which bypasses Llucmajor to Can Pastilla and Palma.*

The restored 16th-century town hall in Campos del Port is the epitome of rural insularity

# Walk: Serra de Llevant

*This comfortable 4km (2½-mile) walk, which includes a fairly stiff climb at the end, takes you to the summit of the Serra de Llevant, the ridge of hills that cuts across the southeast of the island. It begins just below the historic Castell de Santueri (see p121) and ascends to the Santuari de Sant Salvador (509m/1,670ft). A car can be parked at either end, and the walk is equally enjoyable if done in reverse. You will need sturdy shoes.*

*Allow 90 minutes one way.*

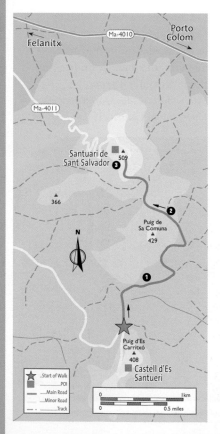

To reach the start of the walk, take the road south from Felanitx towards Santanyí. Turn left after about 2km (1¼ miles) on to a country lane signposted to Castell de Santueri. Continue until the road starts to climb in a sharp bend to the right. At the next bend park on the rough ground to the left, where a track leads east from the road.

## 1 Valleys and orchards

The first part of the walk, which is variously marked by yellow and red paint on the trees and stones, follows a gently undulating route along a valley and through a mixed orchard.

*After about 50m (55yd), turn left along a narrower path, crossing a boundary wall where the ground begins to rise. Joining a forest track, continue to an orchard with carob, almond and fig trees. Turn left to walk through this to a gateway (marked with paint) near a farmhouse. Go straight across the next field.*

## 2 Puig de Sa Comuna

Enjoy the rural views and the many wild shrubs and flowers, such as French lavender, rosemary, heather and the colourful strawberry tree (*Arbutus unedo*). The route crosses several other tracks, then skirts eastward round a hill, Puig de Sa Comuna. As you start to climb, a huge stone statue of Christ will soon come into view.

*Continue up a narrow track, which rises to a small ridge.*

## 3 Santuari de Sant Salvador

From here you can see the great buildings of the Ermita de Sant Salvador. The route now follows a well-worn path that rises steeply. The effort of the climb will be admirably rewarded by the splendid view from the *ermita*, where water, food and an antiquated toilet await the walker. Founded in the 14th century, this magnificent sanctuary has become a magnet for both tourists and religious pilgrims (*see p131*). The Santuari can also be reached by leaving Felanitx in the direction of Portocolom, a 2km (2½-mile) path to Sant Salvador, a stiff climb but easy and well marked; no right-of-way problems.

*Retrace your steps to return to your starting point.*

**Walk: Serra de Llevant**

---

### TREES OF GOLD

The carob tree (*Ceratonia siliqua*), sometimes known as the locust tree, thrives in the hot arid soil of the Mediterranean region. The tree has thick shiny leaves, a gnarled trunk and long seedpods that turn from green to black as they ripen. High in sugar, these are primarily used as animal feed. The fruit of the carob is also made into a chocolate substitute sold in healthfood stores. The word 'carat', used today as a unit of weight for gold and precious stones, derives from the word carob. The Arabs knew the fruit as *kirat*, and the Greeks as *keration*.

---

The Santuari de Sant Salvador was built on the summit of the Serra de Llevant

# Getting away from it all

*The clichéd view of Mallorca as two islands – one passionately devoted to summer holiday fun, and the other real, rural and eternal – is perfectly true. A visit to Mallorca is not complete until you have sneaked off to at least one of its quieter corners. No matter where you stay, all parts of the island are accessible in a day trip.*

## Boat trips

Taking to the sea is a good way to escape the crowds, and at the same time see Mallorca from a different viewpoint. You can observe underwater marine life from aboard a glass-bottomed boat. Some trips call into beaches, coves and sea-caves that would otherwise be impossible to reach – notably the 100m (110yd) long **Cova Blava** (Blue Cave) on the island of Cabrera, where the reflection of light creates an intense blue.

Except in the Badia de Palma, excursions run only in the summer (May to October, in many cases) and often take the best part of a day: check if you need to bring a packed lunch, and put on plenty of suntan cream. Tourist offices and resorts have a detailed leaflet of excursion times and prices. (Signs saying *alrededores* mean a short trip in the waters close to your departure point.)

Nearly every town along the coast has sightseeing boats of some variety, from glass-bottomed so you can see the well-protected marine life around the island

to conventional boats from which you can admire the sea cliffs and bird life.

## Cabrera

The archipelago of Cabrera, a group of islands off the southern tip of Mallorca, also a natural park (*see pp140–41*), can be reached by boat from May to mid-October from the ports of Sa Colònia de Sant Jordi and Portopetra. Both are all-day trips, the first heading for Cabrera and the second to the neighbouring island of Cruceros Llevant. The boat leaves at 9.30am and returns at 5.30pm – take a picnic, swimming costume and snorkel. It's advisable to book the boat in advance in high season.

*Ticket Office at Carrer Gabriel Roca, next to the tourist office in Sa Colònia de Sant Jordi. Tel: (971) 64 90 34. www.excursionsacabrera.com*

## Sa Dragonera

The dramatic island of Sa Dragonera provides a spectacular focus for boat excursions from Sant Elm and Port d'Andratx.

Excursion boats cross the Es Freu channel that separates Mallorca and the island of Sa Dragonera, leaving from Sant Elm and Port d'Andratx. The quickest is the 20-minute crossing from Sant Elm aboard *Margarita*, which operates regularly throughout the day. For bookings *tel: (639) 61 75 45.*

## Cycling

Cycling in Mallorca is a growth industry. The Spanish take it very seriously, and every Sunday the hills appear alive with luridly coloured insects covering great distances and heights with astonishing ease. It is usually too hot in July and August to enjoy a major expedition, but you can have a good time just by hiring a bike in a resort for a day and pottering along the coast. Some hotels have bicycles for hire, or there are specialist shops. Family bicycles with seats for two adults and four children are sometimes available; you may be asked for a deposit.

The Badia d'Alcúdia is obligingly flat, and a cycle path runs between Port d'Alcúdia and Can Picafort. You can also cycle in the S'Albufera nature reserve. Another *pista de bicicletas* (*carril de bicletes* in Catalan, cycle track) curls round the centre of the Badia de Palma from Portixol west to Sa Pedrera, passing right along Palma's seafront; Castell de Bellver makes a rewarding goal. Many other areas are also introducing cycle paths.

If you prefer more of a challenge, ask for the *Guia del Ciclista* map, available from tourist offices. This details six itineraries ranging from 70km (43 miles) to 150km (93 miles), including a masochistic 14km (8½-mile) ascent from Sa Calobra.

## Hidden Corners

There is nowhere on Mallorca that is 'undiscovered', but the following places feel well away from it all.

### Cala Mesquida

In the northeast corner of the island, a once-secluded beach reached by an 8km (5-mile) road north from Capdepera. Though busy in summer, it can be pleasantly quiet out of season.

### Cala Sant Vicenç

*See p97.*

### Cap Blanc

A breezy headland at the southwest corner of the island with white cliffs dropping sheer to the sea 60m (200ft) below. The edges are unguarded, but you can follow an invigorating walk that leads west from the lighthouse.

### Cap de Ses Salines

The flat, southern tip of the island offers views across the sea to Cabrera. Military land restricts walking.

### Castell d'Alaró

*See p70.*

### Ermita de Betlem

A remote mountain sanctuary (380m/1,246ft) reached by a tortuous road that winds for 10km (6 miles) northwest of Artà. Founded in 1805, Ermita de Betlem is still home to hermits, who no doubt find spiritual succour in the stupendous views.

### Galilea

*See p56.*

### Orient

*See p77.*

### Puigpunyent

*See p62.*

### Punta de n'Amer

A respite from the resorts on the east coast, Punta de n'Amer can be reached by walking north from Sa Coma or south from Cala Millor. The 17th-century Castell de n'Amer has a deep moat and ramparts, offers fine coastal views, and is the high point of this 200ha (500-acre) protected headland. It was here that Republican forces from Menorca landed during the Spanish Civil War.

## National parks
### Mondragó

Designated as a conservation area, the park offers a rich flora and fauna amid attractive landscapes of pines, shrubs, small lakes and dunes. The area also borders the sea, and has two of the most attractive coves to be found

along Mallorca's eastern coast. Examples of traditional architecture can also be seen.

Major points of interest, linked by pathways, are the Ca Na Martina, Niu de Metralladores, Ca Na Muda and Aula de Mar, where aquariums display local sea life. An information office gives advice on the area.

*4–9km (2½–5½ miles) east/northeast of Santanyí. For the easiest route take the road northeast to S'Alqueria Blanca. Entry point is to the right, 8km (5 miles) from Santanyí on the Cala Mondragó road. Tel: (971) 18 10 22. Open: daily 9am–4pm. Free admission.*

### La Reserva

On the eastern slopes of Puig de Galatzó (1,026m/3,366ft), this privately owned nature reserve is an easy introduction to the countryside of Mallorca's Serra de Tramuntana. A network of steps and purpose-built

---

### CHARCOAL BURNERS

Among the ancient mule tracks and goat-trodden paths that criss-cross the Mallorcan countryside are routes forged by the island's *carboneros* (charcoal burners). Until the arrival of the gas bottle in the 1920s, Mallorcans used charcoal as fuel. The burners and their families would move into the forests for the summer, building temporary homes and circular mounds of stones where the charcoal was made. Vast quantities of wood needed to be gathered using only axes and saws, and the fires had to be constantly tended. Walkers will encounter abandoned moss-covered *sitjas* (charcoal ovens) – forlorn monuments to an arduous trade.

formations and bird life. Additional points of interest include a charcoal burner's hut, a 1,000-year-old olive tree and the **Cova del Moro** (Cave of the Moor, Point 9).

The walk takes 90 minutes. If you are going by car, try not to arrive too late so that you can avoid having to drive your vehicle back down the mountains in the dark. On Fridays in the summer, you can also visit the park on a coach excursion from Santa Ponça and Peguera.

*18km (11 miles) west of Palma, 4km (2½ miles) west of Puigpunyent, signposted on the Puigpunyent–Galilea road. Tel: (971) 61 66 22. www.lareservaaventur.com. Open: daily 10am–7pm. Last admission: 5pm. Admission charge.*

Another Mallorca: the S'Albufera wetlands are an unexpected treat for nature-lovers

paths will lead you through a 20,000ha (49,420-acre) park which has dense woods, 30 waterfalls, springs, caves and rocky limestone outcrops. Wooden plaques provide information along the way about La Reserva's numerous plants: most grow naturally, while the rest have been introduced from around the island.

La Reserva took seven years to be completed – and it shows. There are handrails beside steep steps, plenty of strategically placed benches to regain your breath, and information boards in several languages giving a background on subjects such as unusual rock

### S'Albufera

The name derives from the Arabic *al-Buhayra*, meaning 'small lake.' First mentioned in Roman times, the marshes were later used as hunting grounds, and, in the 17th century, divided into self-irrigating cultivable plots. From the early 20th century to the 1960s, when the northern end was sold off for tourist development, the area was used to grow rice. In 1985, 800ha (1,977 acres) were bought by the Balearic Islands' government for conservation.

Pay a visit to the Parc Natural de S'Albufera today and you will encounter a wholly unexpected aspect of Mallorca. Marked paths, some of which can be cycled, guide visitors around the level marshland – a hushed world of bridges, hides and observation points tucked away among the lakes, reed beds and grassy undergrowth.

Birds are the main attraction – more than 200 species have so far been recorded, including ospreys, falcons and numerous marsh birds. Frogs, snakes, insects and colourful wild flowers such as the grape hyacinth and elegant orchids add to the natural show.

*5km (3 miles) south of Port d'Alcúdia. Turn west by the Pont dels Anglesos on the Alcúdia–Artà road. Tel: (971) 89 22 50. Open: daily Apr–Sept 9am–6pm; Oct–Mar 9am–5pm. You can obtain a free visiting permit from the reception.*

### Walking

With its absorbing variety of mountain, coast and plain, along with countless sanctuaries, watchtowers and castles to provide rewarding goals, Mallorca is ideal for walkers. Good launch pads, with generally quiet accommodation, are Banyalbufar, Port d'Andratx, Port de Sóller and Port de Pollença. There is a good case for staying in or near Palma, as it is the focal point for all bus routes.

Several specialist books on walking in Mallorca are available. Try to buy them before you leave home. Some local tourist offices, notably those in the Calvià area, produce free booklets with suggested routes.

The Serra de Tramuntana, with its cool forests and wide-ranging views, is the most appealing area for walking.

The island's good bus service means that in many cases you do not need to hire a car – Sóller and Lluc are popular starting points. Caution is always required: beware the fierce heat and sun in summer, and mists and wet ground at other times of the year.

### Cabrera

Cabrera ('Goat') island lies 18km (11 miles) off Mallorca's south coast – and at roughly 7km by 5km (4½ miles by 3 miles) it is the largest among all the scattered islets. Cabrera's coastline is indented and craggy, rising no higher than Na Picamosques (171m/561ft), the 'Fly Bite'. In 1991 Cabrera became a protected Parque Nacional Marítimo Terrestre (National Land–Sea Park), the first of its kind in Spain, and a symbol of the triumph of ecological lobbying.

Today, the island is virtually uninhabited, but its rocks are forever stained by a grim episode during the Peninsular War when 9,000 French prisoners of war were dumped here following the Spanish victory at Bailén in 1808. Left with only meagre water and rations, the defeated soldiers fell victim to disease, indiscipline and chronic thirst. By 1814, when the survivors were finally taken off, more than 5,000 prisoners had died. A monument near the small port remembers the victims of this tragedy. In 1916 Cabrera was taken over for military use, and a handful of soldiers are still stationed on the island – now joined by visiting scientists, naturalists and day trippers from the mainland.

Cabrera has a superb natural harbour, and the island was often used as a stepping stone for pirates raiding the Balearic Islands. The shell of a 14th-century castle-cum-prison still stands on a nearby hill top, but is officially out of bounds.

The appeal of Cabrera today is its rarity: a wilderness island in the midst of the overdeveloped Mediterranean. Among the many birds attracted to the island are Eleonora's falcons, cormorants and a colony of rare Audouin's gulls. Wild goats, an exclusive subspecies of Lilford's wall lizard, and a rich marine life all thrive here.

*Information on the island is available from the Sa Colònia de Sant Jordi tourist office, see p129. For boat excursions, see p136.*

### Sa Dragonera

A steep, bare wedge of rock rising to 353m (1,158ft), it can be explored on foot via walking trails to the summit of Puig de Sa Pòpia (the highest point on the island), to the Tramuntana lighthouse (at the northeast tip) and the Llebeig lighthouse, to the southeast. Walking times vary from 30 to 90 minutes and all trails are well signposted from the little museum and visitors' centre at Cala Lladó, the arrival point for boats. At Cova de sa Font are Roman remains.

*For boat excursions, see pp136–7.*

The 14th-century castle of Cabrera

# Shopping

*Palma is the place to shop in Mallorca. Specialist factories making glass, artificial pearls, leather goods and carved olive-wood items are also worth visiting. Their wares are not necessarily cheaper than in normal shops, but it is always fun to know the provenance of your purchases.*

## OPENING TIMES

Shops generally open up between 9am and 10am depending on what they deal in – those selling fresh produce open earliest. By 1.30pm they are closing down for lunch. They reopen around 4.30–5.30pm, then remain open until 8pm. Shops tend to have longer opening hours in the summer, and in the resorts some stay open through the lunch break, as do hypermarkets. Department stores and fashion shops in Palma also stay open during the siesta. On Saturday, shops are open only in the morning. For the truly indefatigable shopper, the great department store El Corte Inglés has two branches in Palma, at Avinguda Alejandre Roselló 1216a and Avinguda Jaume III 15. These are open Monday to Saturday from 10am to 9–9.30pm. English is spoken in many shops.

Spain is a procrastinator's paradise, and the spirit of *mañana* ('Why do today what can be put off till the morrow?') thrives in a happy-go-lucky island like Mallorca. In some country shops it can take so long to be served it might be necessary to check the sell-by date on your purchases.

## PRICES

Shoes, T-shirts and casual clothing are good value, and 'one euro' shops, where all goods are theoretically that price or less, is a purse-friendly way to indulge the children. Many shops appear to be in a permanent state of sale (*rebajas* in Spanish, *rebaixes* in Catalan). Sizes of clothes and shoes will be in metric and European sizes (*see p179* for conversion tables). Bartering is rarely necessary, though the itinerant market vendors from West Africa found in markets and seafront pitches will oblige. It is a common diversion at Palma's Rastrillo flea market.

## SOUVENIRS

The range of items for sale bearing the word 'Mallorca' or a relevant image is a tribute to the ingenuity of the islanders.

Pottery, glass and fabric make good souvenirs

While some goods are mesmerisingly unnecessary to world progress, glass, kitchen pottery, olive-wood utensils, candlesticks, tableware, tea towels and beachwear are worth considering. A comprehensive range of Spanish and Mallorcan souvenirs can be found at the Poble Espanyol complex in Palma (*see p45*). Local craftmaking skills are also displayed here.

## MARKETS

Mallorca's markets are worth visiting for their local character as much as for the articles on sale. Local fruit is well worth buying, and you may see some pottery or leather goods that appeal. Beware pickpockets and importuning ladies selling flowers and tablecloths.

Of the regular weekly markets listed below, the most worth seeking out are the daily produce market in Palma's Plaça de l'Olivar, the traditional Wednesday livestock-and-everything jamboree in Sineu, and the sprawling Thursday-morning market in Inca. Unless otherwise stated, all are morning markets (and are usually fading fast by 1pm).

## In Palma
### Plaça Major
A number of crafts stalls selling a variety of jewellery, souvenirs, folk art. *Mon, Fri & Sat.*

### Plaça del Olivar
This is a good place to buy the best of local and imported produce as well as specialities like *sobrassada* and cheese from Menorca. In addition to fruit and vegetables there is a meat hall upstairs, a fish hall to the side, several *tapas* bars and even a small public library. *Mon–Sat (fish hall closed Mon)*

### Rastrillo (Flea market)
Junk, secondhand household goods, reject china, lurid plastic toys and the odd antique. Expect to barter for your bargains. *Lower part of Avinguda GA Villalonga. Sat.*

## West of Palma
**Andratx** *Wed*
**Calvià** *Mon*

## The Northwest
**Alaró** *Sat*
**Binissalem** *Fri*
**Bunyola** *Sat*

(*Cont. on p146*)

# Island crafts

*'The first difficulty that a stranger encounters on a shopping expedition in a Majorcan village is the absence not only of shop signs but of shop fronts. Everybody knows where the shopkeeper lives, so why should he announce it?'*

**GORDON WEST**

*Jogging Round Mallorca,* 1929

It is ironic that the best souvenirs Mallorca produces are also the most breakable. Among the glut of holiday merchandise on sale around the island, the brittle, curious *siurell* is the one craft product that feels truly Mallorcan. Made from clay and often painted white with flashes of red and green, these ancient tokens of friendship usually take the shape of a figure on a donkey in a hat or playing a guitar. The origin of the *siurell* is uncertain. They are known to have existed in Moorish times but probably date from much earlier. Artist Joan Miró was fond of these naïve works,

Handmade: attractive semi-glazed brown pottery made in Felanitx …

... and carved olive wood

which are mostly made around Marratxí. They come in varying sizes and incorporate a crude whistle at the base.

Glass is another exceptional product and has been made on the island since Roman times. In the 16th century, Mallorcan glassware rivalled that of Venice, and today's bestselling products often reproduce historic designs. Since the 1960s the island has had three glassmaking centres – the best known is Casa Gordiola at Algaida. Here visitors can see craftsmen hand-blowing the glass, which is made in dark green, cobalt and amber hues. Jugs, drinking glasses, vases and candle-holders are popular buys.

A robust, semi-glazed brown pottery is made in Felanitx, and the Sunday-morning market here is a good place to pick up cooking bowls or jugs.

Local olive wood is carved into domestic utensils and ornaments at the Oliv-Art factory near Manacor; the mellow-grained wood is hard-wearing and makes worthwhile presents.

*Roba de llengües*, literally 'cloth of tongues', is a striking feature of the Mallorcan home. Made mainly in Pollença and Santa Maria del Camí, this durable and reversible cotton material often comes in zigzagging red, green or blue patterns and is used for curtains, bedspreads, wall furnishings and upholstery.

Campanet *Tue*
Consell Flea market *Sun*
Pont d'Inca *Fri*
Santa Eugènia *Sat*
Santa Maria *Sun*
Sencelles *Wed*
Sóller *Sat*
Valldemossa *Sun*

### The northeast
Alcúdia *Tue & Sun*
Artà *Tue*
Cala Ratjada *Sat*
Can Picafort *Fri*
Capdepera *Wed*
Costitx *Sat*
Inca *Thur & Sun*
Lloseta *Sat*
Llubí *Tue*
Maria de la Salut *Fri*
Montuïri *Mon*

Muro *Sun*
Pollença *Sun*
Port de Pollença *Wed*
Sa Pobla *Sun*
Sant Llorenç des
Cardassar *Thur*
Santa Margalida *Tue &
Sat*
Selva *Wed*
Sineu *Wed*
Son Servera *Fri*
Vilafranca de Bonany
*Wed*

### The south
Algaida *Fri*
Campos *Thur & Sat*
Can Pastilla *Tue & Thur*
Felanitx *Sun*
Llucmajor *Wed*
Manacor *Mon & Sat*

Porreres *Tue*
Portocolom *Tue
& Sat*
Portocristo *Sun*
S'Arenal *Thur*
Sa Colònia de Sant Jordi
*Wed*
Santanyí *Wed & Sat*
Ses Salines *Thur*

### SUPERMARKETS
All the resorts have well-stocked supermarkets. Years of experience have taught owners about the money to be made from selling tomato ketchup, Heinz beans and Marmite, and there is little need to take such staples out to Mallorca. Imported goods tend to cost more than Spanish brands. Vegetables are sold by the kilo, and at fish, meat or delicatessen counters remember that you usually have to take a numbered ticket from a machine to be served in turn.

If you pay by credit card, you will always be asked to present some photo ID (passport, driving licence).

If you are staying in a self-catering apartment or inland villa, it may

A seafood stall at Santa Maria market

A shrine to *sobrassada* (spiced sausage) at Carrer de Santo Domingo, Palma

help to load up your rented car at one of the hypermarkets on the outskirts of Palma. You need a €1 coin to get a trolley; in some premises, any other shopping must be sealed in a bag before entering. Hypermarkets are generally open from 10am to 10pm, Monday to Saturday (*see pp146–8* for shops).

## WHERE TO BUY
### In Palma

All the useful shops are within the boundary of the city's old walls. Most of them are to the east of Passeig des Born where many streets are traffic-free. Whether you actually have things to buy or just enjoy the bustle of a city at play, the streets and squares listed below are all worth getting to know. The most enjoyable time for exploration is early evening, when the Palmese go window-shopping, how-do-you-do-ing and buying cakes – all traditions of the Spanish *paseo* (stroll).

**Avinguda Jaume III**
Palma's quality shopping street.
**Carrer de Jaume II** Fans, umbrellas, boutiques.
**Carrer de Platería**
Jewellery shops galore.
**Carrer de Sant Miquel**
Links Plaça Major and the market.
**Carrer de Sindicat**
Bargain clothes, shoes, spices.
**Plaça Major** Revamped underground shopping

centre with leather clothing, handbags and shoes. Souvenirs and supermarket.
**Porto Pi** Enormous shopping centre on two floors with branches of well-known Spanish fashion chains (e.g. Zara, Mango), ethnic shops, home accessories and handmade chocolates.
**La Rambla** Flower stalls and newspaper kiosks.

### Antiques
**Linares** Close to the cathedral, it sells good-value items.
*Plaça Almoina 4.*
*Tel: (971) 71 72 19.*
**Midge Dalton** Antique jewellery and small articles. Mostly silver.
*Plaça Mercat 20.*
*Tel: (971) 71 33 60.*
**Persepolis** High-class antiques.
*Avinguda de Jaume III.*
*Tel: (971) 72 45 39.*

### Books
**The Trading Place**
English and other languages, new and secondhand books.

*Carrer Pou 35.*
*Tel: (871) 94 13 50.*
*www.*
*mallorca-books.com*

**Cakes and chocolates**
**Forn d'es Teatre** Most photographed cake shop in Palma.
*Plaça Weyler 11.*
*Tel: (971) 71 52 54.*
**Forn Fondo** The place for *ensaimadas.*
*Carrer de l'Unió 15.*
*Tel: (971) 71 16 34.*
**Xocoa** Homemade chocs including a range of body products.
*Carrer Tous 1 Ferrer 4.*
*Tel: (971) 71 85 96.*

**Crafts**
**Alpargatería Llinás** A huge range of *espadrilles* – the Queen of Spain is a customer.
*Carrer de Sant*
*Miquel 43.*
*Tel: (971) 71 76 96.*
**Cestería del Centro** Straw-woven baskets and other articles.
*Carrer d'en Brossa 6.*
*Tel: (971) 72 45 33.*
**Fet a Mà** Traditional and contemporary pottery and glass from around Spain.
*Carrer Sant Miquel 52.*

**Rosario Pérez** Hand-painted silk scarves, belts and other accessories in original styles.
*Carrer de Sant Jaume 20.*

**Food and drink**
**Agape** A range of delicacies (cheese, sausages, olives, etc) from the Balearic islands is on sale in this shop.
*Carrer Argentería 12.*
*Tel: (971) 72 52 13.*
**Catavinos** Spanish and Mallorcan wines with regular evening tastings.
*Carrer Guillem Massot*
*45. Tel: (971) 76 05 85.*
**Fosh Food** Celebrated chef Mark Fosh (of Read's Hotel) has opened a gourmet grocery store.
*Carrer Blanquerna 6.*
*Tel: (971) 29 01 08.*

**Glass**
**Gordiola** You can buy *vidrio soplado* (hand-blown glass) in their workshop.
*Carrer de Victoria 2.*
*Tel: (971) 71 15 41.*

**Home accessories**
**Casa Bet Merceria** Cotton, lace, belts, tapestries.

*Carrer de Bosseria 6.*
*Tel: (971) 72 20 69.*
**Josefa Segura** Hand-embroidered articles and household linen.
*Pescateria Vella 5.*
*Tel: (971) 71 67 03.*
**Nobile** Kilims and oriental rugs.
*Carrer de Sant*
*Miquel 75.*
*Tel: (971) 71 30 98.*
**La Oca** Chain with funky, reasonably priced, contemporary furnishings.
*Carrer Berenguer de*
*Tornamira 9.*
*Tel: (971) 72 15 10.*

**Hypermarkets**
**Carrefour** *Avinguda Cardenal Rossell, Coll Rebassa.*
*Tel: (971) 44 83 82.*
**Carrefour** *Avinguda General Riera 156–72.*
*Tel: (971) 76 63 00.*
**El Corte Inglés** A branch of the excellent Spanish department store, with everything from electrical goods, to books, to fashion. There is a very good supermarket too.
*Avinguda Jaume III 15.*
*Tel: (971) 77 01 77.*

**Pearls and jewellery**
**Carrer d'Argenteria**
and **Carrer de Plateria**
are full of jewellery
shops.
**Perlas Orquídea**
Artificial pearls.
*Plaça Rei Joan Carles I.*
*Tel: (971) 71 57 97.*
**Pamela & De Diego**
Stunning contemporary
jewellery presented in a
chic boutique.
*Carrer Montenegro 3.*
*Tel: (971) 42 54 56.*
**Shoes**
**Camper** Flagship store
of this quirky, Mallorca-
based shoe company.
*Avinguda Jaume III 16.*
*Tel: (971) 71 46 35.*
*www.camper.com*

**Around the island**
**Antiques**
**Antonia Sa Coma**
**Antigüedades** *Carrer*
*Vacario Oastir 9,*
*Port de Sóller.*
*Tel: (971) 63 08 65.*
**Galeria Rústic** *Bernat de*
*Santa Eugènia 78, Santa*
*María del Camí.*
*Tel: (971) 62 07 31.*

**Ceramics**
**ArteArtesania** *Carrer*
*de sa Lluna 43, Sóller.*
*Tel: (971) 63 17 32.*

**Ceramicas C'an**
**Bernat** Traditional
Mallorcan pottery
articles.
*Bartolomeu Pascual, s/n,*
*Santa María del Camí.*
*Tel: (971) 62 13 06.*

**Food and drink**
**Estel Nou** Non-profit
organisation making
jam, olive oil and fig
bread.
*Camí des Dragonar 8,*
*Soller. Tel: (971) 63 81 34.*

**Sa Botiga** Specialities
from around the island.
*Camí de Ronda, Alcudia.*
*Tel: (971) 54 96 32.*

**Tunel** You'll find any
alcohol you can think
of including Tunel's
own herb-based
liqueurs in this vast
shop.
*Avinguda Principes de*
*España 3, Marratxi.*
*Tel: (971) 22 97 13.*
*www.tunel.com*

**Glass**
**Casa Gordiola** Hand-
blown glass.
*Carretera Manacor,*
*km19, Algaida.*
*Tel: (971) 66 50 46.*
*www.gordiola.com*

**Lafiore** *Carretera Vella de*
*Valldemossa, km11.*
*Tel: (971) 61 18 00.*
*www.lafiore.com*

**Household accessories**
**Henriettas** Household
accessories, mirrors,
lamps and glassware.
*Carretera França 2,*
*S'Arraco. Tel: (971) 67*
*29 16. www.*
*majorcainteriordesign.com*

**Leather goods**
Inca is the centre of
Mallorca's leather
industry and there is a
very wide choice.

**Olive wood articles**
**Artesanía Olivo Bernat**
**Fiol** *Carrer Bon Jesús 10,*
*Consell.*
*Tel: (971) 62 21 58.*

**Pearls and jewellery**
**Cesare**
Gold and diamond
jewellery.
*Carrer Mariners 13,*
*Port d'Alcúdia.*
*Tel: (971) 54 63 02.*
**Perlas Orquídea**
*Carretera Palma–*
*Manacor, km30,*
*Montuïri.*
*Tel: (971) 64 41 44.*
*www.perlasorquidea.com*

# Entertainment

*In the resorts, the music, shows and nightlife are geared to the international tastes of the briefly visiting holidaymaker. Alongside this popular entertainment, the Mallorcans have their own cultural activities, including a busy calendar of religious and secular celebrations.*

## WHERE TO GO

*On Anar? (Where To Go?),* a free quarterly in English with an up-to-date listing of sporting and cultural activities in the Balearic Islands, is available from tourist offices. You can also sign up for a free weekly e-mail newletter at *www.illesbalears.net*

World news, sports reports and local issues are all covered by the English-language *Majorca Daily Bulletin*, affectionately known as the *Daily Bee*.

Bear in mind that the Spanish are not very punctual and like to party late, and local *festes* may not really get going till well after the times advertised. In July and August many open-air concerts and musical events will not start before 10pm. The choice of bars, clubs and discos is dramatically curtailed out of season, but there is always something going on.

## ART GALLERIES

Mallorca has a buoyant art scene, and several art galleries have bars and bookshops attached – notably Fundació CaixaForum and the museum Es Baluard in Palma.

### In Palma
**Fundació Barceló**
*Casa del Marqués de Requer, Carrer de Sant Jaume 4. Tel: (971) 72 24 67. www.barcelo.com*
**CaixaForum Palma**
*See pp34–5.*
**Fundació Sa Nostra**
*Carrer de Concepció 12. Tel: (971) 72 52 10. www.sanostra.es*
**Pelaires**
*Carrer Can Veri 3. Tel: (917) 72 04 18. www.pelaires.com*

### Around the island
**Maior**
*Plaça Major 4, Pollença. Tel: (971) 53 00 95. www.galeriamaior.com*
**S'Estació**
*Carrer d'Estació, Sineu. Tel: (971) 52 07 50. www.sineuestacio.com*

## BARS AND PUBS

All the resorts have a strip of wall-to-wall pubs and bars. In Palma, the area around the Carrer de Apuntadores is always lively. The up-and-coming Santa Catalina neighbourhood has plenty of stylish new dining holes.

## CASINO

Mallorca has one casino, Casino de Mallorca, combined with the Casino Palladium, which offers dinner and occasional variety shows and is available as an organised excursion. Gaming includes roulette, blackjack and slot machines. A jacket and tie for men, and passport, are required.
*Urbanització Sol de Mallorca, at the end of the motorway to Andratx (turn off at Cala Figuera), Calvià. Open: daily 8pm–4am. Tel: (971) 13 00 00. www.casinodemallorca.com*

## CINEMAS

Programmes and times are advertised in the local newspapers as well as online at *www.aficine.com* and *www.balearics.angloinfo.com*. Films are usually dubbed into Castilian Spanish so check that the film you want to see is followed by the letters 'VO' (*versió original*), which means that it will be shown in its original language with subtitles. The following cinemas are all in Palma and all show some English-language films.
**Cines Renoir**
World and arthouse films.
*Carrer Emperatriz Eugenia 6. Tel: (971) 20 54 53. www.cinesrenoir.com*
**Ocimax**
Multi-screen cinema with a café.
*Carrer Leocàdia Togores. Tel: (971) 75 06 73. www.ocimax.com*
**Porto Pi Centro**
Multi-screen cinema in a shopping mall.
*Avinguda Gabriel Roca 54. Tel: (971) 40 55 00.*

## DISCOS AND NIGHTCLUBS

There are more than 150 discotheques and nightclubs in Mallorca providing sounds for everyone.

Serious clubbers should consider buying the **Magaluf Club Pass** which allows entry to five of the resort's best clubs (Banana's, Boomerang, Tokio Joe's, Buffalo Girls and Honeys) in one night. Available from each of the clubs, all situated on Carrer Punta Ballena. Visit *www.magalufclubpass.com* for more information.

The best alternative discos tend to change their names regularly to suggest they are moving with the times. To find the beat, you need to ask around in bars, or chat up the beach Adonises handing out flyers. Nightclubs catering to refined spenders and dressers can be found in some luxury hotels.

The glossy magazine *d-palma* lists the most fashionable bars, clubs and restaurants. Pick it up at featured places, or at newspaper kiosks (Spanish only). There's an online version at *www.d-palma.com*

## In Palma

**Abaco**

Famously over-the-top décor in an atmospheric old mansion, which serves great (but pricey) cocktails.

*Carrer Sant Joan 1. Tel: (971) 71 49 39.*

**Abraxas**

Long-time favourite with the international clubbing set, it tends to attract a young, fashionable crowd. Cliff-side location offers sweeping views over the bay.

*Passeig Marítimo 42. Tel: (971) 45 59 08. www.abraxasmallorca.com*

**Blue Jazz Club**

Classical jazz in stylish surroundings on the 8th floor of Hotel Saratoga, accompanied by dinner if you're peckish.

*Hotel Saratoga, Paseo Mallorca. Tel: (971) 72 72 40. www.bluejazz.es. Open: Thur–Sat from 9pm for dinner. Shows at 11pm and 1am.*

**King Kamehameha**

Super-cool club, bar and café that welcomes big-name international DJs.

*Passeig Marítimo 29. Open Thur–Sat 10pm–6am.*

**Tito's**

Ibiza-style clubbing for the *beau monde* in ultra-modern surroundings.

*Plaça Gomila 3. Tel: (971) 73 00 17. www.titosmallorca.com*

## Around the island

**BCM**

Mallorca's largest club with a state-of-the-art light show and foam parties. Attracts the likes of Judge Jules and David Guetta.

*Avinguda S'Olivera, Magaluf. Tel: (971) 13 15 46. www.bcm-planetdance.com*

**Paladium** and **Pygmalion**

Two clubs on Peguera seafront – the former has a chill-out room and the latter hosts an 'over 21s night' on Fridays.

*Avinguda de Peguera. Tel: (971) 68 65 57. www.paladiumdisco.es*

**Sala Fónica**

Electro-dance and house music for a young, hip crowd.

*Carrer Germanies, s/n, Muro. Tel: (678) 72 37 46 (mobile). Sat only.*

**Virtual Club**

Glossy beachside bar, restaurant and nightclub.

*Passeig d'Illetes 60, Illetes. Tel: (971) 70 32 35. www.virtualclub.es*

## Folklore and dinner shows

Exhibitions of Mallorcan music and dance are staged regularly in the summer at La Granja and Valldemossa (*see pp56–7 & pp84–5*), and often coincide with coach excursions. Floorshows, barbecues, pirate adventures and medieval banquets can also be booked through your hotel.

**Casino de Mallorca**

*See p151.*

**Es Fogueró**

Variety show with dinner.

*Carretera de S'Aranjassa Km 10, Platja de Palma. Tel: (971) 26 52 60. www.esfoguero.com*

**Pirates Adventure**

Acrobatics, gymnastics, dancing and comedy for families in this swashbuckling spectacle. There's also a

late-night 'adults only' show.
*Carretera La Porassa, Magaluf.*
*Tel: (971) 13 04 11.*
*www.piratesadventure.com*
**Son Amar**
Comedy, singing, magic and dance
accompanied by dinner.
*Carretera de Sóller km10.8, Bunyola.*
*Tel: (900) 71 23 45.*
*www.sonamar.com*

## MUSICAL EVENTS
Concerts and music festivals are
staged in Mallorca throughout the
year, including a programme of
musical and popular events between
April and September. All the following
are in Palma unless stated otherwise.
Ask at a tourist office for more details.
**January:** classical and light music for
Sant Sebastià *festa.*
**March:** international week of organ
music.
**March–June:** spring opera season at
Teatre Principal.
**July:** international folk dancing at
Sóller.
**July–August:** international music
festival in Pollença (*www.
festivalpollenca.org*) and Chopin festival
at Valldemossa (*www.festivalchopin.
com*). Summer serenades in Castell de
Bellver and music festivals in Deià,
Artà, Sóller and Santuari de Cura (Puig
de Randa).
**September–October**: festival of
classical music in Bunyola
(*www.festivalbunyola.org*).
**September–December**: jazz Voyeur

Festival (*www.jazzvoyeurfestival.com*).
**October:** week of organ concerts in
local churches, festival of classical
music in Port de Sóller
(*www.festivalportdesoller.com*).

## THEATRES AND CONCERT HALLS
### In Palma
**Auditòrium**
*Passeig Marítim 18, Palma.*
*Tel: (971) 73 47 35.*
*www.auditoriumpalma.es*
**Teatre Principal**
*Placa Weyler 7, Palma.*
*Tel: (971) 72 55 48.*
*www.teatreprincipal.com*
**Ses Voltes**
*Parc de la Mar, Palma.*
*Tel: (971) 72 87 39.*

### Around the island
**Auditòrium Alcúdia**
*Plaça Porta de Mallorca 3.*
*Tel: (971) 89 71 85.*
*www.auditorialcudia.net*
**Teatre de Manacor**
*Avinguda del Parc. Tel: (971) 55 45 49.*
*www.teatredemanacor.com*

Other venues for one-off music
and dance events are the Bendinat
Golf Club (west of Palma), Castell de
Bellver (Palma), Son Marroig,
Valldemossa, Sa Calobra (all three in
the northwest of the island), Casa
March gardens (near Cala Ratjada
in the northeast), and in several
churches and monasteries around
the island.

# Packaging paradise

Mallorca's phenomenal development as a tourist island is now the stuff of textbooks. The French even coined a derogatory verb, *baléariser*, to describe this evolution, and the Mallorcan model has been copied in coastal resorts from North Africa to the Caribbean. Today, tourism is taught as a subject in the island's state-run university, and in Palma a private Escuela de Turismo (School of Tourism) draws hundreds of students from around the world to learn the art of running hotel chains, creating paradise and packaging up holidaymakers for profit.

Though well-heeled tourists were discovering the island in the late 19th century, it was only after World War II that visitors began coming here in great numbers. In 1931 Mallorca

Have fun while you see the island – sailing boats for hire in Port de Pollença

welcomed 43,000 tourists; by 1950 there were 127,000. This sudden influx was chronicled with alarm by the island's resident sage, Robert Graves. 'Around 1951,' he wrote, 'British, French and American travellers accepted the fantasy of Majorca as the Isle of Love, the Isle of Tranquillity, the Paradise where the sun always shines and where one can live like a fighting cock on a dollar a day, drinks included.'

Mallorca still draws an artistic crowd, though most impecunious bohemians now prefer Ibiza. The drinks aren't so cheap either, and the well-documented days of the lager-fuelled *gamberros ingleses* (English hooligans) and their Continental equivalents are over.

Today, Mallorca is going upmarket and green – new beaches and promenades, better hotels, ring roads and development controls. In 2008, the tourist industry was awarded €50 million for improvements and a €660 million injection will upgrade and expand the rail network over four years.

The figures suggest that the island is moving in the right direction: more than 13 million tourists visited Mallorca in 2008.

Magaluf with its fine white sands offers the typical package-holiday experience

# Children

*Mallorca is most suitable for children. Besides offering plenty of sandy beaches with safe, shallow water, the island's resorts all have purpose-built activities and amusements to bankrupt mum and dad. In the high season, facilities can get stretched and care is required with the strong sun, but Mallorca has everything you need for a family holiday by the sea.*

Children's facilities lean towards physical activities rather than mind-stimulating amusements. Large hotels also put on children's shows as part of their entertainment programme and all hotels organise mini-clubs for children.

Beach games, sports and fishing equipment can be bought in seaside shops, and bicycles with child-seats hired. Some riding clubs have small ponies for young riders, and a mini-golf course is rarely far away.

## ATTRACTIONS
### Palma
**Palma–Sóller train ride**
(*See pp86–7*).

### West of Palma
**Aqualand Magaluf**
Water-themed fun park with slides and exciting rides.
*On the Magaluf–Cala Figuera road.*
*www.aqualand.es.*
*Open: Jul–Aug daily 10am–6pm.*
*Admission charge.*

**Go-Karting**
Suitable for age two and above.
*Circuit at Carrer de la Porrasa s/n Magaluf, right next to Aquapark.*
*Tel: (971) 13 17 34.*
*www.kartingmagaluf.com*

**Golf Fantasia Palma Nova**
Miniature golf among caves, waterfalls and tropical gardens. 54 holes.
*Carrer de Tenis, Palma Nova. Tel: (971) 13 50 40. www.golf-fantasia.com. Open: Mon–Fri 10.30am–6pm, Sat–Sun 10.30am–8pm. Admission charge.*

**House of Katmandu**
A fantastical Tibetan-style mansion which appears to have dropped from the sky and lodged upside-down in the ground.
*Carrer Pedro Vaquer Rami s/n, Magaluf. Tel: (971) 13 46 60.*
*www.houseofkatmandu.com. Open: 10am–midnight. Admission charge.*

**Marineland**
(*See p57*).

**Palma Aquárium**
(*See p39 & p42*).

## Northwest
**Aqualandia and El Foro de Mallorca**
Waterpark with a wax museum.
*On the Palma–Inca road, Km25,
Binissalem. Tel: (971) 51 12 28.
Museum open: daily 9.30am–1.30pm &
2.30–7pm. Waterpark open: daily
10am–6pm. Admission charge.*

## Northeast
**Hidropark**
Water slides, chutes and mini-golf. For
younger children.
*Avinguda de Tucan s/n, Port d'Alcúdia.
Tel: (971) 89 16 72. www.hidropark.com.
Open: May–Oct daily 10.30am–6pm.
Admission charge.*
**Museu de la Jugueta**
3,000 toys and childhood objects from
Spain and elsewhere.
*Carrer Antonio Maura 6, Sa Pobla.
Tel: (971) 54 23 89. Open: Tue–Sat
10am–2pm & 4–8pm, Sun 10am–2pm.
Admission charge.*

## South
**Aqualand El Arenal**
*(See p129).*
**Jumaica**
Family-run banana plantation with
animals, plants and tropical birds.
*Carretera Portocolom-Port Cristo, Km
4.5, Ca'n Pep Noguera. Open: 9am–5pm.
Tel: (971) 83 33 55. Admission charge.*
**Natura Parc**
Biggest butterfly enclosure in Spain.
Huge walk-in aviary and petting corner.
Paths designed with prams, pushchairs
and wheelchairs in mind.

*Carretera de Sineu, Km154, Santa
Eugènia. Tel: (971) 14 45 32.
Open: 10am–7pm. Admission charge.*

Tourist trains run along the seafront
between Can Pastilla and S'Arenal, and
in Cala d'Or between the town centre
and marina.

## BEACHES
### West of Palma
**Magaluf**
Busy, plenty to do (*see p57 & p60*).
**Santa Ponça**
Broad family beach (*see pp62–3*).

### Northeast
**Cala Millor**
Golden sands (*see pp96–7*).
**Platja de Muro**
Backed by dunes and low pines (*see
p108*).
**Port d'Alcúdia**
Clear, shallow water (*see p108*).
**Port de Pollença**
Easy-going (*see p108*).
**Sa Coma**
Busy resort (*see pp96–7*).

### South
**Cala Llombards**
Small, shallow cove (*see p133*).
**Cala Pí**
Sheltered, out-of-the-way cove (*see
p132*).
**Can Pastilla**
Classic holiday beach (*see p119*).
**S'Arenal**
Seaside fun (*see pp128–9*).

# Sport and leisure

*The range of sports available on Mallorca is wide. Water sports, sailing and golf are the main attractions for visitors, while football, basketball and cycling appeal to many Mallorcans. In summer the heat and strong sun should be taken seriously, but facilities and activities are usually available in the evening. Enquire at your hotel reception or visit a tourist office to find out what sporting opportunities are close to where you are staying.*

All package tourism hotels encourage their guests to remain on the premises. They have gymnasiums and fitness clubs, and arrange such sports as archery and shooting, tennis, table tennis and pool. Games and activities run by experienced monitors will be arranged for children. All water sports are available on the nearby beaches – pedal boats, water skiing, windsurfing, diving, sailing, jetskiing. All equipment can be hired.

## ADVENTURE SPORTS
### Ballooning
**Mallorca Balloons**
Get a bird's eye view of the Mallorcan coast and countryside by heading up, up and away.
*Carrer Pins 30, Cala Ratjada. Tel: (971) 81 81 82. www.mallorcaballoons.com*
### Canyoning and coasteering
**Món d'Aventura**
Discover the Sierra Tramuntana and neighbouring coast in this exciting way.
*Carrer Plaça Vella 8, Pollença. Tel: (971) 53 52 48. www.mondaventura.com*

### Climbing
**La Reserva**
Ziplines, rope bridges and rock climbing in the Glatzó Park.
*Carrer Predio Son Net, Puig Punyent. Tel: (971) 61 66 22.*
*www.lareservaaventur.com*

### Flying
**Helicentre Mallorca**
Learn to fly a helicopter in a half-hour or hour's trial lesson. Special occasion? Book a sightseeing flight.
*Aerodromo de Son Bonet, Palma.*
*Tel: (971) 60 70 32.*
*www.helicentremallorca.com*

## BOWLING
**Bowling Porto Pl**
*Avinguda Gabriel Roca, Palma.*
*Tel: (971) 70 38 72.*
**Diverland Bowling**
*Ocimax, Carrer Leocadia Togores, Palma. Tel: (971) 49 87 00.*
**Festival Park**
*Carretera Mallorca, Marratxi.*

*Tel: (971) 22 68 22.*
*www.festivalpark.es*

## BULLFIGHTING

The Spanish consider a bullfight more
an artistic performance than a spectator
sport. In Mallorca, bullfighting is held
in high esteem by its *aficionados,* but
does not have the same status as on the
mainland, so, if you have never been to
a bullfight, Mallorca is not the best
place to experiment.

Every summer is bullfight season
in Palma's Plaça de Toros. There
are bullrings in Inca, Muro, Felanitx
and Alcúdia too, where fights are staged
to coincide with a local celebration.
Seats in the sun (*sol*) are cheaper than
those in the shade (*sombra*).

**Plaça de Toros**
*Avinguda Gaspar B Arquitecte 32,*
*Palma. Tel: (971) 75 52 45.*

## CYCLING

Spring is the main season for
competitive cycling when a round-
island race is staged. To unleash your
inner Chris Hoy, rent a bike from
Wheels Sport and follow one of their
scenic itineraries.

**Wheels Sport**
*Crta Alcúdia–Artà 31, Port d'Alcúdia.*
*Tel: (971) 89 14 19. www.wheelssport.net*

## DIVING

Many scuba-diving clubs and schools
on the island take advantage of the
clear waters off the Mallorcan coast.
Diving is held in several caves and on
two wrecks. Dive schools are usually
only open from April–October.

**Albatros Diving**
Visit six underwater grottoes.
*Son Servera. Tel: (971) 58 68 07.*
*www.albatros-diving.com*

**El Buceo**
Explore caves and wrecks.
*Avinguda Gabriel Roca 42, Port*
*d'Andratx. Tel: (971) 67 42 17.*
*www.el-buceo.com*

**Mero Diving**
Diving in caves.
*Cala Ratjada. Tel: (971) 56 54 67.*
*www.mero-diving.com*

**La Morena**
A 60m (66yd) long cave, with air
bubbles and stalactites to explore.
*Avinguda Bienvenidos 12,*
*Cala d'Or. Tel: (629) 88 13 80.*
*www.lamorena.de*

**5oceanos**
*Avinguda Ma Pas, Port d'Alcúdia. Tel:*
*(971) 54 99 57. www.5oceanos.com*

## FISHING

Portocristo is a favourite spot for
underwater fishing, and used for world
championships. Licences are required
for fishing in Mallorcan waters.

For information on fishing and a
list of regulations, contact **Direcció
General de Pesca** (*Carrer Foners 10,
Palma. Tel: (971) 17 61 00*).

**Tramuntana Tours**
Organises deep-sea fishing trips.
*Carrer de La Luna 72, Sóller.*
*Tel: (971) 63 24 23.*
*www.tramuntanatours.com*

## FOOTBALL

Mallorca is home to Real Mallorca and Atlético Baleares. Matches are normally played on Saturday or Sunday evening, 5pm onward, at **Son Moix Stadium** (*Camí dels Reis s/n.* *Tel: (971) 22 12 21*). *www.rcdmallorca.es*

## GOLF

The best-known clubs are at Santa Ponça and Son Vida. Competitions are frequently held, including the annual Balearic Open. Golfing holidays to Mallorca can be arranged as a package, and golf passes, giving access to all the island's clubs, can be bought. All courses have 18 holes unless stated otherwise. For information contact: **Federación Balear de Golf** (*Avinguda Jaume III 17, Palma. Tel: (971) 72 27 53. www.fbgolf. com*). Some of the main golf courses are:

### West of Palma
**Golf de Poniente**
*Tel: (971) 13 01 48. www.ponientegolf.com*
**Golf de Andratx**
*Tel: (971) 23 62 80.*
*www.golfdeandratx.com*
**Golf Park Mallorca**
*Near Palma. Tel: (971) 60 38 51.*
*www.golfparkmallorca.com*
**Son Muntaner**
*Tel: (971) 78 30 30.*
*www.sonmuntanergolf.com*

### The north
**Golf Pollença** (9 holes)
*Tel: (971) 53 32 16. www.golfpollensa.com*

**Golf Son Termens**
*Tel: (971) 61 78 62.*
*www.golfsontermens.com*

### The northeast
**Canyamel Golf Club**
*Tel: (971) 84 13 13.*
*www.canyamelgolf.com*
**Capdepera Golf**
*Tel: (971) 81 85 00.*
*www.golfcapdepera.com*
**Club Golf Son Servera** (9 holes)
*Tel: (971) 84 00 96.*
*www.golfsonservera.com*

### The south
**Club de Golf Vall d'Or**
*Tel: (971) 83 70 01. www.valldorgolf.com*
**Golf Maioris**
*Llucmajor. Tel: (971) 74 83 15.*
*www.golfmaioris.es*
**Son Antem Golf Resort and Spa**
*Tel: (971) 12 92 00.*
*www.sonantemgolf.com*

## HORSE RACING

Trotting races (*carreras*) are popular. There are two race tracks, near Palma and Manacor.
**Hipódromo de Son Pardo**
*Carretera Palma–Sóller, Km3.*
*Tel: (971) 76 38 53.*
**Hipódromo de Manacor**
*Esplá, Carretera Manacor–Artà, Km48.*
*Tel: (971) 55 00 23.*

## HORSE RIDING

There are several good riding venues. Classes for beginners and advanced riders are available at several centres around the island.

**Club Equítació Es Pas**
*Carretera Puigpunyent s/n, Calviá.*
*Tel: (639) 66 00 32 (mobile).*

**Club Escuela Equitación de Mallorca**
*Carretera Palma–Sóller, Km12, Bunyola.*
*Tel: (609) 60 28 02.*

**Club Escuela Equitación Son Gual**
*Carretera Establiments–Puigpunyent,*
*km2. Tel: (629) 42 68 78.*

**Club Escuela Son Menut**
*Cami de Son Negre, Km3, Felanitx.*
*Tel: (971) 71 /1 22.*

**Club Hipic es Raiguer**
*Carretera Vieja de Lloseta, Inca.*
*Tel: (639) 026 701.*

**La Paz**
*Carretera Militar 52, S'Aranjasa, Palma.*
*Tel: (697) 54 88 82.*

## SAILING

Mallorca is a prominent Mediterranean sailing and yachting centre, with over 40 marinas. The Club Nautico (Nautical Club) in each port is the focus of this activity.

Several resident companies offer yacht charter services. National and international competitions include the King's Cup and Princess Sofía Cup, and in August historic sailing boats take part in the Trofeo Conde de Barcelona.

There are sailing schools at Peguera and S'Arenal, and dinghies can be hired in many resorts.

**Federació Balear de Vela**
*Avinguda Joan Miró, Palma.*
*Tel: (971) 40 24 12.*

## SPORTS CENTRES

Some hotels have saunas and fitness centres, while those catering specifically for sports enthusiasts have gyms and a programme of exercise classes.

Mallorca has many municipal sports centres (Palau Municipal d'Esports or Poliesportius) with a high standard of equipment.

## TENNIS

Many hotels have their own courts and the larger resorts have tennis centres. Tuition in English is available.

**Federació Balear de Tenis**
*Carrer Uruguay, Palma Arena.*
*Tel: (971) 72 09 56. www.ftib.net*

## TRADITIONAL SPORTS

The ancient slinging skill of the Balearic *hondero* (*see p34*) is still practised by enthusiasts in *tiro con honda* (*tir de fona* in Catalan) competitions.

**Federació Balear de Tir de Fona**
*Bar Espanya, Carrer Oms 31, Palma.*
*Tel: (971) 72 62 50.*
*www.tirdefona.com*

## WATER SPORTS

Windsurfing tuition and board hire can be found in many resorts, and jet-skiing and water-skiing in larger ones.

**Escuela de Vela Portals**
Sailing, windsurfing, kayaking.
*Port de Portals. Tel: 666 591 159.*

**Sail and Surf**
*Passeig Saralegui 134, Port de Pollença.*
*Tel: (971) 86 53 46.*
*www.sailsurf.de*

# Food and drink

*The Mallorcans, along with the million visitors a year from the Spanish mainland, enjoy a good meal out. Traditionally based on fish, pork and lamb, the islanders' cuisine is at heart simple, robust fare. Now catering to international tastes, Mallorca's restaurants run the full range from the terrific to the terrible. Price is no automatic guarantee of quality and, as with all mass holiday destinations, you have to be selective.*

## Mallorcan specialities

The pig lies behind two of Mallorca's best-known comestibles. *Sobrassada* is a blood-red, pork-based sausage, often spiced with peppers and made to the butcher's personal recipe. Try them as *tapas*, the small dishes of food served in many Spanish bars. Pigs also provide the lard essential to the delicious *ensaimada*, a light, spiral, sugar-dusted pastry sometimes filled with 'angel's hair' (pumpkin jam) – a favourite way to start the Mallorcan day. Sold in dartboard-sized octagonal boxes, they make interesting and conveniently light presents to take home.

Options for vegetarian travellers are slowly increasing. There are a few purely vegetarian restaurants, and many others offer some meat- and dairy-free meals.

Some restaurants specialise in *cuina Mallorquí* (Mallorcan cooking) – the best are in Palma or out in the countryside. In the latter, service may be slow as your food is being freshly prepared.

The following dishes often appear on their menus.

**Arròs brut:** ('dirty rice'), usually a savoury saffron-flavoured soup with small pieces of meat and vegetables

**Arròs negre:** rice blackened with squid ink

**Botifarró:** highly seasoned cured pork and blood sausage

**Caracoles** (*Cargols* in Catalan): snails, often served with garlic and mayonnaise

**Empanadas** (*empanats* in Catalan): pastry-covered pie with meat and vegetables

**Escaldums:** stew made with chicken, potatoes and almonds

**Espinagada:** eel and spinach pie

**Frito mallorquín:** fry-up with liver, kidney and peppers

**Lechona asada:** roast suckling pig

**Lomo con setas** (*Llom amb bolets* in Catalan): fried pork with mushrooms

**Pa amb oli:** bread smeared with olive oil, garlic and tomatoes

**Sopes mallorquines:** vegetable soup with bread and garlic

**Tordos con col:** thrushes wrapped in cabbage

**Tumbet:** a seasoned dish similar to ratatouille, made with red and green peppers, aubergines and potatoes. Other dishes feature rabbit (*conejo*; *conil* in Catalan), chicken (*pollo*; *pollastre* in Catalan), lamb (*cordero*; *xai* in Catalan) and kidneys (*riñones*; *rinyons* in Catalan). Meat cooked *al horno* (*al forn* in Catalan) is slow-roasted in a brick oven.

### Fish

Good-quality fresh fish is no longer cheap, but the range is astounding. Restaurants often have the day's catch out on display for customers to make their choice. The fish is sold by weight – a good waiter will always tell you the price before it hits the pan. It is quite acceptable to ask for a sizeable fish to be divided between two. Menus in fish restaurants often include the following dishes.

**Arroz marinera:** fish soup with rice

**Caldereta langosta:** pieces of lobster in a tomato sauce

**Chipìrones** (*xipìrones* in Catalan): baby squid

**Gambas:** prawns

**Lubina con sal:** sea bass baked in a mountain of rock salt

**Salmonetes** (*mollets* in Catalan): red mullet

**Sardinas a la plancha** (*sardines a la planxa* in Catalan): grilled sardines.

Fresh seafood is delicious

### Cakes and desserts

Beside the ubiquitous *flan* (crème caramel), and *helados* (*gelats* in Catalan) (ice cream), better restaurants will stock *menorquina* and other brands of frozen desserts. Cakes featuring almonds are a safe bet, such as *tarta de almendras* or *gato* (almond cake), the most typical Mallorcan dessert. The best cheese made in the Balearic Islands comes from Menorca.

### Alcoholic drinks
#### Wine and beer

Mallorcan wine is worth trying, particularly the more expensive reds from the José Ferrer label or those from the dynamic young producers at Bodegas Ánima Negra. Wines from Binissalem, the island's viticultural

Food and drink

centre, have now gained DO status (*Denominación d'Origen*), a sign of their improving quality. There is another DO area on the eastern side of the island, Pla i Llevant. But some of the best wines opt out of the DO system and are called *vi de terra*. Although foreign grape varieties have been introduced, all red wines from here include at least 50 per cent of the local Manto Negro (Black Cloak) grape. Those marked *vino de crianza* (*ví de criança* in Catalan) have been aged in oak casks and are at least two years old.

Wines imported from other regions of Spain are always available, along with many beers from around Europe. Beer (*cerveza*), the first and only Spanish word learned by an over-publicised minority of visitors to Mallorca, is cheaper if bought draught – ask for *una caña*. If you get carried away, *boquerones* (fresh anchovies), available in any *tapas* bar, are a good hangover cure.

### Spirits

Mallorca's contribution to the befuddling choice of Spanish spirits and liqueurs is *hierbas*. These are aromatic herb- and aniseed-based liqueurs which come *seco* (dry) or *dulce* (sweet). Free tasting of the various flavours, such as those sold under the Túnel label, is a feature of excursions visiting *bodegas* or large souvenir emporia. *Palo*, a dark aperitif made from crushed and fermented carob

Palma sign: if you always keep your drink at arm's length it will last longer

seeds, will appeal to the intrepid experimenter.

The best and most palatable spirit to take home is gin made on Menorca – the Xoriguer brands come in a distinctive brown bottle with a windmill label. The production of gin on that island is a legacy of the British presence there for much of the 18th century.

### Non-alcoholic drinks

With so many orange trees on the island, freshly-squeezed orange juice (*zumo de naranja*; *suc de taronja* in Catalan) is an appropriate drink, particularly in the Sóller area. Try it mixed with lemon (*limón*) for additional tang, or refreshingly packed with ice (*granizado*; *granissat* in Catalan). Some bars, such as the Abaco in Palma (Carrer de Sant Joan 1), make a feature of their juicy combinations. *Horchata* (*orxata* in Catalan), a milky drink made from almonds, is also sold. Coffee comes black (*café solo*), white (*café con leche*), with only a little milk (*café cortado*; *tallat* in Catalan), laced with brandy (*café carajillo*), or iced (*granizado de café*). Tea (*té*) is also widely available wherever there are English tourists.

Tap water in Mallorca is safe to drink but can taste salty. It is better to drink bottled water – it is not expensive and can be bought in 5-litre containers from supermarkets.

Water with bubbles is *agua con gas*, without is *sin gas*.

## What's on offer

In the resorts the choice of cuisine and dining venues verges on the exhausting. Many restaurants have similar menus offering adequate but unmemorable international fare. The Spanish employ a fork system to grade their restaurants, but this can be ignored completely.

Instead, look for signs of quality. Has the computer-printed menu been there since last winter? Are there any Spanish diners inside? Ask about the *especialidad del día* (speciality of the day) – not to be confused with *menú del día*, a set meal all restaurants have to offer by law (very competitive in resorts, excellent in Palma, and very good value in country villages).

*Tapas* bars get their name from the Sevillian practice of putting a lid (*tapa*) of ham on top of a glass of sherry. They can be anything from a saucer of olives to a terracotta dish of spicy meatballs. *Tapas* can easily mount up into a hefty bill, but they are a

quintessential Spanish practice and a few *raciones* (portions) are a great way to snack while shopping and sightseeing in Palma. Try La Boveda in Plaça La Llotja.

Some restaurants describe themselves as *cellers* – like cellars, though not necessarily underground. Their hallmark is a rustic atmosphere with solid furniture and vast vats of wine lining the walls. Celler Ca'n Amer in Inca is a sophisticated example, and there are others in and around Carrer de Apuntadores, Palma's principal wining and dining street.

Outdoor menu at a restaurant in San Telmo

**Food and drink**

## WHERE TO EAT

The star rating indicates the price of a 3-course meal, without wine or beer, per person, in euros.

★       under €15
★★      €15–€30
★★★     over €30

Many restaurants open on fewer days of the week during the low season. Some take a holiday in July or August. Many close entirely for the winter, particularly in the main resorts. If you are making a special journey, check if your destination is open. A tax of 7 per cent IVA (value added tax) is added to restaurant bills. Any list of restaurants in Palma and the island must of necessity be a very arbitrary one as there are hundreds of really excellent restaurants.

## PALMA

**Bon Lloc ★**
Vegetarian restaurant with a good-value four-course *menú del día* (set meal).
*Carrer Sant Feliu 7.*
*Tel: (971) 71 86 17.*
*Open: Mon–Sat lunch.*

**Ca'n Juan de S'Aigo ★**
Landmark café serving home-made ice cream, *ensaimadas* and thick hot chocolate.
*Carrer Can Sanc 10.*
*Tel: (971) 71 07 59.*
*Open: Wed–Mon.*

**Cellar Sa Premsa ★**
One of the oldest, most well-known and popular restaurants in Palma.
*Plaça Bisbe Berenguer de Palou 8. Tel: (971) 72 35 29. Open: Mon–Sat lunch & dinner.*

**Natural ★**
Healthy salads and a seasonal menu.
*Plaça Espanya 8.*
*Tel: (971) 72 22 32.*
*Open: 8.30am–midnight.*

**Nineing ★**
Trendy tapas and wine bar in La Llonja district.
*Carrer Apuntadores 24.*
*Tel: (971) 21 40 11.*
*Open: Wed–Mon lunch & dinner.*

**Santa Eulàlia ★/★★★**
An arty café downstairs which serves a good-value *menù del día* and a smart restaurant upstairs for refined Mediterranean fare.
*Carrer L'Església de Santa Eulàlia 7. Tel: (971) 71 57*

17. *Open: Mon–Sat lunch & dinner.*

**Arrosseria Sa Cranca ★★**
Intriguing and substantial rice dishes overlooking the seafront.
*Passeig Marítim 13. Tel: (971) 73 74 45. Open: Mon–Sat lunch & dinner, Sun lunch.*

**Café Fusion ★★**
Grilled meats plus Asian-inspired menu.
*Carrer Trafalgar 33, Ciudad Jardín. Tel: (971) 26 66 59. Open: Tue–Sun lunch & dinner.*

**Shogun ★★**
Elegant and popular, this Japanese restaurant serves excellent sushi and sashimi.
*Carrer Camilo José Cela 14. Tel: (971) 73 57 48. Open: lunch & dinner.*

**Baisakhi ★★★**
Creative, gourmet Indian cooking.
*Passeig Marítim 8.*
*Tel: (971) 73 68 06.*
*Open: Tue–Sun dinner.*

**Es Baluard ★★★**
'New' Mallorcan cuisine.
*Plaça Santa Catalina 9.*
*Tel: (971) 71 96 09.*
*Open: Mon–Sat lunch & dinner. Closed last two weeks of Aug.*

**Fabrica 23** ★★★
Excellent contemporary
Mediterranean cuisine
in fashionable
surroundings.
*Carrer Cótoner 42–44.*
*Tel: (971) 45 31 25.*
*Open: Tue–Sun lunch*
*& dinner.*

**Reial Club Nautic** ★★★
Fish and chips with eye-
pleasing harbour views.
*Muelle San Pedro 1.*
*Tel: (971) 72 63 83.*
*Open: Mon–Sat lunch*
*& dinner.*

## WEST OF PALMA
## Banyalbufar
**Son Tomás** ★★
Seafood and local dishes.
*Carrer Baronia 17.*
*Tel: (971) 61 81 49.*
*Open: Wed–Sun lunch &*
*dinner, Mon lunch.*

## Estellencs
**Montimar** ★★
Mallorcan cuisine in a
lovely location.
*Plaça Constitució 7.*
*Tel: (971) 61 85 76.*
*Open: Tue–Sun lunch*
*& dinner.*

## Génova
**Meson Ca'n Pedro I** ★★
A favourite Sunday lunch
venue. Snails a speciality.

*Carrer de Rector Vives 14.*
*Tel: (971) 70 21 62.*
*Open: lunch & dinner.*

## Palma Nova
**Sopranos** ★★
Italian and
Mediterranean cuisine.
*Avinguda Cas Saboners 4.*
*Tel: (971) 68 13 27. www.*
*restaurantesopranos.com.*
*Open: Mon–Sat lunch &*
*dinner.*

## Port d'Andratx
**A Dorada** ★★
Fish, Mallorcan cuisine
and great views.
*Tel: (971) 67 16 48.*
*Open: lunch & dinner.*

**Rocamar** ★★
Fish and seafood
specialists.
*Almirante Riera*
*Alemany 27.*
*Tel: (971) 67 12 61.*
*Open: lunch & dinner.*

## Portals Nous
**El Bistro de Tristán** ★★
Run by the same chef
as the famous Tristán
next door.
*Marina de Puerto Portals.*
*Tel: (971) 67 61 41.*
*Open: lunch & dinner.*

**Flanigan** ★★
Glassy restaurant-bar
overlooking the port.

*Marina de Puerto Portals.*
*Tel: (971) 67 91 91.*
*Open: lunch & dinner.*

## Santa Ponça
**Meson del Rey** ★★
Traditional Mallorcan,
family-friendly
restaurant serving
snails, suckling pig, and
the usual seafood and
steaks.
*Carrer Puig del Teix 7,*
*Santa Ponça.*
*Tel: (971) 69 08 15. Open:*
*daily lunch & dinner.*
*Closed: 1 Nov–15 Dec.*

**Gala** ★★★
Trendy restaurant and
bar with an international
menu.
*Avinguda Jaume I 92.*
*Tel: (971) 69 93 33.*
*Open: dinner, cocktails*
*& dancing.*

## THE NORTHWEST
## Alaró
**Es Verger** ★★
This restaurant serves
lamb roasted in a wood-
fired oven. It also offers
a very good-value
*menú del día* at
lunchtime.
*Camí Castell 143.*
*Tel: (971) 18 21 26.*
*Open: Tue–Sun lunch*
*& dinner.*

## Jardines d'Alfàbia

**Ses Porxeres** ★★★

Long-established restaurant well suited for a long Mallorcan lunch. Game a speciality. *Carretera de Sóller. Tel: (971) 61 37 62. Open: Tue–Sat lunch & dinner, Sun dinner.*

## Deià

**El Barrigon** ★★

Tapas and wine in an arty setting. *Carrer Archiduque Luis Salvador. Tel: (971) 63 91 39. Open: Tue–Sun 12.30pm–1am.*

## Fornalutx

**Ca'n Antuna** ★★

Charming and rustic, with home-cooked food and sublime views. *Carrer Arbona Colom 6. Tel: (971) 63 30 68. Open: Tue–Sun lunch & dinner.*

## Inca

**Celler Ca'n Amer** ★★★

Award-winning local cuisine – try the suckling pig. *Carrer Pau 39. Tel: (971) 50 12 61. Open: Mon–Fri for lunch & dinner.*

## Orient

**Dalt Muntanya** ★★

Traditional local fare, including roast lamb. *Carretera Bunyola-Orient, Km10. Tel: (971) 61 53 73. Open: Tue–Sun lunch & dinner Feb–Nov.*

## Port de Sóller

**Randemar** ★★

Pizza, pasta and Mediterranean fare. *Carrer Es Traves 16. Tel: (971) 63 45 78. Open: daily lunch & dinner.*

**Es Faro** ★★★

Celebrated seafood restaurant by the lighthouse. *Faro de Punta Grossa. Tel: (971) 63 37 52. Open: lunch & dinner.*

## Sóller

**Luna 36** ★★

Café and restaurant with an international menu. *Carrer de la Luna 36. Tel: (971) 63 47 39. Open: Mon–Sat lunch & dinner.*

## Valldemossa

**Valldemossa Hotel** ★★★

Stylish dining in an exclusive hotel. *Carretera Vieja de Valldemossa.*
*Tel: (971) 61 26 26. Open: lunch & dinner.*

## THE NORTHEAST

### Alcúdia

**Ca'n Costa** ★★

Try classic Mallorcan fare such as *tumbet* (ratatouille) and *frit mallorquín* (fried-up offals) on a lovely flower-filled patio. *Carrer Sant Vicens 14. Tel: (971) 54 53 94. Open: Tue–Sun lunch & dinner.*

### Canyamel

**Porxada de Sa Torre** ★★

Spacious rancho-style barn with wooden tables. Mostly meat dishes. Suckling pig roasted in the courtyard. *Carretera de Canyamel-Artà, Km5. Tel: (971) 84 13 10. Open: Tue–Sun lunch & dinner.*

### Petra

**Sa Plaça** ★★

Specialises in local dishes such as roast suckling pig. *Plaça Ramón Llull 4. Tel: (971) 56 16 46. Open: Wed–Mon lunch & dinner.*

## Pollença

**La Font del Gall ★★**
International cuisine
with a Scottish twist!
*Carrer Montesion 4. Tel:
(971) 53 03 96. Open:
lunch & dinner.*

## Port de Pollença

**Ivy Garden 49 ★★**
Lovely terrace.
*Carretera Formentor 49.
Tel: (971) 86 62 71.
Open: Tue–Sun dinner.*

**Corb Marì ★★★**
Highly regarded
traditional cuisine.
*Avinguda Anglada
Camarasa 91.
Tel: (971) 86 70 40.
Open: Tue–Sun for lunch
& dinner.*

**Stay ★★★**
Incredible seafront
location offering
exquisite gourmet
entrées.
*Passeig Saralegui, on the
pier. Tel: (971) 86 40 13.
Open: lunch & dinner.*

## Sa Colònia de Sant Pere

**El Pescador ★★**
Fresh fish caught from
the owner's boat.
*Carrer de Sant Joan 68.
Tel: (971) 58 95 36.
Open: lunch & dinner.*

## Son Servera

**S'Era de Pula ★★★**
Mallorcan and fish
specialities.
*Carretera de Son
Servera–Capdepera Km3.
Tel: (971) 56 79 40. Open:
Tue–Sun lunch & dinner.*

## THE SOUTH/ SOUTHEAST

## Algaida

**Cal Dimoni ★★**
Popular restaurant
specialising in
Mallorcan food.
*Carretera Palma–Manacor,
Km21. Tel: (971) 66 50 35.
Open: Thur–Tue.*

**Es 4 Vents ★★**
High standard of
Mallorcan cooking.
*Carretera Palma–
Manacor, Km21. Tel:
(971) 66 51 73. Open:
Fri–Wed lunch & dinner.*

## Cala d'Or

**Port Petit ★★★**
Upmarket seafood
restaurant.
*Avinguda Cala Llonga.
Tel: (971) 64 30 39. Open:
Wed–Mon lunch & dinner.*

## Felanitx

**Ca'l Patró ★★**
Spiny lobster stew is the
house speciality.

*Cala Barques.
Tel: (971) 53 38 99. Open:
lunch & dinner.*

## Manacor

**Es Congress ★★★**
Inventive market cuisine
in stylish surroundings.
*Crta Palma–Arta Km48.
Tel: (971) 55 47 66. Open:
Tue–Sun lunch & dinner.*

## Portocolom

**HPC ★★★**
Fashionable and stylish
bar-café-restaurant serving
breakfast, lunch, dinner
and drinks. Paella and
pizzas are the specialities.
*Carrer Cristofol Colom 5.
Tel: (971) 82 53 23.
Open: daily.*

## Portopetro

**Ca'n Martina ★★**
Fresh fish, paellas and
delicious home-made
cakes and tarts.
*Passeig des Port. Tel:
(971) 65 75 17. Open:
9am–midnight.*

## Sa Colònia de Sant Jordi

**El Puerto ★★**
Fresh fish and paellas.
*Carrer Lonja 2.
Tel: (971) 65 60 47. Open:
lunch & dinner.*

# Accommodation

*The bulk of accommodation on Mallorca consists of hotels and apartment complexes catering for holidaymakers. As the island's tourist boom started back in the 1960s, some buildings are now outdated – even abandoned. Today there is a more intelligent attitude to architectural style and the planning of resorts. Standards are rising, alternative forms of accommodation are on the increase, and the days of predictable, repetitive hotels appear numbered.*

## Resort hotels

Most visitors to the island have pre-paid accommodation as part of a package deal. This is by far the cheapest way of staying on Mallorca. It is possible in the low season to take a flight and get bargain accommodation, or to negotiate favourable rates for a long stay – as some over-wintering senior citizens do. Package holidays with accommodation allocated only on arrival are even more economical.

Spanish hotels are graded by stars from 1 to 5. Tour operators also have their own classifications based on different criteria: whether balconies have a sea view, for instance. The difference between a 2- and 3-star hotel is not always significant. Even though the holiday market is highly competitive, the adage that you get what you pay for generally holds true.

## Luxury accommodation

There is a marked contrast between the world of mass tourism and the very special, extremely expensive and luxurious hotels in Mallorca. These hotels are world-class, highly individual establishments and include the five-star chains **Hilton**, **Sheraton** and **Marriott**.

Luxury hotels in or near Palma include the **Palacio Ca Sa Galesa, Hotel Nixe Palace, Castillo Hotel Son Vida** and **Valparaiso Palace**. In the north of the island, the **Hotel Formentor** on Cap de Formentor has been pampering the rich and famous since 1926, while **La Residencia** in Deià attracts a well-off, hip clientele. Villas with a swimming pool and domestic staff can also be rented (*see p172*). There are no *paradors* (state-owned luxury hotels).

## Apartments

The Spanish authorities grade their *apartamentos turísticos* (AT) into four classes symbolised with keys. Apartment complexes can be found in all the resorts but are particularly common along the Calvià coast, and at Peguera, Cala Millor and Port d'Alcúdia.

## Reservations

Hotel reservations can be made through **Central de Reservas de la Federación Empresarial Hotelera de Mallorca** (*tel: (971) 70 60 07*). For on-line reservations: *www.mallorcahotelguide.com* or *www.visitmallorca.com*. For discounted hotels or holidays see *www.lastminute.com* or *www.travelsupermarket.com*

Seven per cent IVA (value added tax) is added to hotel bills. Unless you are on a package holiday, breakfast is not normally included in the price of a room.

## Complaints

In the event of a major grievance, or if you feel you have not received value for money, gather all possible evidence to back your case, perhaps by taking

A pool and a place in the sun are facilities almost all hotels provide

Accommodation

photographs. All hotels and restaurants have a complaints book which you can ask for and you can officially lodge a grievance.

## Villas and farmhouses

Recent initiatives to widen the appeal of the island have led to an increase in opportunities to holiday in the tranquillity and beauty of the Mallorcan countryside. Select country houses have now been turned into hotels, such as **L'Hermitage** in Orient, and a number of rural homes and working farms have also been converted into appealing villas to stay in for a week or two. All quite individual, these are usually stone buildings decorated with rustic furniture and Spanish textiles. Facilities are of a high standard, with a garden, patio, swimming pool and open fire.

Accommodation in converted old country estates and rural hotels can be booked through **Associació Agroturisme Balear** (*Tel: (971) 72 15 08*; online booking service: *www.agroturismo-balear.com*).

## Budget accommodation

Last-minute or off-season package holidays provide a cheap and easy way to stay in Mallorca. There are few youth hostels or student-orientated dormitories on the island. Palma's main youth hostel is at *Carrer Costa Brava 13. Tel: (971) 26 08 92. Email: reserves@tjove.caib.es*. For low-priced accommodation there are 1- and 2-star

hotels, *hostales* (H) which are rated 1 to 3 stars, and *pensiones* (P).

These classifications, along with *fondas* (F) (inns) and *Casas de Huéspedes* (CH) (guesthouses), are of interest only to bureaucrats and provide no easy guide to price, cleanliness or comfort.

Palma offers the greatest selection of such accommodation, but most towns and ports have a *hostal* or two – though finding vacancies in the summer can be a problem. Always ask to see the room before you accept it.

## Monestirs i Santuaris (Monasteries and sanctuaries)

Mallorca's many religious sanctuaries have a long tradition of hospitality, offering simple accommodation to passing visitors. Their remote locations will appeal to people happy to be away from the bright lights, but they are not intended as a source of a cheap holiday.

If you are content to stay the night in premises solely concerned with the worship of God, most likely in the company of other pilgrims, places like the **Ermita de Sant Salvador** (near Felanitx, *see p124*) and **Santuari de Cura** (Puig de Randa, *see pp127–8*) continue to offer sanctuary to those who desire it. Rooms are spartan, with only a wash basin, and guests are expected to make up their bed and take breakfast communally.

At the **Monestir de Lluc** (*tel: (971) 51 70 25; www.lluc.net*) (*see pp76–7*) the atmosphere is slightly more relaxed, and during the summer, religious students, pilgrim families from abroad and casual visitors all stay in its dormitory-style accommodation. Meals are available here and in other sanctuaries. The monastery is very popular with Mallorcans who camp within its walls in August every year. Rooms can accommodate between one and six people, and have small kitchens to be used by two or three people.

Accommodation is very basic at **Refugio del Castell d'Alaró** (*Puig d'Alaró. Tel: (971) 18 21 12*), and supplies can be carried only by donkeys for the last couple of kilometres.

There is accommodation at **Santuari de Sant Salvador** (*Felanitx. Tel: (971) 82 72 82*), while at **Ermita de Bonany** (*Petra. Tel: (971) 82 65 68*) there is lodging but no food.

## Mountain refuges

The government in Mallorca has restored and signalled numerous walking paths in the last two years. The two main routes are La Ruta de Pedraensec (the dry-stone wall route), which has four refuges (*refugis*) along the way, and the Arta-Lluc route which has two refuges. Information on these refuges can be found at: *www.conselldemallorca.net/ mediambient/pedra.*

These provide simple dormitory-type accommodation, popular with hill-walkers. They must be booked in advance at the Nature and Environmental Department (Departament de Medi Ambient i Natura), *Carrer General Rieva III. Tel: (971) 17 37 00.*

For a different experience, Lluc monastery offers accommodation in its dormitory

## PRICES

The prices are based on the average summer time price for a double room.

| ★ | under €60 |
| ★★ | €60–120 |
| ★★★ | €120–180 |
| ★★★★ | above €180 |

## PALMA

**Hostal Brondo ★–★★**
Tasteful budget accommodation in an ancient house. No breakfast.
*Carrer C'an Brondo 1. Tel: (971) 71 90 43. www.hostalbrondo.com*

**Augusta Apartments ★★**
Family-friendly self-catering in a quiet area.
*Carrer Corb Mari 22, La Bonanova. Tel: (971) 70 08 13. www.bqhoteles.com*

**Hotel Dalt Murada ★★★–★★★★**
Characterful and elegant mansion.
*Carrer Almudaina 6A. Tel: (971) 42 53 00. www.daltmurada.com*

**Hotel Tres ★★★★**
Boutique hotel in the old town.
*Carrer Apuntadores 3. Tel: (971) 71 73 33. www.hoteltres.com*

## WEST OF PALMA
## Cala Fornells

**Hotel Petit ★★**
Attractive seaside hotel with four pools and lovely gardens.
*Tel: (971) 68 54 05. www.petitcalafornells.com. Open: Jan–Oct.*

## Port d'Andratx

**Hotel Villa Italia ★★★★**
Luxury lodging known for its gastronomic restaurant.
*Camino de San Carlos 13. Tel: (971) 67 40 11. www.hotelvillaitalia.com*

## Santa Ponça

**Casablanca Hotel and Apartments ★–★★**
Smallish complex close to beach and resort centre.
*Via Rei Sancho 6. Tel: (971) 69 03 61. www.hotelyapartamentoscasablanca.com. Open: May–Oct.*

## THE NORTHWEST
## Deià

**S'Hotel D'es Puig ★★**
Charming, small hotel.
*Carrer Es Puig 4. Tel: (971) 63 94 09. www.hoteldespuig.com. Open: Feb–Oct.*

## Fornalutx

**Can'n Reus ★★★**
Cosy, attractive accommodation.
*Carrer de l'Auba 26. Tel: (971) 63 11 74. www.canreushotel.com*

## Port de Pollença

**Hostal Bahia ★★–★★★**
Renovated building overlooking the bay.
*Paseo Vora Mar. Tel: (971) 86 65 62. www.hoposa.es. Open: Mar–Oct.*

## Port de Sóller

**Hotel Espléndido ★★–★★★★**
Stylish hotel and spa on the seafront.
*Carrer Es Traves 5. Tel: (971) 63 18 50. www.esplendidohotel.com. Open: Mar–Nov.*

## Sóller

**Casa Bougainvillea ★★**

Gorgeous B&B.

*Carrer del Mar 81. Tel: (971) 63 31 04.*
*www.casa-bougainvillea.com*

**Hotel Salvia ★★★★**

One of the best small hotels in the Med. Stunning views.

*Carrer de la Palma 18. Tel: (971) 63 49*
*36. www.hotelsalvia.com.*
*Open: May–Oct.*

## THE NORTHEAST
## Alcúdia

**Hotel Cas Ferrer ★★★**

Minimalist chic in an old blacksmith's house.

*Carrer Pou Nou 1. Tel: (971) 89 75 42.*
*www.nouhotelet.com*

## Canyamel

**Hotel Can Simoneta ★★★★**

Luxury farmhouse perched on a cliff in golf-course country.

*Carretera Artà–Canyamel Km 8, Finca*
*Torre Canyamel. Tel: (971) 81 61 10. www.*
*cansimoneta.com. Open: mid-Feb–Nov.*

## Colónia de Sant Pere

**Hotel Rocamar ★★**

Small, stylish hotel in a little fishing village. Also has an apartment.

*Carrer Sant Mateu 9. Tel: (971) 58 96 58.*
*www.hotelrocamar.net*

## Santa María

**Read's Hotel ★★★★**

Relais & Châteaux hotel and spa with Michelin-starred restaurant.

*Santa María. Tel: (971) 14 02 61.*
*www.readshotel.com*

## Sineu

**Hotel León de Sineu ★★★**

Delightfully refurbished 15th-century stone house.

*Carrer desl Bous 129. Tel: (971) 52 02 11.*
*www.hotel-leondesineu.com*

## THE SOUTH/SOUTHEAST
## Llucmajor

**Finca Son Sama ★★–★★★**

*Agroturismo* with rooms and apartments plus an on-site riding school.

*Carretera Llucmajor–Porreres Km3.5.*
*Tel: (971) 12 09 59. www.sonsama.com*

## Manacor

**Hotel Reserva Rotana ★★★★**

A 17th-century manor with its own golf course and vineyard.

*Cami de S'Avall Km3. Tel: (971) 84*
*56 85. www.reservarotana.com.*
*Open: Mar–Dec.*

## Portopetro

**Hostal Nereida ★–★**

Quaint, simple hostal overlooking the bay.

*Carrer Patrons Martina 3. Tel: (971) 65*
*72 23. www.hostalnereida.com.*
*Open: May–Oct.*

## Sa Colónia de Sant Jordi

**Hostal Playa ★–★★**

Charming, family-run *hostal*-restaurant.

*Carrer Mayor 25. Tel: (971) 65 52 56.*
*www.restauranteplaya.com. Open: Jan–Oct.*

# Practical guide

## Arriving

### Documentation

Citizens from the United Kingdom and the Republic of Ireland must show a valid passport when entering Spain. Visitors from other EU countries need a valid passport or national identity card. Visitors from Canada, the USA, Australia and New Zealand (among other countries) need a valid passport and may remain in Spain for a maximum period of 90 days without a visa. Citizens of most other countries, including South Africa, must apply for a visa at their nearest Embassy or Consulate before travelling to Spain. These regulations are subject to change and you should always check with the Spanish Embassy or Consulate before travel.

### By air

Mallorca's airport is one of the busiest in Europe. It is well served by charter flights, and numerous standard and no-frills airlines operate services from airports around the UK. Prices are usually cheapest if you book well in advance. Many airlines charge a fee for telephone bookings, so book your flight online if possible. To find out which budget or charter airline serves airports near you, go to *www.whichbudget.com*. *www.skyscanner.net* is dedicated to charter flights and often offers the best prices.

**British Airways**: *Tel: (0844) 493 0787. www.ba.com*
**bmibaby**: *Tel: (0905) 8 282828. www.bmibaby.com*
**easyJet**: *Tel: (0871) 244 2366. www.easyjet.com*
**FlyBe**: *Tel: (0871) 700 2000. www.flybe.com*
**Iberia**: the Spanish national airline. *Tel: (0870) 609 0500. www.iberia.com*
**Jet2**: *Tel: (0871) 226 1737. www.jet2.com*
**Monarch**: *Tel: (0870) 040 5040. www.flymonarch.com*
**Ryanair**: *Tel: (0871) 246 0000. www.ryanair.com*
**Thomsonfly**: *Tel: (0871) 231 4787. www.thomsonfly.com*

**Son Sant Joan** airport, 8km (5 miles) east of Palma, is connected to the capital by motorway. Airport Express No 1 runs from the airport to the centre of Palma, or you can take a taxi.

The airport's terminal is immense. Moving walkways help cover the distances involved in getting around, and trolley cars are available on request (or for travellers with disabilities). The airport has a full range of facilities, including car rental, hotel booking services and a tourist information counter in the arrivals lounge.

On departure, you can visit the large duty-free shop after passing passport control. If you are travelling at peak times on charter flights, make sure you have some change and entertainment on hand in case of delay (*Retrasado* on

the flight information screen;
*Embarcando* means 'boarding').
**Airport information desk**
*Tel: (902) 40 47 04.*
**Online live arrivals and departures**
*www.aena.es*

## By sea
Regular car ferries link Mallorca with
Barcelona (journey time 7 hours, or
3 hours 45 mins in the fast catamaran)
and Valencia (8 hours, or 4 hours
30 minutes) on the Spanish mainland.
There are also several services a day
to the Balearic islands of Ibiza
and Menorca.

## Trasmediterranea
*Tel: (+34) 902 45 46 45.*
*www.trasmediterranea.es*
**Balearia** *Tel: (+34) 902 160 180.*
*www.balearia.com*

## Children
Nappies, baby food and formula milk
can be bought in Mallorca, but if you
have a preferred brand of quality take
it with you. Very few hotels and
restaurants have highchairs, so if you
have your own travel chair take it. If
you need to hire a car seat for a child,
double-check availability. (*See also*
*pp156–7.*)

## Climate
Most people visit Mallorca between
April and September when the island
is usually warm and sunny. July and
August are the hottest, driest months.

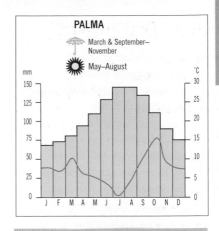

PALMA

March & September–
November

May–August

## WEATHER CONVERSION CHART
25.4mm = 1 inch
°F = 1.8 × °C + 32

Rain is most likely between October
and March. Although it rarely gets very
cold in winter during the day, nights
can be really chilly.

## Consulates
**UK**: Convent dels Caputxins 4, Edificiò
Orisba B, 4-D 07002 Palma. *Tel: (971)*
*71 24 45. www.britishembassy.gov.uk*
**USA**: *Carrer Porto Pl 8, Palma. Tel:*
*(971) 40 37 07.*

## Conversion tables
*See p179.*
Clothes and shoes in Mallorca follow
the same sizes as the rest of Europe.

## Crime
Beware of pickpockets in markets,
outside tourist sights and in crowded
places. If you are harassed by what the

tour reps call 'colourful characters' trying to sell carnations, tablecloths or watches, keep moving and never get any money out as it will only exacerbate the problem. Avoid flower-toting gypsies at all costs.

Thefts can be carried out by your fellow holidaymakers too – apartments are particularly vulnerable in this respect. Never carry large amounts of cash or valuables, and always use safe deposit boxes in hotels; the small fee is worth it. Leave nothing you care about in your car or unattended on a beach. If you are unhappy about carrying your passport, get a photocopy of it verified and stamped at a police station.

## Customs regulations

Spain is part of the European Union, so there are no restrictions on the movement of duty-paid goods for personal use between Mallorca and other EU countries. The allowances for goods bought in duty-free shops (in airports or on board ships and planes), sold free of customs duty and VAT, apply to anyone visiting Spain from a country outside the European Union.

The allowances here are (per person aged over 17): 200 cigarettes or 100 cigarillos or 50 cigars or 250g of tobacco; 1 litre of spirits or 4 litres of wine, 16 litres of beer and other goods up to a value of €430.

## Dress

The Spanish believe beachwear and swimming costumes belong at the seaside. You may be refused entry to Palma cathedral and other churches, as well as some banks, shops and restaurants, if you are considered improperly dressed. Topless sunbathing is common on many beaches, but nudism is confined to more remote beaches.

## Driving

A car is not essential to enjoy Mallorca, but it is the best way to see the island at your own pace. The following are a number of tips to keep in mind.

### Car rental

Mallorca is overrun with car rental companies. If you intend to collect a car at the airport, or need a child seat, make arrangements before you leave home. Compare prices well in advance on websites such as *www.travelsupermarket.com* to get the best deal. Drivers normally have to be over 21 and to have held a licence for at least one year. It is advisable to take out comprehensive insurance and Collision Damage Waiver. Your travel insurance should be topped up to provide cover against your liability to a third party if involved in a motor accident. Check whether the seven per cent IVA (VAT) is included in the price.

**Al Terry's Car Hire** *Carrer Bellamar 8, Can Pastilla. Tel: (971) 26 78 49. www.terryscarhire.com*
**Avis** *Passeig Marítim 16. Tel: (971) 28 62 33. General reservations: tel: (902) 24 88 24. www.avis.es*

## On the road

Drive on the right. Speed limits are 120km/h (75mph) on motorways, 100km/h (62mph) on dual carriageways, 90km/h (56mph) on other roads except in urban areas, where it is 50km/h (30mph) or as signposted. Seat belts are compulsory in front seats and back seats where fitted.

Vigilance is required at all times, particularly on mountain roads. If you meet a coach, you are obliged to reverse. Alcohol limit: 0.5gm per litre; 0.3gm per litre for new drivers with licences less than two years old.

Palma is usefully bypassed by a ring road known as Via Cintura. An *autopista* (motorway) runs west to Peguera, and another northeast beyond Sa Pobla. A third extends south past the airport to beyond Llucmajor.

## Parking

Parking restrictions are enforced by a scheme known as ORA. In town centres, parking lots marked in blue with *Zona Blava* (Blue Zone) signs can only be used with a ticket bought in advance from a nearby machine. These are valid for 30–90 minutes must be displayed in the car. Failure to do this can result in fines, wheel-clamping or towing away.

In Palma, ORA is in force within the boundaries of the old city walls from 9.30am to 1.30pm and 5pm to 8pm, from Monday to Friday. Rules are strictly enforced. If you need to stay longer, go to a public car park.

## CONVERSION TABLE

| FROM | TO | MULTIPLY BY |
|---|---|---|
| Inches | Centimetres | 2.54 |
| Feet | Metres | 0.3048 |
| Yards | Metres | 0.9144 |
| Miles | Kilometres | 1.6090 |
| Acres | Hectares | 0.4047 |
| Gallons | Litres | 4.5460 |
| Ounces | Grams | 28.35 |
| Pounds | Grams | 453.6 |
| Pounds | Kilograms | 0.4536 |
| Tons | Tonnes | 1.0160 |

To convert back, for example from centimetres to inches, divide by the number in the third column.

## MEN'S SUITS

| UK | 36 | 38 | 40 | 42 | 44 | 46 | 48 |
|---|---|---|---|---|---|---|---|
| Rest of Europe | 46 | 48 | 50 | 52 | 54 | 56 | 58 |
| USA | 36 | 38 | 40 | 42 | 44 | 46 | 48 |

## DRESS SIZES

| UK | 8 | 10 | 12 | 14 | 16 | 18 |
|---|---|---|---|---|---|---|
| France | 36 | 38 | 40 | 42 | 44 | 46 |
| Italy | 38 | 40 | 42 | 44 | 46 | 48 |
| Rest of Europe | 34 | 36 | 38 | 40 | 42 | 44 |
| USA | 6 | 8 | 10 | 12 | 14 | 16 |

## MEN'S SHIRTS

| UK | 14 | 14.5 | 15 | 15.5 | 16 | 16.5 | 17 |
|---|---|---|---|---|---|---|---|
| Rest of Europe | 36 | 37 | 38 | 39/40 | 41 | 42 | 43 |
| USA | 14 | 14.5 | 15 | 15.5 | 16 | 16.5 | 17 |

## MEN'S SHOES

| UK | 7 | 7.5 | 8.5 | 9.5 | 10.5 | 11 |
|---|---|---|---|---|---|---|
| Rest of Europe | 41 | 42 | 43 | 44 | 45 | 46 |
| USA | 8 | 8.5 | 9.5 | 10.5 | 11.5 | 12 |

## WOMEN'S SHOES

| UK | 4.5 | 5 | 5.5 | 6 | 6.5 | 7 |
|---|---|---|---|---|---|---|
| Rest of Europe | 38 | 38 | 39 | 39 | 40 | 41 |
| USA | 6 | 6.5 | 7 | 7.5 | 8 | 8.5 |

# Language

Catalan is similar to Spanish (*Castellano*), but it is definitely a language of its own with its own peculiarities. Like English, Catalan uses the unstressed 'uh' sound that appears in nearly every multi-syllable word. Thus 'How are you?', which is '¿Cómo estás?' in Spanish, with every vowel pronouned, becomes '¿Com estàs?' in Catalan, with the first vowel in 'estàs' being an unstressed 'uh' sound. Consonants coming at the end of a word are often unpronounced. For example, *senyor* ('sir') is pronounced Sen-yoh, with no 'r' sound. 'V' is pronounced like a 'B', so *vosté* (the formal 'you') sounds like Boo-steh.

## BASIC WORDS AND PHRASES

| | CATALAN | SPANISH (CASTILLAN) |
|---|---|---|
| **Hello** | Hola | Hola |
| **Goodbye** | Adéu | Adiós |
| **Yes** | Si | Sí |
| **No** | No | No |
| **Please** | Sisplau | Por favor |
| **Thank you** | Graciès | Gracias |
| **You're welcome** | De res | De nada |
| **Do you speak English?** | Vostè parla Angles? | Habla inglés? |
| **I don't speak Catalan/Spanish** | No parla Català | No hablo español |
| **Good day** | Bon dia | Buenos días |
| **Goodnight** | Bona nit | Buenas noches |
| **Excuse me** | Perdoni | Perdón |
| **Sir** | Senyor | Señor |
| **Madam** | Senyora | Señora |
| **How are you?** | Como està? | Cómo està? |
| **Very well, than you** | Molt bé, gràcies | Muy bien, gracias |
| **My name is ...** | Em dic… | Me llamo … |
| **What's your name?** | Come et dius? | Cómo se llama Usted? |
| **How do I get to ?** | Per anar a …? | Para ir a ….? |
| **Where is ...?** | On és …? | Donde està …? |
| **The subway** | El metro | El metro |
| **The airport** | L'aeroport | El aeropuerto |
| **The train station** | El estació de tren | La estación de tren |
| **The bus** | El bus | El bus |
| **The street** | El carrer | La calle |
| **A taxi** | Un taxi | Un taxi |
| **A hotel** | Un hotel | Un hotel |
| **The bathroom** | El lavabo | Los aseos |
| **A pharmacy** | Una farmàcia | Una farmàcia |
| **A bank** | Un banc | El banco |
| **The tourist office** | L'oficina de turisme | La oficina de turismo |
| **What time is it?** | Qina hora és? | Qué hora es? |

## EMERGENCIES

| | CATALAN | SPANISH (CASTILLAN) |
|---|---|---|
| Help! | Socors! | Socorro! |
| I am sick | Em trobo malament | Estoy enfermo/a |
| I am hurt | Estic ferit/ferida | Estoy herido/a |
| Hospital | L'hospital | El hospital |
| A doctor | Un metge | Un médico |

## DAYS AND MONTHS

| | CATALAN | SPANISH (CASTILLAN) |
|---|---|---|
| Monday | Dilluns | Lunes |
| Tuesday | Dimarts | Martes |
| Wednesday | Dimecres | Miércoles |
| Thursday | Dijous | Jueves |
| Friday | Divendres | Viernes |
| Saturday | Dissabte | Sábado |
| Sunday | Diumenge | Domingo |
| January | Gener | Enero |
| February | Febrer | Febrero |
| March | Març | Marzo |
| April | Abril | Abril |
| May | Maig | Mayo |
| June | Juny | Junio |
| July | Juliol | Julio |
| August | Agost | Agosto |
| September | Setembre | Septiembre |
| October | Octubre | Octubre |
| November | Novembre | Noviembre |
| December | Desembre | Diciembre |

## NUMBERS

| | CATALAN | SPANISH (CASTILLAN) |
|---|---|---|
| Zero | Zero | Cero |
| One | Un/Una | Uno |
| Two | Dos/Dues | Dos |
| Three | Tres | Tres |
| Four | Quatre | Cuatro |
| Five | Cinc | Cinco |
| Six | Sis | Seis |
| Seven | Set | Siete |
| Eight | Vuit | Ocho |
| Nine | Nou | Nueve |
| Ten | Deu | Diez |

In Palma there are car parks on the seafront and beneath Plaça Major. There are also several underground car parks. If the weather is hot, a sunshield under the windscreen is advisable. Leave no valuables behind, or, if you must, keep them out of sight.

### Petrol

Petrol is *gasolina* and unleaded *sin plomo*. Many petrol stations are open 24 hours. Some are self-service. There are a number of petrol stations throughout the island, and all take credit cards. No change is given between 9pm and 8am.

### Electricity

The supply is 220–225 volts. Sockets take round, two-pin plugs, so an

Fruit and vegetables at Vilafranca de Bonany

adaptor is required for most non-Continental appliances and a transformer if the appliances normally operate at 100–120 volts.

### Emergency telephone numbers

**Fire, police, ambulance** *112*.

### Health

There are no mandatory vaccination requirements for entering Mallorca, but tetanus and polio immunisation should be kept up to date. As in many parts of the world, AIDS is present. Take a strong suntan cream, anti-diarrhoea pills, and, particularly if you are staying in the Badia d'Alcúdia area, mosquito repellent. If you need to consult a doctor (*médico*) (*metge* in Catalan) or dentist (*dentista*), ask at your hotel reception. All Mallorcan towns and resorts have a public health centre, called *Centres de Salud*.

When you arrive in your hotel or apartment check that balcony railings are secure, there is an unobstructed fire exit, cots and children's equipment are safe, and that you cannot lock yourself out by the balcony door. Report any smell of gas, check swimming pools for concealed walls before diving in, and avoid food that appears undercooked or reheated.

All EU countries have reciprocal arrangements for reclaiming the cost of medical services. UK residents should obtain the European Health Insurance Card, free from any UK post office or *www.ehic.org.uk*. Claiming is laborious and covers only medical care, not secondary examinations (such as X-rays) or emergency repatriation. You are advised to take out adequate travel insurance, available through branches of Thomas Cook and most travel agents.

### Insurance

Medical insurance is highly recommended and is a pre-travel requirement with many package holidays. In the UK this can be purchased through Thomas Cook and most travel agents. Note that travel insurance does not cover liability arising from the use of a hire car, for which a top-up policy is needed (*see also* Car rental, *p178*).

### Lost property

If you lose anything of value, inform the police (*see p184*), if only for insurance purposes. The loss of a passport should be reported to your consulate (*see p177*). In theory, objects that are found and handed in make their way to the local *ajuntament* (town hall). In Palma, this is at Plaça Cort 1, *tel: (971) 22 59 00.*

### Media

The English-language *Majorca Daily Bulletin* provides useful local information. British and international press are widely available. Satellite TV is everywhere. Spanish TV regularly broadcasts such English classics as the Boat Race and the Grand National.

The local newspapers are *Diario de Mallorca, Última Hora, Diari de Baleares* and *El Día 16.* Television channels broadcast in both Catalan and Castilian.

### Money matters

As an EU member-state, the currency in Spain is the euro. Coins are available in denominations of €1 and €2, as well as *céntimos* of the value 50, 20, 10, 5, 2 and 1. They have a common European face, but the obverse is decorated according to the designs of each member-state. The notes are €500, €200, €100, €50, €20, €10 and €5. They have no national side. Credit cards can be widely used in Palma and the resorts, but take cash as a back-up if you are going to shops or restaurants off the tourist track. Currently, Nationwide, Santander and Post Office all offer credit cards which don't charge a fee for transactions made abroad.

Traveller's cheques avoid the hazards of carrying large amounts of cash, and can be quickly refunded in the event of their loss or theft. While ATMs abound in the major resorts, it is safer to take some cash with you on excursions to smaller villages.

### Opening times

**Banks** Mon–Fri 8.30am–2pm, Sat 8.30am–1pm (tourist resorts only). **Churches** Usually 8am–1pm & 5–8pm, but there is no set pattern. On Sunday churches are open as services permit (sightseeing is not welcomed while acts of worship are in progress).

**Museums** Variable, but around 10am–1pm & 4–6pm, often longer. Opening hours are reduced in the winter, and most close for at least one day a week, usually Monday.

**Shops** Mon–Fri 9–10am until 1–2pm, then around 4.30–8pm or even later in summer. On Saturdays, smaller shops open only in the morning. (*See pp142–3.*)

## Pharmacies

Chemists (*farmacias*) in Spain are obvious from the green cross outside. Unlike *droguerías*, which sell toiletries and perfume, they are devoted to dispensing medication and can be useful sources of advice and treatment for minor ailments. Addresses and opening times of duty chemists (*farmàcies de guàrdia*) open outside normal hours are posted in pharmacy windows and printed in local papers, including the *Majorca Daily Bulletin*.

## Places of worship

Mallorca is mainly Roman Catholic. Visitors are free to attend Mass in local churches, some of which hold services in English. A comprehensive list of places of worship catering for different faiths and nationalities is available from tourist offices. The larger hotels can often supply details of local services.

**Anglican Church** Carrer de Núñez de Balboa 6, Palma. *Tel: (971) 73 72 29.* Services on Sunday at 11am.

**Palma Cathedral** High Mass on Sunday and holidays at 10.30am. *www.catedraldemallorca.org*

## Police

There are three types. The urban-based Policía Local wear blue and have the thankless task of keeping the traffic under control. The Policía Nacional wear blue and uphold law and order in towns and cities. The Guardia Civil wear green and control the highways and country areas. If you need a police station, ask for *la comisaría.*

**Policía Local**
Carrer de Sant Ferran, Palma. *Tel: 092 or (971) 22 55 00.*

**Policía Nacional**
Carrer de Ruiz Alda 8, Palma. *Tel: 091 or (971) 22 52 00.*

There are plenty of trains between Palma and Inca, promoted as the 'Leather Express'

### Guardia Civil

Carrer de Manuel Azana 10, Palma.
*Tel: (971) 72 11 00* (but you should call
the Emergency number *112*).

## Post offices

The main post office (*correus*) in Palma
is just east of Passeig des Born at Carrer
de Constitució 5 (*tel: (971) 72 18 67.*
*Open: Mon–Sat 8.30am–10pm, Sun*
*noon–10pm*). Letters can be sent to a
post office for collection. Take your
passport when you collect them.
Stamps can also be bought from
tobacconists; look for a brown-and-
yellow sign saying *estanco*. Many hotels
stock them, as do most smart-thinking
shops that sell postcards. Postboxes
are yellow.

## Public holidays

**1 January**
New Year's Day
**6 January**
Epiphany
**Variable** (March/April)
Good Friday/Easter Monday
**1 May**
Labour Day
**Variable** (May/June)
Corpus Christi
**15 August**
Assumption
**12 October**
Discovery of America
**1 November**
All Saints' Day
**8 December**
Immaculate Conception

**25 & 26 December**
Christmas
For additional local holidays and
festivities, *see pp20–21*.

## Public transport
### Bus

The bus system in Mallorca is good.
Services are cheap and efficient, and the
timetables posted at *paradas* (bus
stops), available free from tourist
offices, are generally reliable. Pay as
you enter and keep hold of your
ticket as inspectors frequently board
the buses.

The island's central bus station is
in Carrer Eusebi Estada in Palma,
where there is an information kiosk. In
the city, buses are run by EMT. Useful
routes include:
**1** Passeig Marítim–Plaça d'Espanya;
**15** S'Arenal-Can Pastilla–Plaça
  d'Espanya;
**17** Aeroport–Plaça d'Espanya;
**21** Palma Nova–Plaça
  de la Reina–Plaça d'Espanya.
**EMT (Palma) bus information:**
*Tel: (900) 700 710. www.emtpalma.es*
The tourist information office has
leaflets showing the timetables.

### Horse-drawn carriage

Sunday is the best time to ride
round the historic centre of Palma
by horse and carriage. There are ranks
of *caleras* along Passeig de Sagrera
and beside the cathedral in Costa de
la Seu. A sign displays tariffs, and a tip
is expected.

Flags outside the Consulat del Mar on Palma's seafront

## Taxi

Taxis are white and can be hailed in the street or picked up at ranks in Palma and major towns and resorts. A green light and sign saying *Lliure/Libre* indicates they are available for hire. Prices are reasonable, but increase at night and weekends. If you are travelling a long distance, negotiate the fare first. To call a taxi (24-hour service):

**Radio taxis**

**Andratx** *Tel: (971) 13 63 98.*
**Calvià** *Tel: (971) 13 47 00.*
**Palma** *Tel: (971) 40 14 14.*
**Pollença** *Tel: (971) 86 62 13.*

## Train

Mallorca has two narrow-gauge railway lines. Trains depart from adjacent stations in Plaça d'Espanya, one route running north to Sóller (55 minutes) and the other – with a more frequent service – travelling east to Inca (35 minutes) and on to Sa Pobla and Manacor.

For information:
**Palma–Inca–Sa Pobla–Manacor**
*Tel: (971) 17 77 77.*
**Palma–Sóller** *Tel: (971) 72 20 51.*
*www.trendesoller.com*

## Tram

A historic tram line runs between Sóller and Port de Sóller, and the journey time is 30 minutes (*see pp86–7*).

## Senior citizens

Mallorca attracts a good number of senior citizens, particularly in the low and 'shoulder' seasons when life is more relaxed and prices more reasonable. Some tour operators offer special extended stay deals if you want to escape to Mallorca for the winter. It is advisable to take out full medical and travel insurance before departing.

## Sustainable tourism

Thomas Cook is a strong advocate of ethical and fairly traded tourism and believes that the travel experience should be as good for the places visited as it is for the people who visit them. That's why we firmly support The Travel

Foundation, a charity that develops solutions to help improve and protect holiday destinations, their environment, traditions and culture. To find out what you can do to make a positive difference to the places you travel to and the people who live there, please visit
*www.thetravelfoundation.org.uk*

## Telephones

The Spanish telephone system is good, although prices remain slightly higher than most other European countries. All the major mobile phone networks have offices in Palma if you want to buy credit for mobile phones. Phonecards (*tarjeta telefonica*) can be bought from post offices and *tabacaleras* and are worth €6.

### Payphones

A public telephone (*teléfono*) takes a variety of coins. Garner a pile of coins if you are calling abroad. The coins should be lined up in the slot before you dial. (Rates are cheaper between 10pm and 8am.) Many bars have a payphone.

You can also make calls from a *Locutorio*. These *locutorios* can usually be found near bus or train stations and pop up and disappear with alarming frequency – you pay a cashier after making a call, which is metered.

### Dialling codes

If you are calling the Balearic Islands from within or outside Spain you must start with 971. When dialling within the Balearic Islands, you must still dial the 9-digit number. To make an international call from Mallorca you must dial *00* then the country code.

### International codes
**Australia** *61*, **Canada** and **USA** *1*, **Irish Republic** *353*, **New Zealand** *64*, **UK** *44*.
### Useful numbers
**Operator** *1009* (within Spain).
**International operator** *1008* for Europe, Algeria, Libya, Morocco, Tunisia and Turkey; *1005* for all others.
**Directory enquiries** (Mallorca and Spain) *11811*.
**International directory enquiries** *11825*.
**Emergency numbers** *See p182*.

## Time

The time in the Balearic Islands is the same as that on mainland Spain. Spain is one hour ahead of Greenwich Mean Time (GMT). Spanish Summer Time, when the clocks are put forward an hour, is from the last Sunday of March to the last Sunday of October, as in the UK.

## Tipping

Although locals rarely tip in restaurants or elsewhere, there are different expectations of tourists. Leave a few coins for bar staff or waiters, and give coins to porters, maids, coach drivers and guides. Consider 5–10 per cent for meals and taxis if you are happy with the service.

## Toilets

Public toilets are uncommon in Mallorca. It is generally accepted that you have to be a customer to use the services of a bar or restaurant.

Toilets (*servicios* and *aseos*) are heralded by entertaining pictograms intended to show the difference between the sexes: *señores, hombres* (*senyors* in Catalan) and *caballeros* are for pipe-smoking dudes, while ladies with dark curls and dangerous-looking earrings should go for *señoras* (*senyores* in Catalan) and *damas*. Facilities are generally modern, but don't be surprised by a communal entrance that then divides into two.

## Tourist information

For information on Mallorca before you leave home consult the following.

**Canada** Tourist Office of Spain, 14th floor, 2 Bloor St West, Toronto, Ontario M5S 1M8. *Tel: (416) 961 3131.*
*www.spain.info/ca/tourspain*
**UK** Spanish Tourist Office, 2nd floor, 79 New Cavendish St, London W1W 6XB. *Tel: (0870) 850 6599.*
*www.spain.info/uk/tourspain*
**USA** Tourist Office of Spain, 666 Fifth Avenue, New York, NY 10103.
*Tel: (212) 265 8822.*
*www.spain.info/us/tourspain*
**Mallorca**
Information is available from tourist offices in **Palma** (*see p34*),
*www.infomallorca.net,*

*www.illesbalears.com,*
and in the following towns and resorts (*see the individual resort entries for addresses*).
**West of Palma** Cala Major (Ses Illetes), Palma Nova (Magaluf), Peguera, Santa Ponça.
**The northwest** Sóller, Port de Sóller, Valldemossa.
**The northeast** Cala Millor, Cala Ratjada, Can Picafort, Port d'Alcúdia, Port de Pollença.
**The south** Cala d'Or, Cala Figuera, Portocristo, Sa Colònia de Sant Jordi.

In summer, offices are generally open Mon–Fri 9am–8pm & Sat 9am–1.30pm. Small offices may be open shorter hours. Most resort tourist offices close in winter.

Birdwatchers should go to the website *www.ausdebalears.org*

## Travellers with disabilities

Facilities for travellers with a disability have improved dramatically in recent years but there is still a long way to go. Modern hotels, restaurants, museums and galleries are required to provide wheelchair access. Most of the public bus network is now wheelchair accessible and there are special taxis for visitors with a disability. For further information about travelling abroad see *www.tourismforall.org.uk*
*(tel: 0845 124 9971),*
*www.radar.org.uk*
*(tel: (020) 7250 3222) and*
*www.balearics.angloinfo.com/*
*information/35/disabled.asp*

# Index

# Acknowledgements

Thomas Cook Publishing wishes to thank the photographers, picture libraries and other organisations, to whom the copyright belongs, for the photographs in this book.

FLICKR HARRYFN (43), A BALAKO (146), SOCRATES (163)
DREAMSTIME F Esteve (10), J Ontel (11), J Martinez (15), Jf Llado Sabater (18), A Drosta (22), Tugores (29), F Fabian (44), R Jones (48), Dga1958 (67), S Palmer (75), R Philipp (83), P Bellido (102), F Amer Serra (104), A Latt (109), P Lockyer (115), V Llorente Garcia (141),
MANUELA MUNOZ 19, 21
MARY EVANS PICTURE LIBRARY 74
PICTURE COLOUR LIBRARY A COX (57), J MILLER (70, 127), SPAIN PIX (129)
SPECTRUM COLOUR LIBRARY 9, 122, 171
THOMAS COOK TOUR OPERATIONS LIMITED 81, 155
WORLD PICTURES/PHOT

The remaining pictures a
with the exception of pa

For CAMBRIDGE PUBLISI
**Project editor**: Diane Te
**Typesetter**: Trevor Doub
**Proofreader**: Melanie G
**Indexer**: Karolin Thomas

## SEND YOUR THOUGHTS TO
## BOOKS@THOMASCOOK.COM

We're committed to providing the very best up-to-date information in our travel guides and constantly strive to make them as useful as they can be. You can help us to improve future editions by letting us have your feedback. If you've made a wonderful discovery on your travels that we don't already feature, if you'd like to inform us about recent changes to anything that we do include, or if you simply want to let us know your thoughts about this guidebook and how we can make it even better – we'd love to hear from you.

Send us ideas, discoveries and recommendations today and then look out for your valuable input in the next edition of this title.

Emails to the above address, or letters to traveller guides Series Editor, Thomas Cook Publishing, PO Box 227, Coningsby Road, Peterborough PE3 8SB, UK.

Please don't forget to let us know which title your feedback refers to!